On a Raven's Wing

ALSO BY STUART M. KAMINSKY

FICTION

Toby Peter series

Inspector Rostnikov series

Lew Fonesca series

Abe Lieberman series

CSI: New York

Rockford Files novels
Devil on My Doorstep • The Green Bottle

Kolchak: The Night Stalker
Kolchak: The Night Stalker Chronicles (story anthology, includes "The Night Talker" by Kaminsky) • Kolchak the Night Stalker, Volume I (graphic novel, with Joe Gentile and Jeff Rice) • Fever Pitch (graphic novel, with Christopher Jones and Barbara Schulz)

Non-series
Exercise in Terror • When the Dark Man Calls

Story collections
The Man Who Beat the System and Other Stories (Audio) • Hidden and Other Stories

As editor
Show Business Is Murder • Mystery in the Sunshine State • Opening Shots

NONFICTION

Behind the Mystery: Top Mystery Writers Interviewed (Interviews by Kaminsky; photographs by Laurie Roberts) • American Television Genres • Writing for Television (with Mark Walker) • Basic Filmmaking (with Dana H. Hodgdon) • Coop: The Life and Legend of Gary Cooper • John Huston: Maker of Magic • Ingmar Bergman: Essays in Criticism • Don Siegel, Director • American Film Genres: Approaches to a Critical Theory of Popular Film • Clint Eastwood • A Biographical Study of the Career of Donald Siegel and an Analysis of His Films

On a Raven's Wing

NEW TALES IN HONOR OF
EDGAR ALLAN POE

BY

MARY HIGGINS CLARK,
THOMAS H. COOK, JAMES W. HALL,
RUPERT HOLMES, S. J. ROZAN,
DON WINSLOW, AND
FOURTEEN OTHERS

Edited by Stuart M. Kaminsky

HARPER

NEW YORK · LONDON · TORONTO · SYDNEY

HARPER

Copyright notices for individual stories appear on page 393.

HarperCollins books may be purchased for educational, business, or sales promotional use. For information please write: Special Markets Department, HarperCollins Publishers, 10 East 53rd Street, New York, NY 10022.

FIRST EDITION

Designed by Joy O'Meara
Illustration from iStockPhoto.com

Library of Congress Cataloging-in-Publication Data is available upon request.

ISBN 978-0-06-169042-6

09 10 11 12 13 OV/RRD 10 9 8 7 6 5 4 3

Contents

Contents

About Edgar Allan Poe

Edgar Allan Poe (1809–1849), while a mainstay of literature today and the recognized creator of the modern genres of horror and mystery fiction, spent much of his life chasing the public and literary acclaim he craved.

Born to David and Elizabeth Poe, young Edgar knew hardship from an early age. His father abandoned the family a year after Edgar's birth, and his mother died of consumption one year later. Taken in, but never legally adopted, by John and Frances Allan, Edgar traveled with his new family to England in 1815, then continued on alone to study in Irvine, Scotland, for a short time. Afterward he studied in Chelsea, then a suburb of London, until 1817. He returned to Virginia in 1820, and in 1826 he enrolled at the newly founded University of Virginia to study languages. During his college years, he became estranged from his foster father, claiming that John Allan didn't send him enough money to live on, but the reality was that Poe was losing the money gambling.

In 1827 Edgar enlisted in the U.S. Army at age eighteen, claiming he was twenty-two years old. It was during this time that he began publishing his poems, including an early collection, *Tamerlane and Other Poems*, printed under the byline "A Bostonian." He attained the rank of sergeant major of artillery and expressed a desire to attend West Point for officer training. Once accepted to the academy, however, he was dismissed for not attending classes and formations.

After the death of his brother, Henry, in 1831, Edgar decided to try making a living as an author. He was the first well-known American to make such an attempt, but because of the lack of an international copyright law and the economic effects of the Panic of 1837, he was often forced to press for the monies owed him and compelled to seek other assistance. After winning a literary prize for his story "Manuscript Found in a Bottle," he was hired as the assistant editor of the *Southern Literary Messenger*, but he was fired several weeks later for repeated drunkenness. This pattern of dissipation would haunt Poe for the rest of his life.

After marrying his cousin Virginia Clemm in 1835, Poe returned to the *Messenger*, where he worked for the next two years, seeing its circulation rise from 700 to 3,500 copies. His only full-length novel, *The Narrative of Arthur Gordon Pym of Nantucket*, was published in 1838 to wide review and acclaim, though once again Poe received little profit from his work. The year after saw the publication of his first short story collection, *Tales of the Grotesque and Arabesque*, which received mixed reviews and sold poorly. He left the *Messenger* and worked at *Burton's Gentleman's Magazine* and *Graham's Magazine* before announcing that he would start his own literary publication, *The Penn*, later to be titled *The Stylus*. Tragically, it never came to print.

Virginia first showed signs of tuberculosis in 1842, and her gradual decline over the next five years caused Edgar to drink even more heavily. The one bright spot in this time was the publication in 1845 of one of his most famous works, "The Raven," which brought him widespread acclaim; unfortunately, he was paid only nine dollars for the poem itself.

Shortly afterward, the Poes moved to a cottage in the Fordham section of the Bronx, New York, where Virginia died in 1847. Increasingly unstable, Edgar tried to secure a position in government, unsuccessfully courted the poet Sarah Helen Whitman, and eventually returned to Richmond, Virginia, to rekindle a relationship with Sarah Royster, a childhood sweetheart.

The circumstances surrounding Poe's death remain shrouded in mystery. Found on the streets of Baltimore, Maryland, delirious and dressed in clothes that weren't his, Poe was taken to Washington College Hospital, where he died on October 7, 1849. It was reported that his last words were "Lord help my poor soul," but this cannot be proven as all records surrounding his death have been lost. Edgar Allan Poe's death has been attributed to various causes, including delirium tremens, heart disease, epilepsy, or meningeal inflammation. He was buried in a Baltimore cemetery, where since 1949 a mysterious figure has toasted Poe on the anniversary of his birth by leaving cognac and three roses at his headstone.

Poe was recognized primarily as a literary critic during his lifetime, but after his death, his work became popular in Europe owing mainly to Charles Baudelaire's translations of his stories and poems. Sir Arthur Conan Doyle cited Poe as the creator of the modern mystery story with his C. Auguste Dupin stories, saying, "Where was the detective story until Poe breathed the breath of life into it?" Poe's work also inspired later authors of science fiction and fantasy, including Jules Verne and H. G. Wells. Today he is recognized as a literary master, who both created new genres and reinvigorated old ones with a unique combination of story and style.

About the Mystery Writers of America's Edgar Award

In 1945, when the Mystery Writers of America was being formed, the founders of the organization decided to give an award for the best debut American mystery novel, as well as awards for the best and worst mystery reviews of the year. Initially they were going to call it the Edmund Wilson Memorial Award (partly in revenge for Wilson's disdain for the genre), but calmer heads prevailed. Although it is unknown exactly who came up with the idea of naming the award for "the Father of the Detective Story," it was an immediate success, and the "Edgar" was created.

The first Edgar Award was bestowed in 1946 on Julian Fast for his debut novel *Watchful at Night*. In the more than fifty years since, the stylized ceramic bust of the great author has become one of the top prizes in the field of mystery fiction. The award categories have been expanded over time to include Best Novel, Best Short Story, Best Paperback Original, Best Young Adult Novel, Best Juvenile Novel, Best Fact Crime, Best Critical/Biographical, Best Play, Best Television Episode, and Best Motion Picture, in addition to the original Best First Novel. The Edgar has been won by many noted authors in the field, including Stuart Kaminsky, Michael Connelly, T. Jefferson Parker, Jan Burke, Lisa Scottoline, Laura Lippmann, Laurie R. King, Steve Hamilton, Peter Robinson, Edward D. Hoch, S. J. Rozan, Thomas H. Cook, Joseph Wambaugh, Jeffery Deaver, Rupert Holmes, Anne Perry, Patricia Cornwell, Ira Levin, Thomas Harris, Dick Francis, Ruth Rendell, Lawrence Block, Elmore Leonard, Ken Follett, Frederick Forsyth, Harlan Ellison, Doug Allyn, and many, many others.

Introduction

Stuart M. Kaminsky

Half an hour ago, as I was about to start writing this introduction, I looked up at the pale-faced, closed-eyed bust of Poe that I received as Grand Master. It resides on a bureau just across from the desk at which I work. There is a continuing problem with the bust, however. The paint on Edgar's head is slowly peeling away. As I've done before, I went to the garage, got some black paint, and dabbed at the places in his hair showing white where black should have been.

I was careful, but the paint began to drip across Edgar's face, forming a startling set of black tears that ran from the outside corners of both of his eyes down his cheeks.

Was Edgar trying to tell me what to write? Was he saddened that I had put together this anthology? Was I reading something into the moment that was not there?

My answer to the last question was a tentative yes. Edgar was no more weeping black paint than I am the only person who will be left after the Rapture.

But still, I felt that chill, the one that makes my shoulders shiver. It is also the shiver that comes to me whenever I read one of Poe's tales of terror.

I have felt it stepping into Poe's preserved dormitory room at the University of Virginia. I have felt that shiver sitting at the desk Poe used at *The Southern Literary Messenger*. Part of the Koester Collection at the University of Texas, Austin, it was in a well-guarded tower on an upper floor, against a wall in a room that reminded me of the vast warehouse at the end of *Citizen Kane*.

You can go to the Internet to find an odd list of Poe artifacts (www.eapoe.org/geninfo/POEARTFS.HTM), the very reading of which reminds me of something one of Poe's morose characters might compile: locks of Poe's hair; fragments of Poe's original coffin; a pen holder made from a fragment of Poe's original coffin; the bed in which his child bride, Virginia, died; Poe's rocking chair; Poe's Bible; and much more.

Things we know about Poe and often say and hear include the assertions that, in his forty years of life, he created the short story, the detective story, and the modern horror story. As far as I am concerned, it does not matter if he was first or if he created any literary genre. What matters is that his stories and poetry have the power to send me into a near syncope.

One of my earliest encounters with Poe was through a half-hour live teleplay in the 1950s of "The Cask of Amontillado." The production was a disaster. Actors muffled and mumbled lines. Painted sets rattled in the breeze of passing performers. And still, just before the last painted cardboard brick was set in place, I felt the horror of that imprisonment as the actor called out, "Fortunato."

Poe's life and work have inspired radio episodes; television tales; popular music by, among many others, the Beatles and Joan Baez; classical music; and even operas by Claude Debussy. There are Poe T-shirts, candies, bobble-head dolls, and action figures. And don't forget Raven Beer.

The revenue from the T-shirts and bobble-heads alone would almost certainly come to far more than Edgar's estimated lifetime earnings, even adjusted for inflation.

I know there are many, writers included, who do not share my appreciation of the odd-looking, wild-eyed Poe. I think, however, many of the writers who have contributed to this collection have similar feelings to mine about him.

At my regular poker game a few months ago, I said something about Poe and was asked if I would like to meet him were it magically possible. I said no. Poe, haunted and besotted, was as morose and difficult as any of his characters. I think a meeting with the man would depress me and probably end with him asking me for ten dollars, which I would gladly give him.

I am content to look up and see the bust of Poe and be inspired, depressed, transported, and even, on some occasions, happy.

I like to think that the ghost of Poe, wafted by his prose or poetry, inspired the stories in this collection honoring him.

When I sent out word that I was putting together a collection of stories to honor Poe, I gave but one condition. Poe himself or his work had to be central to the story. I expected sequels. I expected Poe as detective. What I did not expect was what I got, a dazzling collection of contemporary terror, mystery, and literary game.

Some of the tales (P. J. Parrish's "The Tell-Tale Pacemaker," Angela Zeman's "Rue Morgue Noir") are outright funny. Some are new tales as Poe might have written them (M.W.A. Grandmaster Dorothy Salisbury Davis's "Emily's Time"). Others (John Lutz's "Poe, Poe, Poe," Paul Levine's "Development Hell," Rupert Holmes's "A Nomad of the Night") are tongue-in-cheek games; while others still are poignant gems (Thomas H. Cook's "Nevermore," Daniel Stashower's "Challenger"). There are sequels, modern-day retellings, detective stories, con games, literary homages, and puzzles.

There is also one story, "The Poe Collector," the last story by the late Ed Hoch, which I am particularly pleased to have. It is fitting that the most prolific writer of quality mystery short stories and an M.W.A. Grandmaster should be included in an anthology honoring the father of the mystery story.

Now, open the pages, and if you hear a rattling of teeth, the painful yowl of a cat, or the distant peal of a bell, you will know you are in the right place.

On a Raven's Wing

Israfel

Doug Allyn

The clapping started slowly at first. One pair of hands, then another, and yet another, as impatience spread through our audience like an angry brushfire, growing louder and more insistent. Some began stamping their feet, and the rest took that up as well, until the drumbeat of annoyance thundered through the old theater like an invading army on the march.

Backstage in my rat-bitten dressing room, I was giving my Fender Stratocaster a final tune when Duke Martoni, our road manager, stormed in. Big-shouldered, red-faced, Duke has an even temper. Always angry. A good man to have on your side.

A bad one to cross.

"You've gotta talk to him," he snapped. "Five minutes to show time and he's locked in his dressing room, won't come to the door."

"Whoa, slow down. Who won't come to the door?" Though I already knew. Duke's like a mean dog woofing behind a rail fence. You can't help teasing him a little.

"Izzy, who else?" he snarled, flushing dangerously. "Israfel freaking Markowski. After that fiasco in Detroit, you promised to straighten him out, Roddy. You gave me your word!"

"I promised I'd talk to him, Duke. I never got the chance. After the Detroit show, Izzy disappeared for three days."

"Disappeared where?"

"Don't know. All I can tell you is, he didn't ride down in the tour bus with the rest of the band. Didn't even show up to sound check the PA system or his guitar this afternoon. He arrived at the theater only an hour ago, went straight to his dressing room, and locked himself in. Maybe he's still bummed over the Detroit show——"

"He should be!" Duke snapped, getting redder by the second. "Detroit wasn't a show, it was a freaking disaster! Izzy up on his high riser with his back to the crowd, playing a damn whacked-out solo that went on for forty minutes. He blew our audience right out the stadium doors. Must have been coked out of his fucking mind!"

"Look, I know he's been acting a bit . . . erratic lately, but it's not just the dope. He's been reaching for something, Duke, trying to take our music to the next level——"

"Don't hand me that crap, Roddy. I know a stoner when I see

one. İsrafel's Koven isn't the first band I've managed, or even the twenty-first. I've seen fifty flash-in-the-pan talents like Izzy flush their careers down the toilet exactly the same way. He's destroying himself and he's going to take the rest of you down with him."

"He's not that bad—"

"The hell he isn't! You're a tough kid, Roddy, a street guy like me, so I'll give it to you straight. If Izzy pulls another cockup like Detroit, İsrafel's Koven will be history. The other venues on the tour will cancel us out, and the penalty clauses and lawsuits will bury the band in a financial hole so deep you guys will never crawl out. You're gonna lose everything you've worked for, Roddy. For good."

"Okay, okay," I said, setting my guitar aside. "I'll talk to him—"

"Not good enough," Duke snapped. "We're past talking, Roddy. You've got to cut him loose."

"Cut him loose? Are you nuts? We can't—"

"Just think about it! Plenty of top-flight rock groups have replaced key members and gone on without a hitch. AC/DC, the Rolling Stones, Chicago, Heart—hell, it might be easier to list groups that *haven't* replaced star players. I know you think Izzy's special—"

"He is special! He's a freaking genius!"

"But he's not irreplaceable," Duke pressed on. "Playing on that riser forty feet over the crowd, with all the echo, CO_2 fog, and lighting FX, anybody could be up there. You could be up there, Roddy!"

"No way, Duke! I'm just a blue-collar player. Izzy—"

"Izzy is a goddamn burnout! Whatever talent he had is gone,

and you know it! I've heard you practicing on the tour bus, Roddy. Working like a dog between towns while Izzy's laying back in his berth stoned to the bone. You're as good a guitarist as Izzy ever was. Hell, you're probably better. You're definitely good enough to replace him."

"No! We started this band together. Izzy's been the driving force from the beginning—"

"Maybe he was then, but he's not anymore. Have you looked at him lately, Roddy? Really looked at him? A year ago he was a beautiful kid, but those larger-than-life posters in front of the theater are like pictures of Dorian Gray now. Drugs and the road are killing him, Roddy. I swear, half the audience buys their tickets to see if he'll drop dead onstage. Every show's a dance on the edge of destruction. He's coking himself to death, and his playing is getting so bizarre—"

"You're wrong about that, Duke. He's expanding the structures of our songs, looking for a new approach to the music. You're not a player, you don't understand."

"You're damned right I don't! Neither does your audience. They buy tickets to hear 'Annabel Lee,' 'Lenore,' and 'Berenice's Smile,' the songs that made you guys famous. Not to see Izzy up on that forty-foot riser doing musical masturbation. Nobody's getting off on that noise but him! His solos have been getting weirder every show and Detroit was the last straw."

"Forget it, Duke, there's no way the guys will cut Izzy loose. Period! If his playing seems erratic, it's because he's experimenting. Every creative artist tries things that aren't successful at first. Even Poe had failures—"

"Poe," Duke snorted contemptuously. "And that's another thing. This whole Poe shtick, naming yourselves after his characters, basing your songs on his poems, it's wearing out, Roddy. It worked for the first CD but your second release went straight in the tank. Twelve songs, no hits. The label wants a new direction for your next CD or they'll cancel your recording contract."

"But our entire repertoire is centered around Poe—"

"Then it's time to change it! It's the law of the universe, kid, evolve or die. Jefferson Airplane became Jefferson Starship, Kiss quit wearing makeup! Hell, most of your audience is too young to remember Elvis! That giant painted backdrop of a dead poet glaring out at the crowd bums people out."

"Look, Poe isn't just a stage prop, he's—"

"A downer!" Duke snapped. "Look, losing the dead guy isn't my idea, the orders came from L.A."

"They can't do that!"

"After that mess Izzy made in Detroit, we're lucky they haven't dumped the band already! If you guys are such big Poe fans, you'd better remember something. Your freaked-out hero died flat broke in a charity ward. Which is where you're headed if Izzy blows one more show! You hear that clapping out front? That ain't applause, sport. The animals are getting restless, they want to be entertained. Now round up your stoner superstar and get him onstage, or your careers are going to be deader than Edgar fucking Poe!"

I hustled through the wings to Izzy's dressing room. Onstage, the other members of Israfel's Koven were already in place, tuned up and waiting, eyeing me anxiously as I trotted past. No need to explain where I was going; Duke hadn't told me a thing we didn't already know.

Damn Izzy to hell! It wasn't supposed to be like this.

I grew up in foster care and juvy detention. This band is the closest thing to a real family I've ever known. And it was a hoot at first. Practicing endless hours in Punkin's garage, learning Creed, Aerosmith, and Lynyrd Skynyrd tunes, playing frat parties and roadhouses for chump change.

Until the night Izzy was cruising on crystal, watching TV wide-eyed at four in the morning, some PBS show on great American authors.

And this old black-and-white picture came on the screen.

The guy looked like a stoner. A pasty-faced geek with a high forehead, dark smudges under his eyes, and that thousand-yard stare. And the announcer starts droning on about what a freaking genius Edgar Allan Poe was . . . and Izzy had an honest to God *epiphany*.

Duke was wrong about one thing. Even kids who can't remember Elvis know exactly who Edgar Allan Poe is. They don't have any freaking *choice*!

Poe's picture is in every American Lit text, he's the poster boy for poetry classes. Hell, half the best sellers in the mall have "Edgar Award–Winning Author" on the cover, whatever that means. So maybe kids get Poe mixed up with Vincent Price in *The Raven*, but they definitely know his name, and, more important, they know that face.

Izzy figured that since all of us knew Poe from boring-ass high school English classes, it'd be a perfect payback to put him to work for us.

By making him the star of the show.

Eddie Poe, America's favorite dead pop poet. With his brand-new backup band, Israfel's Koven.

The rest of us thought the idea was totally whack, but there was no talking Izzy out of it. He sold his car to pay for a giant backdrop of Poe's face that we hung behind the band onstage. He started calling himself Israfel and began writing weird love songs to chicks who croaked a hundred years ago. Lines about getting turned on by their "emaciated forms" and humping them in their "tombs by the sounding sea."

Sure it was plagiarism, so what? It was still intriguing. And Poe's been a stiff so long we don't even have to pay him royalties.

Plus, the "hot love with a cold, moldering chick" idea was so sick, so deliciously morbid, that kids absolutely wigged out over it.

We changed the group's name from the Playboys to Israfel's Koven, and quickly went from being just another frat party band into a unique concert act. One with a growing following.

Our new audience were mainly Goth kids, New Age losers in black trench coats, descended from eighties punk rockers and millennium metalheads. Most of them were already dressing like Poe anyway, not counting the tattoos and facial studs. And they loved us. We played songs that grossed out their parents, and gave 'em a dead geek idol that made them look normal by comparison.

They weren't nerdy slackers anymore, they were Israfel's Koven fans. We made them feel trendy, made them feel special.

And after five long, tough years of working dumps for beer money, suddenly Israfel's Koven was an overnight success.

Our first single, "Annabel Lee," cracked the Top Forty at number thirty-two, then our follow-up, "Berenice's Smile," climbed to number sixteen with a bullet.

Our gigs improved too. Duke booked us onto the Lollapalooza tour as an opening act, but after "Lenore" charted, we decided to try our luck as headliners on our own tour. And it worked!

We began filling theaters and arenas with our Goth army. Israfel's Koven was hotter than a rocket on the rise.

And now we were falling just as fast. Our second album stiffed; not one song made the charts. Maybe Duke and the label were right, the Poe shtick had played itself out. But that wasn't the real problem and we all knew it.

Izzy "Israfel" Markowski was the real problem. Edgar Allan Poe drugged himself to death and now Izzy was on that same dead-end roller coaster. Growing up tough the way I did, I'd seen this movie before. Way too many times. The actors may be different, but the ending never changes.

But somehow that didn't matter. Israfel's Koven was Izzy's brainchild. Without him, we'd still be playing weekend gigs in Armpit, Indiana. And if I had to choose between Izzy and big-time success, then to hell with Duke and this tour, the record deal, and all the rest of it.

Izzy was my friend and a brother musician and I wasn't about to cut him loose.

The impatient stomping from the audience was deafening as I hammered on Izzy's door.

"Iz! It's me! Open the hell up!"

He didn't answer, so I reared back and kicked it in! Then froze.

Sweet Jesus. Izzy wasn't close to being ready. He wasn't even dressed. He was sprawled on his cot in his underwear, looking like a death camp survivor, legs and arms gaunt and skeletal as willow wands, tracked with needle scabs. His chest was sunken, his face feverish.

Only his eyes seemed alive, glittering with madness, soulless as an insect.

"What do you want?" he groaned.

"It's showtime, Iz. We were due onstage ten minutes ago."

He nodded slowly, as if hearing me from a great distance.

"Okay," he said at last. He tried to rise, then fell back, coughing. "Help me up."

I put my arms around his slender shoulders, raising him as he swung his pale feet to the floor. He weighed no more than a child.

"Izzy, this is crazy, you're in no shape to play. You need a doctor."

"I-don't-need-no-doctor," he sneered, imitating the lilt of the old rock song. "Just get me to the stage, Roddy. I'll take over from there. And by the way, I'm going on without you tonight. You're fired. All of you!"

"What?"

"You heard me. Fired! Sacked! Laid off! The lot of you! I don't need you clowns anymore. In Detroit, I almost made it. I was on fire, playing like an angel, like the real Israfel. It was the first time I ever really dug what Poe meant by *"his heartstrings are a lute."* I wasn't just playing my guitar, Roddy, I *was* my guitar! I *was* the music. And the music was me! All me! I could have played my way into heaven if you guys hadn't dragged me back."

"Dragged you back?" I echoed in disbelief. "Christ on a crutch, Izzy, you were coked out of your head, playing like a freakin' maniac! You sent the audience streaming for the exits, holding their ears."

"Who cares, they don't know shit anyway. Don't you get it? I'm through playing for that rabble. I don't need them any more than I need you. I'm not pretending to be Israfel anymore, I'm gonna *become* him. An Immortal, like Poe and the others, Gabriel, Uriel—" He broke off, retching so hard I thought he might cough up a lung. If I hadn't held him upright, he would have collapsed.

The seizure passed, and he sagged against me, gasping, blood trickling from the corner of his mouth.

"This is crazy," I said. "I'm getting you to a doctor."

"No! Just give me my guitar and get the hell out of my way."

"Izzy, please, you're in no shape to—"

"Do as I say!" he shrieked. And he slapped me! And I freaking lost it! I grabbed the arrogant bastard by his scrawny neck to shake some sense into him—and I felt it *snap!*

My God! Even over the impatient stomping out front, I heard that awful *snap*. Felt that terrible, final *snap*.

Izzy shuddered in my hands, flopping mindlessly as a beached trout, then went suddenly, utterly . . . limp.

Dead weight.

Dear God! For a frozen moment, all I could do was stare into those lightless eyes. Hoping against hope—

But there was no hope. No flicker of life. His eyes were already glazing over.

I lowered his emaciated form gently to his cot. His head lolled at a crazy, impossible angle, his eyes still focused on mine. There was no message, though. There was nobody home.

Jesus, I'd barely—but that didn't matter now. Izzy was as dead as Hendrix or Elvis, dead as Poe. I'd wrung his neck like a damned chicken. And there was no way in hell I could ever explain it away.

I stood there, staring down at the lifeless body of my friend. Slowly realizing that I'd killed us both.

They'd lock me in a cage for this.

And after growing up in foster care and a long stretch in juvy detention, I knew way too much about cages. Enough to know I could never survive in prison. Wouldn't even want to. I'd rather be . . .

Playing.

The impatient stamping from out front made up my mind. I had nowhere to run. Duke's security crew were all over the building. I had no money, and the only friends I had in this town were already on that stage. Facing ten thousand angry fans. Waiting for me.

Or more accurately . . .

Waiting for Israfel.

Well? Why the hell not?

Duke was right, I'd always wondered if I could match Izzy's guitar work. Tonight would be my only chance to find out.

One way or the other.

Slipping on Izzy's jacket, I pulled the bill of his baseball cap down low to shade my eyes, then grabbed his guitar and trotted out to the stage.

Punkin, our bass player, recognized me as I trotted past him to the steep stairs that led up to Izzy's riser. He yelled after me, asking what the hell was going on. I didn't bother to answer. Slinging the guitar strap over my shoulder, I hurried up the stairway. It was too late for talk. Too late for anything but . . .

The show.

I was still climbing the final flight of stairs when the curtain began to rise. The impatient clapping instantly became a roar of applause, a tidal wave of welcoming whistles and cheers as the rising curtain revealed the stage, the members of Israfel's Koven in black trench coats, backed by a massive wall of amplifiers, bathed in the crimson glow of the footlights. And towering over them, the huge backdrop, the staring face of Edgar Allan Poe.

Suspended a full forty feet in the air, Izzy's riser was closer to the ceiling than the stage, almost level with the dazzling banks of overhead spotlights. Below me, the audience stretched away in a shimmering sea of upturned faces.

But as I hurried up the final few steps, half blinded by the lights, I realized something was terribly wrong.

The carpet on Izzy's platform was soaking wet. Water dripping over the sides. Impossible. There was no way water could get up here, not accidentally. And the safety rail around the riser was wired with a full arsenal of pyrotechnics, flash cannons, propane blasters and starbursts, an array of effects that couldn't possibly be fired up here without . . .

Burning me alive.

No. Not me.

Israfel!

Sweet Jesus! This was Izzy's platform. *He* was supposed to be up here. To give his last performance.

When that crazy bastard said he was going on without us, to play with the Immortals, he really meant it.

He wasn't just quitting the band, he was quitting this life!

A high-voltage cable, stripped bare, was wrapped around the safety rail and the sodden carpet made a perfect contact for electric current. If I touched that rail or even brushed it accidentally, I'd complete the short circuit. And the voltage would toast me like an IHOP bagel.

But as I wheeled to head back down, I noticed a disturbance in the wings. Two policemen were arguing angrily with Duke and gesturing upward. At me.

There was no turning back now. No point. Taking a deep breath, I carefully took the final step up onto Izzy's riser.

Far below, the drummer kicked out the opening beat to "Berenice's Smile." I'd played the song a thousand times, but up here, it sounded different. Fresh and new. The way it sounded that first day we played it together in that garage. Virginal.

And when the band joined in, I did too. Carefully at first, making damned sure to stay clear of that deadly railing. But gradually the music worked its magic, and I settled into what I am, a gear in a musical machine, a functional part of Israfel's Koven.

Perhaps Izzy's guitar was making the difference, because the music seemed to flow from my fingertips like water from a mountain spring, splashing and shimmering.

And though I'd played beneath the enormous backdrop of Poe's face a thousand times too, up here, suspended in space, Eddie and I were practically eye to eye. I could feel the full power of his manic gaze, burning into me, urging me on.

The policemen were at the foot of the stairway, shouting up at me. Let them. I had no time for them now. The guitar solo in "Berenice" was coming up, the place where Izzy had gone off the rails in Detroit.

But when the moment came, instead of ripping into the song with Izzy's cocaine rage, I found myself slowing down, playing more languidly, as if in a dream, the audience forgotten, my troubles forgotten, playing only for Berenice, a woman long dead, calling out to her in a melody as sweet as she must have been in life.

My fingers danced lightly over the strings, touching and discarding each note until I chanced upon . . .

The perfect note.

A pure, impeccable tone, the proper pitch and timbre, a note that began to sustain of its own volition, singing on as the music swirled and roiled around it.

And I held onto it, giving it just the slightest touch of vibrato, creator and listener at the same time, my guitar and my soul in perfect harmony. And in that instant, I knew what Izzy had been seeking so desperately.

I felt transformed. Angelic. Immortal.

I am Israfel!

I seized the rail!

Four hundred forty volts exploded up through my arms, dimming the theater lights, throwing the tower into sharp relief. The massive shock seared through my synapses, a blast of white pain so powerful that my nerve centers flared, then blew out! Instant overload!

I felt only the faintest tingling now, like insects nibbling, as the powerful voltage torched my clothing, charring my flesh, sending flaming fragments pin-wheeling into space as the audience below rose to its feet with a roar, cheering for the most spectacular effect they'd ever seen!

For a heartbeat, I savored their ovation, then it began to fade away. As my final brain functions winked out and shut down, the roar of applause began to wax and wane, washing over me, like great waves breaking . . .

Over a sepulcher by the side of the sea.
A tomb by the sounding sea.

If I could dwell where Israfel hath dwelt, and he where I . . .
A bolder note than his might swell, from my lyre within the sky . . .

———————

Award-winning author DOUG ALLYN is a Michigan writer with an international following. The author of eight novels and nearly a hundred short stories, his first short story won the Robert L. Fish Award for Best First Mystery Short Story from Mystery Writers of America, and subsequent critical response has been equally remarkable. He has won the coveted Edgar Award (plus six nominations), the International Crime Readers' Award, three Derringer Awards for novellas, and the Ellery Queen Mystery Magazine's Readers Award an unprecedented eight times. Published internationally in English, German, French, and Japanese, more than two dozen of his tales have been optioned for development as feature films and television programs.

The Golden Bug

Michael A. Black

1943
Somewhere in the Solomon Islands
0200 Hours

I walked along the beach until my legs gave out, sending me to my knees, my lungs screaming for a breath. Bauer fell from my back and rolled onto the sandy expanse, unconscious but still breathing. I reached into my pocket and pulled it out, the string dangling before me like a ripcord to heaven . . .

Or hell.

But I'd already been there, hadn't I?

Cannibals, a madman, and the golden bug . . .

Its ebony eyes stared back at me, jewels of a meretricious trinket that had driven a man mad. I rolled onto my back, looking upward . . .

•   •   •

It had been the middle of the night when Bauer and I left the submarine. The sea was black in the moonlight, endless; the only sound the slapping of our paddles against the water. The two of us worked furiously to escape the rough wake of the submerging sub. Rising with each wave, we surged forward, then struggled to keep the raft from being drawn back. After an eternity Bauer stopped paddling and held up his hand. I could barely see it in the darkness, but I paused too, trying to catch my breath.

"You hear it, Professor?" he rasped.

I listened, cognizant of nothing but my rapid breathing.

Then I became aware of another sound. Waves hitting the beach. Bauer turned and grinned. At least I thought that's what he did. We both began paddling again with renewed fervor. The sound of the surf increased with each stroke. As the raft crested a particularly high wave, a vague shape, massive and black like some monstrous leviathan, suddenly loomed up in front of us. The island. Sweat ran down my face and my arms ached, but we couldn't afford to stop. We were too close.

A narrow strip of sand suddenly glowed white against the frothiness of the dark water. Beyond it, a dense row of trees. We rode the tide as far as it would take us, our paddles scuffing the solidness of the beach. We'd made it this far, but as we jumped out and carried the raft toward the heavy line of mangroves, I could feel the reluctant tug of the retreating waves pulling at my legs, as if warning me not to go farther. The receding salt water buried our feet, making us fight for each step forward. Finally we broke free and crept into the dense shrubbery.

"How you doing, Professor?" Bauer asked.

Professor. The other guys' nickname for me because I was one of the few enlisted men with a college education. But I didn't mind. My education was something no one could take from me, and I had a teaching job waiting for me when I got back. I flashed him the thumbs-up sign and sucked in a lungful of the humid air. The myriad of insects suddenly went totally quiet. I stared into the thick blackness.

If I ever get back, I thought.

"Note the time," Bauer said.

I looked at the luminescent dial of my watch. Zero three forty. Had it really taken us forty minutes to get only this far? I knew we had forty-seven hours and twenty minutes left until the rendezvous with the sub.

Bauer motioned me forward and now the plants seemed to pull and tear at us as we moved. Bauer paused and we lowered the raft, finding it nearly impossible to negotiate through the bush with the craft's girth.

"You deflate it while I get a compass reading," he said. After unscrewing the plug, I took inventory of our gear. Radio, generator, weapons, ammo, water, and K-rations. The red lens of Bauer's flashlight cast a scarlet hue over his face and hands as he set the compass on the map.

"We're here," he said, his big index finger tapping the paper. "The village is here; the Japs' base here." He swept the red beam over the surrounding area, then said, "Let's look for a good place to bury this stuff, then try to get a little rest. No sense even trying to move through this in the dark."

I looked up through a tangled canopy of black branches toward an unclear sky, then checked my watch.

"Should start getting light in another hour or so," I said.

We busied ourselves with the tasks at hand, finding a suitable hiding place for our equipment, hooking up the generator to send our confirmation signal, and then checking our weapons. I paused to take a sip from my canteen.

"Better go easy on the water, Prof," Bauer said. "Who knows when we'll come across some more that's drinkable."

"Hopefully we'll find Evans and Legrand first," I said. We were talking in whispers, as if the jungle had ears.

"Or they'll find us." Bauer said nothing more.

We tried to find a clear spot where we could secret our equipment, but the ground was covered with thick roots. Bauer chopped at the tendrils with his entrenching tool, then snorted in disgust.

"Let's just cover the stuff with leaves," he said. "We can do a better job once the sun comes up."

And so we did, then waited. Our wait was cut short by an attack of large rapacious ants, crawling over us like scavengers and sinking their mandibles into our flesh. Bauer shone the light over my legs and brushed them off, then I did the same for him. After crushing as many as we could, we moved to another location, took another compass reading, then waited again. I thought about our mission, and the time we had to complete it. Rendezvous with the previous insertion team, supply the natives, and return for removal. Forty-eight hours.

Finally, as the crimson sun ascended from the horizon, we began moving cautiously through the jungle, on the lookout for Jap patrols, booby traps, and snakes. We used our machetes to hack through the brush. The entrenching tool dug into my back; my rifle strap shifted on my shoulder with each swipe. But that wasn't the worst of it. The insects continued to feast on us and, despite the oppressive heat, we had to keep our sleeves rolled down and our hats on. My shirt was soaked through in minutes after we started walking, and the ants left a trail of red marks on my skin. The mosquitoes were especially bad, swarming around us unmercifully. But despite the hardships of the march, the area struck me with its incredible beauty. Verdant trees and plants were everywhere, split in places by long ridges of crusty black volcanic rock. Long, thin poles of bamboo sprouted in clusters, and the limbs of other trees descended downward, piercing the ground like probing tentacles. We tried hard to move carefully, but each step was accompanied by a cacophony of brushing leaves and cracking twigs.

Something flickered behind one of those low-hanging branches to my left, and I caught my first glimpse of him. Dark eyes deeply set in a dark face. Wide nostrils, ebony hair.

"Bauer." My voice was a hoarse whisper.

"I saw him," he said, his fingers curling around the butt of his .45. His rifle was still slung over his shoulder.

I saw another flicker to my right, then still more.

Suddenly a man appeared in front of me, clad only in a loincloth. His skin was dark, and his kinky hair sprung out from his head, contained by a colorful headband. Another strip of the same colored cloth adorned his neck. His right hand loosely held a long spear. He stared at us for a moment. More natives appeared. Neither Bauer nor I moved. They were all around us.

"We're looking for Evans and Legrand," Bauer said finally. He spoke with slow deliberation, the way you speak to a drunk or a child. "Evans and Legrand."

"Leeeegrand," the native said, drawing the word out. Then he smiled. His teeth were blackened stubs. "Massa Will."

He slurred the words so they were hardly understandable. Turning, he scampered off ahead of us, moving through the shrubbery with the agility of a feral cat, motioning for us to follow. The bushes began to rustle on either side, and two dozen more natives filtered out of the green walls. Some carried spears, others bows and arrows. But none raised a weapon toward us in a threatening fashion. We continued our trek at their pace, confident that we were being led in the right direction.

We followed the natives up an embankment, then through some thick foliage. The wispy tendrils of a spiderweb caught my face, and I tried futilely to wipe them off. On the other side a clearing appeared and beyond it a group of thatched huts. More natives moved about within the cluster of huts. Women, naked from the waist up and wearing garments around their hips similar to the men's, stood as we entered the encampment and tugged the curious, gaping children away. One man sitting near a fire rotated a slab of meat on a spigot. Another carved what looked like a large coconut with a knife.

The leader turned and motioned for Bauer and me to sit. We shook our heads, and the native disappeared.

Bauer looked disgusted. "Poor tactics, having a working fire going. Enemy combatants will see the smoke. What the hell's wrong with these guys?"

I stared at the native with the coconut.

He grinned up at me, showing off a mouth full of blackened, discolored teeth.

"Jap," he said, pointing to the round ball he held in his hands.

And then I realized it wasn't a coconut at all, but a human head. The native drew the knife with careful precision from the base of the skull up along the top. Then he set the knife aside and began peeling the skin down along the forehead and cheekbones. It came off relatively easily in one piece, snagging only occasionally. As the skin fell away, it left a whitish layer of tendons and pink muscles. The dark eyes jiggled in their sockets. The separated skin was still intact, looking like a grotesque mask. The native took it and carefully placed it on a long stick above the fire. It was too high for the flames to reach, but waves of heat curled around the drooping skin, and it periodically leaked thick drops of moisture.

Next, the native got up and carried the skull perhaps twenty-five feet beyond the huts. He set it on the ground next to what appeared to be an earthen mound of about the same size. Then the surface of the mound shifted, and I saw what it was. Ants. So thickly crusted over the surface of the mound that they gave it a dark brown color. Within seconds a trail of more ants crept up the front of the skinned skull's jaws and cheeks. Soon it, too, was completely covered with the teeming creatures.

"So the marines have landed," said a strange voice. Bauer, who'd been watching the skull's preparation with me, whirled at the sound. A large shirtless man with a strip of khaki cloth around his forehead stood before us. He was almost as brown as a native but had definite Caucasian features, a shock of unruly, blond hair, and a growth of beard. Every muscle on his frame stood out in taut bas-relief. Instead of the loincloth that the natives wore, he had on cutoff khaki shorts and a pair of ragged boots.

"I'm Sergeant Bauer. This is Corporal Allan." Bauer moved forward, extending his hand. The man stood there looking down at it for a few moments, then took it.

"Will Legrand," he said. He looked at me with two piercing blue eyes.

"Where's Sergeant Evans?" Bauer asked.

Legrand shook his head. "The Japs got him when we first landed." He gestured toward the expanse of trees. "He's buried over there."

Bauer followed the gesture, then said, "Why haven't you been checking in?"

Legrand stared at him.

"We haven't heard from you in more than six weeks," I offered.

"My generator's dead," Legrand said. "Say, you wouldn't happen to have any cigarettes, would you?"

"Let's get that fire extinguished first," Bauer said. "We're risking letting every Jap on the island know where we are."

Legrand laid his hand on Bauer's shoulder. "Hold on. We're safe here."

Bauer stared at the man with a measure of obvious contempt. "For a marine, you look like crap. You lose your razor, too?"

Legrand smirked. He was a big man, as was Bauer. I didn't relish the thought of breaking up a fight between these two.

"I've lost a good number of things in the last six weeks," Legrand said. "Why hasn't anyone come by to pick me up?"

Bauer's lips drew into a line. "There's a war on, in case you've forgotten. You want a cruise ship, you should have stayed aboard the *Jones*."

"I'll be there soon enough. Ahh, those cigarettes?"

I dug my pack out of my pocket and held it toward him, shaking one out. The paper was damp with my sweat. Instead of grabbing the offered cigarette, his hand closed over the whole pack, pulling it away from me.

"Hey," I started to say, but he was already stepping away, holding the pack above his head and yelling.

"Lucky Strike! Lucky Strike!"

Bauer and I exchanged glances. He shrugged. The natives dropped whatever they'd been doing and came running, encircling us like kids at a candy shop. Legrand stuck one of the cigarettes in the corner of his mouth and began handing out the rest to the outstretched hands.

"You got matches?" he asked.

I took out my Zippo, popped open the cap, then spun the wheel. The wick ignited on the first try.

Legrand cupped his hand around mine, leaning in to light the cigarette. I snapped the cap back down, but his fingers curled around my hand. "Give it to me," he whispered. "Now."

I held the lighter tightly for a moment more, wondering if I would get it back, then opened my hand. Legrand plucked it from my palm and turned back to the natives. Holding it up, he flicked the wheel again and the natives' faces lit up with gap-toothed grins. "Jupiter, come here," Legrand called.

One of the bigger natives stepped forward. Legrand flicked the lighter closed, and a pair of dark fingers reached out and my lighter disappeared. The big native began moving around in the crowd, spinning the wheel and lighting all of their smokes.

"Loooky Strike," the native who'd been skinning the head said to me, displaying his blackened teeth again. He puffed copiously on the cigarette, then marched over to the rotating spit and sliced off a long section of meat and handed it to me, nodding his head. It wasn't until he smiled and said "Jap" that I realized what it was.

I recoiled in disgust, but Legrand, the glowing Lucky still tucked into the corner of his mouth, ambled over and grabbed the slice of greasy flesh.

"You mustn't upset our hosts," he said, popping the meat into his mouth after removing the cigarette. "Try some."

I felt a wave of revulsion sweep upward from my stomach. I'd seen a lot of terrible things in my time in the Pacific, but this was beyond all of them.

"Do you know what that is?" My voice was a rasp.

Legrand smirked and nodded as he took another bite.

Bauer put a hand on my chest and shook his head. His eyes were on Legrand as well. The natives, who were still finding joy in watching Jupiter ignite my Zippo, began to meander over to the fire, pulling off loose pieces of meat and chucking them down. Legrand held up his empty hand and waved it, his fingers and face smeared with the grease.

"Legrand," Bauer said, his voice a low growl. "What the hell's happened to you? You're a marine, for Christ's sake."

Legrand's eyes were piercing. "Am I? Like I said, I thought you forgot about me."

"Look," I said, trying to interject some reason into their bickering, "we've got less than thirty-seven hours to accomplish our mission and get out of this hellhole. Let's get to it, all right?"

Legrand looked from me to Bauer, then back to me again. "You guys have a map?"

Bauer nodded and opened his pocket. He withdrew the folded, sodden paper with the metal compass inside. Legrand's eyes lit up when he saw the compass.

"Just what I need," he said. "My ticket off the island. Lost mine when we had to swim for shore. The raft sank. I didn't catch the breaks you two did coming in."

"Looks like Evans didn't either," Bauer said.

They went back to their hostile staring. Wanting to get on with it, I gently plucked the map from Bauer's hand and spread it out on a fallen tree trunk.

"Where's that Jap base at?" I asked.

"Japs?" Legrand said. His voice held a trace of amusement. "On *my* island?"

"Your island?" Bauer said.

"We finished off those bastards about a week ago." Legrand laughed. "The last one was their commanding officer. Helped us out by slicing open his own gut. Guess he felt obligated since he'd failed his mission."

"Are you telling us there are no enemy personnel left on this rock?" Bauer sounded incredulous.

Legrand gestured toward the facial shroud, still hanging above the flames. "I think that's the last one. Or what's left of him."

Legrand's grin was broad, and I thought I detected something strange in his eyes. A primitive savagery. But then again, this was a man, a civilized man, who had just eaten the flesh of another human being in my presence a few minutes ago.

Bauer reached out and grabbed Legrand's arm, pulling him toward him. "Listen, you son of a—"

Before he could finish the sentence a dozen natives descended upon us, spears pointing at our throats and abdomens. I felt if we tried to move, our skins would end up cooking over one of those campfires. The big native, the one Legrand had called Jupiter, pressed the tip of his spear against my throat. I felt a trickle of blood run down my neck as the point sliced into my flesh.

"Massa Will," the native said, "we kill?"

Legrand laughed and leaned in close to us, his whiskered face almost rubbing mine. I could smell burned flesh on his breath. "One word from me"—his voice a hoarse whisper—"one little word, and they'll stick more holes in you than a pincushion."

"You bastard," Bauer said. "I'll see you're court-martialed for this."

Legrand backhanded him. A line of blood welled from Bauer's lips and trickled down his chin.

"I'll see you in hell first," Legrand said. His blue eyes looked more demented than ever as they swept over our faces. The last lines of an old poem raced through my mind: . . . *From the thunder and the storm, and the cloud that took the form when the rest of heaven was blue of a demon in my view.*

His mouth twisted into a maniacal grin. "But wouldn't you rather be . . . rich?"

"Go to hell," Bauer said, and spat.

Legrand recoiled from the bloody spittle. One of the natives clubbed Bauer on the head and he went to his knees. Another grabbed his hair and pulled his head back, drawing a long knife from a scabbard. I felt a blade edge my neck, too. But just as I was certain we were both going to have our throats slit, Legrand said something I couldn't understand. The natives looked up at him. His expression was demented, his smile deranged, his eyes the bluest I'd ever seen. Pure cerulean.

A blue-eyed demon in my view.

It was the last thing I remembered before feeling the heavy blow to the back of my head.

I don't know how long I was out, but when I woke I couldn't move. My arms were asleep, my bare legs tied together with some hemp-like rope.

"We're trussed up tighter than a torsion spring," Bauer said.

I managed to roll over and look at him. He was naked, except for his underwear, and bound just as I was, our arms secured by heavy twine and braced with a stout branch.

"Any chance we can untie each other?" I asked.

"Doubtful. I can't even feel my fingers, these damn ropes are so tight." He rotated his head. "That son of a bitch has gone dancing mad."

I wondered about the time. Through the open doorway I could see that it was still light out, and that the natives were jumping around a huge fire. Several women gyrated and shook themselves, their small breasts shaking. One male, resplendent in a crown-like headpiece, sat at the front of the fire. One by one, the women moved forward and lay objects at his feet. At first I thought they were some sort of rocks, then one rolled over and I was staring at a shrunken Oriental face. The dead Jap's skin had been stretched over a rock to give it support.

I shuddered, thinking our faces would end up like that. I thought about our rendezvous point and wondered how much longer we had to make it there.

"How much time we got left?" My voice was edged with desperation.

"I'd estimate we still have the better part of thirty-two hours." Bauer snorted. "Maybe it'd be better if we had less."

"They'll send a patrol to look for us when we aren't there, won't they?"

His silence told me the answer. We were two dead men, waiting on a madman's whim.

I struggled against the bonds, trying to break free. After minutes of fruitless straining, I lowered my head to the sandy earth.

So this is how it ends for me, I thought.

We listened to the howls of delight from the campfire celebration, neither of us talking. Periodically I could hear Bauer grunting as he tested the strength of the bonds. I did the same until exhaustion and frustration won out. I'm not sure when it was that I drifted off to sleep, but my dream—of a raven strutting and periodically pecking at my guts—was interrupted when I felt a more substantial prodding. I opened my eyes, my mouth parched, and saw the outline of Legrand against the moonlit sky.

"Wha—" I started to say, but he kicked me harder.

"Shhh." He brought his fingers to his lips, then squatted down next to me. He reached over and shook Bauer awake. "Do you both want to live?"

More of his demented teasing. I turned my head away, but his fingers gripped my chin and twisted my face toward his. He spoke in a croaking whisper. "I asked you if you wanted to live."

"Yes."

He looked at Bauer, then back to me. "You both have an opportunity to come with me and live, and be rich men for the rest of your lives."

"What the hell are you talking about?" Bauer asked.

"There's a treasure buried on this island," Legrand whispered.

"A treasure?" Bauer said. "You're nuts."

Legrand's face contorted with sudden rage. I had to do something to keep him from slitting our throats. "Treasure? Where did it come from?"

The question eased Legrand away from his anger. "Pirates, probably. They say Captain Cook circumnavigated the globe through here."

"He was no pirate," Bauer said.

"Who's to say?" Legrand's face contorted again. "You?"

"How did you find out about it?" Desperation washed over me.

"It's been here forever." Legrand suddenly seemed calm again.

"The natives worship it like a shrine. It's ours for the taking, if we play it smart."

"Like you've been doing so far?" Bauer said.

"What about your friends?" I asked.

Legrand looked down at me.

"Like I said, the natives worship it. They'll never give it up. We're all civilized men. It's ours for the taking, if we can dig it up and get it back somewhere safe."

"Marine Corps regulations," Bauer said. "They'll never let you keep it."

"The Japs had a boat." Legrand ignored him. "It's in good shape, anchored in a cove. We can use that to get away. With the treasure."

"You're talking desertion," Bauer said. "In a time of war."

"I'm talking the difference between living rich and dying in this godforsaken hellhole."

"And we're supposed to believe you?" Bauer made no attempt to hide the derision in his voice.

Legrand withdrew something from his pants pocket. In the dimness it looked like a large hickory nut on a string, but as he dangled it between us, I saw that it was something more . . . A beetle . . . A golden beetle with two dark gems for eyes.

"Take a look at this bug," Legrand said. "It's solid gold."

"Fool's gold," Bauer said, his voice still full of contempt.

Legrand drew a big knife from a sheath on his belt. The silver blade gleamed in the moonlight. "Time to decide." He held out his hands, one with the knife, the other with the gold bug. "Are you with me, or ready to die?"

I caught a glimpse of Bauer's face, frozen with a determined bravado. My bladder felt on the brink of release. "I'm with you."

Legrand nodded, then looked to Bauer. "Okay, sarge. It's your turn."

Bauer ran his tongue over his lips, waited a few seconds more, then nodded.

"How are we going to find this place?" I asked.

"Jupiter will show us." I felt a flood of relief as Legrand cut through the twine binding me. The blood began flowing freely in my arms and legs and I massaged them as Legrand crept over and cut Bauer loose. It was a full three minutes before I could feel anything. I worked my fingers open and closed, trying to stem the cramps that were seizing them. Jupiter came in carrying our clothes and, most important, our boots. He set them down between us and we rummaged through the pile trying to sort out which was mine and which was Bauer's.

"Where're our weapons?" Bauer said.

Legrand's teeth shone white against the darkness. "I may have adopted some of their ways, but I'm not stupid." He patted his side and I saw he had on Bauer's pistol belt and holstered .45. I also noticed then that the rifle slung over his shoulder was one of ours. "And I'm warning you. Step out of line after we get out of here, and I'll blow your head off and leave you where you lay." He stared at each of us in turn, then mumbled something to Jupiter.

The big native crept to the side of a nearby hut and glanced around. He turned and nodded, waving his hand for us to follow. In another moment, he disappeared outside. Legrand motioned for us to get up. I stood, only to collapse onto my knees after half a step.

Legrand's mouth was next to my ear, the whisper sounding like a staccato burst of gunfire. "Get your damn ass going."

I felt Bauer help me up, and we slipped out into the night. Legrand was behind us, shoving us toward the tree line. I had no idea which way we were going until I felt Legrand direct me. In no more than thirty seconds we'd traversed the camp and found ourselves in the bushes.

"There. Stop." Legrand pointed to two packs. "Pick those up."

They'd obviously found our secreted supplies. The knapsacks contained our canteens, our entrenching tools, and little else.

"Like I told you," Legrand said. "I'm the only one with a weapon, and I'll use it if you try to cross me."

"Where's my watch?" I asked.

Legrand held up his left arm and the greenish spot on the dial glowed before my eyes. "You mean *my* watch?" He grabbed a spear that was stuck in the dirt.

We followed Jupiter along a small path, enabling us to pass through most of the wooded areas fairly quickly. If we'd known about this trail on the way in, we could have made it in half the time. They kept us on a forced march, Jupiter leading us through the darkness with the assurance of a mountain goat negotiating a hillside, and Legrand behind us, occasionally prodding with the long spear when we slowed. After what must have been hours of walking, the sun began to climb in the sky above us and bright rays filtered through the coniferous canopy, making random spots of light on the pathway before us. I noticed for the first time that the trail winding its way through the dense vegetation was bare earth, indicating that this was a well-traveled pathway, known to the natives. I wondered if the rest of them would come after us when they discovered we'd left under the veil of night. It made desecrating some sacred site seem like not such a good idea, though not because of any reverence for the beliefs of these savages. My concern was that it would make them even angrier at us.

But then again, I thought, *an unpleasant death was probably in the cards no matter what.*

I managed to get close enough to Bauer to whisper, "What's your take on this?"

His head shook fractionally. "Wait for the right time. Try to escape." His lips barely moved, but I felt Legrand prod my back with the spear.

"Keep your mouths shut. Both of you."

Ahead, Jupiter stopped and held up his hand. Crouching, he pushed apart a row of bushes and turned with a wide, gap-toothed grin.

"Massa Will," he said, pointing.

I looked in the direction of his finger and saw a dip in the terrain. The ground descended on an incline perhaps forty feet, then leveled off only to run into a rocky bluff that went almost straight upward. Legrand prodded us again with the spear.

"There. Do you see it?" he said.

"See what?" Bauer asked.

"There. Look. On the mountain." His voice was full of excitement. "The rocks form a skull."

It was far from being a mountain, but it was tall enough to

give a good high-ground advantage. If we could somehow get up there with some weapons, there was a chance we could hold off any marauding natives until the sub came back. I suddenly found myself doing mental calculations as to what time it might be and how much time we had left.

"I don't see nothing," Bauer said.

"Then you're blind as well as stupid." Legrand glanced at my watch. "Get down that hill. We got work to do."

It took us another half hour to get to the bottom of the ravine and make our way across. As we drew close the shape of the rocky bluff became clearer. It did resemble a crude skull, the large oval holes being the eyes, the protrusion of smooth rock looking much like a forehead. More rocks had been laid at the foot of the bluff, forming two long rows about three feet high. A primitive altar was my guess. Legrand pushed us toward the middle of it and turned to Jupiter.

"Where?" he asked, making inquiring gestures with his arms.

The native walked around, looking up toward the rock skull, then back to the ground. After about five minutes of pacing, he shrugged.

Legrand's face tightened. "Come on, you ignorant cretin."

Jupiter looked toward the sky. The sun was almost directly overhead, which most likely meant it was around noon. We had about fifteen hours before the sub would come back and surface at our rendezvous point on the other side of the island. If we could get away from this madman . . .

Legrand gestured again, and Jupiter pointed to the skull, then stepped forward and hurled his spear toward the bluff. It stuck in the center of what appeared to be the left eye. The native then traced the shadow of the shaft onto the ground, got down on his hands and knees, and sniffed the earth. He rose with a grin and pointed.

Legrand nodded and backed up a few steps. "Start digging there."

I pulled my entrenching tool out of the knapsack and straightened its blade. I wasn't sure how much the futile digging attempt after we'd first landed had dulled it, but it would still make a passable weapon, should the chance arise. Legrand must have read my thoughts in my expression because he backed up a few more steps and took out the .45.

"Dig. Now."

Bauer and I exchanged glances, and he withdrew his shovel, too. We set to work and, despite the heat, managed to dig a fair-sized hole in an hour.

"I hope we're not digging our own graves," Bauer whispered to me.

I had the same thought. But if we found any treasure, and it was substantial, Legrand would at least keep us alive to help him transport it to this boat he'd secreted. That could buy us more time.

"Where the hell is it?" Legrand's voice was growing more impatient. He turned to Jupiter. "Where?"

The native, who had been working his knife into a coconut and drinking the milk, seemed befuddled.

Legrand withdrew the gold bug from his pocket and dangled it in front of the dark face. "Where?" He pointed to the hole. We'd gone down at least four or five feet.

Jupiter tilted his head back and held the coconut up to drink some more juice, but Legrand slapped it from his grasp.

"Where?" he yelled.

Jupiter's face lost its happy expression, and he stood, ambling over to check our progress. He licked his lips, then retrieved his spear, which was still sticking outward from the bluff. Testing the weight with one hand, then the other, he jumped forward and hurled the spear at the bluff again, this time striking it in the center of what was the right eye. He once again traced the path of the spear's shadow onto the ground. It was several feet away from our current hole.

"Dig there," Legrand said.

"This is crazy," Bauer said. "You can dig it yourself, dammit."

Legrand aimed the pistol at him. "Do it now, or I'll let Jupiter cut your head off and make it into another of his shrunken trinkets."

"Bauer," I said, still harboring the faint hope that we could escape once darkness fell. If we could both stay alive until then. "Come on."

I climbed out of the hole and jammed my shovel into the packed earth.

"What time is it?" I asked, after about fifteen minutes of digging.

"Never mind," Legrand said. "Dig."

"I need some water," Bauer said.

"Find my treasure and I'll give you water." The madness in his blue eyes seemed a permanent fixture now, and I began to wonder if he'd even keep us alive to carry his booty, should we find it. I felt as futile as Sisyphus, rolling the boulder up the hill. I had to keep digging to stay alive, which in this heat was a slow death in and of itself, but we'd be able to stop digging only when we found the treasure, which would be equally deadly.

Suddenly Bauer's shovel made a scraping sound and he looked up at me. I scooped more of the earth away and used my fingers to explore. I felt something metallic. A large ring. We dug deeper on each side and brushed off what appeared to be the edge of a large wooden chest.

"It's there!" Legrand yelled. "It's there!" His maniacal laughter echoed in the declivity. "I found it. I'm rich. I'm rich." He straightened and pointed the pistol at us again. "Pull it out of there."

Bauer and I grabbed the ring and tugged. The chest wouldn't budge.

"Do it, dammit," Legrand yelled. "Do it."

We braced our legs and pulled harder. After more straining, there was a sudden cracking sound and we both fell backward. The section of the chest attached to the ring had broken off. Legrand scrambled over to the edge of the hole and looked down. I did, too, seeing what appeared to be a large pile of gold coins through the broken side of the chest. His mad laughter continued.

Exhausted, I tried to catch my breath. Jupiter, indifferent to us all, leaned against the bluff, working his knife into another coconut. A few feet over his shoulder, where the spear rested in the soft earth, a green snake twisted out of the skull's eye. It slithered outward, coiling along the shaft, and dropped down on the big native's shoulder.

Jupiter jerked spasmodically, dropped the coconut, and gripped the serpent with both hands. He threw the slim creature to the ground and sliced it in half with his knife. Both pieces of the snake writhed for a few seconds, then ceased. Jupiter touched his shoulder, near the juncture with his neck, muttered, "Massa Will," took two steps, and collapsed.

As Legrand turned to look, Bauer swung his shovel into the man's left leg. Legrand whirled, firing the pistol in our direction. I recoiled as the ejected casing did a slow-motion semicircle in the air above me. Bauer reeled backward into the hole, holding his side.

My feet found purchase on the edge of the hole and I was surging upward, my entrenching tool at the ready. Holding it like a spear, I had a vision of slicing Legrand's throat.

But the madman moved too quickly, dancing away from me despite the red blood that cascaded down his bare leg where Bauer had struck him. He raised the .45 and grinned. I knew I had mere seconds to live, even less, when I heard the crack of the round.

I waited for the impact, but felt nothing. Legrand's face went from a look of enraged dementia to almost complete idiocy. The hand holding the pistol slowly lowered and he looked down at his chest. A large red stain was working its way from between his pectoral muscles, where, in the center, a jagged hole oozed blood. He looked up just as another report sounded, and this time his head jerked to the side. He fell to his knees and rolled into the hole with Bauer. The ground next to my feet erupted and I knew the sniper, or whoever had shot Legrand, was now concentrating on me. I dove back into the hole, scrambling to get hold of the .45 and return fire.

"Who's shooting?" Bauer's voice sounded weak.

I shook my head. "How bad you hit?"

"I think it went clean through the other side. Hurts like hell but it's not bleeding that bad."

I managed to peel the pistol from Legrand's death grip and then peered over the edge of the hole. Back where the ground dropped off a ragtag group of three Jap soldiers were moving steadily downward.

"Japs," I said, crawling over to pull my watch off Legrand's wrist. The son of a bitch had placed the rifle about ten yards away from our holes. If I could get to it, we might stand a chance. A half-assed chance, but a chance nonetheless. I felt a bulge in Legrand's pocket and worked my fingers inside. I pulled out the gold bug he'd shown us and something worth far more. A grenade.

"Reach in there and get me one of those gold coins," Bauer said. "I want to die a rich man."

"We're not going to die yet," I told him, and reached between the broken shards of the chest, withdrawing a handful of gold coins. I was about to grab more when two coiled snakes began working their way upward through the shattered wood. I grabbed Bauer and pulled him to the side. "It's full of snakes."

We worked our way over to the side of the hole as the snakes coiled over Legrand's blank face. Reptiles seeking the fading warmth. Or were they merely seeking one of their own?

I told Bauer my plan: I'd throw the grenade at the Japs, then make a break to recover the rifle, leaving the pile of gold coins on top of the ground. He was to make for the trees and we'd work our way in the direction of the beach. Hopefully, the Japs would be momentarily stalled by the sight of the treasure and figure they could deal with us later. In any case, it was our only shot.

"Ready?" I asked, as I straightened the flattened wires of the pin.

Bauer nodded.

I slid the pin from the hole and held the lever tight. If ever I'd thrown to home plate from the outfield playing baseball as a kid, I needed that true aim now. I launched myself out of the hole, ran three steps, then let the grenade fly. I sprinted toward the rifle and reached it just as I heard the resounding explosion. Grabbing the long gun, I pivoted and ran, seeing Bauer making his way toward the tree line, just like we'd planned.

We pushed through the dense brush, bullets crashing into the vegetation around us. We kept moving, knowing certain death was behind us. The bullets ceased after a while, but we continued to press onward. The denseness relented slightly and we found something akin to a path. The light was beginning to fade and we were soon plunged into a growing darkness. Our throats were parched, our limbs weak, I didn't know how much longer we could go on. Bauer fell. I slung the rifle over my shoulder and picked him up, draped his arm over my neck to help him along. Each step brought groans of pain, but as long as he was groaning, I knew he was alive.

"I . . . have t—to stop," he said. "Can't go on. You . . . leave me here."

I dropped to my knees, taking him down with me. If I left him here, he'd die. I'd never find him again. But I didn't think I could go on carrying him. I panted, trying to catch my breath, then heard something. A not so distant sound of surf slapping the beach.

Renewed, I stood, raising my depleted companion with me, and surged forward. After a few more minutes, we were at the beach. Not knowing exactly where we were, I chose the direction I thought was correct and began walking. The smell of the water and its cool wetness lapping over our feet gave me new strength. Bauer seemed renewed, too.

"You think we're going the right way?" he asked.

I replied that we were, and silently prayed I was right. Bauer soon lost what little strength he had left. I shifted his body and got him on my back. All I could think of was to keep moving. I teetered on the edge of the abyss.

After walking for an eternity more, I collapsed to my knees, my chest heaving, my lungs screaming for a breath. Bauer fell off me and tumbled to the sandy expanse, unconscious but still breathing. I reached into my pocket and pulled it out, the string dangling before me like a ripcord to heaven . . .

Or hell.

But I'd already been there, hadn't I?

Cannibals, a madman, and the golden bug . . .

Its ebony eyes stared back at me, jewels of a meretricious trinket that had driven a man mad. I rolled onto my back, looking upward. The dark sky, full of stars, was a brightly spotted canopy above me. Then it transformed into a vision of Legrand's maniacal face, as a jagged line split the heavens and a peal of thunder swept over us, followed by a soft, but drenching, rain.

From the thunder and the storm, and the cloud that took the form . . .

I woke up groggy and bandaged with IV lines taped to my arms. An angelic face leaned over me and smiled.

"Am I in heaven?" I asked.

"No, marine," the angel said. "You're on the USS *Relief*. I'm Nurse Lee."

The hospital ship? I closed my eyes and thanked God. Then managed to say, "Bauer?"

She smiled again. "He's here, too." Turning, she pointed and I saw him lying in an adjacent bunk, snoring. "He's a bit worse off than you, but you'll both survive."

I tried to swallow and she gave me a sip of cool water. After coughing a few times, I managed to get down some more.

"Don't try to drink too much," she said. "You were both so dehydrated when they found you, you were almost dead. Plus your friend had been shot." The nurse patted my forehead with a damp cloth. "God only knows what you've been through." She wiped the cloth over my face again.

What had we been through? Had it all been a dream? Some terrible dream? Her eyes were the purest azure I'd ever seen.

"When the rest of heaven is blue," I managed to say.

She put her fingers to her lips. "Don't try to talk. When you're stronger, I'm looking forward to hearing all about it. Especially about how you got this." She raised her hand, a string wound around her finger, the golden bug suspended above my face, its dark jewel eyes glaring down at me.

"We found this clutched in your fist," she said. "What is it? Some kind of good luck charm?"

"It's"—I searched for the right words—"a demon in my view."

MICHAEL A. BLACK grew up reading Edgar Allan Poe's stories and poems and is even rumored to have had a pet raven at one time. He is the author of ten books, eight of which are mystery and thriller novels. The most recent are *Random Victim* and *Dead Ringer* (cowritten with Julie Hyzy). He also has more than fifty short stories to his credit. Black majored in English and was always impressed with Poe's versatility. Not only was he the originator of the detective story, but his work also included thrilling science fiction and adventure tales. "The Golden Bug" is Black's homage to Poe's story of a similar title.

William Allan Wilson

Jon L. Breen

Monday, September 3, 2007

Today brought an occurrence that in recent months has been only slightly less singular than a total eclipse: a telephone call from my literary agent. It was heartening to hear from him for a change. More often, it is I punching out his number and struggling to get through his dragon of a secretary—excuse me, personal assistant.

"Is that William Allan Wilson, master of detection?" he said with his usual facetiousness.

"It is."

"Hard at work, Willie?"

"It's Labor Day, Phil. I always labor on Labor Day."

"That's good, 'cause I've been working for you, too. Last week, I was talking to your old pal Sloane Ghormley over at Westcott Press."

"Not my pal exactly."

"Well, I know you guys go back a long way."

"We were never close."

"That's not what he says. Anyhow, he values your work. We had a few drinks together—booze always helps when you're dealing with Ghormley—and we kicked around some ideas for you. I never thought anything would come of it. I mean, who knows what a guy like that will remember when he sobers up. But he called this morning and he's ready to offer a contract. The money isn't great, but the prestige may be."

"Pay me enough money and you can keep the prestige, Phil."

"Ha ha. Believe me, you're not getting enough money to blow off the prestige. Willie, you know I love this retro stuff you write, but it's not that easy to market, okay? And I know you really prefer short stories."

"Which you don't handle."

"Normally, I don't, no, but an agent's gotta make a living, too, you know."

"The short story is the original and ideal vehicle for the tale of detection, starting with Poe and continuing with Doyle and Chesterton and—"

"Funny you should mention Poe. He's part of the deal. The bicentennial of Poe's birth is coming up in 2009. Sloane wants a sort of homage volume for his winter list, and we both agreed that you are the most Poe-inspired mystery writer on the scene. Now you know my opinion of Poe in today's market, so I don't have to repeat it."

"But you will anyway."

"He wouldn't get anywhere. He'd be publishing online for

nothing or in small-circ poetry and horror mags that pay in copies. I keep telling you that, but do you ever listen to me?"

"No."

"Anyway, what Sloane wants is a collection of new stories about that great detective of yours, Archie Swan—"

"His name's Archer Swain, Phil. You know that."

"Whatever. A collection of stories all based on motifs from Poe. A big house like Westcott commissioning an original collection, I don't have to tell you, is more than unusual. It's like man bites dog, you know what I mean?"

Unusual indeed. Why, continuing the canine metaphor, would Sloane Ghormley of all people want to throw a bone my way? I said nothing of this to Phil, sticking to business.

"How soon does he want this?"

"His target for publication is Poe's birthday in January 2009, so the timeline is kind of tight. He says he needs all the stories in his hands by the first of May next year. That's asking a lot, I know, but you're a fast worker when you have to be, Willie. I know you can get that done."

"And how much of an advance are we talking about?"

"This won't sound like a lot, but you gotta remember the prestige of Westcott and the publicity hook of the Poe bicentennial. They're promising to get behind it, so it's sure to earn out fast, and I can negotiate a favorable royalty."

"How much money, Phil?"

He told me, and I grumbled for form's sake, but truthfully it wasn't bad. For an original collection of detective short stories, even by a writer as respected and accomplished as myself, it was quite generous. The way Phil had downplayed it was simply agent psychology: lower expectations and your client will be favorably surprised. In any event, I am in no position to turn down work, so of course I agreed.

"Give him a call, Willie," Phil said. "Touch base. Talk about what he's looking for and what ideas you have for it. Meanwhile, I'll take care of the business details."

The idea of talking with Sloane Ghormley was unappetizing. It had been years since we had spoken, and there were good reasons. I was not truthful when I said we were never close. We had been close friends once, but Ghormley had taken something from me that I valued beyond measure. Still, I promised Phil I would telephone his office at Westcott tomorrow.

After hanging up the phone, I told myself the request was not so incredible, strictly from a publishing standpoint. It would be obvious to anyone knowledgeable in the genre that I am the ideal person for this job. After all, how many current practitioners of the classical detective story are there? And of that handful, how many write about a peerless supersleuth whose cases are recounted by an admiring friend? Archer Swain's Watson is named Wally Weston, and I must constantly emphasize that he is not me, no more than the anonymous narrator of the Dupin stories was Poe, although Charles Raymond Macauley drew him to look like Poe in illustrating the collection *Monsieur Dupin* (McClure, Phillips, 1904), of which a very fine copy is a treasured feature of my library.

My short stories about Archer Swain, albeit less lucrative than his novel-length cases, are palpably superior and certainly have afforded me greater pleasure. The novels weary me, especially with the increasing editorial demand for greater and greater length, which my aesthetic standards demand I satisfy with greater complexity of plot and theme rather than lumpy dollops of soap opera.

But I confess to astonishment that Sloane Ghormley should offer me an opportunity like this. He never evinced any interest in the Swain novels. Was it guilt? But it is pointless to conjecture. Mine not to reason why, mine only to do the work and cash the check.

I had not really been laboring on Labor Day when the telephone rang, but I begin my labors now. As soon as I lay aside my pen, I shall take down from my shelves as a source for inspiration the definitive Thomas Ollive Mabbott edition of Poe's tales and sketches.

Tuesday, September 4, 2007

Before I could telephone Sloane Ghormley this morning, a prospect I was preparing for with a second mug of strong coffee, he telephoned me. I mean the man himself, not some secretary (or personal assistant) to establish my identity and ask me to hold for Mr. Ghormley. He was hearty and ingratiating. I was polite and civil. While it is fresh in my memory, I shall reproduce our dialogue.

"Willie Wilson! My God, it's been too long. How are you?"

"Quite well, Sloane. And yourself?"

"Fine."

"And Mrs. Ghormley?"

"Ah, she's fine as far as I know, but alas, no longer Mrs.

Ghormley." I intrude to note the sad words were belied by a cheerful delivery. "And how is Mrs.— Oh, but you never married, did you?"

"I think you know that, Sloane."

"Of course, I do, forgive me, but it's been so long. Now, I know Phil told you roughly what I'm looking for in this collection. Could we meet for lunch maybe and talk about it?"

"I think not. I rarely leave my house these days."

"Why not? Agoraphobic?"

"Nothing like that, but every comfort I require is here, and venturing into the city has come to seem a major expedition. And anyway, this proposed deadline of yours is so short that I must get to work immediately to meet it. So you'll forgive me if we have what conversation is necessary by the present means of communication. Or perhaps e-mail would be even more efficient."

"Sure, whatever you say. I was figuring on ten or twelve stories, all with your man Archer Swain on the case, of course, but each based on a motif from Poe's work. You could do a locked-room story, for example, in homage to 'The Murders in the Rue Morgue.' I'd say have a situation as much like Poe's as you can but solve it without an orangutan."

"No problem," I said. Truthfully, it was a big problem. Locked rooms are not my specialty. But I would come up with something.

"Then you could do a hidden-document mystery like 'The Purloined Letter.'"

"Easy enough," I said, quite truthfully.

"The one I look forward to most is a code or cipher story like 'The Gold Bug.'"

"Oh, yes. You always did enjoy codes and ciphers, didn't you, Sloane?"

"Love them."

"You were good with numbers, too, as I recall." If he sensed any innuendo, he let it pass. "And handling money." With that addition, I had thrown subtlety out the window, but still he chose to ignore it.

"Do me a good code story, Willie. You know, I've always loved your work. We should have a least-suspected-person variant in salute to 'Thou Art the Man.' You get the idea of what I'm looking for, don't you?"

"Certainly," I said, grudgingly admitting to myself that he seemed to know his Poe, though there had been one notable omission from his listing of the detective tales.

"Now let's see. That makes four stories. What else could you do?"

Eschewing the obvious for the moment, I said, "I might draw some inspiration from his exposé of Maelzel's Chess Player. And certainly the horror and science fiction stories have some elements I could use. Perhaps I'll even get into the poetry."

"Sure, that's great. In Hollywood pitch terms, 'The Raven' meets 'The Bells,' right?" A rather strained laugh from his end, none from mine. "Well, I guess you're on your way then, Willie. It's been great talking to you after all these years. Really."

"But you forgot one story, Sloane."

"What do you mean?"

"Another Dupin story. What about 'The Mystery of Marie Roget'? Don't you want Archer Swain to have a crack at a real-life murder case?"

"Oh, yes, of course. How could I forget that? You have a case in mind? Something from Swain's period, I suppose."

You who are reading these words, whoever and whenever you are, surely know the Archer Swain series—you wouldn't be much of a mystery fiction scholar if you did not—so I hardly need tell you the great sleuth's cases are not set in the present but rather in the late 1930s and early 1940s, much more suitable to a Golden Age crime-solver. I decided early on I didn't wish to concern myself with DNA and modern forensics, and the wisdom of my decision was only fortified when that annoyingly ubiquitous atrocity known as the cell phone came onto the scene. I don't even own one. I have no objection to advanced technology if it serves a useful purpose—I write my fiction quite happily on a computer, and the Internet, if explored with caution, can be a boon to research—but most so-called modern advances, always excepting the medical, are anything but a step forward.

"No," I replied, "not from Archer Swain's period."

"A current case then?"

"No, not that either. A case from a few years ago. From around the time we were in college."

A long silence at the other end of the line. He knew what I was talking about. Finally he said, "You can't live in the past, Willie."

"Oh, can't I? I thought my residency in the past was the reason I was being given this assignment."

"You need to let old wounds heal."

"Some never do heal, Sloane. Now, if you expect me to meet your deadline, I had best get to work, had I not?"

"Sure. We'll talk again. Can't wait for that code story. Call me anytime. Or e-mail me. Way back in our days on the college paper, I hoped we could one day work on a book together, you know that?"

No, I hadn't known that actually.

So to work. If the demanding schedule should cause me to neglect this journal, you future scholars will, I hope, forgive me.

Thursday, September 19, 2007

The initial story is done at last. My locked-room mystery in homage to "The Murders in the Rue Morgue" came to me surprisingly smoothly. I replicated Poe's crime just as Ghormley had asked and provided what I think is an acceptable solution, sans orangutan, with Archer Swain in excellent form. Next I'll move on to the hidden-document tale. It should go faster. But the code or cipher story worries me, frankly, speaking as one who cannot even hold the difference between *code* and *cipher* in his head. How can I come up with something truly original in that line that will impress a connoisseur of deception and hidden meanings like Sloane Ghormley?

Tuesday, January 1, 2008

If posterity peruses my humble journal, what will a gap in entries of more than three months cause you hungry scholars, you desperate graduate students, to speculate? Where, I hear you asking, was William Allan Wilson between September 19 and January 1? Involved in a torrid love affair or on a secret mission for the United States government or recovering from a mysterious wasting disease? No such drama, I fear. Merely working, working, working. Three more stories done: the document tale (fairly easy), that worrisome code (or is it cipher?) puzzle in the fashion of "The Gold Bug" (from an inspiration that came to me in a flash while sitting at my computer keyboard one dark and stormy night), and for comic relief, a variation on "Thou Art the Man" (though instead of one exaggerated innocent, I have a complete cast of them).

Fatigued but laboring at a high creative level, I take your leave once again.

Thursday, February 14, 2008

Valentine's Day. A happy day for united lovers, a sad one for lovers separated, or sadder yet for those never joined. I am gripped by a melancholia with origins beyond my identification with Poe. I once was in love, you see, and when that love was lost to me, I resolved to be, if not precisely celibate, solitary. The life of a bachelor has its advantages, to be sure, but I would happily have traded it for life with her.

Enough of this bathos. The writing continues to go well, thanks, I believe, to my genuine affinity for Poe. I was not, as many believe, named for his character William Wilson, with my middle name added as a secondary clue to the intent. Wilson of the tale, you may remember, was a caddish card cheat thwarted at every turn by a mysterious doppelgänger from his school days. Hardly a character to celebrate. (Though I, too, am haunted by my school days, some of my schoolmates, but I mustn't dwell on that.) In fact, my newspaperman father cared little for Poe, and my generous-hearted but uneducated mother might never have heard of him. My father named me for the great journalist William Allen White. When I became enamored of Poe's writing, I changed the spelling of my middle name to match his own. And why do you imagine a person like me, brimming with what an antic friend once called ancien fogiosity, would willingly be called by the undignified diminutive Willie, associated in commonplace minds with jockeys or center fielders or racial stereotypes or the male member? Ah, but was not Poe known, by those who loved him most, as Eddie? And what would I not give to hear called the name of Willie in certain soft, musical, and now ever-lost tones?

There I go again, sinking into melancholy. Now you will forgive me. I must return to Archer Swain, and the problem of why the raven rang the bells.

Wednesday, March 12, 2008

It was a cold, cold February, but all the month my fingers danced a roundelay on the computer keyboard. This mode of creation is soundless, sterile; it lacks the elegant aestheticism of cursive script or the satisfying impact of keys striking a typewriter platen; it includes no satisfying end-of-line ding to measure progress. Still, withal I find the computer no barrier to fine writing. Would Poe have spurned such a device had it been available to him? More practical than generally credited, surely he would not.

Eleven stories now done. At times, it has felt almost like automatic writing, as if Poe himself were guiding my flying fingers from beyond the grave. It is with satisfaction that I shut down the computer, pour a generous measure of Armagnac, pick up my pen, and open the pages of this sadly neglected journal. Not once were midnights truly dreary, never did I feel too weary. Is this the best work I have done? Whether 'tis or not, 'twas fun. In my book-lined writing chamber, I wrote a tome they won't remainder—but ah the phone is ringing, ringing, the twenty-first century may be bringing telemarketers with that bell. Excuse me, while I give them hell.

Back again now after a longer than anticipated interruption. It was my agent on the phone.

"Willie, it's Phil," he said. Not the usual sarcastic recitation of my entire byline. Was he under some additional pressure? "How's it going? Hard at work?"

"Writing in my journal as it happens."

"You still doing that crap? You're wasting your time. If you have to keep a journal, at least do it online, make it a blog, get a little publicity out of it anyway. So how's the book going? We on target?"

"Eleven stories done."

"Great! So is this a wrap?"

"Not quite. The twelfth is not quite finished."

"You sure you need it? Eleven might be enough."

"I've saved what may be the most interesting job, quite possibly the crowning achievement of my writing career, for last. Archer has to solve a real-life case, as Dupin did in 'The Mystery of Marie Roget.' Just as Poe moved Mary Rogers from New York to Paris and changed her name to Marie Roget, I'll move whomever from her time to Archer's and change her name." That slighting word *whomever* was a red herring, I'll confess to you now.

"Her name?"

"Murder of a young woman. Has to be. Won't work otherwise."

"You have a case in mind?"

"I do, yes."

"And how long will this take?"

"Not long at all if you get off the phone and let me get to work."

"But you said you were writing in your damn journal. And you sound like you've been drinking, Willie."

"In moderation. In celebration. For cerebration. Imagine if you will American literature without the helping influence of alcohol."

"Work how you like, Willie, I'd never interfere. But Sloane Ghormley is getting a little antsy. He'd really like to have a look at something."

"Tell him to have a drink and relax."

"You never have to urge Ghormley to have a drink, but it doesn't always make him more mellow. Do me a favor, will you? Let me have the eleven you've done already. I'll forward them to Sloane to ease his mind and tell him there's one more to come."

"Certainly. But not all eleven. Ten should suffice to dazzle him. I want to hold onto my 'Gold Bug' story a little longer."

"Why? It needs more work?"

"Something like that."

"Okay, ten then, with two to come. Can you do that right now?"

I sighed. "I'd have to turn on the infernal computer again."

"I thought you said you were writing in your journal."

"With a pen, Phil. A fountain pen. With ink in it. On paper."

"You mean you still——? I can't believe it."

"Never fear. You shall have the ten stories."

As soon as I rang off, I sent Phil an e-mail attachment of the criminous decalogue—I am a man who if not of his time can operate adequately in his time—and returned to my pen and my journal.

I am not drunk, by the way. I exaggerated my condition to torment Phil, as I do sometimes. Alcohol does help lubricate the creative gears but only up to a point, and I take pains never to pass that point, a lesson Sloane Ghormley never seemed to learn.

As for my "Mary Roget" homage, you have undoubtedly guessed the case I was adapting was from back in my college days, when Ghormley was still my friend, when the girl I loved yet lived, when life was fresh and full of hope. To give Archer Swain no greater advantage than Dupin had, I shall require him to confine himself to print reports in reaching his conclusions about the case. Certainly I have saved them over all these years, though they lay yellowing in a bottom drawer of my desk. Reading them was too painful even as I clipped them from those long-ago newspapers, but I can face them now that I have a purpose in doing so. Rather than paraphrase the facts, I shall place a clipping of that first report below:

A twenty-year-old student at Murgatroyd University fell to her death yesterday from the old clock tower. Esther Collingwood, a senior majoring in English literature, was apparently alone at the time, though many horrified students and staff witnessed her fall.

Roommate Carla Peabody denied that Esther had been depressed,

indeed said she had everything to live for and that she could not imagine a
person less likely to take her own life. Other students living in her dormi-
tory recalled her taste for danger, on one occasion climbing a trellis and
crawling along a ledge three stories up to sneak into her room after curfew.
Campus police attribute the death to an unfortunate accident.

Not the whole story, but newspaper reports seldom are. How I
loved her. And I know she was not alone the day she climbed that
clock tower.

Tuesday, March 18, 2008

The final story is well under way. I will fold a printout of an early
draft of the opening scene between the pages of this journal for
the aid of scholars to come. I see the course of the narrative in my
mind, or most of it. But an ending must be determined, and I cannot write it alone. I need help.

Archer Swain, entering his second week as a housebound invalid, was
proving an uncooperative patient.

"He insists he is ready to get up, Mr. Weston," his nurse told me,
frowning prettily, "but the doctor forbids it. Can you find something to
occupy his mind?"

As it happened, I could. At my old alma mater, Mangletraub College
(class of 1928), a young woman named Hester Collingworth had died in
what was being called an accident. My nephew Argus, an acquaintance of
Miss Collingworth, suspected it was actually murder and had been writ-
ing about the case for the student daily.

"She would not have killed herself, Uncle Wally," he said. I suspected from his fervency the young woman was more than a mere classmate to him, but I did not probe further, merely taking a handful of clippings of his articles and promising to ask the great Archer Swain for his opinion.

I had fond memories of Mangletraub College. In some ways, the thirteen years that had passed since those carefree days of my youth seemed but the blink of an eye, despite all that had happened to me and to the world in the intervening time. Then we had all the options of life before us, oblivious to whatever warnings there were of the Great Depression that would limit our dreams—I certainly did not anticipate it, and I was an economics major. Now, as that cataclysm appeared to have run its course, we were about to encounter another, more foreseeable and even less welcome, brought upon us by the gathering clouds of war.

These events and these portents had not changed Archer Swain perceptibly. Nothing did. His impervious wealth protected him from the cares of the everyday. Only his books, his fine art collection, his dog breeding, and his enthusiasm for arcane crime puzzles that could be solved by, to use an old-fashioned term, ratiocination, were important to him. As I entered his bedroom that day, I found him propped up with one book in his lap and several others stacked on the table at his elbow.

"I'm a prisoner, Wally," he said. "I'm stir crazy. Break me out of here. I rhythmically slam my cup on my breakfast tray, but it does no good."

"You need to be an armchair detective, Archer," I said.

"Ha! An armchair would be an improvement. Seriously, though, you have something for me? I always wanted to see if I could solve a case at one remove, in the style of Dupin or the Old Man in the Corner."

I gave him the handful of clippings. "As thorough an account as my journalist nephew can provide. But I'll bet you can't solve it from that."

"You're on, Wally! Come back at seven tonight. I'll talk that nurse of mine into some brandy for us both, and I'll tell you my conclusions."

"That fast? Do you have a fever, Archer?"

"Always, Wally. Detective fever, and there's no known cure."

That last, you scholars will surely recognize, was a reference not to Poe but to Wilkie Collins. The scene could do with some judicious pruning and tightening, I think, and I'll have to decide exactly what has Archer Swain laid up—a traffic accident, an operation, a heart attack? Many conditions could send one to his bed in 1941, but at least hiring a resident nurse was possible. Now I'll reread all my clippings and try to work out some brilliant deductions Archer Swain can make to conclude what I already know: the identity of Esther/Hester's killer.

Wednesday, March 19, 2008

Today, I printed off on a single sheet of paper in sixteen-point type from an esoteric font among many offered by my computer the following painstakingly composed message:

697 i8oo3e 3w5y34 d9oo8ht299e

I chose another font and printed out the same message on another sheet, then another font the same message, and another, and another, and one more, six versions in total, each in a different font. I put each message in an envelope and addressed them all to one man: Sloane Ghormley. Three I addressed to his home on

Long Island. Three I addressed to his office at Westcott Press in Manhattan. I included no return address. I drove a few miles to a mailbox in the next city and posted two of these envelopes, one to each address. Tomorrow I shall do the same from another mailbox, on Thursday the same with the final two. Thursday evening, I shall, using an anonymous e-mail address not easily traced to me, send Sloane Ghormley the same message electronically.

He will have them all by Friday, the anniversary of Esther Collingwood's death.

Tuesday, April 1, 2008

"Hard at work, Willie?"

You know by now, my diligent scholar, who my caller was. One month to deadline, and Phil was checking in.

"Just a few finishing touches," I assured him. "I should have that last story ready within days."

"I talked to Sloane Ghormley yesterday. He sounded worried, Willie."

"Why worried? He has ten stories in hand. Were I to drop dead in my chair this morning, he'd have enough for a book. And my death might even help sales in today's decadent commercial market, don't you think?"

"I don't think it was the book he was worried about. I think something else was bothering him."

"Did he tell you what?"

"No."

"What did you think of the code story I sent you?"

"Great stuff, Willie. Damn clever idea."

"I'm rather proud of it. It works equally well in the present and in the time of Archer Swain. Of course, it could not have existed in Poe's time but with a little explanation, I think he would have approved it and saluted his student's ingenuity. Why don't you send that on to Ghormley with my assurance that the final tale is on the horizon?"

"Great. Take his mind off his troubles."

"And April Fool's Day is the perfect day to send it to him."

"What do you mean by that?"

"Nothing much. Except that detective fiction is all about fooling people, isn't it?"

I will confess that I was not completely candid in my explanation to Phil. Eventually he may understand the true nature of the joke on Sloane Ghormley.

By the way, my scholar, I know what you're thinking about me and the death of Esther Collingwood. That I climbed the clock tower with her that day, that I myself was her murderer. But that I would never do. I don't mean the act of murder but the act of literary imitation. That particular trick has been done too many times before and too well. Give me credit for a little originality and fairness to my readers even of this journal.

Now how about my code? Have you figured it out? Cogitate on it a little longer before you read the following excerpt from my Archer Swain code story over the next leaf.

"Don't you see it, Wally?" Archer Swain said with exasperating casualness.

"No, I don't. I was counting the letters, looking for the most common symbol to represent the e, the most common letter in the English language in the days of Poe's 'Gold Bug' and I believe still. But the message is too short. My method doesn't work. Yours, I am sure, is more sophisticated."

"It's damnably simple. You are a touch typist, are you not?"

"I need to be to keep up with your adventures."

"And when you type, you don't have to look at the keys before you strike them?"

"Certainly not."

"Imagine you want to code a message quickly—and it would be quick, though the interpretation might take a little longer. A touch typist's fingers, as I understand, rest on the second to bottom line of keys, with two keys, the G and the H, untouched between the index fingers. From that position, the typist can reach all the letters easily."

"Yes, yes, Archer. So what?"

"What if you moved your fingers to the line directly above, the second from the top, and then typed your message in the normal way. What came out on the paper would appear nonsensical, but a touch typist receiving the message would be able to reconstruct your message, is that not so?"

"Swain, that's remarkable!" I exclaimed.

April 8, 2008

Do I regret what I have done? No, I do not. I have done justice. I have avenged the one great love of my life. And I take malicious comfort in imagining the final moments of Sloane Ghormley's life. I see him reading my story, finding out the explanation for the code as elucidated by Archer Swain. Then I imagine him thinking about that very strange message with which some anonymous person has tormented him. He may have destroyed one or more of them—that's why I was careful to send multiples—but I feel sure he kept at least one. I imagine him looking at the message, looking at the keyboard of his computer, painstakingly figuring out what the message would read if the fingers of the typist were on the asdfjkl; keys, instead of the qweruiop directly above them. I imagine his horror when he realized what his tormentor was saying:

you killed esther collingwood

In our days on the Murgatroyd University daily, someone stole a large amount of money carelessly unsecured in the newspaper office. Esther and I discovered who must have done it: our esteemed editor, Sloane Ghormley, a young man of such promise. When confronted, he wept, made excuses (a gambling habit along with his already troublesome alcohol habit), promised restitution. We agreed to say nothing. He was effusively grateful.

But Sloane Ghormley stole more than money. He also stole from me the woman I loved. The developing relationship between Sloane and Esther surprised and wounded me. As they gradually grew closer to each other and subtly farther from me, I outwardly evinced sportsmanlike equanimity as they remained outwardly friendly. At the time of Esther's death, I suspected nothing. Only years later, sorting through her "literary" effects at the request of her mother, did I learn that on the day of her death she had an appointment to meet Sloane at the top of the clock tower. Why had she agreed to meet him there? Had she decided to break off their relationship, even come back to me? Had she found the pace of his restitution too slow and threatened to expose his secret? I'm not sure. But I am sure of one thing: Esther had not committed suicide. Neither had she fallen. She had been pushed.

But I knew none of this then. I only wanted to forget this dark chapter in my life. In the numbness of loss, I sought other outlets. I did not reveal Sloane Ghormley's perfidy, but neither did I ever want to deal with him again.

Why did he reenter my life with the offer of this Poe bicentennial collection? Guilt? Was it his way of making some partial recompense to me, the person he had so wronged? Did he suspect I knew his secret and believe this literary bone he had thrown me might close my lips forever? Or, the most troubling and pathetic prospect of all, did this professionally successful but personally anchorless alcoholic want to rekindle a past friendship?

I don't pretend I knew for certain he would immediately put a bullet through his head, but that decision makes a highly satisfactory outcome, don't you think?

Jon L. Breen, author of eight novels and around a hundred short stories, has won two Edgar Awards in the biographical/critical category. He is a regular reviewer for *Ellery Queen's Mystery Magazine* and *Mystery Scene*. His most recent short story collection is *Kill the Umpire: The Calls of Ed Gorgon* (Crippen & Landru), and his latest novel is the comic courtroom mystery *Probable Claus* (Five Star).

The Tell-Tale Purr

Mary Higgins Clark

There comes a time when in the name of common decency grand-mothers ought to die. I confess that in the early stages of my life I had a half-hearted affection for my grandmother but that time is long since past. She is now well up in her eighties and still exceed-ingly vain even though at night her teeth repose in a water glass by her bed. She has a constant struggle every morning to get her contact lenses popped into her myopic eyes and requires a cane to support her arthritic knees. The cane is a custom-made affair de-signed to resemble the walking stick Fred Astaire used in some of his dances. Grandma's story is that she danced with him when she was young and the cane/walking stick is her good-luck charm.

Her mind is still very keen and seems to become keener even as her eccentricities grow. She, who always proudly considered herself frugal, is spending money like water. Thanks to several investments her husband, my grandfather, made, she is downright wealthy and it has been with great pleasure that I have observed her simple lifestyle. But now it is different. For example, she just put an elevator, which cost forty thousand dollars, in her modest home. She is sure she will live to be one hundred and is contemplating building a state-of-the-art gym in the backyard because she read in a Harvard medical report that exercise is good for arthritis.

I submit to you that a better cure for her arthritis is to put an end to it forever. This I propose to do.

You must realize that I am her sole grandson and heir. Her only child, my mother, departed this earth shortly after I graduated from college. In the twenty-six years since then I have married and divorced twice and been involved in many ill-fated ventures. It is time for me to stop wasting my time on useless enterprises and enjoy a life of comfort. I must help to make that possible.

Obviously her demise would need to seem natural. At her advanced age, it would not be unlikely to have her pass away in her sleep, but if someone holding a pillow were to help that situation occur there is always the danger of a bruise that might make the police suspicious. Suspicious police look for motive and I would be a living, breathing motive. I am uncomfortable about the fact that when under the influence of wine I was heard to say that the only present I wanted from my grandmother for my next birthday was a ticket to her funeral.

How then was I to help my grandmother sail across the River Styx without arousing suspicion?

I was quite simply at a loss. I could push her down the stairs and claim she fell but if she survived the fall, she would know that I caused it.

I could try to disable her car but that ancient old Bentley she drives with the skill of Mario Andretti would probably survive a crash.

Poison is easily detectable.

My problem was solved in a most unexpected way.

I had been invited to have dinner at the home of a successful friend, Clifford Winkle. I value Clifford's superb wines and gourmet table far more than I value Clifford. Also I find his wife, Belinda, insipid. But I was in the mood for a splendid dinner in comfortable circumstances and looked forward to the evening with pleasure.

I was seated with Clifford and his wife, enjoying a generous scotch on the rocks that I knew had been poured from a two-hundred-dollar bottle of single malt reserve, when their little treasure, ten-year-old Perry, burst into the room.

"I've decided, I've decided," he shouted, spittle spraying from the space between his upper front teeth.

The parents smiled indulgently. "Perry has been reading the complete works of Edgar Allan Poe this week," Clifford told me.

The last time I was a guest I had endured Perry's endless description of a book he had read about fly-fishing, and how by reading it, he could really, really understand all about baiting and casting and catching and why fly-fishing was really, really special. I wanted desperately to interrupt him and tell him I had already seen *A River Runs Through It*, Robert Redford's splendid film on the subject but, of course I did not.

Now Perry's all-consuming passion was obviously Edgar Allan Poe. "'The Tell-Tale Heart' is my favorite," he crowed, his short red hair spiking up on the crown of his skull, "but I could write a better ending, I know I could."

Barefoot boy with cheek out-Poes Poe, I thought. However, I wanted to show some small degree of interest. I was down to my last sip of the two-hundred-dollar scotch and hoped that by directing attention to myself, Clifford might notice my empty glass and not neglect his duty as my host. "In high school I wrote a new ending to 'The Cask of Amantillado,' " I volunteered. "I got an A in my English class for it. I remember how it began"—I cleared my throat—" 'Yes. I killed him. I killed him a long fifty years ago . . .' "

Perry ignored me. "You see in 'The Tell-Tale Heart' the guy kills the old man because he can't stand looking at his eye. Then he buries the old man's heart but when the cops come he thinks he hears the heart beating and goes nuts and confesses. Right?"

"Right!" Clifford affirmed enthusiastically.

"Exactly. Um-hmm," Belinda agreed, beaming at her whiz kid.

"In my book, the guy kills the old man, but another guy watches him do it, then helps him cut up the body and bury the heart under the floor. When the cops come in, the murderer laughs and jokes with them and thinks he's getting away with it. Then when the cops go, the friend comes back and as a joke says he can hear the old man's heart beating. Isn't that good?"

Fascinating, I thought. *If only Poe had lived to meet Perry.*

"But then the murderer, 'cause he doesn't know it's a joke, be-lieves he really is hearing the heart, and you know what?"

"What?" Clifford asked.

"I can't guess," Belinda gushed, her eyes wide, her hands clutching the arms of her chair.

"The murderer dies of fright because of the heart he thinks he's hearing."

Perry beamed at his own brilliance. *Send for the Nobel Prize*, I thought, not realizing there was more to come.

"And the twist is that his friend was going to split the money the old man had hidden somewhere in London and now he realizes he'll never know where to find it so he's punished for the crime too." Perry grinned triumphantly, an ear-splitting grin that made all the freckles on his cheeks bond together in a henna-tinted mass.

It was I who led the applause and my reaction was genuine. *The sound had scared the murderer to death.* My grandmother's fear of cats rushed into my mind. She shakes and trembles to the point of almost fainting at the sight or sound of one. It goes back, I am told, over eighty years ago to when a rabid cat attacked her in the garden. She still bears a scar on her left cheek from that long-ago encounter.

My grandmother has a new elevator.

Suppose . . . just suppose, Grandma got stuck in her new elevator in the dark during a power failure. And then she hears the sounds of cats yowling and hissing and howling and purring. She hears them scratching at the door of the elevator. She is sure they will break through. She cowers, shrieking, against the back of the elevator, then crumbles onto the floor, the memory of that long-ago attack overwhelming her. No, it is not a memory. It is happening. She is sure that the cat is poised to attack her again, not just one cat but all the cats in this hydrophobic pack, foaming at the mouth, teeth bared.

There is only one way to escape the panic. She is frightened into heart failure and her death would be blamed on her being trapped, alone, at night, in the new elevator.

I was so excited and thrilled at this solution to my problem that I hardly tasted the excellent dinner and was uncommonly responsive to Perry who, of course, dined with us and never shut up.

I planned my grandmother's death carefully. Nothing must arouse even the slightest suspicion. Fortunately there are frequent power failures in her area of northern Connecticut during wind storms. She has talked of installing a home generator but so far that has not happened. Still, I knew I had to move swiftly.

Night after night for the next few weeks, I roamed through the nearby towns, slithering through dark alleys and around abandoned buildings, any place where wild cats gathered. I tossed pieces of meat and cheese to get them fighting with one another, their teeth bared, their ungodly yowls rumbling from their throats, getting it all on tape. One night I was attacked by a cat who, frantic for the food in my hand, sprung on me, her front claw ripping my left cheek in the same spot my grandmother was scarred.

Undeterred, I kept on my mission, even recording cats in animal shelters, where I caught the plaintive meows of discarded felines bewildered by their fate. At the home of a neighbor I secretly caught on tape the contented purring of her cherished pet.

A cacophony of sound, a work of genius. That was the result of my labors.

As I was engaged in my nocturnal wanderings, by day I was also lavishing attention on my grandmother, visiting her at least three times a week, enduring at mealtime the vegetarian regime that was her latest quirk in her battle to stay alive till her hundredth birthday. Seen with such frequency, the annoying habits she was developing became increasingly hard to take. She began to avoid my eyes when I spoke to her as though she were aware everything I said was a lie. She also took on a nervous mannerism of pursing then releasing her lips, which gave the impression she was always sucking on a straw.

Grandma lived alone. Her housekeeper, Ica, a kind Jamaican woman, arrived at nine a.m., prepared Grandma's breakfast and lunch, tidied the house, then went home and returned to prepare and serve dinner. Ica was very protective of Grandma. She had already confided to me her distress that Grandma might somehow get trapped in the elevator when she was alone. "You know how when it gets very windy, she gets power failures that can last for hours," Ica worried.

I assured Ica that I, too, was troubled by that possibility. Then, I impatiently waited for the weather to cooperate and a good wind storm to come along. It finally happened. The weather report was for heavy winds during the night. That evening I had dinner with Grandma, a particularly difficult dinner, what with the vegetarian menu, Grandma's averted eyes, her twitching mouth, and then the dismaying news that she was meeting an architect concerning her idea for building a personal gym. It was clearly time to act.

After dinner, I kissed Grandma good night, went into the kitchen where Ica was tidying up, then drove away. At that time, I lived only three blocks from Grandma. I parked my car and waved to my next-door neighbor, who was just arriving home. I felt it was fortuitous that, if necessary, he could testify that he had seen me enter my own modest rental cottage. I waited an hour and then slipped out my back door. It was already dark and chillingly cold, and it was easy to hurry undetected back to Grandma's house. I arrived through the wooded area, checking to be sure that Ica's car was surely gone. It was, and I slipped across the lawn to the window of the den. As I expected I could see Grandma, hunched up on her recliner, an old fur lap robe wrapped around her, watching her favorite television show.

For the next ten minutes she stayed there, then, as I had expected, promptly at nine o'clock, the fur robe dragging behind her, she turned off the television and made her way to the front of the house. In a flash, key in hand, I was at the basement door and inside. As soon as I heard the rumble of the elevator, I threw the switch, plunging the house into silence and darkness.

I crept upstairs, my feet noiseless in my sneakers, my flashlight a thin beam. From the sound of my grandmother's cries for help I could detect that the elevator was only a few feet off the floor.

Now for the tricky part. I placed my tape recorder on the vestibule table behind a book I had left for Grandma. I reasoned that Ica, if indeed she noticed it, would think nothing of it being there. I had developed the habit of bringing books and little gifts for Grandma.

And then I turned on the tape. The sound that thundered from it was a litany from cat hell, meowing, clawing, scratching, and howling, their shrieks interwoven with the suddenly incongruous rattle of purring contentment.

There was absolute silence from the elevator.

Had the recording done its job already? I wondered. It was

possible, but I wouldn't know for sure until the morning. The tape was twenty minutes long and would play repeatedly until midnight. I was sure that would be sufficient.

I let myself out of the house and walked home at a quick pace, bracing against the sharp wind that was now making tree branches bend and dance. Chilled to the bone, I went directly to bed. I confess I could not fall asleep. The mental image of my grandmother's stiffening body inside her elevator kept me from restful slumber. But then as I allowed myself to imagine finally getting my hands on all her money, my frame of mind improved and from dawn till eight o'clock I enjoyed a refreshing slumber.

But then as I began to prepare breakfast, several possibilities occurred to me. Suppose Grandma's face was frozen into a frightened mask? Would that make anyone suspicious? Worse yet, suppose for some reason the recording had not automatically turned off!

My original plan had been to await Ica's phone call, the one that would convey the sad news that Grandma had been trapped in the elevator and must have had a heart attack. At the frightening possibility that the tape just might still be playing, I leaped up from the breakfast table, threw on some clothes, and rushed over, arriving as Ica was opening the front door. To my vast relief there was no sound from the recorder.

The morning was overcast, which meant that the vestibule was dark. As Ica greeted me she tried to turn on the light. Then she frowned. "My God, there must have been another power failure." She turned and made a beeline for the stairs to Grandma's bedroom. I, on the other hand, raced down to the basement and threw the master switch on the panel. The whir of the elevator rewarded me. I rushed up the stairs and was there when Ica yanked open the elevator door.

Grandma was on the floor wrapped in her mink lap robe. She opened her eyes and blinked up at us. With the fur wrapped around her head, the strands of fur resting on her cheek, for all the world she had the face of a cat. Her mouth pursed in and out as though she were sipping milk.

"Grandma . . ." My voice failed. With Ica's help, she was struggling to her feet, her hands on the floor, her back arched to help regain her balance.

"Eerr . . . Eerr . . ." she sighed. *Or was she saying "Purrrr . . . purrrr"?*

"Eerrr, that's the best sleep I've had in years," Grandma said contentedly.

"Weren't you frightened trapped in there?" Ica asked incredulously.

"Oh, no, I was tired and I just made the best of it. I tried calling out but there was no one to hear me. I decided not to waste my voice."

The record had been playing. I had heard it myself.

Grandma was eyeing me. "You look terrible," she said, "I don't want you worrying about me. Don't you know I'll live to be one hundred? That's my promise to you. So I was stuck in the elevator. The carpet is thick. I lay down and was nice and warm under the robe. In my dreams I was hearing this faint purring sound like water lapping against the shore."

Afraid I would give myself away, I stumbled downstairs and grabbed my recorder from the table, then realized that in my haste

I had knocked a small object off the table. I bent down and picked it up. It was a hearing aid. I started to lay it down and saw there was another one on the table.

Ica was coming down the stairs. "How long has Grandma been wearing hearing aids?" I demanded.

"They're just what I'm coming for. She leaves them on that table every night. She's so vain that I guess she didn't tell you that her hearing has been going steadily downhill and she's practically deaf now. She's been studying lip reading and is quite good at it. Haven't you noticed the way she always looks at your lips when you're talking? She finally got the hearing aids but uses them only for television in the evening and always leaves them right here."

"She can't hear?" I asked, dumbfounded.

"Only a few sounds, deep ones, nothing shrill."

That happened five years ago. Of course, I immediately destroyed the tape, but in my sleep I hear it playing over and over. It doesn't frighten me. Instead it keeps me company. I don't know why. There's something else that's a little strange. I cannot look at my grandmother's face without seeing the face of a cat. That's because of those little whiskers on her cheeks and lips, the odd pursing movement of her mouth, the narrow intense eyes that are always focused on my lips. Also, her bedchamber of choice is now the elevator where, for naps and at night, she curls up on the carpeted floor wrapped in her mink lap robe. Her breathing has even taken on a purring sound.

I can hardly keep my wits about me as I await my inheritance. I do not have the courage to try to precipitate its arrival again. I live with Grandma now and as time passes, I believe I am beginning to resemble her. The scar on her cheek is directly under her left eye; mine is in the same spot. I have a very light beard and shave infrequently. At times my beard looks just like her whiskers. We have those same narrow green eyes.

My grandmother loves very warm milk. She's taken to pouring it into a saucer to cool it before she laps it up. I tried it and now I like it that way too. It's purr-fect.

MARY HIGGINS CLARK's books are worldwide bestsellers. In the United States alone, her books have sold more than eighty million copies. She is the author of twenty-six suspense novels, three collections of short stories, a biographical novel about George Washington, and a memoir, *Kitchen Privileges*. She is a number-one fiction bestselling author in France, where she received the Grand Prix de Littérature Policière and the Literary Award at the 1998 Deauville Film Festival. In 2000, she was named by the French minister of culture Chevalier of the Order of Arts and Letters. She was chosen by Mystery Writers of America as Grand Master of the 2000 Edgar Awards. An annual Mary Higgins Clark Award sponsored by Simon & Schuster, given to authors of suspense fiction writing in the Mary Higgins Clark tradition, was launched by Mystery Writers of America during Edgar week in April 2001. She was the 1987 president of Mystery Writers of America and, for many years, served on their Board of Directors. In May 1988, she was chairman of the International Crime Congress. Her most recent novel is *Where Are You Now?*.

Nevermore

Thomas H. Cook

My father's last request was that I bring him a book. We had not been close, or even very much in communication, since the day my mother left him. Over the years, the many years, my anger with him had not abated. But in his final days, I'd decided to offer him at least an occasion for atonement, despite the fact that he'd never given any indication that he had anything for which he felt the need to atone. At times I'd even felt my presence in his hospital room reduced to that of a Shabbas goy, performing servile tasks like turning on a light or adjusting the volume on the television that hung opposite his bed.

"I'm a rabbi," I reminded him sternly one afternoon when my lowly status in his eyes became particularly irksome.

"So was I," my father said. "Almost."

Almost? I didn't think so. For although he'd been a rabbinical student in his youth, he'd later chosen Columbia over Yeshiva, and from there gone on to the life of a liberal arts professor, complete with pipe, tweed jacket, and, as I'd been told, an occasional mention in scholarly magazines.

"Poe," he said one Friday afternoon when the sun was setting and I was hurrying to leave.

"Poe?" I asked.

"The poems," my father said. "There's a volume of them somewhere around the house."

He'd been in the hospital for several days by then, suffering from the usual infirmities of old age, though this time with the added problem of pneumonia. His breathing was labored, and he seemed generally exhausted, not at all the vibrant man who'd daily escorted me into his study, whipped a book from the shelf, and taught me the classics and ancient history.

"Bring it on Monday," he added with a tired wave of the hand.

I'd recalled my father as a quick discarder of old books, always on the lookout for the latest edition, so when I got around to the latest humble task he'd asked of me, I found it surprising that his Poe was an old volume with yellowed, crumbling pages, a book that had the present look of my father, once sturdy and tightly bound, but now tattered beyond repair.

It had been nearly fifty years since I'd entered my father's study, but I found the look of it quite at one with the man himself. From the time he'd first left the Lower East Side, he'd been a "modern" man, with high, upwardly mobile ambitions. The glass-topped desk seemed perfectly in keeping with his character, as did the sleek leather chair with its gleaming chrome legs. There was a flat-screen monitor and an ergonomic keyboard, and just to the right, an iPod stood perkily in its white plastic stand.

I shook my head at the sheer predictability of it all. How fitting that this was where my father did his thinking, beneath halogen lights, with the silvery louver blinds open to reveal a neat, suburban lawn. For he was not at all the somber black-clothed scholar I thought myself to be, a man of prayers and fasting, immersed in the Torah, not in some lengthy study of imagery in *Lolita*. The fact is, we'd gone in completely opposite directions, and because of that my father's existence now seemed transparently thin to me, the man himself a cellophane soul, utterly without mystery, his life a story without twists or turns, one that surely would have proven an unfit subject for the inventor of the detective story.

"Why Poe?" my wife asked when, after my return home, I showed her the book my father had requested I bring him on Monday morning.

"I don't know," I answered. "He taught Poe only that last summer."

My wife covered her head and prepared to light the Shabbas candles. "Maybe that's what's on his mind," she said.

I shrugged. "If so, it's too late to make amends."

He took a severe turn for the worse two days later, so that when I arrived at the hospital that morning, I found him barely the shadow of the man I'd left the Friday before. He'd clearly been given something, as my mother had in her last hours. Like her, he was unable to speak coherently, though he appeared to be fully conscious. After offering my usual terse greeting I brought the book within view, showed him the spine. "The book you wanted," I said. "Poe." I drew a chair up to his bedside. "I thought I might read a few of the poems to you."

He stared at the book with what seemed the quiet affection and admiration he had once offered me, but which I had long ago rejected and continued to reject.

"So, let's begin." I flipped past the melancholy visage of the author, the title page, the table of contents, to the first poem in the volume. "'Alone,'" I said like a speller cautious to follow the rules of the bee, pronouncing the word before defining it.

From childhood's hour I have not been
As others were; I have not seen
As others saw; I could not bring
My passions from a common spring.

My father's eyes darted about, and for a moment he seemed disoriented.

"You're in Room 1213," I told him. "Clark Memorial."

He squinted hard, like a man trying to bring something small into focus.

"Shtorm," he said, then much more clearly, "Storm."

"Storm?" I asked, glancing at the poem again, now focused on the last line I'd read, *I could not bring my passions from a common spring,*

"Summer storm." One hand rose and floated out and away, like a boat into the vastness, and his gaze went to the middle distance.

"What summer storm?" I asked.

He seemed frustrated, gasping at words, determined to say something that either his weakness or the drugs prevented him from saying. "Poe," he said softly, then louder, more emphatically, "teaching Poe."

So my wife had been right. He *was* thinking about the idyllic three months during which he'd held forth on Poe, often in a little arbor beside Lake Montego, deeply shaded and oddly romantic, with his few exchange students gathered around him.

He struggled to speak again, faltered, then blurted almost vehemently, *"Shiksa."*

I stared at him, stunned. For although before leaving him my mother had often used the old world language of her parents—*meshugana,* for a crazy person, *mitzvah* for a good deed—my father had shunned Yiddish entirely, thought it fit only for comedy, and even then for only the lowest kind. He'd even corrected my English when it slipped into what he called "foreignness." "In America we don't 'close' the light, Alex," he'd once said to me when I'd inadvertently used one of my mother's phrases. "We 'turn it off.'"

"Shiksa?" I asked. "Since when do you . . ."

"Summer, storm, Poe," my father said, connecting all three words, though without giving the connection any decipherable meaning.

"Summer, storm, Poe," he repeated, his tone urgent, as if he were searching through his vast vocabulary, riffling through the great cabinet of his mind for some purloined letter that would explain his life.

"Shiksa," he said, paused, searched, then added, "Sarah."

Sarah was my mother's name, and my father's use of *shiksa* and *Sarah* in such juxtaposition immediately returned me to the climactic scene that seemed most disastrously to connect them. I saw my mother and father in our car on a particularly stormy day, though one whose wind and rain I'd hardly have noticed had not the car come only partway up the drive and then stopped without going into the garage. Abruptly stopped, with a jolt, as if someone had stomped the break.

"I was seven when we left," I said softly, remembering that dreadful, life-altering day, the thudding rain, my mother's anger a quite different storm, one that had proven far more devastating to the landscape of my youth.

But this was a disturbing recollection, fraught with old rage, and so I quickly returned to Poe's poem and began to read again:

From the same source I have not taken
My sorrow; I could not awaken
My heart to joy at the same tone;
And all I loved, I loved alone.

"Never," my father said. "I would never."

He appeared to be rambling now, his focus less clear. I barely acknowledged what he said. For despite the effort, I found myself still fixed in place at the second-floor window, the little boy I'd once been, peering down into the chasm of adulthood, where the family car halted at the rim of the house and my mother dashed out into the rain while my father sat behind the weeping glass, listening to the *thump, thump, thumping* of what I had considered since that storm-tossed day to be his profoundly selfish heart.

"You are . . . ," my father murmured. "You are . . ."

The callous heart of a man my mother had left more than fifty years before, left to his suburban house and big-shot college professorship, left and taken me with her and returned us both to the din of New York, where we'd lived with my grandmother in a crowded neighborhood, Ludlow Street. My mother hence known to all as Surala, speaking Yiddish to the vendors and shopkeepers, using her hands when she spoke, covering her head and lighting the candles for Friday night prayers—*Baruch Atah Adonai*—and from which world, with my father far away, his visits growing more infrequent, I had made my way unfathered into the world.

"Alexander," my father said.

It was the name he'd chosen for me, a conqueror of worlds, and certainly inappropriate for the rabbi I was, with a synagogue on Sixth Street and a little apartment in Stuyvesant Town.

"I'm Ezra," I reminded him starkly. "I've been Ezra since . . ." I stopped, already irritated by my little visit to the past. "Ezra is my name."

My name because it was the name called out in the synagogue, the middle name that had been chosen by my mother, and so, as I saw it, forever my name, shouted in greeting by the pickle sellers on Essex Street and the tradesmen of Delancey, by the old people in the park and the young people in the handball courts, my name to my grandmother, carried on breath laced with herring, past lips crumbed with latkes, my name to all the "old world" my father had despised and back to which my mother, in her brokenness, had fled, and by which she had again been made whole, and so the world I had embraced as my world too, this island, where storms also raged, of course, but always amid the anchorage of the old traditions and blood relations and neighborhood bonds, faith and family and friends.

"Ezra," I repeated, like a man raising a proud old flag.

My father drew in a trembling breath, but said nothing, so I returned to the poem:

Then—in my childhood, in the dawn
Of a most stormy life—was drawn
From every depth of good and ill
The mystery which binds me still:

He poked his chest with a single finger, eyes glaring. "I am the father," he said with an odd fury, like a man declaring an ancient and inalienable right.

I looked up from the page and considered this "father" of mine, a man who had renounced so many holy things—the language of his youth, the history of his people; severed so many sacred bonds—marriage, fatherhood—lost so much that was precious and irrecoverable that he seemed the victim of some monstrous theft, though I knew *he* was the thief. And with that thought I returned to the window, the storm, my mother dashing through the tearing wind, my father silent behind the wheel, his eyes following the rhythmic pulse of the windshield wipers, listening to the *thump, thump, thump,* as I imagined it, of his own tell-tale heart.

My father's lips twitched and jerked as he tried to speak, now moving his head from side to side as if laboring to shake the words from his mind.

"Lenore," he said finally.

Lenore.

So now, I thought bitterly, now when he could no longer speak whole sentences easily, when he was too weak to sustain anything resembling conversation, when he had to rely on some kind of associative code, now, at the very border of coherence, after all the damage he had done, the terrible betrayal he had inflicted upon my mother, now, now, my father finally wanted to talk about her, this young girl who'd listened as he'd pontificated about Poe, this *shiksa* whose life had ended early and violently, in the throes of a passion my father held in the very contempt he'd expressed so starkly in that storm-tossed car, the cruelty of which had caused my mother to stomp the brake. *For God's sake, Sarah, she's just a girl.*

Her name, this "girl," was Lenore. She had pale skin and yellow hair, like the Lenore of Poe's poem, and it was easy for me to imagine just how beguilingly my father had used her name's connection to Poe's pining love song as a way of seducing her, how he must have asked her to linger in the arbor after the other students had left, sat with her in that deep shade, quoted Poe to her, made her believe that she was "fair and debonair," like the lost Lenore.

I never knew how my mother found out about her, or learned any of the details of her immediate response, save the terrible admission that had caused her to stomp the brake of the family car as it had drawn up to the garage that stormy afternoon.

"Lenore?" I said to him now. "Spare me."

My father closed his eyes, but I could see them moving about beneath the lids, back and forth and up and around like a man following a flying bit of paper.

I lifted the volume toward him. "Poe," I said firmly, since my mother had made me promise never to speak of my father's betrayal, a promise it had been easy to keep, since my father had never seemed to feel the slightest guilt concerning Lenore, or my mother's abrupt departure, or even the loss of me. The deep grudge I'd nursed against him, a fire from which he'd finally drawn away, with fewer and fewer visits and phone calls until my bar mitzvah, and after that, as if freed by my full embrace of the faith he had so fully rejected, I could without guilt, and almost as if commanded, hold him in a searing contempt I had made since my thirteenth year no effort to conceal.

After that rupture, my father's phone calls had dwindled into nothing, and we'd retreated into our vastly separate worlds, he the strolling luminary of a grassy college campus, I, a familiar figure on the old fabled streets, Essex and Orchard and Rivington, well known and not without honor in the little shtetl of my life.

I pointed to the open book of Poe's poems. "Shall I go on?"

My father eased back wearily and closed his eyes like a man defeated in some final purpose.

I returned to the poem and began to read:

From the torrent, or the fountain . . .
From the red cliff of the mountain,

I stopped, but why? What did I want? I knew quite well what it was, of course. I wanted an apology. I wanted my father to tell me that he was truly, deeply sorry not only for what he'd done, but for what he was. I wanted him to tell me that he had been wrong in everything, wrong in all he had rejected and in all he had taken up, that his every guiding thought had been wrong, that he'd been wrong at every turn, wrong about my mother, wrong about me, and coldly, cruelly wrong in destroying our family over some nothing of a girl, this poor, distraught Lenore.

He'd gone to her that same wind-driven afternoon. I'd watched from the second-floor window, oddly transfixed by what I'd already seen, and so held by the curious prospect of what would happen next. My father sat, as if in mute suspension, behind the wheel of his spanking-new sedan, while downstairs I could hear my mother as she strode from room to room, her feet pounding angrily against the hardwood floors below.

And so I was still at the window when my father came to his conclusion, slapped the gear into reverse, and guided the car back out of the driveway, where he stopped again, though only briefly, perhaps turning some final notion over in his mind before pressing down upon the accelerator and heading east, toward Lake Montego.

Meanwhile, as the public record later showed, Lenore had also journeyed out into the storm, her body wrapped in an old wool coat, her yellow hair bound in a red scarf, her shoes protected by her very English "wellies," and so, by all accounts, a careful young woman, careful of her clothes, her shoes, her modest ambitions, careful with the feelings of her family and her female reputation, careful in everything, as it had later seemed, save in what she'd let herself feel for my unfeeling father.

My father had driven directly to the little bungalow Lenore shared with two other English girls, one named Betty, who later told authorities that he had looked angry when he came for Lenore, and one named Dotty, who said he looked flustered and a little confused. Neither had known of their summer roommate's relationship with the man they called Professor Green before he'd shown up at their door, though they had noticed a change in Lenore, a nervousness they'd attributed to anxiety about her studies. Her long hours of walking in the nearby woods had taken a toll, they thought, as well as her late hours at the college library. Then, in an instant, it had all come clear to them, they said, Lenore crying, distraught, pulling on her coat and galoshes, barging out into the storm, my father banging at their bungalow door a few minutes later, the motor left running in his car, windshield wipers thumping in the rain.

Back on Giddings Street, of course, I'd heard a very different thumping, first my mother as she climbed the stairs, and after that, the soft thump of her suitcase as she tossed it onto the bed. I didn't hear the whisper of clothes hastily packed, however, and so I had no idea of anything so dire as the decision she'd made until she suddenly called to me from the hallway, "Alexan . . ." A pause. "Ezra."

And so everything had changed.

But less for me, as it turned out, than for yellow-haired Lenore.

She had gone to the boathouse, and when I think of her at the moment my father found her there, I imagine her sitting, wrapped in her own arms, eyes red with crying, the very picture of a broken-hearted young woman, innocent and naïve, the perfect prey for a man such as my father. Professor Green, smooth-tongued, erudite, with his prized Phi Beta Kappa key dangling from his watch chain, this great, learned warship of a man whose seductive wiles the small craft that was Lenore surely could not have resisted.

For as I later learned, Mary Lenore Leeds was a lowly working-class girl, little more than a scullery maid, who'd won a summer semester in America at a Liverpool dance hall. She'd picked my father's course on Poe from the great variety of academic offerings open to her because, according to Betty and Dotty, she'd liked penny dreadfuls, read them by the score, and thus had been surprised when Professor Green disparaged them. But they had had a talk, Lenore told her roommates, and after that . . .

I had always had trouble imagining the "after that" of my father and Lenore, not because it is almost impossible for children to imagine a parent in the act of sexual congress, but because my father had never seemed physical at all. He'd been all brain to me, all books and learning, all authority and judgment, a secular father of biblical proportions. Aristotle, in the inflated way he seemed to think of himself, to my Alexander.

But he had hardly turned out to be that sort of sage, a sad fact of life my mother had often made clear. Rather, he was the phony *ba'al torah* who'd lacked the wisdom to hold his family together, a vain and haughty man, always *farputst*, with his scholar's key and gold watch, a puffed-up *feinshmeker* who'd fallen victim to his own exalted image of himself, taken advantage of a young girl and *murdered her*, to use my mother's phrase, though she well knew he had not done that.

Or had he?

For murder, or at least the possibility of it, was surely what I'd taken from the newspaper accounts of Lenore's death. I'd been a freshman at Yeshiva before I'd actually read them, warned away from the story by my mother, who had seemed to bury the details of her leaving my father in a deep grave of secrecy. But after reading the newspaper stories, the notion of foul play had lingered in my mind, so that once, after watching that sad and frightening scene from *A Place in the Sun* where an ambitious, social-climbing Montgomery Clift rows the distraught, pregnant working girl who loves him out onto a lake and murders her for his own advantage, I'd felt a dreadful question circle through my mind. For Lenore had died like that, drowned after somehow falling over the side of the small boat she'd taken out onto storm-tossed Lake Montego. But had she gone alone? Or had my father gone with her, done what he had to do in order to get rid of this inconvenient little strumpet, one he had himself dismissed as "just a girl"?

It would be easy, I thought, to kill someone who could be dismissed with the very words my father had said in the car that afternoon, words that had always seemed to me the true mark of his cruelty. And if he had done nothing, why had he never gained high position at the college, never become a dean or head of his department, never soared up and up as he'd no doubt expected to soar?

I felt the darkest suspicion of my life rise like a gush of bile in my throat.

"Did you kill her?" I blurted suddenly. "Did you kill that . . . pregnant *shiksa*?"

My father's eyes burst open.

"Is that why my mother left you?" I demanded. "Not just that you *schtupped* that girl, but that you killed her?"

My father began to kick and pull at his sheets, twisting his body and jerking his head. But none of his contortions summoned the slightest pity in me. Let him kick and toss about forever, I thought. Let the dogs of his conscience, the ghosts of all he'd so recklessly thrown aside, even the ghost of Alexander, that little boy who'd loved him so, let them all have their way with him, chew his flesh and drink his blood and break his bones, and finally reduce him to the same dust his betrayal had made of my childhood adoration of him.

Then quite suddenly he stopped, and with what seemed a mighty effort, said *"Nischt mein."*

I'd seen other people revert to words and phrases they'd not used since childhood, people long rooted in the suburbs who'd abruptly returned, as it were, to the shtetl of their parents or grandparents, the blasted villages and charred ghettos of a vanished Poland. But this latest of my father's reversions to Yiddish seemed less natural than calculated, perhaps his way of mocking me.

"I've always wondered if you did it," I said. "If you rowed her out on that lake, into that storm, with nobody around, no other boats on the lake, just rowed her out into that storm and tossed her over the side."

My father jerked his head to the right in a way, it seemed to me, a guilty man would turn from his chief accuser.

I waited briefly, thinking he might look back toward me, actually address the accusation I'd made, but he didn't, and after a time I went back to Poe's poem.

From the sun that round me rolled
In its autumn tint of gold,

My father released a long, weary breath. *"Farblonschet."*

It was an almost comic term for being confused, and again I wondered if he was mocking me.

"So, you're confused?" I asked, now determined to speak to him only in English, as if Yiddish were my language, and could never be his, Yiddish and all that clung to it just another worthy thing he'd brutally renounced, a language that was like me, something he never visited or called, a Yid to this anti-Semite, a piece of *dreck*.

My father twisted around and pointed to me with a shaky finger.

"So, I'm the one who's confused?" I laughed. "About what?"

My father began to squirm, so that I could see the effort he was making, the energy it took for him to say simply, "Sarah . . . never . . . never . . ." A jumble of sounds followed, none of them decipherable. Then, quite clearly, though with failing strength, he said, "Not mine."

He saw that I had no idea what he was talking about, and with a labored movement reached out for the book.

I handed it to him, and watched as he thumbed through the pages until he found the one he wanted, then tapped the title of the poem.

"Lenore?" I asked. "Lenore wasn't yours?"

But that was absurd, I thought, *for had not my mother discovered the whole sordid business, confronted him with it in the car on that stormy afternoon, heard his heartless dismissal of Lenore*—She's just a girl.

"What about the baby?" I asked.

He shook his head furiously, clearly and forcefully denying that Lenore's baby was his.

"Not mine," he repeated. He twisted about, lips fluttering, so that it seemed to me that he was using up the last dwindling energy of his life in some final effort to communicate what I'd once hoped might be an apology, but which was clearly something else.

I leaned forward. "Whose then?"

Again my father seemed to take up a mighty struggle, hands jerking at the sheets, legs ceaselessly moving, lips twisting, his eyes darting about, until they settled on the window, emphatically settled, like a pointing finger.

I looked out the window, the grounds empty, save for the young workman in the distance pushing a lawnmower, and made a wild guess.

"Joey?" I asked. "The kid who mowed our lawn?"

My mother had always called him the Shabbas goy. He'd mowed the lawn and trimmed the shrubbery and done anything else that she required any time one of her girlhood friends from the old neighborhood visited, always frumpily dressed, these now middle-aged women with herring on their breath, and the old country in their voices, and memories of their but recently slaughtered kindred still hanging like hooks in their hearts.

"Joey?" I asked again.

My father nodded fiercely.

I recalled Joey O'Brian as tall and very skinny, with bad skin and bad teeth, a red-headed young man I'd once found staring quizzically at the little mezuzah my mother had tacked up at the front door of our house—*Waz zat, guv?* When I'd answered, he'd chuckled and shaken his head, so distant from it all, not just Jewishness, but college towns, professors and their little boys, rooms lined with books.

"You're saying it was Joey . . . the father?"

My father nodded and his eyes brightened like a man at last understood.

"You and Lenore never . . ."

My father shook his head firmly.

But if this was true, why had my mother ever left him? I wondered. If my father had not even had a fling with Lenore, much less murdered her, then why had my mother packed her bags, called me Ezra, dragged me from the house, and taken me back into the world of her father and out of the world of mine?

I leaned forward and stared into my father's eyes. "Why did my mother leave that day?"

My father shook his head, as if surrendering to silence, to something that would forever remain confused.

"Why?" I repeated.

He closed his eyes, and in the silence that settled over us, I took the book from his hand, returned to the earlier poem, and read its final stanza softly.

From the lightning in the sky
As it passed me flying by,
From the thunder and the storm,
And the cloud that took the form
(When the rest of Heaven was blue)
Of a demon in my view.

My father opened his eyes slowly, and to my surprise, they were glistening. He nodded toward the book, and I could see that he was too tired to speak, that the haze of drugs or perhaps even the weight of his own impending death was exerting an irresistible power over him. Still, he seemed to think that somewhere in those tattered pages he might find words he could no longer say.

And so I began to turn the pages again, through poem after poem, past "Annabel Lee" and "The Bells," on to "The Raven," and past it, too, until I reached "Tamarlane," and heard my father groan, a signal it seemed to me, that this was the poem he wanted.

I put my finger on the first line, and looked at him. He shook his head and so I continued down the page, his head shaking and shaking until I reached these lines:

The rain came down upon my head
Unshelter'd—and the heavy wind . . .

"The day of the storm," I said.

My father nodded and smiled, and it seemed to me at that strange moment we suddenly returned to the world we had once known and loved, he the patient teacher, I the adoring student.

And so I recited the events of that day as I had come to know them.

"Okay, the day of the storm. You and my mother came home. You were in the car together."

He nodded again, paused briefly, like a man gathering up his strength, then with the greatest effort he had made so far, he spoke.

"Argument," he said in a tone very different from the one my mother had described or my bitter imagination had created and which seemed to embody the depth of his loss.

"But it was not over Lenore? Is that what you're saying?"

My father nodded excitedly, as if to say, *Yes, yes*.

"Over what?" I asked.

My father seemed even now reluctant to tell me what had passed between him and my mother on that stormy afternoon. His pause was long and thoughtful before he lifted his hand and pointed to me.

"Me?" I asked. "You were arguing about me?"

The old twinkle came into his eye, as when I'd been a boy in his study, he my devoted teacher, often speaking to each other through verses quoted from the great poems of the West, whole conversations carried out in that erudite, yet oddly intimate way.

"What about me?" I asked.

My father pointed to the book and began waving his hand, a gesture that sent me flipping back through the pages of Poe's poems, slowly one by one, thinking that he sought a poem, perhaps certain lines.

I'd almost returned to the first of those poems by the time he groaned, a signal that I should stop.

I looked at him, utterly puzzled. "Why here?" I asked. "It's a blank page."

He struggled to speak, but only a few slurred sounds came out, nothing I could make sense of.

"It's a blank page," I repeated. "There's nothing on it."

My father shook his head violently, clearly denying what I had just told him.

"There's nothing on this page but the number," I told him.

He nodded fiercely.

I looked at the number. "Thirteen?"

Again he nodded wildly. Then with great effort he said, "Never . . . never."

So the argument had been about me, had something to do with the number thirteen, something my father associated with the word *never*.

"*Me*," I said, turning the first of my father's words over in my mind. "*Thirteen. Never.*"

And suddenly I knew what he was struggling to tell me, what the number thirteen could only mean in relation to me, and what he must have said to my mother about that relationship.

"You told my mother that you'd never allow me to be bar mitzvahed?" I asked.

He nodded solemnly.

I saw my mother as I knew she must have been at that moment in her life, that moment as they sat with the rain thudding around them, and she saw him fall like a man through a gallows floor, fall utterly from the world they'd once shared, the rabbinical student my father had once been, how deeply my mother had expected to live as a rabbi's wife, and how different that life had become, the suburban life of a professor's wife, uprooted and unmoored, as she must have thought of it, though never, never as utterly lost to all that was holy until that moment in the storm when my father had effectively told her, and no doubt bluntly, that her son was not to be a Jew.

I could only imagine the utter fury with which my mother

must have received this final proof of my father's demonic secularism, proof once and for all of how arrogantly he had discarded the sacred values, how deeply and irrevocably he had dismissed the commandments and commentaries, the centuries of accumulated wisdom, and with it, the fierce need she must have felt to flee this dead-souled modernist, this despiser of ritual, of all the honored customs, this pragmatist who believed in quick solutions, in getting rid of obstacles, this radical assimilationist who was ashamed of his own people, felt no pity for the great heaps of European dead, who wished only to throw off the yoke of the past, make himself new . . . this *American*.

He eased himself back into his pillow and released a long deflating breath, so that I saw that even now he remained unsure of what he'd done, whether he'd been right or wrong, though even this seemed to matter less to him at that moment than what I would do with this strange revelation.

He tried to speak, but nothing came. So after a moment, and with what appeared to be the very last of his vital force, he motioned for me to give him the volume of Poe. I rose and sat on the bed beside him, holding the book open and turning the pages until he found the verse he wanted.

"Be that word our sign in parting, bird or fiend," I shrieked, upstarting—
"Get thee back into the tempest and the Night's Plutonian shore!
Leave no black plume as a token of that lie thy soul hath spoken!
Leave my loneliness unbroken!—quit the bust above my door!
Take thy beak from out my heart, and take thy form from off my door!"
Quoth the Raven, "Nevermore."

He placed a single, trembling finger on that final word and looked up at me quizzically, no doubt wondering, perhaps quite desperately, if I could intuit the question his eyes asked. *Will you answer as the Raven does? Will you refuse to abandon me?*

For my answer, I took the book from his hands and read the last stanza of Poe's great poem:

> *And the Raven, never flitting, still is sitting, still is sitting*
> *On the pallid bust of Pallas just above my chamber door;*

I looked up and saw that he understood.

"I won't leave you alone," I assured him.

Had the world been less the thing it is, and more the thing we wish it were, then my father would have recovered, and we would have had a few more years to work out the long confusion of our lives, come to graceful terms, so that by the time his death at last arrived, I would have been a truly loving son, he a loving father, the two of us at last in some accord with what he had done, and I had done, what he was and what I became. But it was too late for that, as I could see by his waning strength. And so I accepted what the Talmud teaches, that no act can be wholly undone. *But then, "The Raven" teaches that, too,* I thought, and so I returned to it and began to read to my father again, this time from the beginning, a land both dark and dreary rising before me as I read, that place denied all true atonement, and where, as Poe so darkly knew, each second turns Forever into Nevermore.

THOMAS H. COOK is arguably America's shortest male crime writer. Utterly lacking in tough guy characteristics, he remains the mystery world's most consistent no-show at sporting events, car races, horse races, and urban marathons. He has never painted his face in anticipation of the Super Bowl and is allergic to beer. His sole experience with law enforcement was being pulled over for speeding, at which time he was given only a warning. As a boy he wanted to be a great writer, then he read some great writers and decided he was nowhere near that good. Since then, he has churned out more than twenty novels and a smattering of nonfiction. He likes writing short stories because they're short and does not like writing long books because they're long. He has never read *Remembrance of Things Past*, though on the street he is often mistaken for Marcel Proust.

Emily's Time

Dorothy Salisbury Davis

No one in the village could say just when or how he came to be called the professor. He could not say himself, for he had taken many courses but never earned a degree. He was self-taught, even self-published, and proud of it. Nevertheless, it was better to be called the professor than the actress's son, as he was known until the actress herself was all but forgotten.

Her only heir, he had inherited one of those Hudson River Gothics, propped up by history, you might say. It had been left to her, along with a sizable trust fund, by an admirer. Such fame as she gained was on the road rather than on Broadway, and her not greatly wanted son was left to the care of almost as many nannies over the years as he had cats. The cats he had been able to choose, at least. He had grown up bearing his mother's name.

With a mother dedicated to her art, he turned early to science, and favored biological studies, most particularly those given to the development of man. He longed to make a contribution; he longed for applause, about which he had heard so much in his youth. At the age of forty, after several unsustainable starts, he was working on a premise he was sure was worthy of his endeavors. Simply stated, his belief was that man, and indeed all life on earth, would at its zenith turn backward and, step by backward step, fall off the edge of time. He suspected, but was not yet sure, the turn had already occurred.

It was his practice to travel into the city by way of bus and subway several mornings a week. Tall and lanky, he carried an overstuffed briefcase and a black umbrella he sometimes used as a cane, and sometimes as a spear to pick up flotsam, which he deposited in the nearest container. Its silver handle was tarnished and looked more to him like a gargoyle than the sheep's head it was supposed to represent. He acknowledged any encounter with a neighbor or, in town, with a familiar out for a smoke on the institution steps, with a smile that disappeared as fast as it came. Wherever he was going, to library or museum, his mind was there far ahead of him. So, it scarcely needs to be said, was his heart. He was followed, accompanied really, to the bus stop every morning by his black-and-white cat. Peasblossom was the most recent of his many cats named from Shakespeare, and far and away the most loving of them. Unless urgently occupied in the pursuit of game, Peasy also came out of the bushes to greet him on his return from the city.

The professor at this time was trying to come to grips with the reality of DNA, and how it was bound to impact on his work. That scientists the world over were going through the same struggle was small comfort. Science always seemed a step ahead of him and before he could go forward, he seemed always to have to catch up. DNA both bolstered and undermined his findings, and he began to feel that his lifetime would not be long enough to judge its impingements. He began to fear he had made another unsustainable start.

This was his frame of mind the afternoon he arrived home to find Peasy waiting for him on the front step with a large, bloodied chipmunk hanging limp from her jaws. Before the professor decided whether to praise or scold the cat, for he was a compassionate man, his housekeeper flung open the door and poured out the story of how Peasy had cornered the chipmunk in the living room. She was sure chipmunks were taking over the house. They had already made the garden look like a pegboard, and now she had found bits of foil behind the sofa cushions, and worse, in a winter shoe when she went to put it away, she found two chocolates, the very ones her nephew had sent her for Easter. Chipmunks were vermin, she wailed, and they affected her allergies. If the professor didn't do something about them she would have to give notice. At the moment the professor did not think that was such a bad idea, but he promised to consult an exterminator. He said, "Good cat, Peasy" and, giving his briefcase and umbrella to the housekeeper, took the stiffening chipmunk round to the back kitchen and put it for the time being in the metal box that once was the repository of milk bottles.

The housekeeper was still complaining of her allergies at dinnertime. Now she did not see how she could make her weekly trip to the farmers' market in the morning. The professor agreed to go himself before leaving for the city.

So it came about that he met Emily.

Emily was a farm girl from upstate who came to the village market with her brother twice a week to sell seasonable produce and their dairy specialty, sweet butter, purveyed in collectable stone jars. They also sold pint containers of buttermilk when available. Both the professor and Peasy loved the buttermilk.

No doubt buttermilk was the most congenial among the professor's concerns when he reached the market, but from the moment he first laid eyes on Emily his spirits soared. At first he thought her only unique, with her unremitting smile, her ruddy cheeks, and her blue, blue eyes even brighter than Peasy's. Then he realized that such quaint old-fashionedness as hers was of another time, another culture, one quite distinct in the ascent of man and now quite gone. Unless, it occurred to him—but something not to be dwelled on at the moment—she was harbinger of the backward turn.

That thought probably made it easier for the professor to ingratiate himself—call it courtship—on his frequent early morning visits to the marketplace that followed. The professor kept their conversation simple. He even exaggerated his ignorance of farm life. However, it was with unfeigned wonder that he discovered cows had only one set of teeth. Emily allowed that might account for how long it took them to chew their cud. She giggled as though delighted with herself. The professor, enchanted but chagrined at his ignorance, went home and looked up the word *cud*.

It's possible the brother made inquiries among his local custom about the professor, and while no one had a bad word to say about him, no one had an especially good one either. He just wasn't like anyone else in the community.

In any case, he and Emily were married a short time later in his house with a few neighbors; Peasy and a weepy housekeeper stood as witnesses. The housekeeper's notice was accepted without her quite realizing she had given it.

Despite the dire advice of the departing housekeeper to Emily to beware of the wily cat and to expect more chipmunks, the professor's household seemed likely to be a happy one. Peasy could come and go at will—she had been kept indoors during the professor's visits to the farmers' market, a circumstance that no doubt also kept the chipmunks out of sight. Either that or they were weaning a late brood, as Emily suggested out of her experience of animal life.

Emily wasn't half the professor's age, but that didn't seem to trouble either of them. In fact, it allowed a deference that might otherwise have needed to be addressed. Peasy shared their bed as well as their board, and sometimes even the professor's midnight vigil when he turned on the lamp and tilted the shade so that he might better study Emily's face in sleep. In daylight her countenance could hardly have been brighter. Her smile seemed etched as might an angel's whose mission was to bear good news. She carried the same angelic smile into sleep, where, if possible, it was enhanced by the delicate pale violet of her eyelids with their curtain of dark silken lashes. She was Sleeping Beauty. A hundred years: he would not dream of waking her.

The professor resumed his regular trips to the city almost ebullient. The presence of Emily in his life gave him back his wavering faith in the regression theory. But now he hoped that by further study of what he called Emily's Time he might point the way to delaying its passing to the era that preceded it.

Whether by good or ill omen, the week the professor returned to work, the eyes of science and much else of the world were riveted on another stunning achievement in genetics: the cloned sheep that had been named Dolly. The very idea of cloning outraged him. It interfered. It destroyed the relevance of both the cloned and the clone by its promise of multiplicity. It sped annihilation. The more he contemplated the consequences of clones begetting clones, as it were, the more distraught he became. He attributed to the phenomenon realities far beyond reason, leaps that defied measure.

It was inevitable that his distress spill out at home, little acts of unkindness to both Emily and Peasy, for which he apologized at once and immediately committed again. There was a night when he came close to waking Emily, to shaking her into wakefulness so that he might watch for changes in her face as she fell back into sleep. He clung to Peasy to restrain himself, and Peasy, with a little moan at first, settled into a purr that lasted until sleep overcame both the professor and the cat.

The professor, by sheer determination, managed to *compartmentalize* cloning. It was a word—and a practice—he had learned in a brief stint of therapy he otherwise considered a waste of time and money. He explained his change of mood to Emily by saying he had stopped counting sheep. It gladdened Emily without enlightening her and pleased the professor for having said it. He didn't have much humor. Indeed, he had a compartment for *humor* to which he added every snippet he might recall in future need.

But spring came on, as always, as if it were the first time. Willow trees turned yellow, forsythia and crocuses bloomed, and the shad ran in the river. Both the professor and Peasy would as soon Emily had not so quickly acquired a taste for shad roe, but it was apportioned equally by the professor's hand as it came from the grill. Confirming the wisdom of the banished housekeeper, a profusion of chipmunks moved outdoors from their basement shelter.

Emily, with or without Peasy, would meet the professor at the bus stop and walk him home, swinging his hand like a schoolgirl might and squeezing the life out of it. The professor thought how ideal a couple they must seem to any observing villager. He could even imagine applause if they were to go to the Firemen's Benefit Ball. He might just use the tickets this year.

One soft spring morning Emily insisted that he come out at once to the garden. It was a Saturday and she wanted him to see Peasy and the chipmunks. The ground had not been cleared of winter rubble so that the holes left over from the fall, or new ones, were not to be seen. What played out like a pageant on a bracken-strewn stage was the sudden appearance and as sudden vanishing of a skittering chipmunk with Peasy bouncing in pursuit. It was a ballet, the professor said, and fell himself to thinking of the night his mother, swathed in veils and calling herself Isadora, danced for him and a gentleman he could remember only by how much he'd hated him. When he'd been taken by his mother up to his turret bed, he'd been more sure than of anything in his life till then that she would go down and dance again, this time without the veils. He'd heard the music. But when he'd tried the door, he found it locked. And that had somehow turned his anger off. He had wept and afterward wished he'd kicked and raged.

Peasy caught the hapless chipmunk and brought it to the professor, who, as soon as it was quite dead, buried it in the potter's field of cats and their prey at the bottom of the garden.

When he threw a last handful of dirt on the little mound and looked up at Emily, her smile seemed molten, her face a golden glow. It seemed the very essence of spring. Was this, then, happiness? She untied the scarf at her neck and tried to get him to wipe his hands on it. "It's too beautiful," he said, and wiped them on his shirttail.

Before they returned to the house, Peasy brought yet another creature to the professor. This time, with a scientist's thrust, the professor dispatched it and gave it back to a whimpering Peasy. "No more," he said. Peasy tore into it and devoured the bits she wanted.

"No more," Emily repeated, mournful suddenly, and said again, "no more." And yet again, "No more."

"Nevermore," the professor said.

Peasy, as usual, was the first in bed that night, occupying as much of it as she could manage until Emily pushed her over. On the professor's arrival, she preened and gave a defiant swish of her tail toward Emily, and as soon as the professor got into bed, she settled in the crook of his arm. Emily turned her back on them.

"You mustn't mind," the professor said, but the truth was he enjoyed the show of animosity between them. He had not missed Peasy's flick of her tail. Nor did he miss now Emily's bare shoulder. It seemed odd to him, as though it didn't belong there, her head tucked in, her face away. He reached across, intending to pull the comforter over her, but at the touch of his hand, she turned to him and threw off more of the quilt. She was quite naked and might have come to him, all smiles, but Peasy would have none of it. She growled.

The professor held her tightly and tried to tell Emily that Peasy sometimes purred that way, a lie that didn't matter. Emily was covering her nakedness and her face was changing, the smile turning down, not up. She sat up and screamed at both of them. "What she needs is kittens, and I don't know what you need!"

"You know she can't have kittens," the professor said. He hugged Peasy tighter, feeling she, too, needed to be comforted.

"I don't care," Emily cried and the tears came freely. They fell on her beautiful distorted face like rain gushing through a gargoyle.

He would never forget the image.

The professor got loose and fled from the room. He banged the door on his own heels.

A solitary night lamp lit the shadowy way to the bathroom. The professor did not stop. He went on to the staircase that circled up in broad steps from the ground floor and then wound upward more narrowly into the turret. He climbed by feel and memory and the seepage of starlight from the one window left unboarded. It was from there, as a child, he scouted the river and every night saw in his mind's eye the British frigate lying in anchor to blockade the passage. At the window now, he wiped away the dust and pressed his face onto the glass to see something, anything, to banish Emily from his mind. A solitary tanker, in a tugboat's tow, came slowly into his vision and passed, unstoppable, into and beyond its periphery. He delved deeper into his memory and conjured the British crew carousing on the anchored warship, even as he'd seen and heard it as a child. They were making fun of the colonials, singing "Yankee Doodle Dandy." He had wakened in the night and heard them, and must have run to tell his nanny, for he remembered now how every morning afterward until she left, she would ask him who he'd seen that night. But it was always the same, and he remembered her, her face pinched up in disgust when she said, "My God, aren't they ever going to come ashore?" And he had said, "Don't you see, they can't."

And those words summoned again the face of Emily the grotesque.

The night chill came over him, a dank dampness. Cold through, barefoot and in his nightclothes, he turned from the window and opened the door to his childhood bedroom. He turned back the spread and crawled beneath it.

It was there that Peasy found him. The professor spoke to her, a whisper really, lost among the many disturbances of an ancient house, "I would never have let them do that to you, Peasy, if I knew you wanted kittens."

Peasy was gone when he awoke from a leaden sleep, and the sun was well up. He knew where he was at once, having dreamed himself there before he wakened. At the foot of the bed was the picture of his mother he had brought up from his bedroom when Emily came to live with him. He could hear a muffled birdsong outside, but no sound of movement within the house. As in a dream within a dream, he went downstairs and dressed in the empty bedroom, staring at the blanket and bed linens where they had been neatly folded and left on the bare mattress. The kitchen, when he went down, was as tidy and pristine as they had left it, as he always left it, before going up to bed. The kettle was cold on the stove. Then he saw Peasy outside the window, her front paws on the sill, her mouth open in a meow he couldn't hear. Before he opened the door to her, he turned back and listened to the inside stillness. He called out Emily's name in a voice he did not recognize as his own. A faint quivering echo came back to him.

The professor sat outside the kitchen waiting for the phone to ring. He felt sure it would. He also felt quite powerless, unwilling, unable to cope with whatever was happening to him. He had known the feeling once before and had never forgotten it. There was a massive rock, bleak and weather-whitened, in the palisades down river. It was known as Eagle Rock and the great birds were said to rest there, perhaps to sight their prey, perhaps to savor it. The last time he had climbed to the rock was to escape the terrible emptiness in the house when his mother had just gone away. He had gone there and he had imagined jumping into the gaping crevice that cleaved the rock and tumbling into a pit of darkness. It had so fascinated him that he lay on his stomach and crawled toward the division. But something had stopped him. He could not remember what—the cry of a lost eagle perhaps, for they had come back—but he had not gone there again.

It was early afternoon when he received a phone call from his lawyer. Emily's brother had been in touch with him. Emily planned to sue for divorce. The professor's lawyer suggested, if what he had heard of the situation was true, that the professor simply seek an annulment: it would not be as messy and it would save him a lot of money. The professor instructed him: "Give them what they want."

The professor tried to heal himself as best he could. He closed out Emily's smiling face whenever it came to mind because inevitably it turned into the grotesque mask it had become in her burst of tears. Peasy was his constant and only companion, indoors and out. He gave away the umbrella with the sheep's head he had thought of as a gargoyle. He paid off the gardener, who was ready to start the spring cleanup, and he didn't answer the door to service people. When a meter man caught up with him out back of the house, the professor bade him find his own way: The cellar door was never locked. Indeed, it was now left open a wide crack for Peasy to come and go by when the professor had to be away. He did his shopping at a convenience store at the edge of town. They ordered Peasy's specials for him.

He did not often think of—and he no longer tried to document—the backward turn of life. As much of daylight as there was, the professor and Peasy spent outdoors. Peasy the indefatigable hunter and the professor, still the bemused recipient of first refusals. He gathered such bones as Peasy left in the milkman's box, where he had put the dead chipmunk in the days of his last housekeeper. He planned to dig a common grave when more remains accumulated. The words *common grave* had a timely feeling, a familiarity, but they were to be passed over quickly because they did not mean what they ought to mean. And no more no mores. He found himself enjoying Peasy's decimation of anything ground level because she took such pride in it, such sprightly pleasure. He even got a hatchet from the tool shed and cleaned the bracken and winter debris from Peasy's happy hunting ground.

Indeed, it was Peasy's good spirits and the way she demanded the same of him—he was sure that was her message—that kindled his all but dormant curiosity: How deep could her feelings be? Were all cats the same in needs, and was the difference in attitudes among them only reflective of whom or what they responded to? The root of what he was asking, he supposed, was whether they had wills of their own. Since he had grown skeptical of the will of man himself, the question ought to be moot.

But it wasn't. Not quite.

The professor began blowing the dust from the books in his own library to search for mention of relationships between man and beast, to put it crudely. He thought the appropriate limit to set for his study, given his own limits, was the emergence of man from beast. Did a common bloodline run through the transition to become more manifest eons later? He asked such questions as the expanding brain of man must have asked, even as his developed brain asked to this day, Who am I? What am I? Why am I?

He could not imagine Peasy asking questions like that. And yet, for the professor, the questions increased and diversified, ranging from mythology to microbiology. He resumed his trips to the city but there was a change in his expectations. Experienced researchers, learned librarians, even a scientist helped him, all, he now came to believe, speculators who scented a rich man's foible and access to his fortune. There was a terrible sameness in this to what had gone before in his life's work, and before and before—all those Before Emilys.

And, in truth, he was no longer a rich man. Except in one way—the devotion of Peasy, or, as he forced its reasonableness upon himself, his devotion to Peasy. He kept his own house in his fashion, and took a kind of delight in the way Peasy rolled in the curls of dust under table and bed, and then, when the professor opened the door, went out and shook herself like a mop. He bought her luxuries he did not provide for himself unless they suited their common tastes.

As fall came on, the bus fares went up, and the professor stayed mostly at home. He would sit for hours in the latent garden watching as Peasy would come and go, bringing him only the occasional mole, poor blind thing. Never a chipmunk. It was time for them to go underground again, and, through old or new channels, probably into the house. They would route themselves through the decaying basement, storing up for winter. Would they remember the fate of their ancestor at the jaws of Peasy? Peasy would remember. He was sure of that.

It was a gray, storm-threatened day when Peasy brought him a rabbit as big as herself. He had been about to go indoors, for one of the chills he often experienced in those days had sent its first waves through him. The rabbit was as dead as could be. Frightened to death. Rabbits knew how to die quickly. While Peasy tore it open, as was her way, the professor gathered his feet beneath him, and mused on how man slaughtered beasts they had themselves made tame, and turned them into what were called choice cuts. And wasn't that what Peasy was doing? The professor bent closer and studied the innards. Huddled and with life not entirely gone from them, was a near-to-be born, now never-to-be born, litter of rabbits. Sightless, they sucked air. The professor kicked at Peasy, who would not now be denied her prey, and then at the prey. He groped beneath the bench for the hatchet he knew was there and swung it wildly at both corpse and Peasy. Peasy leaped clear and let out a scream the whole village may have heard, while the professor made sure there was no life left in the bloody mess of fur and bone and sinew. When he came to himself, he looked round for Peasy, but she had fled.

Although he called her all night long, until, in fact, he had no voice left, she did not come. With daylight, he set out through the rain into the wood, still calling, though he made no sound. He was sure as he had been in all the beginnings of his life that he would find her at Eagle Rock. When he got there and did not find her, he lay down and called her name with what was left of his voice, calling into the dark cleavage in the rock.

Dorothy Salisbury Davis was born in Chicago in 1916. She was married for forty-six years to actor Harry Davis, who passed away in 1993. The author of twenty novels and thirty-some short stories, she was named Grand Master by the Mystery Writers of America in 1985, received the Lifetime Achievement Award at Bouchercon in 1989, and was the guest of honor at Malice Domestic in 1994.

The Cask of Castle Island

Brendan DuBois

It happened on Halloween night in South Boston, as I waited in the Easy Mart liquor store parking lot on East Broadway, hands in pockets, for Tommy Fortune to show up. Next to me was my Ford F-150 pickup truck with extended cab, one of the few luxuries I had allowed myself over the past few years. There was the constant roar of jets arriving and taking off from nearby Logan Airport, the red and green lights bright indeed as the metal birds clawed their way up into the sky, or made deliberate approaches to the concrete runways across the harbor.

I waited. It was dark and not that cold but I shivered. I wondered if Tommy would show up. We had known each other for many years, growing up in the projects of Southie, learning from each other and the streets, and I had put up with a lot from him over the years. But tonight I would right the wrong inflicted years ago on me and my family.

Still . . . part of me didn't want him to show up, didn't want him to come here, face-to-face. Part of the deal, I guess. Traffic went by in a constant stream on East Broadway and there were partiers out and about as well, having fun on Halloween night. Earlier the younger trick-or-treaters had been out on the sidewalks in their little kid costumes, looking adorable of course, but now the pretend tricksters were in bed, and the "for real" ones were out, fueled by booze or coke or any one of a half dozen drugs available on the streets of Southie. The men dressed like monsters or criminals, and for some reason, the women felt compelled to dress like hookers, with skirts up to there, fishnet stockings, and plenty of exposed cleavage. Usually I would have found this Halloween carnival fun to watch, but not tonight.

I took my hands out of my pockets, crossed my arms, tried to relax by leaning back on the polished black fender of my Ford, and stood there for a moment, until a dark blue BMW sportster roared in. Something cold and clammy seemed to catch in my throat, as I saw the BMW pull into a handicapped parking spot and Tommy Fortune step out.

He was my age, about my height but a hell of a lot skinnier, with a ruddy face and red hair done up with some sort of gel or hairspray. In keeping with the occasion, Tommy was in costume, and not being up on costume styles nowadays, I guess I would call it Irish Goth. He had on loose black jeans with safety pins clipped here and there, a leather jacket with decals and buttons, and a black T-shirt commemorating the latest tour of the Dropkick Murphys. From the way he walked and the way he talked, he was wired, and I could tell that he had been up to some heavy-duty partying earlier on.

"Randy!" he called out, stumbling a bit in my direction,

holding out a hand. "So glad to see you, m'man! Been way too long!"

I took his hand, gave it a quick shake, felt like I was touching week-old greasy pot roast. I dropped the clasp and Tommy whistled. "Man, that's one rough and rugged hand. You still working for the bricklayer's union?"

"Yep."

"Pretty boring, isn't it?"

I shrugged. "It's pretty regular, Tommy. That's all I care about."

He nodded and took a breath and leaned back against the fender of my pickup truck. From inside his leather coat he took out a pack of Marlboros and with a practiced move I had first seen in junior high school, he got a cigarette out and lit it. A cool move from so very long ago, and one that had entranced many a young girl, including my sister Katie.

"Regular," Tommy said. "Jeez, just another word for friggin' boring, if you don't mind me saying."

"It's okay, Tommy. I don't mind. After all that's gone on before . . . boring can be good."

He snorted with laughter, took another drag off of his cigarette. "Boring sucks," he said. "Can't stand being bored."

"If you say so," I said.

He eyed me with a casual approach but one that I definitely knew wasn't casual. He was checking me out, investigating me, and I kept my cool.

"So," he said. "You called me. Said you had a deal."

"Yeah."

Another defiant puff of the cigarette. "But word is . . . brick-layer boy, is that you've gone straight. True?"

"True."

"But you still said you had a deal. So what's up with that?"

I shrugged. "I need money. And . . . well, I got a deal. If you're interested."

"Always interested. Whatddya got?"

I hoped my voice was going to keep steady and calm as I pro-ceeded. "It's like this," I said. "I'm working on a renovation project over at Castle Island, the old Fort Independence. Doing support work, replacing old bricks, stuff like that. And for the most part, it's a union gig . . . but they do have some guys there, working under the table. Don't know the ins and outs . . . somebody's get-ting paid off, but we got some nonunion guys there as well, doing manual stuff."

Laughter from the other side of the parking lot, as a crew of teen boys and girls, in various degrees of Halloween dress, were raising hell. There was the sound of a beer bottle being smashed on the parking lot pavement. I took a breath and went on.

"There are these two brothers. Colombian. Up from Miami . . . We got friendly a bit, just because of where we were working together. Don't know why, but most of the union guys, they treat them like crap, you know? Because they're Colombian and here il-legally, nobody will have anything to do with them."

Tommy said, "Look, no offense, but can we skip the civics les-son?"

"Sure." I took another breath. "So these two guys, they came to me with a business proposition. They're here, they don't know anybody except for me, and . . . well, Tommy, they've got some coke they want to move."

Now I had his attention. He looked right at me. "Go ahead."

"Two kilos. Miami flake. Ninety percent pure."

He whistled. "Miami flake!"

"I guess, from what I hear, that the stuff up here in the streets, it's only thirty or forty percent pure, because it gets cut and recut so much, with baby powder or corn starch or flour."

"Miami flake!"

"But they have it here, and they want to sell it. I guess somebody who'd sell it on the street here could make a really good chunk of change. So . . . if you're agreeable . . . I could be the middleman."

"Miami flake!"

I crossed my arms. "So. Interested?"

He slapped me on the shoulder, and I refrained myself from slugging him. "Christ, yes, I'm interested. Let's do it. Can we set a meet?"

I shook my head. "They want me to take care of it, Tommy. They're afraid of getting caught, getting deported. So you make a good offer, I take a finder's fee, and we'll go on for there."

He laughed. "Best trick-or-treat gift I've ever gotten. When do you want to do the exchange?"

"Why not tonight?"

Now he looked suspicious. "Why tonight?"

I rubbed my hands. "Because I've got it, and I want to get rid of it. You can pay me later. And . . . I just don't like having it around. Makes me jumpy."

He smiled. "All right, where is it then? Your place?"

"No, it's at the job site. At the fort."

"Why there?"

"The Colombians felt it was safer there. They're living in an illegal cut-up joint over in Charlestown, don't trust their roommates. They thought the fort would be a safe place to keep it. So we can go there now, if you'd like."

"Isn't it closed?"

"Yeah, but I've worked my way up to temporary supervisor. They trust me enough to give me a key to the joint . . . and I know when the security guards do their rounds. We can get in and out, fifteen minutes or so, and you can go back to partying, maybe even do a test snort if you'd like."

He seemed to think about that for a minute, my Southie neighbor, looking ridiculous in his Halloween getup, and scratched at his chin. "Two keys . . . Miami flake . . . what kind of finder's fee you looking for?"

My mouth was so dry. "Tommy, I don't feel like dickering. Just make it fair . . . for me and the two Colombians."

"All right. Let's do it . . . I'll follow you?"

First test coming up. "No, Tommy. We go over there in my truck."

The suspicious look came back. "Why's that?"

"One vehicle going there after hours, all right, that can be overlooked. But two vehicles, Tommy . . . that's too much. Besides, if something goes south, we've got a better chance of getting out of there with me and my truck. I belong there. Not you and your Beemer."

Another pause to think, and I was hoping that his natural suspiciousness from working and living on the rugged streets of South Boston would be outweighed by his greed, and the thought of getting Miami flake in his hands.

For once my wishes came true.

"All right, Randy," he said, dropping his cigarette to the ground and stubbing it out. "Let's do it."

As we got into the pickup truck, he flipped open his jacket, maybe to settle himself in nice, but I think it was to give me a little demo, for he had on a shoulder holster and some sort of semiautomatic pistol. Just to show me, I guess, that he was in control. Typical Tommy.

I started up my Ford and backed out onto East Broadway. Between us on the seat was a small cooler. I motioned to it and said, "Open it up, Tommy. Have something to quench your thirst as we head over there."

Tommy opened up the lid of the cooler and gave me an appreciative whistle. He pulled out a sixteen-ounce can of Guinness. "Now we're talking." He popped open the can and took a long swallow. "Mmm," he said. "Damn, that's fine." He looked down into the cooler and said, "You want one?"

"Nope."

"You sure?"

"I'm sure," I said, driving along the street, keeping an eye out for tricksters along the side of the road. We passed small stores, old three-deckers and small brick homes with even smaller yards. Southie, my old hometown.

He took another swallow. "I guess what I heard about you is true, then."

"What's that?"

"That you're straight and narrow."

Up ahead, some kids dressed as skeletons waved at us as we sped by. For whatever it was worth, I waved back at them. Took a breath. Here we go.

"Yeah," I said. "Clean and sober, for three years and two months."

Tommy seemed to think about that for a while, and said, "How did that happen?"

I could feel my fingers tighten around the steering wheel. "Ever since Katie . . . ever since Katie."

The can of Guinness halted in midair, and then it came back down. Another possible detour, depending on how Tommy reacted. I stared straight ahead down the road, trees spaced on each side. I stopped and then made a left onto Day Boulevard.

"Yeah, Katie. Look, Randy, it was an accident, you know? This crap . . . it happens. It was an accident."

I had to blink back the tears that had suddenly arrived. "Sure. An accident."

Up ahead was the curve of the causeway, linking the mainland to Castle Island and its fort. I kept on driving into the darkness.

We stopped a few minutes later as the road narrowed, where a gate was blocking the way. I put the truck in park and stepped out. A light mist had now descended over the island and the wetness felt cool on my hands. With a key I undid the lock and opened the gate, and then got back into the truck, drove a few yards, stopped, and locked the gate behind us. In front of us was a parking area for the fort and the surrounding beaches and walkways, and there were a couple of cars parked on the other side, cars I knew belonged to the night security force, such as it was.

I drove to the other side of the lot, where construction trailers and assorted construction gear and debris was parked or piled up, and stopped the Ford. I looked to Tommy and said, "Just a bit of a walk." I opened the cooler. "How about one for the road?"

He snickered. "Or one for the walk."

Outside the mist was still falling, and there were far-off sounds of sirens, car horns, and the roar of jets going in and out of Logan. I shivered and took a small flashlight out of my coat pocket and flicked its switch, pointing it in front of us. I heard a swallow and a burp from Tommy as he kept pace with me, going down a gravel path that led up to the old fort.

The streetlights on some of the walkways cast domes of fuzzy light, as the beams lit up the falling mist. I shivered again, thinking, of all the nights, I would be bringing Tommy out here on Halloween, the night that our old Irish and Celtic ancestors said spirits and ghouls moved about the darkness. He stumbled as his foot caught on a root and said, "Damn, almost fell. But saved my beer. That's what counts, eh?"

"Sure, Tommy, whatever you say."

In the gloom I could make out the bulk of the old fort looming ahead of us, Fort Independence. I said, "See the fort, Tommy?"

"Yeah, I do," he said. "So what. Seen it plenty of times. Mostly when I was in the bag, if you know what I mean," and he laughed.

"But look at it again. You know this is one of the oldest forts in North America? Did you know that?"

He burped. "Maybe. Who knows. Who cares."

My throat tightened. "Katie knew. Katie cared. That's one of the things she cared about, you know? History of Boston and the islands. She knew almost everything about this fort, how it was built, who manned it, the kind of soldiers stationed here . . . Some famous soldiers came here, did you know that?"

Tommy finished off his Guinness and tossed the empty against a tree trunk. "No, I didn't know that. Hey, we almost there? I gotta take a leak."

"Yeah, Tommy," I said. "We're almost there."

Up ahead the path narrowed some and Tommy jostled into my shoulder and I recoiled automatically from his touching me. I could smell the stench of beer on his breath, sweat, and the general stink of someone who seemed to give bathing the same priority as retirement planning. The path then emptied out into another construction area, with temporary chain-link fence and trailers. My trusty key got us in once again, and we were nearer the waters of the harbor, where a wind had picked up. It was colder and Tommy said, "Shit, why in hell didn't these clowns come back in July? This sucks."

I waved the flashlight beam ahead of us. "We'll be out of the wind in a minute, Tommy. Don't worry."

I maneuvered us through piles of rocks and masonry, to a gaping hole in a dirt berm that was underneath one of the great stone walls of the old fort. I flashed the light up and said, "Just a short walk and we'll be done."

We went into the hole and up ahead was a temporary door, made of plywood, some framing, and hinges. I opened the door and with the aid of the flashlight found a circuit box and threw a switch, setting off a chain of temporary lighting that lit up the way. Before us was a long corridor made of brick, curving overhead like some medieval chamber. Despite everything that was going on I flashed the light overhead and said, "Look at the work there, Tommy. Still standing after nearly two hundred years. They did good work back then, stuff that lasted."

Inside it was cool and damp but at least we were out of the wind. "Big deal."

I kept the light up overhead and said, "But these were our ancestors who made this brickwork, Tommy. Didn't you know that? Poor Irishmen, fleeing the famine grounds of Ireland. Millions starved to death because of the potato famine, whole villages emptied out, and so many came here to the United States, to survive, to build a better life. They worked hard and dreamed that their children and grandchildren and their descendants would do something with themselves, would better themselves."

I lowered the light so it briefly shone in Tommy's face. He raised a hand up and I said, "Imagine what your ancestors would have thought, seeing you now. Knowing that they risked starvation, disease, death aboard ship . . . so that their descendant would be a drug dealer."

Tommy said, "Lower the goddamn light, okay?"

I did, cursing myself for pushing too far, thinking he would back out now, for Tommy did have a temper, especially when he had been drinking and taking whatever crap was popular this month, but he surprised me by laughing and said, "You know what I think? I think they would've been proud of me, that I found a job where I could make a ton of money without working too hard, selling junk to stupid white kids from the 'burbs or numb immigrants who don't know any better. So yeah, Randy, don't try to guilt me. I think they'd be proud of me. Now, enough with the history lesson, okay? Show me that Miami flake."

I lowered the light to the ground, switched it off. "Coming right up."

We walked into the brick-lined tunnel, descending lower into the depths of the old fort, water seeping from above, and we came to another temporary door on the left, which I opened up. Another string of lights came on and I led the way. "This is where we did some of the reconstruction work. Some of these old chambers were used to store gunpowder and other supplies, but because the fort is so old, some of the brick started crumbling. So that's what we did. Preserved the past."

Now I could feel my heart thumping harder, as we got closer to where it was all going to end. I had to distract myself so I started talking some more. "We'll be there in a couple of minutes, Tommy. This is where the Colombians were working, and this is where they were storing the Miami flake. You think we could get payment tomorrow if it all goes right?"

We were in Tommy's world now, of deals being struck and made, and he said, "Sure. And look, Randy, I'll give you a fair price, okay? Even more than fair, since you're from the neighborhood and all. And don't be so friggin' generous with the Colombians. Just give 'em enough to make 'em happy, you can skim the rest."

"Sounds good."

Tommy coughed and said, "Christ, it's spooky in here. Imagine if all the lights crapped out on us."

"Don't worry," I said. "Got my flashlight here. And speaking of spooky, you know who was stationed here, back in the 1820s?"

"How the hell should I know?"

"Poe."

"Who?"

"Edgar Allan Poe. The poet and horror writer. He was in the army for a while and was stationed here, in this fort. Don't tell me you didn't know that."

"Christ, why should I care about crap like that?"

A pile of bricks came into view and I forced myself to keep talking. "Because it means a lot, that's why. Edgar Allan Poe wrote his first book of poetry here, and rumor has it that something happened at this fort that inspired one of his short stories. Oh, here we are, just past those blocks. There's a little storage room, right off to the right. One pile of Miami flake, coming up."

Tommy slapped his hands together and said, "Finally."

Set inside the wall was an opening, about six feet tall, three feet wide, and just as deep. A blue tarpaulin hung against the wall, and another tarpaulin was covering something in the corner. On the floor was a brown-wrapped package and I pointed to it and said, "There you go, Tommy. Your Miami flake."

"Man oh man," Tommy said, and he knelt down and picked up the package. Standing behind him, I clenched my two fists together and brought them down hard against the back of his neck.

• • •

He grunted and fell forward. I moved quick, hitting him again with a brick, and then reaching under his coat to pick up his pistol, which I tossed into the corridor, the sound of metal striking the stone echoing. Grabbing him by the scruff of his neck, I hauled him up with one hand and tore at the hanging tarpaulin with the other, revealing chains set into the wall. Tommy was groggy, which made it helpful, for I had spun him around and in a manner of seconds had him secured at his wrists and ankles. I stood back, breathing hard, suddenly nauseous.

Tommy shook his head, looked at me. "What the . . ." and then he unstrung a series of obscenities that echoed throughout the brick-lined chamber. He fought against the chains, making them rattle, tried to kick at me, his feet moving only inches.

"Randy, what the hell is going on?!"

I went over to the other tarpaulin, pulled it off, revealing a pile of bricks, a trowel, a bag of ready-mix cement, and a wide metal pail, filled with water. I opened up the bag and, with a measured eye, poured in enough and started mixing.

"Randy, you let me go, or by God, you're a dead man. A dead man!"

I started mixing with a wooden dowel. "Sure, Tommy. You know about death, don't you? The death you sell in little plastic baggies, week after week. Like the crap you pushed on Katie, when she was barely out of high school."

He pulled at the chains about his wrists. "It was an accident, damn it!"

I checked the cement. Perfect consistency. Ready to get to work.

I picked up the first brick and lifted it up so Tommy could see it. "An accident is something that happens if your brakes fail. Or you're struck by lightning. Or hit by a drunk driver while crossing the street. That's an accident. You weren't an accident, Tommy, not by a long shot."

And then I went to work.

After the first layer was put down, he said, "Randy . . . look, let's be reasonable here, okay? It was a long time ago . . . and she was young and I was young, too."

"Not young enough," I said. "You were older than her, by five years. And you had to pervert her, make her a junkie. And what happened was no accident."

"It was! It was just a screwup, that's all . . . The dose was too high. A simple mistake, that's all."

"Mistakes," I said. "You know what your biggest mistake was, Tommy? You didn't know my sister all that well. You should have listened to her. You would have learned a lot. About this fort. About Edgar Allan Poe."

With trowel in hand, I started work on the second layer. More rattling of the chains. More cursing. I said, "Yeah, Tommy, while you were busy teaching Katie the ins and outs of how to pop a vein and work some junk into her arms, she could have told you about how Edgar Allan Poe was stationed here in the 1820s . . . how the rumor spread when he was stationed here, about a duel."

I was working fast, but I was making sure the lines were tight and the mortar wasn't put on sloppy. Time now for the third layer, and the fourth. Tommy caught his breath after a bout of cursing. He said, "Look, Randy, let me out. Okay? Nice joke and all, but let me out. I'll make it worth your while."

Despite it all, I found some comfort in the work of the brick, trowel, and mortar. It was good work, hard work, work that I had used to forget the cravings for booze, for pot, and for revenge. Work had served me well over the years, but it had failed in one area, of course. Revenge. But what the hell. Two out of three ain't bad.

"You will?" I said, mixing more mortar. "What can you do to make it worth my while?"

"I'll cut you in," he said, his voice moving fast. "You wouldn't have to do a thing. Five hundred bucks a week for doing nothing. Whaddya think?"

"A bribe, is that it?"

"No, not a bribe. Christ, okay, I know you're upset and pissed, and man, you got a right to be, but—"

Plop. More mortar. Another layer of bricks. I said, "So, you want to know the story, do you?"

"What story?"

"The Edgar Allan Poe story," I said. "You see, when Poe was here as a soldier, there was a tale about a duel between two military officers, a popular one and a despised one. The popular officer was killed, and the officer that everyone hated . . . well, one night, friends of the popular officer grabbed him from his quarters, dragged him to a dark corner of this same fort, and bricked him up."

Tommy moaned low, like a coyote with its leg caught in a trap. I looked up at him, chained, wearing his Irish Goth Halloween outfit, looking so ridiculous and frightened, an appearance that cheered me.

I said, "That's the tale. Probably made up. What the hell. But it probably inspired him to write one of his most famous stories, 'The Cask of Amontillado.' About a man taking revenge on another by bricking him up in a set of catacombs, during a time of festival."

"Jesus, Randy . . ."

I held up the trowel to his face. "So if you had listened to Katie, you might have learned something, you dope. Might have known what was waiting for you, for what you did to her, for what you did to me and the rest of her family. And then you wouldn't have come here with me, looking for your Amontillado. Or your damn Miami flake."

I lowered the trowel, scooped up some more mortar, and continued.

By the time the wall had extended to chest height, the cursing had returned. My sexual orientation, my supposed drinking and drug habits, the origins of my family and everyone I had been associated with came into Tommy's view. I kept my head down, kept working. Once I stepped back and looked at the wall with a critical eye. Not bad. Not bad at all.

Something hit my face. I wiped the spit from my cheek and looked at Tommy. "That all you got?"

"You're a dead man, Randy," he said, "a goddamn dead man.

I get out of here, you've got nothing. Southie, Eastie, New Hampshire, California, you can't run far enough to get away from me and my buds."

I picked up another brick. "Pretty bold talk for a guy in your position. See this mortar? Quick-drying stuff. In about an hour, you won't be able to break out of here without a sledgehammer or crowbar."

The chains rattled even louder. "Damn you, you bastard, why are you doing this! Why are you doing me like this!"

More mortar, the automatic movement of the trowel, the bricks rising and rising. "Because of what you did to Katie, because of what you did to me and my family, and because not once did you ever show regret, concern, for what you did."

He started blubbering. "All right, all right, all right, I'm sorry! Okay, is that what you want to hear? I'm sorry . . . I'm sorry I knew her, I'm sorry I gave her the drugs . . . sorry she OD'd at my place . . . but for Christ's sake, Randy, that was long ago."

Plop. Another brick lowered down. "Funny, I close my eyes and it was just yesterday. You damn rat, you couldn't even attend her wake or her funeral, could you?"

I worked some more and now there was just a foot or so of clearance available, and I looked into those eyes and that face, and I remembered something. "You know, Tommy, in the original story, the man being entombed is wearing a silly hat, to commemorate the festival. One with ribbons and bells, to appear the fool. I don't have anything like that to put on your head, but I do have this."

I bent down to my little collection of belongings and grabbed a small plastic bag. From the bag I took out a baseball cap, and I thrust my hand in to the little cavern, to place the hat upon his head.

"You bastard," he whispered.

I laughed. "Relax, Tommy, it looks good on you." And it did, the simple black and white with the intertwined white letters *NY*, the cap of a Yankees fan. "And just think, if and when you're ever found, the first thing they'll think of is that a Yankees fan got himself what he deserved."

He tugged and tugged at the chains. "Randy . . . please . . . don't do it . . . Don't keep me here . . ."

Almost done. I was sweaty and my hands and arms ached. I said, "And Tommy . . . it's Friday night. Don't think that if you hang tight over the next couple of days, that someone might hear you bright and early Monday morning. It's not going to happen. This tunnel out here was finished and inspected months ago. I set up this temporary lighting myself. No one's ever coming down here, except in the spring, when the extended tours start."

More screaming, more cursing, and then, after a bit, he started laughing. Laughing and laughing, an edge of hysteria to his voice. "Okay, Randy," he whispered. "You got me. A good joke. I can take a good joke like anyone. You're not going to finish this, I just know it. So let me out, we'll have some laughs and drinks, and we'll make that deal we talked about earlier. A weekly stipend for doing nothing, nothing at all. You can quit laying brick, can do anything you want, go anywhere you want. Okay? Just . . . just stop . . . I beg you, just stop."

A few more and then there was just a gap now, a gap that would be finished by three more bricks. I stepped closer and said,

"I'm going to stop. In just a minute . . . and you know, Tommy, someone of your intelligence, you might have read about this tale in another story. One written by a guy named Ray Bradbury, when the very same thing that's happening to you happened to someone else. And at the very end, the narrator looks to his captive and says something like, 'If you say, for the love of God, Montresor, I might let you free.'"

It was hard to see his face and the baseball cap in the gloom. "What . . . what am I supposed to say?" he stammered out.

"For the love of God, Montresor."

He coughed, started weeping again. "Oh, Randy . . ."

"Say it," I said. "Say it."

Another cough. "For . . . for the love of God, Montresor!"

"Yes," I replied. "For the love of God."

And, with a few swift movements, I placed the three bricks where they belonged and finished my work.

After a while I had collected everything—my tools, the string of lights, the tarpaulins, and even Tommy's pistol—up into a large canvas duffel bag, which I slung over my shoulder, and I stood before the fresh wall, flashlight in hand.

From behind the wall I heard the murmur of sounds, like the sound of waves crashing on the beach in the middle of the night, while you lay half awake in bed.

I played the beam of light over the new wall and I said in a low voice, "Tommy, at the end of Poe's story, he uses a little Latin phrase: *Requiescat in pace*. Which means 'Rest in peace.'"

I took a breath and, against the newly made brick wall, like

I was looking at some odd movie screen, I could see my younger sister Katie, with her long red hair. Katie the smart one, Katie the tomboy, Katie the book lover. I remember her growing up, remember her becoming a sweet teen girl . . . and then I remember . . .

My Katie. In a casket. Stretched out, cold and gray, while we weeped about her.

I turned the light away from the wall. "But Poe was a romantic. So Tommy?"

I knew he couldn't hear me, but I had to say it anyway.

"Tommy, don't rest in peace," I said.

A pause.

"Go to hell."

And I walked out of there, never to return.

BRENDAN DuBois is an award-winning author of short stories and novels. His short fiction has appeared in various publications, including *Playboy*, *Ellery Queen's Mystery Magazine*, and *Alfred Hitchcock's Mystery Magazine*, as well as numerous anthologies, including *The Best Mystery Stories of the Century*. He has twice received a Shamus Award for his short fiction and has been nominated for three Edgar Awards. DuBois's long fiction includes six previous books in the Lewis Cole mystery series, as well as several other suspense thrillers. He lives in New Hampshire with his wife, Mona.

Bells

James W. Hall

While the stars that oversprinkle
All the heavens, seem to twinkle
With a crystalline delight;
Keeping time, time, time,
In a sort of Runic rhyme,
To the tintinnabulation that so musically wells
From the bells, bells, bells, bells,
Bells, bells, bells—
From the jingling and tinkling of the bells.

"They're back," she whispered. "The bells. They're jingling. Listen. Listen, goddamn it."

Isaac squinted up at the ceiling as if he were straining to hear. A white ceiling. The four-bladed Hunter fan was turned off, the better to hear the bells. They lay silently side by side with the tumble of sheets at their feet. Both of them still sweating from the sex. The scent of their juices ripe in the air.

Isaac said, "I wish I could hear them. I truly do."

Janet pressed her head back in the pillow, squeezing her eyes shut.

She'd cut her hair this week. There was a trendy name for the style, but Isaac thought her stylist must've used a hatchet and a pair of pinking shears, leaving less than an inch of shiny jet black ruffling against her white skin. She'd not told him she was having it done. Just went off and returned with it hacked off, an act of defiance, or self-destruction. Her shrink had labeled her impulsive act with some jargon Isaac couldn't recall.

Janet's hair had been growing uncut for a decade. When he first saw her, Isaac thought she resembled a folk singer, a throwback to their grandparents' era, the ends of her feathered locks teasing at her butt.

Still, the new buzzed look turned him on, this strange woman lying beside him with the fine dusting of hair. While they made love for the first time in months, he'd rubbed his hands through it, feeling the shape of her skull so close to the surface. Not at all like the tangles and layers of her old mane. He was touching her hair during his climax, doggy style, as he preferred. That short, boy's cut making him rock hard, firing him up and out, over a high, cascading ledge that he'd forgotten was there. Sending him freefalling on that thousand-foot plunge into a groaning, wailing release.

He used to go sailing into that void every time they fucked. But after two years together that phase had melted away. Until this new cut. Until her fit of reinvention. All because of the bells. This certainty Janet had developed that there were bells tinkling within the walls of their old house.

For weeks the fixation had been rattling her normal insouciance. Janet's yoga-induced, vegetarian, and chamomile serenity was gone. In recent days, at random moments she would come to an abrupt halt, swing around, stare at the thick plaster of the living room wall, or the kitchen, or the TV room, and she'd point and whisper to him to listen. Listen, damn it, couldn't he hear?

Beside him now she opened her eyes, lifted her shorn head from the pillow, and fixed him with a wretched look.

"They've stopped," she said. "Can you at least hear that they've stopped?"

"That," Isaac said, "I can hear."

Isaac took a joint from the side table, lit it, drew a slow drag, and let the smoke crawl back out his mouth in a yawn.

"You're mocking me."

"I'm lying here smoking."

"You don't take any of this seriously. I'm going crazy and you're just acting like nothing's happening."

He was silent. They'd covered and recovered this ground. He didn't want to argue. He wanted to savor the erotic afterglow, the arousing pretense that she was someone else, a stranger he'd met on the fly. That this encounter had been a wild, zipless fuck. That's what they'd called it back in the day. Hooking up, a one night stand. If she'd only quit talking and let him luxuriate in the last few glowing seconds of his fantasy.

"It feels different this time. More quiet than usual. I can't describe it."

"Maybe they've left." He offered her the joint but she waved it off. "Maybe they've taken their bells and gotten the fuck out of our walls."

"Mocking me," she said. "Again and again and again."

With her toes she tweezered the edge of the sheet and pulled it up to cover her. She had the most prehensile toes. He'd found it sexy once, the things she could do with her feet.

"No, Isaac," she said. "I'm afraid these bells are here to stay."

He wondered how long it would take her to try to validate what she thought she was hearing. Bring a friend over to listen, for instance. Though she had only one friend. Carla, a masseuse at the same spa where Janet worked. But Carla had a new boyfriend and was spending a lot of her off hours with him, so she hadn't made it over yet. Screwing the guy, then massaging the knots in his trigger points, easing the lucky man's tensions inside and out.

Three days ago Janet bought a small Sony tape recorder and she'd been carrying it around with her in the evenings after work, waiting for the next episode of tinkling. Planning to tape the bells and play them back for whoever would listen. So far she'd fumbled with the switch when the bells came, or they'd stopped tinkling just as she got it on. The devilish bells were proving too quick and slippery for validation.

Isaac approved of the recorder. He told her so.

"You're doing something positive, that's good. Is this something Ray suggested?" Ray being her shrink. Wednesdays and Fridays at five thirty, an hour session at one sixty five a pop. Her insurance wasn't covering it, so Janet was using all her tips from the Emerald Spa. Applying facials, six customers a day, extracting blackheads from the cheeks and greasy noses of rich old ladies and goombas from Miami Beach, every cent of that money was going to Ray so Ray could steer her through this obsession and return her to normalcy. Make the bells stop ringing.

He could hear them going back and forth, Ray and Janet, their tango of psycho-blather.

Did bells have any special meaning to her?

Not particularly.

Were there any bells of significance buried in her past?

Well, there were church bells when she was growing up. Presbyterian bells. But she was an atheist now.

Did the bells make her miss her childhood, miss church, miss that time in her life when she still had faith in a higher power?

No, she didn't miss any of that. And anyway, these bells were more like sleigh bells, or chimes, a higher-pitched jingle. They didn't have the seriousness and weight of church bells.

Did you ever go on a sleigh ride as a child? Perhaps something happened on that ride, some trauma? An unwanted sexual advance perhaps.

I grew up in Orlando. No sleigh rides, no hay rides. Nothing but endless traffic, lots of horns, but no bells.

Are there any other bells in your past?

None I can think of.

Stories with bells, movies with bells? Dreams with bells?

Maybe there's a Christmas movie, I don't know, some clichéd

scene with kids in a sleigh in the snow. But it means nothing to me. Just some snippet I can picture, but I can't even remember the movie's name.

One sixty five an hour. All those blackheads, all that pinching and massaging and cleansing the cheeks of the rich, the pampered, and Janet was converting all that into worthless back-and-forth blather. Nothing to show for it week after week as the bells continued to chime within their walls.

Janet reported on her sessions to Isaac. She claimed she was giving him the verbatim replay. Even if it was true, he doubted she caught every nuance of Ray's questioning, or her own responses. How could she? And it was often the nuances, the unspoken revelations hidden in the shadows of the sentences, crouched in the timbre of the voice or lurking in the incomplete phrases, the swallowed word, the unfinished thought that gave away the truth. He wondered if he'd been implicated in Janet's deteriorating mental health, this hallucinatory excursion she was taking. He wondered if Ray had requested that Isaac attend a session. Couples therapy. He wondered if Janet had refused to ask Isaac, for fear he'd decline. Or maybe she was working herself up to ask him. She was right. He would decline. That was certain. He wanted no part of shrinks and their manipulative manner, their insidious tactics for sneaking past the surface into the private regions. Fuck them all. Fuck their neutral questions, their long silences, their slimy trade craft.

He could distinctly hear other conversations between Ray and Janet. Conversations that went unreported, but that Isaac was nonetheless certain had occurred.

Were there any other stresses in her life? Problems. Sexual, marital, work related.

Oh, I forgot.

What's that, Janet?

Well, really it's no big deal. I mean nothing that would explain the bells.

Tell me about it.

Last month I had a miscarriage.

I'm sorry.

You think that could be connected? You think that miscarriage could have set this whole thing off?

Do *you*?

Well, I really did want to get pregnant and have a child. I still want to.

Go on.

But I mean, what? Like the bells might be related to a lost child? How would that work?

I don't know. But the mind is very good at finding images for its pain.

Oh. So like I'm hearing these bells, they're metaphors for the baby somehow. Bells I would've hung on the baby's crib. Is that it? The bells that were meant to be but aren't going to be? That's a stretch. I don't buy it.

Why not, Janet?

Bells on a crib? No. I don't really associate bells and cribs.

Go on. See where that leads you.

Go where? I had a miscarriage. That was real. And now these bells are real. They're in the wall. Like rats or mice. Only bells.

Are they?

Yes, there're real.

But your husband can't hear them.

No, he can't. That's what he says.

You don't believe him?

The bells are real.

Why would Isaac lie?

Sometimes he's not supportive. Like he's unhappy with me. I love him and I know he loves me, but it feels like he's the enemy sometimes. Like he's run out of patience with me.

Is that what you think? Your husband hears the bells and he's lying so you'll doubt your own sanity?

He's very smart. A genius really. I think he's disappointed in me. He seems to have lost interest in me physically. Especially since the miscarriage.

So make the connection. Your marriage is suffering a downturn and then there are these bells you hear in the wall.

Okay, okay. So somehow I created the goddamn bells to make myself interesting to Isaac? To get attention?

Did you?

No, absolutely not.

All right.

But while we're on my marriage, I've been thinking about something. This thing I haven't thought about for years. It's probably nothing.

I'm here. I'm listening.

At the beginning, before we got married, we signed papers. Legal stuff. Prenups, you know. I get half no matter what.

Is that important? Are you considering a divorce?

I'm not. But sometimes I think Isaac may be.

And that connects to the bells how?

Well, you know, there's like a kick out clause or something in the prenups. I don't know what it's called. Something about sound mind, good mental health. Some boilerplate thing that the lawyers put in.

I'm not sure what you're getting at, Janet.

If I'm crazy, I get nothing. If I get committed to an institution or if you diagnose me as unstable. Oh, never mind. That's too weird. It's impossible.

Why is it impossible?

I think I'm hearing bells. But you're not about to commit me to a mental ward, right? I'm not that far gone. Am I? Tell me I'm not that far gone.

Ray would laugh at that.

Janet, calm down. We're just talking. You're not that far gone. Not even close.

Fucking shrinks. Isaac imagined this conversation. Imagined it, but it felt like it happened. And did she report it to him? Hell, no.

Isaac and Janet hadn't discussed the miscarriage or the emotional fallout. That morning when it happened she'd come into his office looking pale. Her face grim. He rocked himself to his feet, followed her to the bathroom.

"I don't think we should flush it. That would surely clog the pipes."

Janet said nothing. She stared at the soupy mess.

So Isaac disposed of it. Scooped it out of the toilet with a garden trowel and dumped it into a garbage bag, then put that in another, and that in another. Three bags for the little red mass. They discussed burying it in the backyard, but Janet said no. She couldn't bear the thought that it would always be so close by. So Isaac dropped the garbage bags into the can outside. The red unfortunate mass in the toilet bowl had to wait inside the garbage can for two days until the Friday pickup.

Isaac wasn't ready for a child. Not even close. So he had to pretend to be grieving, go through the motions. She seemed to buy it, and said reassuring things to him, hugged him. Then sure enough, not long after that she began hearing the bells. So maybe there was a connection. One would think.

A week went by. The bells kept ringing for Janet. Janet, for whom the bells tolled. They didn't toll for Isaac. He smoked his dope, watched sports on TV, bought and sold his stocks. A day trader for the last five years, he was at his computer twelve hours a day making split-second money. In and out of one position, then another, you couldn't get sentimental about anything, or have any doubts; you had to forge on, click and click again, buy and sell and be quick about it, at his computer all day while Janet extracted plugs of wax from the enlarged pores of her pampered customers, the insipid spa music playing overhead.

Isaac rarely left the house. Everything he wanted he could order online. He bought his toothbrushes online, his deodorant, all his needs. Even his dope arrived at the front door. The teenage kid down the street came by every couple of weeks. Stood on the porch and gave Isaac a baggie inside a paper sack, and Isaac gave him white business envelope full of bills. Hydroponic sensimilla, one toke and Isaac was gone. Gone for hours. One freaking toke.

Lately he'd been getting out of the house more often. Twice a week. A round-trip jaunt to his lover's condo on South Beach. Took a couple of hours off from work. Trading one perfectly timed transaction for another.

Was he a shit? Was he a shit for cheating on Janet after her unfortunate biological accident? Was that any way to be supportive? Okay, sure. He was a shit. A jackass, a son of a bitch. Guilty as charged. Hey, he was a guy. What could he do? It was part of the job description. Psychoanalyze that, Ray.

Wednesday night Isaac was watching ESPN, Indiana's tall white guys clobbering the beejesus out of a scrappy all-black Kentucky team. Online he'd placed a five-hundred-dollar bet on the Hoosiers, taking the eight-point spread. And his bet looked safe late in the fourth quarter.

That's when Janet and Carla walked into the TV room. Carla wore a white T-shirt, the material as thin as a film of sweat. Isaac was thinking, Why bother with a shirt at all?

Her boobs were bigger than Janet's, perkier too, and her nipples were the shadows of pennies behind the vaporous fabric. She had shoulder-length blond hair and dark bushy eyebrows. The blond was real, and the dark eyebrows were real. Janet had commented on them. Actually, she said she found Carla hot. If she were a lesbian, she'd hit on her. Slim-hipped, a boyish butt, great legs that she liked to show off. Calves that you might expect on a ballerina. A physical specimen. Isaac had suggested a threesome, but Janet thought he was joking and blew him off. He wasn't joking. He'd never had a threesome. One of his many unfulfilled fantasies.

"Have the bells been ringing?" Janet asked him.

"Not so I've noticed," Isaac said. "Anyone want a toke?"

He picked up the baggie off the side table. Held it up.

Carla smiled, but said nothing.

"We're just going to walk around and see if we can hear the bells," Janet said. "Carla's going to tell me if I'm crazy."

"You're not crazy," Carla said. "Nobody thinks you're crazy. You've just been under stress."

Carla knew about the miscarriage. That made four people in the know, counting Ray. Their little extended family.

They started a tour of the house, searching for bells. Isaac waited till they were in the kitchen, the most distant room, then got up from the lounge chair, went into his office, and jiggled the mouse to wake his computer. He clicked to the program he'd written.

His router was set to activate the wireless modules scattered through the house, each tucked a few inches inside air-conditioning grills, and all of them faced inward so the sound would travel back into the walls. Five chiming units, each with a microprocessor, set to play a few seconds of wind chime music or the tinkle of a xylophone. Small deviations between the bell sounds. He'd ordered the units online as he had his toothbrush and deodorant. The shit you could find online, it was amazing.

Just that morning when he'd been resequencing them to keep things fresh, he found a bug in the system. He wasn't sure where or what it was. Since then, all afternoon, the chimes had been going off and turning on without warning. He rebooted his computer but that didn't stop it. Off and on, on and off. He'd fucked up the program somehow, inserted a line of bad code, or deleted some crucial passage, or the fucker had just gone unstable on its own. He spent hours trying to track it down but couldn't. So the whole bell-ringing system was pretty much fucked. He'd have to wait till Janet went to work tomorrow and take down each chiming unit. Figure out what to do next.

For a minute he fiddled with the program, but it didn't respond. He'd lost control of the damn thing, and now that Carla was here, there'd be no bells. Or maybe there would be. It was no longer his call. Some gremlin was calling the shots.

He went back to the TV. While he'd been gone, Kentucky had employed a full-court press and those dogged ball hawkers had stolen three inbound passes from Indiana and scored each time. Less than a minute he'd been gone, and the Wildcats had erased the comfortable lead and were now endangering the spread. Five hundred bucks about to disappear. More gremlins.

From the dining room Janet gasped. Then she let loose a bright metallic scream. The chimes had decided to ring. Just then, just at that moment, right in front of Carla and Janet together. Like black magic. Like chupacabra blood-sucking voodoo.

Then he heard their voices. Carla's was calm, trying to be reasonable with Janet, comforting her, telling her everything was going to be okay. Just relax, find her center, be tranquil, breathe breathe breathe. Then her voice grew quiet, and a second later a howl so low and forlorn came from Janet you might've thought she was a starving dog.

After a long moment Carla marched into the TV room and sat

down on the couch. He could hear Janet sobbing in the bedroom at the far end of the house.

"I assume you told her you didn't hear the bells."

Carla looked at the TV. She smoothed a hand across her forehead as if trying to ease away a headache.

"I told her I didn't hear them."

She looked at Isaac, then stared off toward the other end of the house, where Janet was sobbing. Frost glazed her blue eyes.

"Okay. Well done."

"I don't like this, Isaac. This is mean. This is shitty."

"You're not mean, Carla. Or shitty. You're a wonderful person. I'm the shitty one. Blame it on me. The twisted husband."

"Are you mocking me?"

"Maybe a little."

"Stop it, Isaac. Just stop it."

"Look, we're almost there," he said.

"I don't like it."

"Okay, sure, it's not pretty. But it's necessary. We need to suck it up, keep our focus."

"This is mean. Just flat-out mean."

"Don't go soft on me, sweetness. You knew what it would take."

"Hearing about it is one thing. But this . . . Janet is my friend."

"Lose a friend, gain a lover. You're having second thoughts; it's normal. Don't worry about it. You'd have to be a heartless bitch not to have second thoughts. I wouldn't like you if you were heartless. Completely heartless. A little heartless, that's fine."

They listened to Janet's sobs die to whimpers.

Carla pinched the bridge of her nose. A pretty nose, maybe a little bigger than textbook, but it gave her a certain exotic flavor. The places that nose had been. That prodding beak.

"It's too much, Isaac, screwing with my friend this way, what, just to weasel her out of her rightful split."

"I made that money. Every nickel."

"It's a marriage, Isaac. Things are supposed to be fifty-fifty."

"Well, it's not just the money. Not really. It's the principle, you know. All those hours of work. Poof, gone."

"I don't like it."

"Be cool. We can talk about it tomorrow. I'll come over at noon. We'll sort it out. Now you just breathe, find your center."

"You're mocking me again."

"Okay, I'll cut that out. I'll never do that again."

"Yes, you will."

She was watching Kentucky celebrate. Come-from-behind assholes.

Janet wasn't sobbing anymore. And the bells were going again. Fucking gremlins. Fucking weird-ass voodoo spirits.

Isaac was wearing his pajamas at three in the afternoon. He was in the TV room watching ESPN. He'd jacked up the volume as high as it would go, but the walls were still alive with the sound of bells.

He'd removed all five units. He'd crushed each one of them with a ball-peen hammer. Pulverized them to smithereens. But there were still bells. They'd started ringing the night Janet told him she was leaving, that she was moving in with Carla. That it was over between them and he could have the entire nest egg, she didn't give a shit. She was so happy and relieved to get away from him, to be free of his asshole mockery, his shit-eating grin, that she would have raided her own small savings account to bribe her way out. Or something to that effect. It sounded rehearsed. In fact, it sounded a lot like Carla's kiss-off lecture the night before. Like maybe they'd put their airheads together, compared notes, and come up with this pathetic termination speech.

That was two weeks ago.

The night she left he took the bells down, but they continued to ring. He pried open all the other air-conditioning grills but could find no sign of any more. Maybe Carla or Janet had snuck in when he was sleeping and planted their own chiming units in other places around the house. That would be just like them. The sluts. The devious bitches.

He searched the closets, the pantry, the drawers, the cabinets. He searched the dirty clothes hamper, the dishwasher, the cushions of the couch, the bottoms of chairs and tables and desks. He looked in every lampshade. He was thorough. He was methodical. He wasn't a raving lunatic. He went from one room to the next, tearing open every place that chimes or bells or any other ringing device could be concealed. And he found nothing. Nothing at all.

So he drowned out the bells with TV noise, with music, with the radio. None of it worked. Faintly, behind the blare of CNN or ESPN or CNBC, he could hear the sweet tinkle of a bell. A hand chime, a wind chime, a dinner bell, a sleigh bell. Some fucking bell or another.

Even now as a beer commercial filled the house with its blather, he could hear the bells clinking like silver coins in a pocket. And he could hear a conversation too. Janet and Carla talking. He could hear it inside his head as though he were there in the room, standing beside Carla's queen-size bed.

Both of them breathing hard. Both of them gasping and giggling and sighing deep.

I didn't know it would be like this.

I always had a feeling about you. I would look at your incredible body, and I had a feeling. You did something to me. I knew this was going to happen. Not like this exactly, but something like this. I knew it.

Are we lesbians now?

I think what we are, Janet, we're broadening our horizons.

I can't get enough of you. I really can't.

There's plenty of me left.

Now?

Whenever you're ready.

Really, you're still horny?

Not horny, no. Hungry, yearning. But for you. Horny's too general. I want what you've got. I want to give you what I have.

Jesus, you're insatiable.

You know what they say, Janet. The best laid women often go astray.

I never thought he was a particularly good lay. Did you?

The shithead was worthless. Nothing like this.

I should be mad at you. Fucking my husband.

Except you're not.

You did me a favor, Carla. You did me a huge favor. Got me out of that hellhole.

Of course, this was happening in Isaac's head. The two of them mocking him, having fun at his expense. It sounded real to him. It felt real. After all, wasn't all conversation just something in your head?

The bells were ringing louder. And there was something different. A different bell. An old familiar bell he couldn't place.

Isaac turned off the TV and got up from his lounge chair and padded into the living room in search of this new blood-sucking voodoo bell.

Halfway into the room he saw through the front window a UPS truck parked at the curb.

The doorbell rang again.

Ah, yes. The doorbell. He'd forgotten its sweet *ding-dong*, a comforting sound, so unique, so different from all the other bells.

The UPS guy was wearing his brown short-sleeve sweat-stained shirt and shorts. The day was hot outside. The man was bald and he was in a hurry like he always was.

"I didn't think you were home."

"I'm home, yes."

They were old friends, he and the UPS man. All the online shit he got delivered over the years. You name it, this man in brown brought it to the door. He never said anything to Isaac about all the parcels. He never even suggested anything obliquely. Very professional deliveryman.

He handed Isaac the two packages and Isaac put them down on the floor just inside the front door. They were heavy. He wanted to tear open the boxes right away and get to work, but he'd had an idea and turned back to the UPS man.

"Could you do me a favor?" Isaac signed his name on the electronic pad.

"Okay."

"Could you step inside? It'll just take a second."

"Inside?"

"I'm not going to hit on you or anything."

"I didn't think that."

"I just want to get your opinion on something."

"My opinion."

Isaac held the door wide open.

"One second, that's all."

The UPS man stepped into the house. For years he'd been stopping at Isaac's house several times a week, but this was the first time he'd ever been across the threshold. When he was inside, Isaac waved at the ceiling, at the walls, at the air filling the room.

"Do you hear anything?"

The UPS man stared at Isaac and tilted his head like a dog decoding a new command.

"Like what?"

The bells were ringing throughout the house. Twenty bells, thirty. A symphony of bells. A tabernacle choir of bells. A horde and great multitude of bells. Church bells, the bells on a tricycle's handlebars, the ice cream man's bell, glass wind chimes, the Salvation Army's Christmas bells, the gong and jangle, plink, chinkle, dong, and peal of bells. The house was ringing, the walls were throbbing with bells.

"I hear your refrigerator going on," the UPS man said. "Is that what you mean?"

Isaac forced himself to go slow. He forced himself to stay disciplined. Using the hand sledge and chisel he'd ordered from an online hardware store, following the blue-lined quadrants he'd laid out against the white plaster, he was working his way around the living room, cracking open the walls, breaking through the drywall, tearing out the insulation, section by section, scooping out the dust and debris with the garden trowel.

Moving down the front wall until he'd peeled it open, then working down the west wall in the same methodical fashion.

No bells yet. No hidden chiming units. But he knew they were there. Ones he had planted himself and forgotten, or ones that Carla and Janet had secreted into some cavity within the wall to sabotage his peace of mind, to destroy his bulwark against the chaos beyond his castle walls. He knew this with the same certainty that he knew what was happening at Carla's South Beach condo.

All of it rang in his ears, their voices, their heaving sighs, their quick, tightly spiraling cries, their orgasmic bellows and yawps and sobs. The creak of her bedsprings, the thud of the headboard against that lavender wall, the shimmy and teeter of Carla's dwarf collection, those little ceramic men and women who stood guard on her bookcase shelf, watching it all, watching Isaac's two women have at it. His lover and his wife joined in unholy union.

And Ray was there. Fucking psycho-babbler, Ray was getting undressed. Shimmying out of his professional clothes, his stylish slacks and shirt falling to the floor, his Calvin Klein fancy-ass un-derwear. Until there he was, Ray, the unshrinking shrink standing naked and at attention beside the bed watching the two of them satisfy each other the way only a woman can satisfy another woman. And Ray waited until he was asked. Which Janet finally did.

What are you waiting for, Ray? An engraved invitation?

Everyone chuckled. Carla snuggled into the embrace of her damp lover, Isaac's soon-to-be ex-wife, and the two of them opened their free arms to Ray.

Permission to come aboard? Ray said.

Granted, Janet said.

Double granted, said Carla. Come anywhere you like.

Where do I start? I've never done anything like this before.

Neither have we, Carla said. Ain't it great?

It's like being reborn, starting fresh, the slate is clean, and this is a whole new me, Janet said.

Follow that thought, Ray said. Follow that thought.

I'd like to get pregnant again, Janet said. There, I've said it.

Whoa, said Carla. Where'd that come from? Pregnant?

I'd like to, Ray. Is that bad? Is that wrong?

No, it's not wrong, Ray said. Nothing you do is wrong. You're perfect just as you are. Don't doubt yourself. And I think you're very brave, very open.

Oh, man, said Carla. Oh, man. Do I get to be the daddy?

Oh, yes, goddamn Ray was there, taking Isaac's seat at the table, satiating himself with those two she-demons. Spreading his psycho-babbling seed. The man was going to father Isaac's son. All this while Isaac worked his way around the house, inch by scrupulous inch, painstakingly, utterly focused on the plaster before him, digging beneath the hard crust to root out those bells, exorcise those jingly, gonging, twinkling, hellish voodoo chimes.

> *Keeping time, time, time,*
> *In a sort of Runic rhyme,*
> *To the throbbing of the bells,*
> *Of the bells, bells, bells—*
> *To the sobbing of the bells;*
> *Keeping time, time, time*
> *As he knells, knells, knells,*
> *In a happy Runic rhyme*
> *To the rolling of the bells,*
> *Of the bells, bells, bells—*
> *To the tolling of the bells*
> *Of the bells, bells, bells, bells,*
> *Bells, bells, bells—*
> *To the moaning and the groaning of the bells.*

JAMES W. HALL is the author of fifteen novels set in South Florida. He's a winner of the Shamus and the Edgar Awards and has taught writing and literature for thirty-five years. He and his wife divide their time between Florida and the mountains of North Carolina.

In My Ancestor's Image
A Rory Calhoun Short Story

Jeremiah Healy

"Rory," said Don Floyd, "this lady tried to call your condo from our guard shack, but didn't get any answer."

Not surprising, since I'd just spent an hour alternating laps with Harry Lewis in the swimming pool at the Lauderdale Tennis Club, where I live, and—more or less—work. Toweling off, I thanked Don for bringing her around to me, and turned to introduce myself.

"Rory Calhoun, Ms. . . . ?"

"I'm Edwina Ellen Poe. When I saw you were named, like me, after somebody else—though a B-movie actor rather than a legendary author—I thought you'd be the right private investigator for my problem. Now"—she looked me up and down—"I'm not so sure."

Swallowing a comeback, I gestured toward the new, wrought-iron furniture on the tennis patio above Court One. "Well, since you're already here, why don't we talk for five minutes, and then you can decide?"

As we sat down and Poe laid her mesh shoulder bag on the tabletop, I did my best to gauge her. Fiftyish and slim, with the premature white hair that I've always assumed comes from an unfortunate gene pool or a lot of stress. Poe wore hers long and straight, though, like photos of the hippies from the sixties and seventies. She had pale blue eyes, like a malamute's, which, with the mane, made her seem a little ghostly.

"Mr. Calhoun—"

"Considering my dress code and our surroundings, how about just Rory?"

A thin smile. "And I prefer Ellen. I don't think either of us has to trade stories of growing up with odd names."

I nodded. My mother had a "screen crush" on the actor, and when she met a man named Calhoun, she married him. I was doomed from the womb.

Poe said, "Rory, can you tell me something about your, uh, background?"

"Sure." I gave her a quick summary of my college and professional tennis career, a wobbly knee knocking me off the tour at age twenty-nine, even for doubles. I apprenticed with an established private investigator long enough to get my own license, doing cases here and there and playing "club" tennis to keep my hand in the sport.

Poe pursed her thin lips. "You won trophies?"

I tried for humble. "A few."

"And you . . . treasure them, correct?"

I did, and said so.

"Well, Rory, I write crime fiction. So far, ten novels and dozens of short stories."

I remembered now seeing ads in the *Sun-Sentinel* and thinking the author must just be ripping off a famous name. "Quite the résumé."

"Yes. Yes, it is, actually. However, I've won only one 'trophy' despite the depth and breadth of my work."

Apparently Poe wasn't trying for humble, but maybe that kind of ego is what drives a writer.

She reached into her handbag and took out two photos. One was of a slightly younger version of herself, dressed in evening wear and holding a little figure about ten inches high and five inches across, with a cartoonish face on it. She was genuinely beaming, a man next to her wearing a tux and smiling, too. The second photo was a close-up of the weird little statue, the man's face now more caricature than cartoon, with wavy black hair and a high forehead narrowing down to a small black mustache over an even smaller mouth. He looked like he could be Latino, or maybe French. And below his chin was a plaque, with some writing on it that I couldn't make out.

I said, "Your trophy."

"Award. It's the Edgar—named, naturally, after my ancestor. I'm the first certified descendant of Edgar Allan Poe ever to win one. In my case, for Best Short Story of the year, as recognized by the Mystery Writers of America."

"And . . . ?"

"Some rat-bastard has stolen it from me, and I want it back."

I glanced between the photos, then at her hands. "From the scale of the bust, about ten inches high?"

"Or a little more. Weighs two or three pounds."

"What's it made of?"

A dismissive wave. "I don't know. Porcelain, papier-mâché, it doesn't matter. I want it back."

So, not much intrinsic value. "Have you contacted this mystery writers' organization? Maybe they could replace the statue for short money, save you the—"

"They told me they'd replace it for free, but that's not the point." Poe made a fist, pounding it lightly but determinedly on the wrought iron. "I don't want a replacement. It's the one god-damned award I've ever won, and I want the goddamned thing itself returned to me."

No intrinsic value, but a boatload of emotional investment. "Well, the place to start would be wherever you kept it."

"My home office. We can go there as soon as you . . . change clothes."

We talked about my fee, and she dipped into her bag for a checkbook.

As Poe was signing and tearing off my retainer, I said, "You have any suspects?"

Now the thin smile again. "Three." She put the checkbook back into her bag and brought out a sheet with names and contact information on it. "The first is another professional writer; he's always been jealous of me, especially about winning the Edgar. The second is a woman who's taken God knows how many writing classes from me and others; she's persistent about getting published, but hopeless. The third is my rat-bastard ex-husband, who would have taken the Edgar just to irk me."

I was beginning to identify with her ex. "Twenty minutes?"

Edwina Ellen Poe glanced at her watch. "Sooner if you can. I've already burned a morning on this."

"Well, at least I know you can follow people."

Poe had given me her address, and happily Fort Lauderdale is laid out in a numbered grid pattern. Once you learn the quadrants (northwest, southeast, etc.) around a central, major intersection, you can find almost any building just by its avenue or street address. But I did make sure to trail behind her Toyota Camry in my Chrysler Sebring convertible, a gift to myself after a successful tournament.

We were standing in a semicircular driveway before a rambling ranch-style house, thick trees and shrubs a bit overgrown around it.

As we walked toward her front door, Poe read my mind. "I like my privacy."

"Me, too. But it makes it a lot easier for a bad guy to try an unlocked window."

She gave me the thin smile and slipped her hand into the shoulder bag again, this time producing a short-barreled revolver. "After my divorce, this was my first purchase. I took the course, and I'm licensed to carry it."

Tread lightly, Rory. "I see."

Poe keyed the front door, then called out, "Maria, are you still here?"

"*Sí, Señora Poe,*" from a few rooms away. "I am now in the kitchen."

We moved through the foyer and living room, both floors covered in sixteen-inch square tiles. When we reached the kitchen threshold, Maria was standing by the sink, Lysol and paper towel in hand.

Poe said, "This is Maria Vasco. She's the one who first noticed the Edgar was missing."

I looked at Vasco. Around my client's age, stolid more than pudgy, with brown hair and eyes, currently downcast, probably because she'd been introduced to a strange male.

"My name is Rory Calhoun, Ms. Vasco."

She glanced up at me, then again at her feet. "How can I help?"

Poe nodded for me to continue. "I'm trying to recover the writing award that was taken. Can you show me where it used to be?"

Vasco looked at Poe, then back in my direction. "Please to follow?"

The ranch had a labyrinthlike layout, confirming my initial impression that it might have gone through a couple of additions. When we got to a bedroom/den with floor-to-ceiling bookshelves, I saw the available wall space occupied by framed, enlarged book covers with Poe's name above the titles.

"Impressive," I said.

Poe might have chuckled. "As it's intended to be. This is where I'm interviewed for print or broadcast media."

The concept of "humility" just didn't seem to be part of her character. "Where was the statue?"

"*Aquí,*" said Vasco, pointing to a shelf over the computer desk, the middle of the wood plank noticeably empty compared to the rest of the home office.

Poe said, "And when did you first notice it missing?"

Vasco looked at her feet again. "The last time I come to clean for you, when you are away on the book tour. So . . . two weeks in the past?"

I addressed Poe. "You waited two weeks before contacting me or anybody else?"

She shrugged. "I'd hoped it was a prank. Or, at worst, a juvenile attempt by my ex to irk me, as I told you before." Some steel crept into Poe's voice. "Now, I fear it's permanent."

"Ellen, you gave me a list of suspects. Did they all have access to the house?"

"As I showed you at the front door, Rory, I value my privacy, but I carry my own security. The doors and windows are occasionally open and almost always unlocked."

Great. "Ms. Vasco, did you see anyone in or near the house around the time the statue was taken?"

More examination of her feet. "No, but I would not have been here for two weeks before I see the statue is not there."

Poe nodded, confirming the scheduling.

"Ms. Vasco, thank you for your time." I gave her a business card. "Please call me if you remember anything else."

"*Sí, Señor. Inmediatamente.*"

"Well," I said to Edwina Ellen Poe in her semicircular drive, "I think we can rule out Ms. Vasco."

"It never crossed my mind to rule her in. Maria is a Castro Cuban, Rory. She and her family had to run for the boat with just the clothes on their backs. Her father died getting Maria and her brother off the island."

Sadly, as I knew from my time in South Florida, not a unique experience. "Okay, then. I'm going to interview your list of suspects, then get back to you, probably via cell phone from my car, so you're not paying twice for my time."

The sly smile. "I can blow out my candle."

I didn't get it. "Sorry?"

Poe seemed disappointed. "The Greek legend: Demosthenes carried a lit candle with him until he met an honest man."

Somehow I thought he was the guy who spoke with pebbles in his mouth, but then, like a lot of jocks, I kind of skipped the classics. "Thanks for the implied compliment."

"Pity you didn't appreciate it without explanation."

Edwina Ellen Poe turned on her heel and walked to the Camry. I decided then to save her ex-husband for last and treat him to a commiserating drink.

"So, the scarecrow's award has gone missing, eh?"

I sat down on a pool chair near Jason Buford, hair dyed a ridiculous shade of copper and combed over his forehead. The Speedo trunks on the beefy body were just an assumption. "I think she prefers 'Ellen.' "

"Hah," Buford shifted in his chaise lounge to be able to look at me more directly. "Who wouldn't?"

The ripped young man who'd met me at the door arrived with two iced teas. He gave Buford a bedroom-eyes glance as he left the tray on the little resin table between us.

"Thank you, Paolo."

Just a nod.

Buford waited until Paolo was out of earshot before saying, "From Brazil. Lovely, isn't he?"

There were gay players on the tour with me, so I hoped my attitude was as tolerant as their orientation seemed to make them. "I'm glad you're happy together."

"Yes, well, one does have to compensate, eh?"

An opening you could drive a truck through. "For . . . ?"

"Mr. Calhoun, Edwina told you I was a fellow crime writer, correct?"

To be polite, I sipped some iced tea. "Yes."

"Well, I write about a homosexual private investigator. My reviews are superlative, my recognition within the sorority/fraternity of my peers somewhat less so."

"Ms. Poe said you'd never won an Edgar Award."

"Correct," a slurp of the iced tea through the straw in his glass. "Industry prejudice, and—honestly—probably a misguided homage to her ancestry."

"Nevertheless, somebody's hooked the thing."

Another slurp. "And Edwina suggested you speak with me about it."

"Yes."

A rumble from his chest that could have been a laugh. "Mr. Calhoun, I've been nominated six times in eight years for that Short-Story Edgar. I do not resent her receiving one. I *do* resent my being passed over, time and time again."

"Enough to snatch the statue from her?"

"Hah," followed by a more contemplative sip from his iced

tea. "Poe-etic justice, don't you think? I just wish I'd thought of it before you came to visit."

Sensing a definite strike-out with Jason Buford, I moved on to the second suspect on Edwina Ellen Poe's list, Suzanne Murray. I tried her home first, but no answer. Then I tried her cell phone.

"Murray, here."

An accent. Irish, Scottish? "Ms. Mur—"

"Oh, please. Just Suzanne, okay?"

Okay. "My name's Rory Calhoun. I'm a private investigator, and I'd like to speak with you about a case I'm working."

"Ach, now I'm intrigued. But I'm also . . . 'working.' Can you swing by the Fort Lauderdale Executive Airport in half an hour?"

Scottish, I was pretty sure. "Yes, thank you."

"In fact, if you can hit the half-past precisely, I'll do my best to drop in on you."

Not quite knowing how to respond, I simply said, "See you then."

I have to say, it was pretty impressive.

There were four legs dangling from the parachute, which looked like a giant, pink caterpillar suspended illogically in the air. The tandem of diver and master kissed the ground for a near perfect landing.

I walked over as the female mentor was congratulating the sixty-something guy in the front harness and he was babbling his thanks to her. She was in her late twenties, with short blond hair and gray-green eyes.

Once the guy moved off, I addressed the woman. "Suzanne Murray?"

"Yes?"

"Rory Calhoun."

"Ach, the private eye. Let me just get clear here."

She did so efficiently, but gently, even elegantly, and I commented on it.

Murray looked up. "I might not be the next instructor to dive tandem with a rook." She took in the parachute and its spider-strands. "Mr. Rory, I've lost five friends in two years to accidental death on a tandem, and all the equipment gets shared between instructors. Tends to make you a wee bit more careful."

I couldn't see how to top that. "Actually, I'm here about a writing issue."

"A writing . . . ?"

I took out my holder with the laminated copy of my investigator's license. She looked at it long enough to read and process it, then raised her eyes to me. "So, what 'writing issue' could you be wanting to raise with a 'prepublished' Suzanne Murray?"

I told her.

"Edwina, Edwina. A right bitch who's just had better luck than most of us."

"My client told me that she taught you. Trying to help you get your works into print."

"Have you ever attended a writers' conference, Mr. Rory?"

"Can't say that I have."

"Well, it's basically a secular pulpit kind of thing, with these writers who have been published gloating over those of us still knocking on the church door. And the great pooh-bahs imply that if the more attractive students are willing to participate in a little extracurricular 'tutoring,' there might be a referral—even a recommendation—to the teacher's literary agent."

It didn't take a genius to see what she was suggesting. "Ms. Poe hit on you?"

"Like she had war clubs in both hands. However, I tend to prefer younger, athletic males."

As I was processing that, Murray said, "Rather like you, in fact. Ever gone diving . . . tandem?"

"Tandem, yes. Parachuting, no."

"Pity. You might have two incredible experiences . . . simultaneously."

I told Suzanne Murray that I would definitely be back in . . . touch with her.

The problem for most guys, I think, is that when you believe you'd like to empathize with somebody, he or she turns out to be a cockroach.

Current example: Larry Sutcliff, Edwina Ellen Poe's ex-husband.

He lived in a one-bedroom apartment not a mile from the Lauderdale Tennis Club. Pretty soon he'd have to move to a bigger place, or begin throwing out a ton of books.

I found him on his lanai, the sun setting in front of him. He was reading—and highlighting with a yellow Magic Marker—a very thick book. I guessed him to be pushing seventy, but in good, loose-limbed shape, wearing a one-piece, black-vinyl track suit.

"Why should I talk with you?" said Sutcliff, keeping his place in the book with an index finger.

"I've been hired by your former wife to look into the theft of her writing award."

Sutcliff seemed stunned. "Ellen won an award for that schlock she writes?"

Not "Edwina," but "Ellen," her preferred name. "One of the most prestigious in her field."

A horse laugh. "Now that, young man, is a truly left-handed compliment."

"Meaning . . . ?"

"Meaning I could never be bothered to read her pulp." Sutcliff raised the hefty volume from his lap. "I study Hegel, Proust, Kant. Giants." He lowered the book again. "What Ellen produces is the equivalent of network television, only it takes longer."

"So, you don't know anything about her missing award."

"Like I said, I can't believe anybody would actually give her one." Then Sutcliff drew in and let out a deep breath. "You wouldn't know it to look at her now, but Ellen was a genuine hottie in her twenties. Which is when she hooked and landed me, a sugar daddy who was happy to support her in exchange for intergenerational sex. But after maybe book number five, Ellen started thinking she was a literary star, and the bedroom time suffered from her computer time. Then came the Internet, and I knew it was time to cut the cord."

"You divorced her?"

"Yes, but I had a prenup, so it was like canceling a contract that went bad. She didn't get much, though I guess it was enough of a grubstake to let her keep writing." Larry Sutcliff looked up at me. "But some organization giving her an award? If I were dead already, I'd be spinning in my grave."

Driving back to the Lauderdale Tennis Club, the sunset was a chamber of commerce dream come true. Pink, charcoal, then gray as the failing light, helped by car pollution, turned the sky into a pastel palette.

Only I was no further along in finding Edwina Ellen Poe's missing award than when I'd first spoken with her after my swim.

As I drew even with our guard shack, Harold—a friendly man from South Asia—greeted me. "By how you are dressed, Rory, I think you have been working today rather than playing."

I glanced down. Polo shirt, long pants, loafers, even black socks. "Tough case, Harold."

A frown of genuine concern. "And how so?"

I tried to summarize it for him. "A statue is missing, and the owner suggested three possible suspects. But, after interviewing all of them, I can't see a clear winner."

"Well, then," Harold rubbed his chin with the palm of his left hand, "perhaps you have not talked with all the suspects?"

Another car was pulling up behind me, so I just said, "Thanks for the suggestion."

Taking a stretching, yogalike half hour in the hot tub next to the club's pool, I thought about what both Edwina Ellen Poe and Harold had said to me. Then I thought about my first impression of the award from the photographs she'd shown me of it.

And then Harold's advice hit home.

On the phone with Poe, I made up what I hoped was a convincing cover story about why I needed an address not on her list of suspects. After clicking off, I drove to it.

A small bungalow, meticulously landscaped and maintained, in Aventura, just south of the Broward County line. Nobody in sight, except for a neighbor four doors down watering his lawn.

I left the Sebring at the curb and walked up to the front entrance. I don't really believe in ESP, but when Maria Vasco undid the locks and swung open the door, she already seemed to know what I was thinking.

"Mr. . . . Calhoun?"

"Yes."

Her trademark look down to her shoes. "You have discovered my . . . secret?"

"The 'what,' but not the 'why.'"

A resigned nod. "Come into my house, please."

It was as pristine as Vasco maintained Poe's home. We sat on opposing but matching chairs. "You took the Edgar statue."

Eyes to shoes again. *"Sí."*

"But why?"

A wave of the hand, but, unlike Poe's dismissive one, Vasco's seemed to embrace all she could see. "My family flees Cuba after Castro."

"Ms. Poe told me."

"We could take nothing with us."

This time I just nodded.

Vasco's eyes filled with tears. "My father, he was killed by the Communists. And I had nothing to remember him. Not even a photograph."

I watched her.

"Then, when I begin to work for Ms. Poe, I see the award on the shelf in her office. It is my father, Mr. Calhoun. Even to the expression on his face."

I thought back to seeing the caricature as Latino, maybe French.

Vasco said, "But Ms. Poe, she does not treat it with . . . the proper respect, you know? More like it is a trophy than a . . . *tesoro?*"

Treasure. "And so you . . . ?"

"Every other week, I come to her house to clean it. And there is always dust on the statue, like Ms. Poe does not care about it except as an award for her work. To me, it is an . . . icon of my father, the only thing I have of him."

"Ms. Vasco, where is the statue now?"

Another downcast look. "In my bedroom."

I tried to think it through. Then I believed I saw a way out.

"Ms. Vasco, you care about the statue because it reminds you of your father, not because Ms. Poe received it as an award, right?"

The eyes came back up to mine. *"Sí?"*

"And you know that Ms. Poe cares about this particular statue because it is the only award she has ever won?"

A nod before, *"Sí, sí."*

I came to a decision, though without much hope that I could execute it. "Relax for now, and don't say anything to Ms. Poe. I'll be in touch with you."

• • •

My telephone call to New York City was answered by a cheerful, "Mystery Writers of America."

"My name's Rory Calhoun, from Florida."

"The pro tennis player?"

I was flattered. "Former."

"Ohmigod, I saw you play in the U.S. Open. Three times. You were so good."

Unfair to trade on a fan relationship? Hopefully not. "And you are?"

"Margery. That's M-A-R-G-E-R-Y. I can't believe I'm actually talking with you."

"I'm a private investigator now, and I have a problem you might be able to solve."

"Shoot."

I told her the whole story.

Margery hummed on the other end of the line. "I can't make that decision myself, but I could ask our executive vice president if he'd okay it."

Much more than I could have hoped for. "That would be terrific."

"Give me your number down there."

They say that plumbers merit the big bucks because they know exactly where to hit the pipe with their wrenches. If so, I was very lucky to speak with Margery.

Six days later, a bust of Edgar Allan Poe was in my mailbox at the tennis club. No plaque, but the caricature was identical to the photos Edwina Allan Poe had shown me.

The next day, I made the exchange with Maria Vasco, and I discovered a small plaque also on the back of the original. And that afternoon, Ms. Poe had back her trophy. My client wanted to hear all the details, but I told her I'd made a confidential commitment that was necessary to the return of the award. I'm not sure she believed me, but Poe did say, "Keep the balance of that retainer. You earned it."

Wish I had more clients—humble or not—with that sense of gratitude.

JEREMIAH HEALY, a former sheriff's officer and military police lieutenant, is a graduate of Rutgers University and Harvard Law School. Healy is also the creator of the John Francis Cuddy private-investigator series and (under the pseudonym Terry Devane) the Mairead O'Clare legal-thriller series, both set primarily in Boston. Healy has written eighteen novels and more than sixty short stories, sixteen of which works have won or been nominated for the Shamus Award. He served as the president of the International Association of Crime Writers (IACW) from 2000–2004 and was the international guest of honor at the 34th World Mystery Convention in Toronto during October 2004. Currently, Healy is a member of the Mystery Writers of America's national board of directors.

The Poe Collector

Edward D. Hoch

I first met the Poe collector at one of those impressive auction houses in midtown Manhattan. He was a short dark-haired fellow with a mustache and a slight limp. I would have guessed his age to be around forty. Like him, I'd been attracted by a promise of rare and collectable editions of nineteenth-century American writers. I rarely purchased anything at these events, but being in the used-book business I liked to know what was going on.

It was Monday, the day before the auction itself, and I was at the auction house perusing a plastic-wrapped copy of the Philadelphia *Saturday Courier* for January 14, 1832. "That's a real rarity," the short man told me. "It's Edgar Allan Poe's first short story, 'Metzengerstein,' in its original publication."

"I know. Are you a collector?" I asked.

"Only of Poe." He held out his hand. "Evan Petrick. I live upstate, outside Albany." I told him my name and admitted I had a small bookstore in the Village. "How do you keep going these days with those big chains and the Internet?" he wondered.

"It's mostly mail order," I told him. "I have quite a few regular customers and I know what they like."

"Are you bidding on anything tomorrow?"

I shook my head. "The going price for these items would be a bit rich for my blood. How about you?"

"I might try for this Poe item." We strolled around a bit longer, until Petrick decided he'd seen enough. "Maybe I'll see you here tomorrow," he said as we parted.

That night I met up with Cheryl Blanding after I closed the bookshop. She came back to the apartment with me. "Did you find anything interesting at the auction house?" she wondered.

"Nothing I could afford. I met a chap who's a Poe collector, though. He sounded as if he might bid on the initial publication of Poe's first short story."

"What would that be worth?" she asked, reaching into my liquor cabinet for her favorite bottle of Chivas Regal.

"Hard to say. I'd never seen the real thing before, although a facsimile was published back in the 1930s. They're starting the bidding at ten thousand and it could go a lot higher. Philadelphia's *Saturday Courier* was a weekly newspaper that held a short story contest with a hundred-dollar prize. That was big money in those days and Poe, already a published poet, submitted five tales. He didn't win the prize, but the editor liked what he saw and published the tales anonymously, starting with 'Metzengerstein.' These were youthful efforts, and all were revised by Poe prior to their book publication."

"You know a lot about old books," she said, pouring a drink for me too.

"It's my business."

"Are you going to the auction tomorrow?"

I thought it over while I sipped my drink. "I might, just to see how the bidding goes. Len could take care of the shop."

Cheryl was in her late twenties, a decade younger than me, with sparkling brown hair and eyes to match. We'd hit it off at once after meeting at a wine-and-cheese party at my shop back in the spring. She'd worked as an intern for a literary agent on the Upper West Side during a semester at college. Her memory held a vast knowledge of nineteenth-century literary trivia, even though she'd ended up in a different profession. That first night she'd looked me in the eye and said, "You know, in those days authors often rolled up their manuscripts and sent them to magazines in mailing tubes rather than envelopes. That's how Arthur Conan Doyle usually submitted his stories."

I decided this was someone I should get to know better. So now she came to my apartment a couple of times a week after work and often stayed over. She liked my Scotch and I liked her. It was a perfect match. Along the way I discovered her reading interests extended to modern mystery writers as well as Poe and Doyle. Often she'd bring a collection of short stories along, claiming she needed something to read if things got dull. I made sure that didn't happen too often.

By Tuesday morning I'd decided to attend the auction. While Cheryl made breakfast and got dressed for work, I phoned Len to tell him I wouldn't be in till late afternoon. "Want to come with me?" I asked Cheryl.

"Got to work. The city can't do without me. Let me know if you buy anything."

The auction house was crowded by the time I got there. I accepted a numbered bidding paddle from the attendant at the door, even though I wasn't planning to bid. There was no one in the crowd that I knew, and I took a seat near the back of the room. The auction started promptly at ten, with an announcement that lot fifteen had been withdrawn. Flipping through my catalog, I found:

15. Poe (Edgar Allan, contributor) Saturday Courier, a weekly newspaper containing Poe's first published story, "Metzengerstein," a few tears on edges. Philadelphia, 14 January 1832.

Almost at once I noticed Evan Petrick, the collector I'd met the previous day. He'd left his seat on the other side of the hall and hurried up the aisle to the podium. The auction halted for a moment before it had actually begun, as Petrick waved his arms and attempted to get some sort of explanation from the auctioneer. Finally he gave up and headed for the exit. I decided to follow him out.

"What was that all about?" I asked, catching up with him in the corridor.

"What?" he asked sharply, then seemed to remember me from the previous day. "Oh, it's you. I came to bid on that Poe item and they told me it had been withdrawn. They wouldn't say why."

"I didn't know they could do that."

"It's rare but it happens occasionally."

I tried to sympathize with his frustration. "Did they tell you who the seller was?"

"It says in the catalog that it's from the collection of Quentin Oakes. I met him once. An old guy, with gray hair and a beard. Apparently he decided to sell some things before he died. But I don't understand why it was withdrawn. I have a nice collection of Poe material and I really wanted this item."

"Your collection sounds interesting."

He turned to give me a measured look. "It is. You can see for yourself if you'd like. My apartment is only a ten-minute taxi ride from here."

I shrugged. "Why not?"

His place was on West Ninety-second Street, just off Broadway, in an older building that I figured might still be rent controlled. There was an elevator but no doorman, and we ascended to the fourth floor without encountering any other residents. The apartment itself was a bit dingy, in need of painting and general sprucing up. Against one wall was a locked cabinet toward which he gestured with pride.

"Before I show you my treasures, can I get you a beer or something?"

"Beer would be fine." I thought about relaying my day's adventure to Cheryl later, who'd no doubt tell me Evan Petrick was probably gay.

Petrick handed me a can of beer and a glass, and then turned his attention back to the cabinet. He unlocked it and brought forth his treasures. "True first editions of Poe are rare, but there've been numerous illustrated editions in the nineteenth and twentieth centuries, some of them quite valuable. Rare limited editions illustrated by Sangorski or Rackham can bring as much as fifty or a hundred thousand dollars. I have nothing like that, of course, but this 1919 British edition with illustrations by Harry Clarke is something of rare beauty."

I glanced through it and was indeed taken by the bizarre illustrations that perfectly conveyed the tenor of Poe's tales. "Very impressive."

"It's a limited edition signed by Clarke. Cost me nearly seven thousand dollars and that was a few years ago. Here's an even older set, the 1902 Putnam edition of the complete works. This goes for more than twice as much as the Clarke."

There were three shelves full of books of all sizes, most of them recent compilations of Poe's work. Some were leather-bound, others were illustrated, and on the bottom shelf were a few plastic-wrapped magazines and even a handwritten letter from Poe to his editor, dated February 18, 1845, and signed with his characteristic flourish. "I'll bet that cost you a pretty penny."

He merely smiled. "I won't even tell you how much. You can see why I really wanted that copy of the *Saturday Courier*."

I hadn't noticed them before but on top of the cabinet were a number of Poe figurines, one with a raven perched on his shoulder and another with an enlarged bobble head like a ballplayer. "I wonder what Poe would think of that," I commented.

"Probably not much."

"It's a very impressive collection," I remarked as he closed and locked the cabinet. "I hope you're well protected against thieves."

"Oh, it's insured. And this building is pretty safe. Sometimes my work takes me away for weeks at a time."

I finished my beer and decided to move on. "Thanks for showing me your collection. What's next for you?"

"I haven't given up on Poe's first story. I may try contacting old Oakes directly."

I phoned Cheryl that evening to tell her what had happened. "You went to his apartment?" she repeated. "You should have asked me to come along as a bodyguard."

"Sure. You can come over now if you'd like to guard my body."

"I'd better get some sleep for a change. See you tomorrow."

My shop didn't open till eleven, so I stopped by the auction house Wednesday to speak with Matt Caine, one of the auctioneers. He was a jovial fellow about my age, always ready to kid about my status as a perennial bachelor. "Good to see you, fella. You married yet?" A picture of his own wife and kids was prominently displayed on his desk.

"I'm working on it, Matt." I sat down opposite his desk.

"What can I do for you? Got a signed first edition of *To Kill a Mockingbird* or *A Farewell to Arms* that you want auctioned off?"

"Wish I did. No, I was just wondering about yesterday's auction. The Poe first edition that got pulled . . ."

Matt Caine nodded. "Odd old guy named Oakes, came in with

it about a month ago when he heard about our nineteenth-century literary auction."

"Ever dealt with him before?"

"I haven't, but one of our staff, Sam Fargo, knew him and vouched for him. Fargo told me the item certainly seemed of value."

"What happened?"

"Bit of a tragedy. Sam fell onto the subway tracks last week and was killed. When Oakes heard about it he came back two days ago and pulled the item. I told him the catalog was all printed, but he still wanted it pulled. I told him we'd have to charge a fee equal to our average commission on the sale, but it didn't matter to him. He took the *Saturday Courier* with him."

"Unusual."

"But not unheard of. It might not have had anything to do with Sam's death at all. Sometimes a seller decides he or she simply can't part with an item. And sometimes they discover they can sell it on their own without the auction house. That's why we have to charge a fee."

"Do you have Oakes's address?"

"Right here. Are you planning to make him an offer?"

"Hardly." I put the address in my jacket pocket and departed after a bit more small talk.

I don't know what I intended to do with that address, and when I took off the jacket that evening my thoughts were more on Cheryl's imminent arrival than on Quentin Oakes. But the following day when I went out for the lunch I rarely ate, I took the subway up to the address he'd given me. It was another of those aging West Side buildings off Broadway, but there was no Quentin Oakes on the mailboxes. I wondered why he'd given a false address to the auction house.

The following morning, Friday, Evan Petrick came by my bookshop.

"Hello, Evan," I greeted him. "Come to look over my collection?"

He glanced around at the shelves and smiled. "It's a bit larger than my little cabinet."

I swiped a customer's credit card through the machine and slipped his purchase into a bag. Then I turned my attention back to Petrick. "What's up?"

He glanced around, noting that my assistant, Len, was helping the only other customer. "Is there someplace we can talk?"

"Come into my office." I led the way, removing a stack of books from the visitor's chair.

He sat down and nervously started to talk. "Look, I hate to ask you this, but something's come up. I talked to Quentin Oakes about his copy of Poe's first story in the *Saturday Courier*. He says he withdrew it because the auction house had placed only a ten-thousand-dollar minimum on the bids. He wanted at least twenty thousand for it. I told him I'd pay that much for it and he agreed to sell it to me, but it had to be within forty-eight hours. He's flying to his home in Aruba on Sunday."

"Good, I'm pleased for you."

"The problem is that I have only ten thousand in cash available. I couldn't get more until next week and that's too late for him. He'd rather take the Poe to Aruba and try to sell it there, or on the Internet."

"Well, I—"

"Look, we hardly know each other. I'm not asking you for the money—"

"That's good," I said with a smile.

"But if you could loan it to me until next week, I'd put up my Poe letter as collateral."

I held up my hand. "Wait a minute. Just what are you proposing?"

"That I give you the Poe letter as collateral for a loan of ten thousand dollars, which I will repay next week. The letter is worth far more than that."

"I don't have that much money sitting around."

"The shop must have a bank account."

"Well, yes. But we have expenses. Ten thousand would be quite a hit. And what if you were delayed in repaying me?"

"Then you could sell the letter and keep all the proceeds. There are dealers on Madison Avenue who specialize in rare books, manuscripts, and letters. That letter could bring fifty thousand dollars."

"You should sell it to a dealer, then."

"Don't you see?" His voice was growing desperate now. "I want to keep the letter as part of my collection. If I sell it to a dealer it's gone!"

"I don't know, Evan."

"I'd give you a signed agreement stating that if I don't repay your money in one week's time, the Poe letter is yours to keep. You've got nothing to lose!"

I sighed and told him, "Let me think about it overnight. Call me in the morning."

I should have told him straight out that I couldn't help him. Perhaps the reason I didn't was because the letter did interest me. Even if I kept it for only a few days I could photocopy it and have a nice keepsake. It wasn't Cheryl's night to stop by after work, but her hours had changed and by the time I closed the shop she was waiting for me. Later, over a couple of drinks, I told her about it and described the Poe letter as best I could remember it. I told her about Quentin Oakes too, and that I'd been unable to find him at his address.

"This Petrick wants to borrow ten thousand dollars from you and you've known him only a few days?"

"What do you think?"

"I think you're crazy, but if you want to do it I'd make sure I had the Poe letter in hand, plus the agreement signed by him."

"Okay," I said and shifted the subject to more agreeable topics.

Before I could phone Petrick on Saturday morning he called me at nine thirty. "What have you decided?" he asked.

"I'll loan you the money."

I could hear his voice relax on the phone. "That's great. He said he'll need it in cash because he'll be gone before the banks open Monday."

"I don't deal in large amounts of cash, Evan. My bank is open till noon. I'll give you a bank draft and you can cash it yourself or give it to him."

"That's fine."

"Come by the bookshop around eleven."

He was there a good ten minutes early, carrying a slender black attaché case. I directed him to my back office and he opened the case, carefully removing the letter in its clear plastic envelope. "Here it is."

I examined it carefully, making certain it was the Poe letter he'd shown me at his apartment. A letter from the previous owner accompanied it, vouching for its authenticity. "And the agreement from you?"

"Right here." I read it through and it was exactly what he'd promised. He signed it Evan A. Petrick with a flourish.

"I should have guessed your initials were EAP."

He grinned. "I suppose that's what got me started as a collector."

"Is your middle name Allan?"

"Ambrose. I never use it, but it seemed only right that I include it here."

"Certainly." I opened my desk drawer and took out the bank draft for ten thousand dollars. "I'll expect to see you next week with the money so I can return your letter."

"Don't worry. I'm already anxious to have it back."

Cheryl showed up as I was closing the shop that evening. It was unusual for her to turn up three nights in a row because of her work schedule, but I certainly wasn't one to complain. She was wearing her maroon suede jacket that usually signaled a night out, but the first thing she asked about was the Poe letter.

"Let me see it."

I took out the plastic envelope. "Be very careful. It's nearly a hundred and sixty years old."

She studied it for only a moment and then handed it back. "This man who is selling him the Poe story—Quentin Oakes?"

"That's right."

"You said Petrick had to have the money today because Oakes is flying to his home in Aruba tomorrow?"

"That's what he told me." I turned out the lights and headed for the front door. "You coming over to my place?"

She smiled. "Not tonight."

"I've got good Scotch."

"I know you do. Save it for tomorrow."

I usually slept late on Sunday mornings, but the ringing telephone awakened me before eight o'clock. It was Cheryl's chipper voice. "Are you still in bed?"

"I usually am at this time on a Sunday."

"Alone?"

"Of course."

"I'll pick you up in twenty minutes."

"What? What for?"

"We're going out to JFK to see Quentin Oakes off on his flight to Aruba."

"What are you talking about?"

"Twenty minutes," she repeated, and hung up.

I dressed quickly, swallowed a glass of orange juice, and went downstairs. She pulled up right on time. "Hop in!"

"What's this all about?"

She gave me her best smile. "I intend to astonish and amaze you."

"You could have done that in the bedroom."

The Sunday morning traffic was light if not polite, and we made it out to JFK in record time. Cheryl parked in the JetBlue lot and we hurried inside. "I've never laid eyes on Quentin Oakes," I told her. "I hope you're not expecting me to identify him."

"Leave that to me."

She punched some numbers into her cell phone as we walked and said simply, "I'm here." She listened to the response and replied, "Okay."

Once inside we skirted security and went down a corridor to an unmarked door. "What's this?" I asked.

"The holding room." She knocked and we were admitted at once. Three men were in the room, an official-looking type with a name tag that read Security, a uniformed guard wearing a pistol, and a much older man with gray hair and a beard. He was seated at the table, looking bewildered.

"That's him," I told Cheryl. "Petrick described him to me."

She ignored me and walked over to the table. "Quentin Oakes?" she asked.

"Yes. What's this all about?"

She held out her badge and ID. "Detective Blanding, NYPD. You're under arrest for grand larceny, fraud, and forgery. You have the right to remain silent and consult a lawyer. Anything you say from this point on may be used against you in a court of law." She hurried on, reading him the rest of his rights.

I was indeed astonished. I'd never seen her make an arrest before. And I was amazed when she reached over and yanked away the beard, revealing the face of the much younger Poe collector, Evan Petrick.

Cheryl phoned for a squad car to take him in, and I swore out a formal complaint against him. She went with her prisoner and I drove her car back to my apartment where she could pick it up later. When she arrived late in the afternoon I wasn't about to let her get away without an explanation.

"I've got a few questions," I told her.

"Fire away."

"How'd you know Petrick was swindling me? How'd you know he'd be at the airport, in disguise, and with a passport in the name of Quentin Oakes?"

"The first part is easy. As collateral on that ten-thousand-dollar loan, he gave you a handwritten letter from Poe to one of his editors. If it was real, it might well have been worth fifty thousand dollars, but it was a fraud. The Edgar Allan Poe signature was no doubt copied from a real one, but Poe stopped signing his middle name after about 1831. By 1845, the supposed date on that letter, his autographs and letters were all signed Edgar A. Poe. It's mentioned in biographies and even in a story by Ellery Queen."

"Really?"

"Honestly, for a bookseller you don't read nearly enough. His performance at the auction, protesting the withdrawal of the Poe story, was just an act, since he'd withdrawn it himself in his guise as Oakes."

"How'd you know he'd be on that plane under Oakes's name?"

"That was guesswork, but fairly logical guesswork. He'd told you Oakes was flying to Aruba today, yet Oakes wasn't at the address you had. That might have been enough to make you suspicious. You might have checked the flights. So he bought a ticket in Oakes's name, and decided to disguise himself and take the flight himself on a forged passport. If you or the police checked the flights later, they'd have Oakes on it, looking just as Petrick and the auction house had described him to you. He'd get off the plane in Aruba, throw away the wig and beard, and Quentin Oakes would be gone forever. So would Evan Petrick and your ten thousand dollars. He could have returned at a later date to collect the other Poe volumes from his apartment."

"And if I tried to sell the letter, someone at the auction house probably would have noticed that mistake in the signature. They deal with that stuff all the time."

"I think someone already did, and maybe that's why Sam Fargo was killed by a subway train."

"You mean . . . ?"

"We're reinterviewing witnesses now. We might be able to tie Petrick to it."

"How did he know I'd strike up a conversation with him? How did he know I'd loan him the ten grand?"

She shrugged. "He had plenty of other suckers to work on."

"All this for just ten thousand?"

Cheryl smiled. "Oh, you weren't the only one. We've already learned of two other cases like yours and there may be more. It seems Petrick was an expert when it came to forging Poe letters."

EDWARD D. HOCH (1930–2008) was a past president of Mystery Writers of America and winner of its Edgar Award for Best Short Story. In 2001 he received MWA's Grand Master Award. He was a guest of honor at Bouchercon, twice winner of its Anthony Award, and recipient of its Lifetime Achievement Award. The Private Eye Writers of America honored him with its Life Achievement Award as well. He was the author of more than 950 published stories, and his work had appeared in every issue of *Ellery Queen's Mystery Magazine* for the past thirty-five years.

A Nomad of the Night

Rupert Holmes

Andris Riga, twenty-two and justifiably confident that 1969 was his year, walked up the subway steps and onto Hudson Street. The long-limbed, chestnut-maned graduate student, who'd been regarded as a six-foot weakling at his Bronx high school until Mick Jagger became the new standard for sexy, strode north on Varick and turned onto Carmine.

Edgar Allan Poe had once lived on this street, but Andris had an appointment with a different practitioner of horror.

The narrow four-story brownstone was flanked on its left by Tilio's Auto Body Shop and on its right by a decomposing duplicate of itself. It was as if the two brownstones were Siamese twins and a decision had been made to let one die so the other could live.

There was a service entrance (which had once been a servants' entrance) four steps below the sidewalk, its portal gabled by the tall flight of steps leading to the main doorway high above the street. Andris took the front steps three at a time and found a solitary doorbell button with only one name above it: TWILL.

He pushed the button and thought how remarkable yet inexorably logical it was that he would be standing here, about to meet the man who had inspired him to create the work that had now motivated the man to want to meet with him.

A few months earlier, for his master's thesis in film direction at NYU, Andris had made a feature-length motion picture. Admittedly, it weighed in at barely eighty-one minutes, and this only with the assistance of an interminable series of end credits in which the names of the hairstylist and script supervisor were each given fifteen seconds of solo screen time. But even granted that most of the film equipment was supplied gratis by the university, and that the student production team had worked for Twin Donuts and coffee, the feat of making a not-altogether-awful feature for under seven hundred dollars was a stunning achievement.

And his film was not some head trip (to use the vernacular of the time), indifferent to such foolish concerns as plot and characterization. Andris Riga's first movie belonged to that most commercial of bargain-basement genres: it was a good old-fashioned horror flick.

That he had opted to earn his graduate degree by creating a cheapie shock film would hardly have surprised Andris's old friends from the Grand Concourse. As youngsters they had shared a normal boyhood fascination with all things ghoulish, and when in elementary school the Riga boy was called upon to read aloud in English class his latest book report, he could be relied upon to invoke some grim, grisly passage from one of Poe's most horrific tales—and joy of joys, there was nothing his teachers could do to silence or punish him. It was literature!

"'His whole frame at once crumbled—absolutely rotted away beneath my hands. Upon the bed, before that whole company, there lay a nearly liquid mass of loathsome, detestable putridity!'"

"Thank you, Andris, you can sit down now."

Early on, Andris's heroes had been the great pragmaticians of fright films. His NYU college classmates may have spent their lives deifying directors, but Andris had always revered such financially shackled producers as Val Lewton, whose work for RKO he'd savored on late-night TV; Roger Corman and company at American International, with their highly profitable exploitations of Poe's titles; and, his all-time favorite, New York independent filmmaker Canaan Twill, whose neo-Gothic homages to Poe had, for financial reasons, lately evolved from "lost Lenore to newfound gore," as *Variety* had once put it.

Perhaps it was Andris's upbringing that caused him to so admire these frugal producers who podged together tolerable horror flicks employing over-the-hill actors en route to the Will Rogers Home, sets unworthy of a junior high play, stock footage of thunderstorms, and a philosophy that going for more than one take on any given scene was a tad self-indulgent.

Andris's father, an immigrant, had owned a small butcher shop on Allerton Avenue, and the boy had been fascinated by how little of each carcass went to waste. Hard fat was delivered to a tallow factory in Sheepshead Bay; shins, tendons, and eyeballs to Chinatown; stomach to a Normand bistro for their acclaimed tripe; snout and hooves to a vet for doggie chews. Bones were sold for soup, or ground into offal for tropical fish, or combined with the steer's own blood for fertilizer.

Andris was raised to respect this nothing-wasted mind-set, and when he read in *Famous Monsters of Filmland* that Roger Corman, finishing a movie shoot a few days ahead of schedule, had used the bonus time to create, on the fly, a second feature called *The Terror*, and had further insisted that a young Peter Bogdanovich use outtakes from the same shoot in a feature called *Targets*, Andris thought, "Man, I'm going to be *that* kind of filmmaker."

He'd shot his film in sixteen-millimeter color (blown up to thirty-five for the final print) on Taiwanese film stock purchased literally under the table in the monochromatic coffee shop alongside the Film Center building. The transaction had felt as illicit as a drug deal, and very likely was.

When processed, the anemic tints proved to be members primarily of the green family. It was not a pretty picture, but then neither was his movie. He'd called it *A Nomad of the Night*, though privately he referred to it as a *Catcher in the Rye* in which Holden Caulfield is searching for truth while also drinking other people's blood.

One way to look at the film was as an artsy (translation: grainy) update of the low-budget teen rebel films of the 1950s, except that switchblades had been replaced by fangs.

Another way to look at the film was squinting.

Andris's master stroke had been to shoot the entire film in the Italian style, with no attempt to record live dialogue or ambient sound. He planned to dub the entire movie in postproduction, as if it were a foreign-language feature. The ability of any cast member to speak his dialogue convincingly, or even remember it, was not a requirement. The actors needed only to look right for their parts and work for free.

Andris's contention, stated in the notes accompanying his submitted celluloid thesis, was that if Americans could admire French and Italian films whose dubbed dialogue tracks held only passing allegiance to the actors' lip movements, U.S. filmmakers could avail themselves of this technique as well. (This also allowed him to rewrite dialogue *after* a scene had been shot.)

A few short days after completing the final, silent cut of his motion picture, Andris dubbed *A Nomad of the Night* in the university's primitive recording studio, using the best voices he could cull from the school's drama department. The result was a film that felt like a foreign movie in which an entirely American cast, speaking their native tongue, had been dubbed in English. This strange overlay lent a surreal ambience to the work that proved artfully appropriate to the movie's tone and theme.

The length of Andris's film had entitled him to an evening screening essentially his own, with his girlfriend Sally Dahlzell's twenty-minute documentary on de facto sweatshops in modern-day Manhattan serving as an opening short subject.

Afterward, at a little reception (Yago Sant'Gria on ice in plastic cups) outside NYU's auditorium, Andris basked pleasantly in the outpouring of compliments from his graduate adviser, Herbert Brodkin.

"Jesus, Andy, when you decided not to record live audio, you just knocked the hump right out of the camel's back! You did away with renting a Nagra tape recorder, an operator, microphones, I mean, the whole goddamn sound department!" Brodkin enumerated on his thick fingers. "No scene could get screwed up by some actor muffing his line or a microphone boom creeping into frame. Right on!" Brodkin was the kind of professor who liked being one of the guys, and he encouraged his students, particularly the more attractive females, to call him Herb.

"Andy is so decisive," said Sally, looking at her boyfriend with such immense adoration that he wished he could wear her on his arm wherever he went.

"You should try to sell your film," Brodkin advised him, as was his job.

"Really?" The idea had never been far from Andris's mind, but he pretended it was the first time he'd thought of it.

Brodkin shrugged. "Why not, man? It's a feature. It's color. It's a horror movie, sort of."

"Andy doesn't think of it that way," said Sally, who'd always been uneasy about the quantities of stage blood Andris had employed during the five-day shoot. She had strong principles and wealthy parents, the latter making it easy to maintain the former. "It's an allegory. Sacramental. A statement."

Andris would have explained to Sally that it actually *was* a color horror movie and that, as usual, she was granting him an artistic integrity that he would seek to achieve only when he had a five-picture deal at United Artists. But her fine spirit, splendid body, and weekly stipend from the folks back home made him choose not to correct her.

Brodkin gave Sally the same patient and inviting smile he'd been offering her all semester. "Of course, it's a metaphoric use of the vampire genre. But there's a chance some independent distributor might pick it up for loose change, for drive-ins or triple bills. It's kind of a drag you didn't have any nude scenes." Brodkin's eyes panned down to Sally's T-shirt. "That might really up its salability. Of course, you could probably do some pickup scenes, if you could convince a couple of your cast members to . . . you know." He looked around at Andris's young cast and crew. "Any help I could give you . . ."

"A contact in the film business would be good," Andris replied.

"If you had nudity, maybe we could talk," said George Mueller of Globe International Film Distribution, Room 514B, 630 Ninth Avenue. Mueller looked like a large, clothed thumb upon which a face had been drawn, and after viewing Andris's reels, the face was frowning. "Herbie Brodkin was my best editor, and I'd like to help, but you need to have something like a nude scene or a name. Doesn't have to be a big star, just enough to hang a poster on. Hire John Carradine, or Chaney's son. Add a few scenes with them, maybe we could talk."

Andris didn't want to mention that the actors in his movie had worked for the absolute most he could afford to pay them, which was nothing. As far as his financial resources went, it was a good thing Sally loved him, because otherwise he didn't know how he'd get by.

"Besides," Mueller continued, "I do mainly exploitation and motorcycle movies nowadays. Maybe you should take it over to Canaan Twill. He hasn't made a film of his own for a couple of years, but he distributes other people's crap now and then. I can give you his number, but you better get yourself a selling point first. Sex, or a star. Corman's using this LSD thing, and he's still working Edgar Allan Poe . . ."

"I love Poe."

"Always solid box office. They're just running out of titles. The lush wrote only so much. Twill got some mileage out of him, but then he started making those slaughterhouse flicks. I don't know if he can pay you anything, though. He says he doesn't have anything more to say on the screen, but I think it's that he doesn't have any money."

It had been debated among horror cultists why Canaan Twill had abandoned his comparatively genteel Poe adaptations for epic stories of flesh-ripping and blood-letting. Andris recalled that once, a few years ago, he had stayed up until four a.m. to hear his role model interviewed on Long John Nebel's radio show.

"I make films that are offensive to the community in order to give the public what it wants," Twill had stated drolly. "But I find myself frustrated by the endless constraints of that silver rectangle—a movie screen—boxed in by a cinema's four walls."

Long John had called Twill a "mad genius." Twill replied that he was half right and left it at that.

Returning to Sally's one-bedroom apartment—Sally's father had raised no objections to his daughter's roughing it in the West Village as long as her building had a doorman and central air— Andris immediately consulted *The New York Times Index of Films,* a massive black tome that had been his favorite reading (and weight-lifting) since Sally had bought it for his birthday.

Sally was fresh out of the shower and dewy as anything.

"How'd it go?" she asked, dabbing at her shoulders with a big white towel, then tying it around her like a sarong.

Andris indicated a copy of *The Village Voice* on an orange beanbag chair. "Check for any movies based on Edgar Allan Poe playing around here. Don't forget the Elgin and Thalia . . . Wow." He'd located the listing for Poe in the thick volume. "There've been more Poe movies made than Poe wrote stories. Look at this: *The Haunted Palace*, 1963, Roger Corman. That was just a poem within "The Fall of the House of Usher." And here, *House of Usher*, 1960, Roger Corman. Way to go, R.C.! Two movies for the price of one."

The half-naked Sally set aside her disappointment at her half-nakedness being ignored. "Does it cost a lot to get the rights? From Poe's estate?" she asked, thumbing the pages of the *Voice*.

"Not a cent. Public domain. Anybody and his sister's cousin can make a *Masque of the Red Death, Murders in the Rue Morgue, Tell-Tale Heart*—"

"*The Conqueror Worm*," offered Sally.

"No, that's another poem, and it doesn't have a plot."

"I wasn't suggesting—"

"You could never make a movie out of it."

"Tell that to whoever did," she said, indicating a quarter-page ad for "Edgar Allan Poe's *The Conqueror Worm*," starring Vincent Price.

On the IRT up to the Loews Capitol Theatre at Broadway and Fifty-first, Andris wondered how he himself would have constructed a film based upon an allegoric elegy with no characters or plot. It would be like trying to make a sitcom out of the Twenty-third Psalm.

They found an empty row to themselves. The smell of hot popcorn and toasted hashish wafted pleasantly from the back of the loge. The movie's credits began with the opening lines of Poe's poem. Vincent Price intoned the disturbing words as if they were stewed prunes in tawny port and he were savoring each one of them.

Lo! 'tis a gala night within the lonesome latter years!
An angel throng, bewinged, bedight in veils, and drowned in tears . . .

Then flashed a screen credit incongruous with this invocation. "Based on the novel *The Witchfinder General* by Ronald Bassett."

"I thought this was Edgar Allan Poe," murmured Sally.

Andris frowned and concentrated on the unreeling tale of anti-Satanic crusades in seventeenth-century England.

About an hour into the movie, Sally whispered, "So when does the giant worm appear?"

But no promised conquering *tuberculata* raised its ugly peristomium for the duration. When a doom-laden freeze-frame turned from color to black and white, indicating that the movie had now officially ended, the last lines of Poe's poem were again intoned, Price's plummy voice giving the benediction.

While the angels, all pallid and wan, uprising, unveiling, affirm
That the play is the tragedy, "Man," and its hero the Conqueror Worm.

"It had nothing to do with Poe at all," Andris marveled as they left the theater. "It's as if—" He looked at Sally. "Come on, there's an out-of-town newspaper place on Forty-second."

Dead center between Sixth and Seventh, commanding a sweeping view of Tad's Steak House (home of the $1.89 steak dinner), the international newspaper and magazine shop reeked pleasantly of European slick paper. In the British rack toward the rear, Andris found several back issues of *Films and Filmmakers*. Moments later, he tapped a page with the back of his hand.

"Exactly what I thought. We just saw a cheapie British horror film—budget under a hundred thousand pounds—called *Witchfinder General*. But for the States, the distributor added a new main title and end title, hired Vincent Price to read a totally unrelated poem by our pal Edgar, and changed the name of the movie to make it seem like it was the newest Poe flick from Roger Corman's crowd." Andris led Sally to the front of the store, where *Variety* was on sale, and quickly flipped through the box-office grosses around the country. "And doing good business at that. Huh."

They ended up on stools at Grant's emporium at Times Square, eating a couple of twenty-five-cent burgers off a small paper plate. It was Sally's treat. It always was.

"*A Nomad of the Night*," Andris mused. "That could be the title of a story by Edgar Allan Poe, don't you think?"

Sally moved a little scoop of chocolate ice cream around in the paper cup that housed a modest ice cream soda. "I suppose. But of course, your story is set in the present."

Andris sipped from his small pilsner of ale. "So? It's a modern-day retelling of a great Poe classic. Like *West Side Story*."

"Poe wrote *West Side Story*?" Sally asked.

"Don't be a wiseass."

Sally swiveled toward him. "I don't get the point."

"A film is made. It has nothing to do with Edgar Allan Poe. But someone says it's based on Poe, even though it isn't, which immediately makes the film more sellable. Poe's work is public domain, so there's nobody with a legal right to complain, except the cheated moviegoer." He downed a last rivulet of ale from the bottom of the glass. "Why couldn't that happen to my movie?"

Smoke undulated madly over a surface of cratered onyx. As it began to clear away, a small lake of dark blood appeared, its surface still and dead. But soon the blood started to ooze and form shapes that coagulated into ominous letters raised upon the black stone. They formed the words:

Edgar Allan Poe's
A NOMAD OF THE NIGHT

The footage ended. Andris, standing by the Moviola's preview screen, bowed slightly at the waist.

"Far out," Sally said with admiration. "How'd you do it?"

"Made the letters by dripping red sealing wax on a black cast-iron griddle, put the griddle on top of a double burner, used NYU's camera in an overhead animation mounting to film the letters melting, toward the end blew cigar smoke between the pool of melted wax and the lens, then had it processed at high-speed and in reverse. I'm slugging this footage right into the master print. It'll play in silence, and I'll cut to the first downbeat of music on the next credit, which is the word *STARRING*. Hopefully, it'll look and sound like I meant it to be that way."

"But why didn't you say it was based on some *real* Edgar Allan Poe story?"

"Because then people could look it up and see that my movie bears no resemblance. And before you ask me why I don't just use a poem to bookend the film, like *The Conqueror Worm*, you can pull that trick only once. Everyone'll be wise to it now."

Sally, who unlike Andris was hampered by a conscience, asked, "So . . . what would you say if a distributor tried to locate the story and couldn't find it in any library, anywhere?"

Andris called Canaan Twill the next morning at the number George Mueller had given him (despite the shocking lack of nudity in his film). An answering service took his message. His mentioning that the film was a modern retelling of Edgar Allan Poe's "A Nomad of the Night" must have helped, because the next day a man who was Twill's assistant called Sally's apartment, instructing Andris to drop off the print at a screening room alongside the Rizzoli Bookstore on Fifth Avenue. Andris felt funny leaving his only print with the projectionist there, but Twill had not invited Andris to view the film with him.

Two days later, the same assistant left a message with Sally. Would Andris call Twill to arrange a meeting that afternoon?

A minute after Andris had rung the doorbell at 109 Carmine, a somewhat patrician-looking man in his fifties opened the door and smiled pleasantly. His thin copper-colored hair was combed straight back and had a pleasing sheen to it. He wore a light gray corduroy smoking jacket with charcoal lapels over matching shirt and pants, and a paisley ascot at his throat. He looked casually formal, or perhaps it was the other way around.

"Andris?" inquired the man, whom the student instantly recognized as Canaan Twill. If a smile could also be a wink, his was it. "In you go," he said, holding the oak door open wide.

Making his way in, Andris saw what might have been a set for one of Twill's series of Jack the Ripper films and then realized that of course it was precisely that. In fact, he realized he probably knew most of the house, as it had passed for a Victorian drawing room (*Jekyll Meets Hyde*), a parlor in a 1920s bordello (*I Must Be Killed*), and a cozy New England boardinghouse (*Dracula Is Among Us*). The guest bathroom just inside the front door had been the setting for the almost unbearable-to-view finale of *Brain Drain*.

"I ran your movie yesterday. I liked it, it's quite good," said Twill, indicating a central staircase Andris was meant to ascend. "I realize I've just killed the suspense, but some critics insist that's my trademark." He laughed heartily at his own joke as he led the way into an office, the width of the brownstone, at the head of the stairs. Windows behind an impressive Jacobean desk overlooked a narrow garden and patio that were wedged in between Twill's house and the back of a dry-cleaning facility.

On one side of the room was the examination table used in *No One Can Hear You*, with the six straps whose securing had underscored a chilling speech by a very aged Otto Kruger. The other side of the room was all bookshelves, the final resting place for a slew of awards and trophies (none of them Oscars, needless to say) that formed a kitschy wall of metal-painted plastic and cheaply framed certificates "bequeathed" to Twill at various horror and comic-book conventions.

However, one shelf, located dead center, was home to a row of old bindings, some ornate, some worn and drab, and a number of slipcases and clamshell boxes undoubtedly protecting more fragile or valuable publications from exposure to the sun or the overcurious.

"Let me get straight to it," said Twill, whose voice was seasoned with a dash of a British accent. He sat behind the massive desk and indicated that Andris should take the chair opposite. "I think the film has its charm. It's not going to be a big moneymaker, but it would fill out a double bill without causing the audience to storm the box office for refunds."

"Thank you," said Andris. Not bad from a lifelong hero.

"I'm a bit concerned about the lip sync. I mean, I know what you were doing, and to some degree it works, but the audience may feel . . . What would be the chance of getting your cast to use French names in the credits? So we could palm it off as a foreign film?"

Andris explained that since his actors had donated their services, he'd hoped to at least get them a film credit in return. But he quickly offered, "Maybe we could add a lot of fictitious French names to the opening credits, alternating them with the real cast."

"Giving the impression of a French coproduction—*Parfait, mon ami!* I can see you're my kind of filmmaker."

"*Et vous*, maestro," said Andris, passionately sincere if linguistically awkward. "Your body of work, the tapestries you've woven—"

"On threadbare budgets?" offered Twill wryly. "Still, I suspect you may actually have underspent me with your fledgling feature.

My God, even *Hotel from Hell* cost me the price of a motel room for three nights—though the crew did get a continental breakfast." He laughed as he rose and moved to the bookshelf, posing by an award shaped like two conjoined masks, one of Tragedy with its traditional frown, the other of Tragedy frowning even further. This was clearly a ceremonial moment, even if he and Andris were the only ones to witness it. He announced to the room, "I can offer you what you say it cost you to make the film, plus two thousand dollars."

He paused as if expecting Andris to say something. Andris was silent in the hope that Twill would say more.

At last, the producer shrugged. "That's all, I'm afraid. If you were thinking you'd clean up, I'm very sorry. As it is, I'll have to sell one or two of these to make copies of your print." He indicated the row of old volumes, waving Andris over. "You might want to take a look before I bid them good-bye. My modest collection of Poe, first editions and otherwise. Not the best in Manhattan, but up there. I call this brownstone the House at Poe Corner. He lived just down the street for a while, don't you know."

Twill opened up a clamshell box to reveal a first edition titled *Eureka*. "There were only five hundred printed. And perhaps I'll let go of . . . this one." He reached for a slipcase and withdrew an old tan volume with a drawing of shells and snails on the cover. "*The Conchologist's First Book,* by one 'Edgar A. Poe.' A scientist's guide to seashells, a subject about which Poe knew nothing. He just lent his name to the volume for fifty dollars because he needed the money. Your generation probably finds that reprehensible."

Andris shook his head. "Not me, but then, maybe I'm not 'my

generation.' What matters is getting the work out there at any cost or, better yet, at no cost at all."

Twill smiled approvingly. "Well, your work will certainly get out there. I'll distribute through the old channels and hopefully turn enough of a profit to make another film for myself. Fair exchange. I'm exploiting you exploiting me." He put back the volume and confided chummily, "I believe I've got you right where you want me."

Andris displayed a maturity beyond his youth by knowing when a gracious surrender, unblemished by quibbling, can be a rain check for victory. "To be exploited by the master of exploitation is an honor," he offered. "All I would . . ." He thought it diplomatic to hesitate.

"Go ahead."

"I would want to work on your next film, as your assistant director. College is behind me. Now I want to learn something."

Twill was pleased but cautioned, "The credit may not bolster your résumé. I've never been asked to speak at an NYU seminar on how I made *Blood Pudding*. No Canaan Twill retrospectives at the Museum of Modern Art."

"Your film career is far from over," Andris assured him.

Twill looked unconvinced. It made Andris ill at ease to see a god appear so mortal. "I don't know. I hope you're right. I think I strayed, artistically, trying to find new images of horror . . . went on a bit of a binge with *Gut Wrench*, you know. *Brain Drain* as well. Lost my bearings—or marbles, some say—with that one." Twill retreated to his side of the desk and resumed a more businesslike manner. "Which brings us to the subject of your movie, and also to the—uhm—well, the *subject* of your movie. The fact that it's a

fresh title among film adaptations of Poe is our strongest market-
ing point. But although I'm an avid, even ravenous, collector of
E.A.P., constrained only by my financial limitations, I've never
heard of 'A Nomad of the Night.' Explain, please."

"This might be the strongest selling point of your campaign,"
Andris confided, leaning across the desk. "It's a lost story."

"What on earth are you saying?"

"Privately printed in a magazine that never reached the public.
A story I alone have been privileged to read, outside of the person
who owns it."

The director seemed bewildered. "But a truly lost story *found*,
especially one with the horrific elements your adaptation suggests,
would be worth a tremendous sum." He gestured to a ledger book
on his right. "You certainly wouldn't need this trifling check I'm
about to write you."

"Unfortunately, the story isn't mine, or in my possession. I was
allowed to see it once, that's all, just enough to take the notes on
which I based my film." Andris produced several rumpled pages
torn from a spiral-bound notepad. "You can see how I derived my
plot from them."

The hastily scrawled notes did indeed accurately parallel the
plot of *A Nomad of the Night*, which was hardly surprising since Andris had manufactured them that morning to match the storyline
of his movie.

"But how'd you learn about this collector, and why was he or
she willing to let you see the magazine?"

"I learned about it from my girlfriend," Andris said, naming
the only person who was in on the scam and who would be willing

to lie for him. "As for why she . . . Let's just say the collector has his or her reasons."

"Your girlfriend? Sally? The one I spoke to on the phone?"

Andris repressed a smile as he realized that the "assistant" who had set up the appointment had been Twill himself. "I can tell you only that her family is pretty well-connected."

Twill scanned the notes quickly. "But I'm uneasy, with only your word and these notes to back up your claim. I wish I could see it myself. How I envy your eyes. I'd give up my entire collection—"

"You don't have to," said Andris, playing his last card. He was seeing uncertainty in Twill's expression and felt the deal might be drifting away. "While I was alone with the old magazine, a large corner of the upper right column tore off in my hand, although I'd been extremely careful. A pure accident, of course."

"Of course," muttered Twill.

"I thought the best thing to do was to, uhm . . ."

"Keep it?" asked Twill, his eyes burning with hope.

Andris reached into his shirt pocket and withdrew a clear plastic case, suitable for displaying, say, a block of stamps. It contained a dry, yellowed corner of a very old magazine page, brittle-looking and jagged as bad teeth, upon which could be read a broken paragraph from the top right column. He offered the plastic case to Twill, who studied the words as if committing them to memory.

like a shroud the sheet was wound about his frame! Yes; it was a corpse, in its burial-clothes. Suddenly, the fixed features seemed to move, with dark emotion. Strange fantasy! It was but the shadow of the fringed curtain,

waving betwixt the dead face and the moonlight, as the door of the chamber
opened, and a girl stole softly to the bedside. Was there delusion in the
moonbeams, or did her gesture and her eye betray a gleam of triumph, as
she bent over the pale corpse—pale as itself—and pressed her living lips
to the cold ones of the dead? As she drew back from that long kiss, her
features writhed, as if a proud heart were fighting with its anguish. Again
it seemed that the features of the corpse had moved

And the page ended. The reverse side showed part of a seemingly unrelated illustration of a horse.

"Oh, Lord," said Twill in something like a moan. He regained
his composure and pronounced authoritatively, "That's his voice.
That's Poe."

"Like I said," seconded Andris, displaying a modicum of
resentment that his word had for even a moment been doubted.
The fact that the text was written by Nathanial Hawthorne didn't
hamper his performance one bit.

Andris proudly reflected that he was indeed made of the same
scrappy resourcefulness as the men he admired, although in the
"Special Thanks" credit he would have to give Sally first billing.
She'd actually been the one to find a ragged and nearly unreadable
copy of *The New England Magazine* in a stack of "offer us anything"
closeouts at the Old Print Shop, and been clever enough to locate
a paragraph that might pass for Poe. She'd bought the magazine,
if you could call the remains of its tattered pages that, for a dollar.
Andris knew that he'd have to take Sally out to dinner once he
was reimbursed for the reasonably marked-up receipts he planned
to present to Twill.

But the director had one last concern. "And have you considered what would be the legal ramifications if the owner of the magazine decided to come forward after the film's release?"

"None," the student assured him. "Privately owned or not, the story itself is in the public domain. Anyone can make a movie of it, if they can find the story and read it, as only I have." He lowered his voice, although there was no one else there to hear him. "But that's the beautiful part: Since no one else can claim to have seen the story, any filmmaker who tries to do their own version of it will obviously be plagiarizing us."

Twill liked this immensely. "So if Corman ever tried to make his own *Nomad of the Night*, or *Bride of the Nomad*, even though it's Poe and public domain, I'd be able to sue his sainted ass?"

"Sure, what could he be basing his movie on except *our* movie? It's a neat little trap we can pray he or somebody else steps into. I tell you, there are all sorts of ways this film can make money."

Twill rose to his feet. "God, you're the old school born again. With your wiles and my experience, who knows what we could accomplish." He opened the right-hand drawer of his desk and took out a typed sheet of paper, one that had clearly been waiting there all along. With a fountain pen he crossed out something on the page, wrote some numbers, initialed them, and thrust the sheet of paper toward Andris. It was a simple letter of agreement and bill of sale, transferring all rights to the film version of *A Nomad of the Night* to Canaan Twill for Andris Riga's expenses and an advance of two thousand dollars—only that amount had been crossed out and upped to four.

Andris knew he might easily bargain Twill up to five thousand.

He could also demand in writing his granted request to participate in future projects. But he also knew it wouldn't matter what was in the contract; Twill would keep him around as long as it pleased him and was to his advantage. And it would be the same the other way around. One man would leave the other soon enough. He offered the director his hand. "If we can shake on my being your assistant director, I'll be glad to sign."

Twill nodded. This was the way it used to be done. They shook hands, Andris signed the agreement, and the director wrote a check for four thousand dollars, which Andris tucked gratefully into his shirt pocket. "You really needn't give *A Nomad of the Night* another thought, except for the glowing reviews I hope it will receive in the cult magazines," Twill reassured him. "As the first new Poe feature I've released in ages, it has to be only a modest success to pave the way for the film I've wanted to make for almost twenty years now. Serendipitously, it too is based on a version of a Poe story that few people have seen—and, my young sir, I think you might be just the fellow to write the screenplay."

Andris more than welcomed the sound of this. If he was the screenwriter and this new film was to continue a line of Poe titles that had begun with *Nomad*, surely number three in the series would have to be his baby.

Twill impulsively started to walk from the room. "Would you like to see the story? It's the most valuable Poe I own, and I don't keep it out in the open."

Twill led Andris back down the stairs into a charming old kitchen, and then they descended toward what had likely been the servants' dining and common rooms on the lowest floor of the house.

"What's the title of the story?" asked Andris, trying to keep pace with the older man.

"When you see it, you'll think, 'What's all the fuss?' But the edition I own has a few interesting differences that could be cinematically stunning, even on a tight budget." Twill walked over to a large black door with a dull copper handle and swung it open. "I keep it in this room where it's cool and dry." He gestured toward the open door. "There's a light switch on the far left."

Andris entered the room and felt around. "Well, you've got me intrigued. Which story is it?"

"'The Cask of Amontillado,'" said Twill, smoothly closing the door to the small vault with Andris Riga inside it.

Twill walked slowly up the two flights of stairs to his study and smiled at the magazine fragment sitting on his desk. Yes, it was Poe's work, there could be no doubt about it.

He went to a decanter and poured himself a small sherry, which really was wonderfully ironic, except that it was a Fino.

For a moment, he imagined he could hear the cries of the young student, but he knew from past experience that this was just his admirable imagination. He was not the sort to relinquish control to the Imp of the Perverse, or allow a fleeting moment of guilt to induce a confession to whatever policeman might come to call, in the unlikely instance one ever did. He was impervious to imagined screams, walled-up black cats, and tell-tale hearts that go thump in the night.

In that regard, he'd always thought Poe a bit silly.

He took inventory. The film was in his possession with a signed letter of agreement serving as bill of sale. Twill's check had been safely deposited in the vault—tucked away in the boy's shirt pocket, where it would never be cashed. Andris's strange disappearance off the face of the planet would only hype the publicity and deepen the mystery surrounding *A Nomad of the Night*. In fact, if the film was decently received, Twill would make further films bearing the cryptic directorial credit "Nomad." Speculation would be encouraged that Andris Riga was still alive but working in total secrecy.

Further, Twill had in his possession the fragment of Poe's story and Andris's notes. These, combined with the motion picture, would help buttress and authenticate the existence of the lost story, raising the market value of the fragment—should he ever choose to sell it.

All this meant funding, blessed funding, so he might once again direct scenes of unspeakable pain and savagery for the screen—rather than only getting to rehearse them with untrained performers in makeshift settings, the final results maddeningly unpreserved and unrecorded.

What an unexpected turning of the tide. It was almost more happiness than he deserved.

And lest he forget, there was something more to anticipate with the toe-wriggling expectation of a child on Christmas Eve: the locating and acquiring of Poe's "A Nomad of the Night," by whatever means it would take. A most pleasurable calling.

Calling.

He picked up the phone and dialed the number at which he'd left his message for Andris earlier that day.

"Hello?" said a female voice.

"Hello, is this Sally?" Twill did his best to sound as if he were in his twenties, and frightened.

"Yes?"

"Listen, Andris has had an accident. No, don't get upset, I think he'll be just fine, but it would be best if you helped him get home."

"Hold on, who is this?"

He passed over the question. "It's awkward . . . Andris was using some, uh, *remedies*, if you understand me, with a lady friend of his—"

"A girl?"

Yes, he thought, *I've got you now.* "They've both had a bad reaction. Andris gave me your name and number before he started throwing up."

"Where are you?"

"Well, as I say, it's a little awkward, because of the nature of what Andris was doing. There's a pay phone at the corner of Varick and Carmine."

"Varick and Carmine."

"Go there and I'll meet you," Twill lied. When from the front parlor window he saw her arrive, he would call the pay phone: 249-9173. Others had been directed to that corner, and they always answered by the tenth or eleventh ring, never failing to follow his directions to the letter, and to his door. "Tell me what you look like so I'll know it's you. Gee, this is so awkward."

"I'm twenty, five-foot-six, light brown hair."

"Okay, hurry here, he really needs your help."

Twill hung up the phone, stepped over to the examination table from *No One Can Hear You*, and removed a black velvet cloth from a pallet mounted to its side, revealing an array of surgical instruments. The implements dated back to the Victorian era, but they had been sharpened last year and used only a few times since. He wasn't sure how long it would take him to extract the location of "A Nomad of the Night" from young Sally, five-foot-six, light brown hair. But he would certainly be in no hurry.

Over and over that night and through the next day, as he honed Sally's performance, she was privileged to hear the masterful director call out after every take:

"*Cut!*"

―――――――――――

Rupert Holmes has twice received Edgar Awards from the Mystery Writers of America and a combined eight Tony and Drama Desk Awards for his Broadway comedy-thrillers, which include *The Mystery of Edwin Drood* (Tony Award for Best Musical), *Curtains*, *Accomplice*, and *Solitary Confinement*. His first novel, *Where the Truth Lies*, published in six languages, was a Nero Wolfe Best American Mystery Novel nominee, a *Booklist* Top Ten Debut Crime Novel, and a film directed by Atom Egoyan. His second novel, *Swing*, was a *San Francisco Chronicle* top ten bestseller. His "Monks of the Abbey Victoria" has been chosen for *Best American Mystery Short Stories 2008*. Next, for Twelve Publishing, is *The McMasters Guide to Homicide: Murder Your Employer*.

Rattle, Rattle, Rattle

Stuart M. Kaminsky

> *Misery is manifold. The wretchedness of earth is multiform.*
> —Edgar Allan Poe

The rattle. The rattle. Recalling a Louisiana witch doctor's voodoo bones or the clacking ivory of dice? As it is now, I can make no sense of when the rattle, rattle, rattle will stop and when it will start. Would it be better if it never stopped? No checking of the clock, no examination of the tides, no code in the intervals makes sense, though I probably shouldn't have been looking for pattern or reason.

I'm getting ahead of myself. The present should be my rock firmly in place but it is an infinity of horror and madness. I sit in hope that I have but dreamed, but I know and feel full well that it has been all too real.

The year is 1901. The season is fall. The time is just before midnight. The place is Egeaus, my crumbling estate just outside of Baltimore. These things are true.

I am in the library of the mansion I have inherited. I am determined to finish writing this. The writing will be my rock. Like Ulysses on the coast of Phaeacia I will cling to a jagged boulder with Ino's veil around my shoulders. When I have no more to write . . . I can't allow myself to think about that.

I shall begin.

When I first saw Egaeus Manor in its Gothic majesty, I had trouble believing my luck.

On closer inspection and a tour of the forty rooms, three towers, and catacombs I became a true believer, not in my good luck but in what I called "my nightmare." Little did I appreciate at the time what a nightmare really was.

"It's not all that bad," said Mr. James W. Tolliver, executor of my uncle Michael's estate. "The land itself is worth close to one hundred thousand dollars in a good market, possibly more. I'd hate to see Egaeus torn down but . . ."

Tolliver and I were standing in the great hall that stands off the corridor along the east side of the decaying mansion. The corridor is at least thirty feet high and fourteen feet across with floors hewn from local stones. Along the corridor, in the floor, are four mosaics depicting some kind of story.

It was impossible to determine from which end the story began. Moving from the north, the first mosaic showed a young man and woman being married. Their clothes were from the early part of the last century. Man and woman were smiling at each other. There was something in his slightly slumped shoulders and skin more pale than his bride's that made the next mosaic almost predictable.

The young man, now quite pale, sat in the same library in which I now sit. He was looking up at his bride, who was in a flowing white night dress. The young woman's expression was pained and the glow of health was gone.

In the third mosaic, the man, now gaunt, looked at what appeared to be a pile of clothing in a corner of the chamber. An old man, possibly a servant, stood next to him. On the face of both servant and master was a look of horror.

The last mosaic was the strangest of all. It was a box, a closed wooden box with what appeared to be brass hinges, held in the pale hands of someone lost beyond the edge of the creation.

"What's this?" I asked.

Tolliver looked down at the box and back at the other three mosaics. He had a peculiar and slightly annoying habit of gently pulling at his lower lip when he was about to speak. It seemed to be a habit he was trying without success to break.

"Your great-uncle was a bit . . . peculiar," Tolliver said, pretending to be absorbed in looking at the four images laid into the floor.

"Peculiar as in . . . ?"

"He is reported to have gone quite mad shortly after his fiancé died. Bernice was her name. No one is certain what caused this madness. It does have some genetic roots in the vague family history."

The rest of the tour through covered and spiderwebbed corners was interesting if uneventful, here a cracked wall or ceiling, there a wooden table with worm-rotted legs. And then there was the scurrying of rats in the wall.

"Should you decide to remain here," Tolliver said, touching finger to lip, "the house can be restored and the rats and other vermin exterminated. The cost, I warn you, will take much of what you have inherited along with house and land."

We were in a round room in one of the towers, accessible only by a narrow winding stairway that Tolliver chanced only after I insisted. I was the one in frail health, suffering from severe asthma, yet it was I who was willing to climb those stairs.

"And the graveyard?" I asked standing at the window and looking down at the half acre of overgrown land with tombstones peeking over the top of tall weeds. Some of the headstones had fallen. Others stood at an angle ready to totter.

"Your ancestor left specific instructions in his will that the graves be maintained in perpetuity. His instructions, as you can see, have long been forgotten. I'm sure the law would uphold the complete plowing under of the entire plot of land."

"I've decided to keep Egaeus," I said. "Can you arrange for at least four contractors to come to me with plans for restoration?"

"You are sure?" he asked, finger now clicking against his lower lip.

"Quite sure," I said.

Tolliver put me in touch with an old woman named Mrs. Carstairs in Baltimore. Mrs. Carstairs had a niece named Sophie who, with her husband, was willing to live at Egaeus and take care of it and me.

As it turned out, complete restoration of Egaeus Hall had to wait for a while. When I had paid for and received satisfaction in the restoration of a little more than half of the estate, I began to see my wealth take a downward dip due to a weak stock market. With Tolliver's help, I sold some of the land and much of the old furniture, paintings, and fittings in the as-yet-to-be restored section of the house. The sale refilled my coffers nicely.

Sophie and her husband, who preferred to be known only as Bascomb, were a perfect match for me. They were neither interested in nor equipped for conversation beyond the most mundane daily business. Neither were they particularly handsome creatures. She had a rotund pink look about her that reminded me of a small pig. He had a body and face that suggested a Goya grotesque.

It was on the second night after I had officially moved into the house that I heard the sound. At first, I was certain it was the scurrying of rats, but if it was rats, they were playing with something in the walls.

The restoration of Egaeus Hall had gone well. The only problem was the electrical wiring. The walls were solid stone so hollow spaces did not exist. For months I had to endure noise, dust, and the voices of ignorant workmen using foul language.

I'm not a prude. I've been known to utter the occasional choice word. It just seemed inappropriate in this house and in my hearing.

I probably would have complained had it not been for the morphine. My asthma had grown worse in the dusty atmosphere of the house. Morphine was the only thing that helped me through the days and nights of fright when I awoke certain that the breath I was trying to draw would never be achieved.

During the days I worked with all manner of contractor in the hope of getting the first phase of the restoration finished. At night, I worked on my book.

I had experienced some minor success with my writing, a few articles on early-eighteenth-century British epistolary novels, two short stories in the Cumberland University literary magazines, a one-act play about Lord Byron that won a $50 third place prize in a British play competition. I had been told for more than two years that the play was about to be produced. It never happened.

Now I concentrated on my novel, a sequel to Horace Walpole's *The Castle of Otranto*.

Each morning I shaved, inhaled camphor, and struggled without success to ward off the need for morphine by midday. My image in the mirror showed no marked deterioration. To the contrary, each morning I saw the same lean, decent-looking bespectacled face in the mirror. My uniform was a pair of often-washed pants, a black sweater with rolled-up sleeves, and comfortable slippers.

For a few weeks, colleagues from the university came to see Egaeus Hall and stay overnight.

I always included a pause at the mosaics in the corridor and asked what they made of the four-image tale. Some explanations were very creative. None satisfied me. We usually talked till late, often about the mosaics, had breakfast prepared by Sophie and Bascomb, and they invariably left saying they looked forward to returning another time. It was evident that they had no such intention.

One night, while trying to entertain a married couple—he in

the Geography Department, she in Literature—I mentioned the rats in the wall.

"Sorry about that," I had said. "I've been trying to get rid of the pesky creatures but nothing seems to work. They appear to be a particularly hearty breed."

"I didn't hear anything," he said.

"I think I did," she said.

"A rattling," I said.

"Maybe," she said. "Maybe."

And, after my ritual pause at the mosaics, that ended that. They left early the next day, never to return.

Aaron Wynch was my last visitor unless you count Dr. Silvius and Lawyer Tolliver as visitors. Aaron had been my roommate at the University of Virginia. We had often joked about having the honor of living in former slave quarters with no indoor toilet and cold winter winds as our reward.

Aaron was an alienist. I suppose that was one of the reasons, but not the only, one for visiting me. He readily admitted that a former visitor to Egaeus Manor had told him that I was not doing well.

Over a glass of brandy after dinner, we sat in the warmth of a fire prepared by Bascomb.

"Your housekeeper is a fine cook," Aaron said, looking at the blood-red brandy in his glass.

"Is she? I suppose," I said.

This time he looked at me over his glasses and said, "Oliver Twede says you've been hearing odd noises at night."

"I have," I admitted. "Rats, creaking of old timbers, constant resettling of the wooden floors."

"What do these noises sound like?" he asked.

"Rattling," I said.

"What kind of rattling?"

"I don't know. Rattling of dice, maybe a dozen dice," I said. "Or bones, old chicken or rabbit bones, the kind of rattling we heard that old conjurer woman make with her box of bones when we went that time to New Orleans. Remember that?"

"I remember," Aaron said with a grin. "Do you hear the rattling now?"

"No," I said. "Do you?"

He laughed. We drank. We talked.

At the door we said good night, though it was past night and into early day, Aaron said, "Come see me in Baltimore."

We shook hands.

"You have a doctor here?"

"Yes," I said, "one no older than we are with the face of a cherub and an earnest look that masks confidence. I like him."

"You don't look well," he said.

"I'm feeling better. The pain is under control."

"Do you have odd dreams?" he asked.

"Who doesn't?" I said.

I thought he was about to say something more, but he said only, "Good night. Take care of yourself."

"I will," I said.

As soon as the door was closed, the specious smile on my face disappeared. It was clear that he had not heard the rattling that had begun almost an hour earlier and I was not about to mention it.

When I was about eight, I had an ear infection. I was certain a pump was drumming somewhere. I asked my mother to turn it off so I could sleep. When the infection was cleared, the pump stopped.

But this was no pump. If it was an infection, it was an infection of a very different sort. Perhaps it was a manifestation of the disease that was slowly rubbing its fine-grained sandpaper fingers against my liver.

Morphine, defense against pain and the real or imagined rattling, detained me for an agony, which kept me from writing.

The rattling was louder than before. It was distant, but definitely inside the house.

When in my initial year at the University of Virginia, I joined a militia in which we marched twice each week to the cadence call of old Sergeant William Barley Mead. Sergeant Mead had been a drummer with the 93rd Corps New York Infantry. His favorite marching songs, sung in a moist and toothless caw, were "Always Stand on the Union Side," "Marching Through Georgia," "When Johnny Comes Marching Home Again," and "John Brown's Body." To mute the horror of the insistent rattle, rattle, rattle, I evoked the pace of old Mead cackling "John Brown's body lies a-mouldering in the grave." I followed the sound through the dining room.

I marched past the servants' rooms and into the great corridor, where dull orange triple-lighted sconces faced each other across the quartet of mosaics. There was now no longer any doubt.

He's gone to be a soldier in the Army of the Lord.

The rattling stentorophonic echoed from twelve-foot-high

stained-glass windows to stone walls and across the ceiling, where soot-stained cherubs with small white wings dashed about with wide smiles on their once pink faces.

John Brown's knapsack is trapped upon his back.

I knew now the origin of the sound. I stood over the last mosaic, the one of the hinged box, and looked down.

I knelt and with careful searching found, surrounding the image of the box, a line of stones slightly more separate from each other than those in the rest of the mosaic.

The sound grew deafening.

The stars above in Heaven now are looking kindly down.

Why had the servants not heard and come rushing in? With difficulty and some bruising I wedged my fingers into the crevice. I had to stop for a moment to cover my ears, but soon went back to my task. This time I joined old Mead in singing.

His soul goes marching on.

I found purchase and pulled. The entire image of the box rose with the effort of my thrust and I slid the stone slab to the side. It screeched as I pushed it along.

His soul goes marching on.

There, in the space below where the image of the box had lain, was the real box, one identical to that in the mosaic in every way but size. The one that I now lifted from the ground was much smaller, no larger than a thick cigar box. I tucked it under my arm and shoved the howling slab back into place.

John Brown's body lies a-mouldering in the grave.

I did not march. Did Sergeant Billy Mead laugh as I ran with the prize, trying to ignore the rattling that came from inside it? When I got to my room, I placed the box on my bed and opened it. It wasn't locked. As soon as I began to lift the lid, the rattling stopped.

I sat back, taking shallow breaths, knowing that I needed my camphor and my morphine. I looked inside the box at a sight so strange and unexpected that I laughed.

Inside the box were small teeth that appeared to be human. Ancient blood still tainted their valleys. Next to the teeth there rested a grotesque steel instrument, a kind of curved pliers that, since it rested so close to the teeth, I took to be a dental instrument. I touched it, held it up to the light. It opened and closed easily with no sign of rust or wear. I counted the teeth now without touching them. There were thirty-two.

There was also a sheet of paper in the box. Still holding the pliers I unfolded the sheet. The penmanship was of a kind and at a level that none use save calligraphers and Jewish specialists who painstaking copy the first five books of the Old Testament and roll them in a scroll called a Torah.

I read:

And when my Beatrice, my once gossamer bride,
Called of our damnation from the profundity of Hell
With a rattling even devils chose to hide,
I could not bear to view the box or hear the knell
Of thoughts so purple tenebrous and ink black wide.
I pressed the vessel into a welcome seeping earth,
Covered it and wept for one who all too soon died.

I opened that box but this once to press inside
This warning note to myself, a maddening Egaeus,
And any other who may find this box, Lord pity us.

I read it again and again, clicking the dental pliers like a demon's castanets. I dared not touch those teeth again. I closed the box and put it on a high shelf behind old and yellowing books.

And then I slept.

I expected a sleepless night, but I awakened from dreamless rest to the brightness of morning sun through the windows. There were no unbidden sounds. The books on the top shelf had not moved. I heard no rattling teeth. And yet I was not content.

If the servants noticed the displaced mosaic, they said nothing. But then they were a dull and unobservant pair. I ate a large breakfast of oatmeal and brown sugar, feeling far better than I had in weeks.

"Fine breakfast," I said to Sophie as she cleared the table.

"Thank you," she acknowledged.

I could see she had something on her mind. There was no intelligent veil between that bland face and weak intelligence.

"Something you want to say?" I asked.

Her eyes were down, looking at the remnants of my breakfast in the bowl in her hands.

"My husband would like to talk to you," she said.

"Send him in."

She slouched off and I reached for my coffee. Bascomb entered almost immediately, trying to hide a dry-mouthed gulp, and said, "Mr. Egaeus, my wife and I give notice."

"Why?" I asked.

"If it's all the same, we just want to leave."

"Have you been overworked, offended?"

"No," he said, not meeting my eyes. "We just have decided to seek employment elsewhere."

"The sounds at night," I said. "You're frightened."

"Frightened, yes, but not of sounds at night. My wife and me are concerned about your . . . moods."

"My moods? Yes, well I have those under control now. I can offer you both a raise. Would that change your mind?"

"No."

"And you'll tell me no more?"

"I will not."

"Then I'll have to find new help won't I?"

"I think you'd do best to seek it from outside the town."

"Thank you, Bascomb."

"Welcome. We'll stay one more night if you want it."

"Yes, thank you."

He left. Had my behavior been so erratic? Had they come upon my medication and mistaken it for an opiate drug of choice?

Bascomb was right about my moodiness, but with the box where I could easily reach it, I allowed myself to acknowledge that my imagination may have been at work. The poem of my ancestor suggested that there may have been a fever of the mind as part of my inheritance.

I made two calls, one to Tolliver and one to Dr. Silvius. Both, after some pressure and pleading, agreed to spend the evening with me and perhaps the night in Egaeus Manor.

"I'd like to discuss disposing of the house," I told Tolliver. "And then, depending on the doctor's assessment of my health, seek a far more modest home."

I thought about the box, wondered if I had missed something in my haste to put it on the shelf. Were those hinges truly brass or were they gold? Were those really teeth or small creations of wood or ceramic? I had seen perfectly formed Japanese ivory tiger teeth.

Perhaps the Bascombs or someone else—Tolliver, the doctor—was trying to drive me mad. It wouldn't have been difficult to do to someone of my ill health and heavy medication.

I hurried to my room, locked the door from inside, and, wheezing as I did so, stood upon a chair and recovered the box. It felt heavier. I placed it on my bed and opened it. Nothing had changed. The teeth were there in no particular pattern. The pliers was there, jaws open, and the poem was there, neatly folded. I touched teeth, poem, and pliers to be sure they were sensible to feeling as well as sight. They were.

I closed the box and put it back on the shelf.

I spent the rest of the morning and the afternoon at the window looking out at the cemetery. An occasional bird rested on a faltering tombstone. Something scurried and scrambled out of sight into the earth. Shadows of the manor slowly moved over headstones and untrimmed grass and weeds. Silence. I closed my eyes but was soon aroused by a knock at my door and Sophie announcing, "The doctor is here."

The early part of the evening after dusk went without mark or moment. The doctor examined me immediately after a spare dinner of pork and potatoes and declared that it would probably be a good idea for me to move to a smaller, far less damp home where I would be close to medical support. Tolliver noted the improvements that had been made to Egaeus Manor since I moved in and declared that it could rather easily be sold and the proceeds used to support me for the rest of my life. I had the distinct impression that he did not expect me to extend my days beyond a decade or so.

"A buyer," said Tolliver, "will probably want to tear down the manor."

"So be it," I said. "Contents and all. I think . . ."

And then I heard it. The rattling. At first I was sure it was only my imagination. The sound was far away and could easily have been rats.

"Mr. Egaeus," said Tolliver.

"Yes?"

"You seem distracted."

"Just considering where I'd like to move and when."

"I think the city would be best," the doctor said.

I knew where the rattling sound was coming from now, yet I said nothing. What would be the point of confessing my delusion or addressing their conspiracy?

"It's late," I said. "I'm tired. You know where your rooms are."

"We do," said Tolliver. "I think the doctor and I will stay up a bit longer and talk about taking care of your future."

"Thank you," I said. "You know where the wine is. Take what you please."

I did not run, though I felt the urge. I walked slowly, evenly, with sober determination from the room, knowing the two men at the table were watching me. Then I heard their voices forming questions and Sophie and Bascomb answering them.

The stairs were manifold. I took them slowly, drawn upward, fighting the urge to go back down and announce to guests and servants that I wished to leave instantly and forever. My clothes could be packed and sent to me wherever I decided to go.

But I didn't leave. I continued to my room, the rattling now so loud that it almost drowned out a new sound, as of some creature being tortured.

In my room, I mounted a chair, almost fell from it, retrieved the box, and took it once more to the bed. This time I examined it carefully before opening it. My head was pounding, my fingers slipping. There were thumbnail-sized little faces all along the box along the base. Why had I not noticed them before? On one side the little faces laughed. On another they wept. On the third, they were filled with sorrow, and on the fourth, a dozen tiny faces looked out in wide-mouthed, wide-eyed horror.

As soon as I began to open the box, the rattling stopped and the teeth ceased their motion. I could not tell if they had moved while I was gone. I took my morphine dose and lay back on the bed, arm over my eyes, box at my side. I intended to rise, bathe, shave, and reread the poem in the box before sleeping, but I fell asleep almost instantly.

I dreamed, not of rattling teeth, madness, or conspiracy, but of my mother and wretched father, both long dead. It was no nightmare. They sat at the dining table where I had eaten with the lawyer and physician. They sat without speaking, smiling with a secret. And then I was aware of a figure behind them, a beautiful woman in a diaphanous nightgown standing between them. She was the woman in the third mosaic. Her face went through each of the countenances of the faces on the box. First she smiled. Then she saddened. Then she wept, and finally her eyes and then her mouth opened in horror.

There was only blackness and a languid pink tongue in that open mouth. No teeth.

Sharp pain pierced the back of my head and neck. The pain paralyzed me for an instant and then chilled my spine. I awoke, sat up weakly, and looked around. I was alone.

And then I turned my eyes to the box. It was closed. I was sure it had been open when I fell asleep. Maybe I had bumped it as I slumbered. I opened the box with trembling fingers and looked inside.

The number of teeth had more than doubled. The new ones were covered with blood, as was the pliers whose jaws were now open. I closed the box and backed away, scrambling weak-kneed off the bed.

Whose teeth were these?

As if in answer to my question, the rattling began again, ten times louder than it had been before. I hurried to my bathroom, closed the door, and switched on the small night light over the sink. The rattling was deafening.

And then, as I looked up at the mirror, opening my eyes in fear and horror, I saw myself. The look was exactly that of the woman in the gown. Eyes wide open. Mouth agape. And I knew whose teeth were rattling in the box.

They were mine.

STUART M. KAMINSKY is the author of more than sixty mystery novels, seven produced screenplays, and two produced plays. He has also worked on and written for television series, including Nero Wolfe Mysteries. Nominated nine times for Edgar Awards in five different categories, he has received an Edgar for Best Mystery Novel and has been named a Grand Master by the Mystery Writers of America. A former professor at Northwestern University and Florida State University, he earned his Ph.D. in Communications from Northwestern. For the past two decades he has lived with his wife and family in Sarasota, Florida, where he writes ten pages a day, plays softball twice a week, and enjoys tai chi under a banyan tree.

Development Hell

Paul Levine

Marvin Beazle slipped off his tinted shades, tugged at his ponytail, and studied the emaciated writer sitting across from him. Skin the texture of paraffin. Stained trousers, moth-eaten frock coat, and a silk cravat dangling like a tattered curtain.

"Love the Johnny Depp look," Beazle said. "But why the long face?"

The writer stared back with rheumy eyes. "Like absinthe with its cork askew, I do not travel well."

A scarecrow in a wool coat, Beazle thought. *One of those writers who could use a tanning salon, a tailor, and some Zoloft.* "Okay if I call you Eddie? Or do you prefer Al?"

"I have never stood on ceremony."

"My man!" Beazle beamed, a tiger dreaming of tasting lamb.

They were in the executive offices of Diablo Pictures on Sunset Boulevard, and Beazle had a rights deal to close. In his experience—and he'd been doing this forever—writers were worms. Drowning in doubt, strangling on self-loathing. A little money, a little flattery, and most scribblers would sell their souls along with their scripts.

Beazle vaulted from his ergonomically correct swivel chair and pointed toward the floor-to-ceiling window. "What do you see out there, Eddie?"

The writer squinted into the afternoon sun. "Houses on a precipitous hillside. A hideous white sign. 'Hollywood.' As if the inhabitants need assistance recalling their whereabouts."

That snooty East Coast attitude, Beazle thought. *Like Baltimore is the Garden of Eden.* "It can all be yours, Eddie."

"All of what, sir?"

"Okay, not my digs on Mulholland. But a big chunk of this burg is yours for the taking."

Beazle peeled off his black silk Armani suitcoat and tossed it onto his leather sofa. He plopped back into his chair and swung his five-hundred-dollar Matteo sneakers onto the desk. The sneakers—alligator hide dyed red and gold—made Beazle recognizable to everyone who counted, especially the maître d's of Prime, Mastro's, and The Grill, where he ate his steaks bloody.

"Gotta hand it to you, Eddie. You're a helluva wordmeister."

"So you have read my story?"

"Devoured it. The coverage, I mean." Beazle picked up a three-page synopsis and skimmed through it: "Condemned prisoner wakes up in a dungeon. Nearly tumbles into a deep pit. Falls asleep, wakes up strapped to a board, a pendulum above his head with a razor-sharp scythe, swinging lower and lower." Beazle looked up from the document, sniffed the air. "I smell franchise, Eddie."

"I beg your pardon."

"Slasher flicks keep on trucking. Sequels, prequels, spinoffs."

"*Slasher?* What a macabre word."

Beazle returned his gaze to the document. "Then you throw in some moving walls for a second-act complication, and finally the guy's rescued by the French army. A little deus ex machina, but we can fix that. Our reader—a top film student who happens to be my niece—says you've got a bold voice and a literary style. Don't worry about that 'literary' part. We can fix that, too."

"I am not certain I take your meaning."

"Forget it. Let's talk money, Eddie. How much you making now?"

"The *Southern Literary Review* pays me fifty dollars a month. Occasionally, there is extra remuneration. I was paid ten dollars for 'The Raven.'"

Like a fisherman with a woolly bugger, Beazle baited the hook. "Diablo Pictures wants to option your story, Eddie. A quarter million bucks for one year against a cool million pickup price."

"The devil you say!"

"I shit you not, Eddie. Plus three points of the net, which of course is zilch, seeing how *Gone With the Wind* still hasn't turned a profit. But you'll get the usual boilerplate regarding sequels and merchandising."

"Merchandising?"

"If McDonald's wants to license the 'Pit Burger,' you get some dough. If Gillette markets the 'Double-Bladed Pendulum,' you get a slice of the pie. Assuming we don't change the title."

"Is this really happening, Mr. Beazle, or is this some phantasm of my imagination?"

"It's real, pal. You're talking to the guy who greenlit three of the top ten grossing pictures of all time. Adjusted for inflation, of course. And here's the foam on the latte. We want you, Eddie Poe, to write the script. In fact, we insist. Half a mill for a first draft, a rewrite, and a polish. Whadaya say?"

"I fear I might swoon."

"As long as you don't piss yourself. Fitzgerald did, right in that chair."

The writer's forehead beaded with sweat. Either it was the excitement or the heavy wool coat on an August day.

"You look a little dry, Eddie. You want something to drink?"

"Laudanum, perchance?"

"What a kidder! Okay, let's do some business." Beazle pulled out a thick sheath of papers stapled to luxurious blue backing. "All I need is your signature, and it's a done deal. Check's already written. A quarter mill up front."

He brandished the check, waving it like a pennant in a breeze. Handing a pen to the writer, Beazle said, "Before you know it, Eddie, you'll be sitting in a director's chair with your name on it, eating craft service omelets, and banging the script girl."

The writer searched for an inkwell before figuring out that the pen had its own supply. His hand poised over the contract, he said, "What did you mean a moment ago? About changing the title."

"The jury's still out, Eddie. But we may have to lose *Pendulum*. It's three syllables."

"And that presents a conundrum?"

"Titles need punch. *There. Will. Be. Blood.* Get it? Too bad *Saw* is already taken."

"But the pendulum is essential to the predicament. The scimitar swings ever closer, magnifying the horror."

"So who wants to see a circumcision? It's a movie, not a bris."

Confusion clouded the writer's face like fog over Malibu. "But I thought you liked my story."

"Exactly. Liked it. Didn't love it. That's why we gotta make some changes."

The dark bags under the writer's eyes seemed to grow heavier. "Am I not free to write the script as I see fit?"

"Sure you are. When hell freezes over." Beazle drummed a manicured fingernail on his desktop. "Look, Eddie. Do you want the deal or not? I got Bram Stoker and Mary Shelley dying to get their projects out of turnaround."

"I daresay some cautious editing might be appropriate," the writer ventured.

Like taking biscotti from a baby, Beazle thought. "That's the spirit, Eddie. So I gotta ask you. Where's the girl?"

"What girl?"

"You got a guy strapped to a board. Talking to himself. *Boring!* Maybe Tom Hanks can schmooze with a volleyball for two hours, but he had the beach, the ocean, the great outdoors. You got a dark hole in the ground."

"The solitude represents man's existence."

"Deal-breaker, pal. If you're gonna ask Leo or Cuba or Russell to spend the entire shoot in a hole, at least give 'em Scarlett Johansson for eye candy."

"Scarlett . . . ?"

"In a torn blouse. And instead of those rats chewing off the guy's straps, she unties him."

"The rats represent our primal fears."

"Box office poison, Eddie. A one-way ticket straight to video."

"But a woman . . ." The writer's voice trailed off and he scratched at his mustache as if it had fleas. "Writing from the distaff point of view is hardly my forte."

"*No problema*, Eduardo. We'll bring in Nora Ephron to punch up the he-said, she-said dialogue."

"Another writer?"

"Read me your first sentence, Eddie."

The writer recited by heart. " 'I was sick—sick to death with that long agony.' "

"Downer. Maybe we get Judd Apatow to lighten the mood, toss in some fart jokes."

"But that would dilute the horror."

"Hold the phone, Eddie! Just got a brainstorm. The prisoner falls in love with Scarlett, but she's got a fatal disease."

"Good heavens. What would that accomplish?"

"*Halloween* meets *Love Story*. Boffo B.O."

The writer's face took on the pallor of a drowning victim. "Perhaps the theme of the story is unclear to you."

"Hey, you want to send a message, use e-mail. You want foreign box office, you need stars, action, sex."

"I assure you my work is quite popular in France."

"Sure, you and Jerry Lewis. The point is, we're going after the masses, not the art-house crowd."

The writer still held the pen in a death grip. He stared at the check. Picking up sunlight from the window, the paper seemed to be made of burnished gold. He exhaled a long sigh and said, "I suppose you know best, Mr. Beazle. So if there are no other changes . . ."

Beazle smiled, his double row of porcelain crowns gleaming. He loved breaking a writer. It was better than sex. Maybe not sex on coke, but straight sex, yes. "One more thing, Eddie. What's the setting? Where the hell's this prison?"

"Spain, of course."

"Fine. We'll shoot in Vancouver. But no subtitles and we gotta update."

"How? It's the Spanish Inquisition."

"Period piece? No can do. With all respect, Eddie, you're no Jane Austen. And as for the ending, we gotta lose the French army. Who's gonna believe they could win a battle? I'm picturing a SEAL team, maybe the Rock in a cameo."

The writer's alabaster hand trembled as he fiddled with a loose button on his heavy coat. Beazle made a mental note to send the guy to Melrose Avenue for some new threads before letting him on the set.

"That is it, then?" the writer asked. "A new title. Another writer. A naked woman. No rats. A SEAL team. And Canada."

"Almost there. But tell me. Who the hell's the heavy?"

"A faceless evil. The horror is intensified by the anonymity of its source."

"Muddled storytelling, Eddie."

The writer's shoulders sagged. "I suppose you could say the villain is the unseen executioner."

"Unseen? It's motion *pictures*, not radio. How about Anthony Hopkins? Those creepy eyes will pucker your orifice."

The writer's forehead knotted like burls on pine. "Putting a face to the evil is unnecessary. The man in the pit believes he is going to die. True horror is not physical pain. It is the anticipation of pain, the realization that death is a certainty, whether by falling into the pit or being eviscerated by the pendulum. Do you understand, sir?"

"Sure. You don't like Anthony Hopkins. You want to go younger? My daughter says Clive Owen makes her panties wet. Whadaya say?"

"Mr. Beazle, I cannot surrender my integrity."

"Not surrender. Sell! I'll get you a suite at the Peninsula. Room service. Blow. You want a hooker? I got a chippie you'll love. Name's Lenore."

The writer pulled himself up, knees wobbling. "If I agreed to your terms, it would indeed be a midnight dreary."

"Sit down, Eddie!"

"I think not." He took a step toward the door.

"You're saying no to money, pussy, and drugs? What the hell kind of a writer are you!"

But he was already out the door.

Beazle couldn't believe it. A moment earlier, the bastard was perched on the edge of the abyss. Beazle grabbed his suit coat and hurried into the corridor, alligator sneakers *clomping* on the tile. He caught up with the writer at the elevator bank.

"Eddie! Is it the dough? I'll double it."

Two elevator doors opened simultaneously. One attendant, a smoking-hot redhead in a black leotard festooned with orange flames, winked and said, "Down?"

The writer recoiled as waves of heat rolled from the open car.

In the other car, the attendant, a petite blonde in a white leotard with snowy wings, smiled angelically and said, "Up?"

"Last chance Eddie!" Beazle implored.

"Nevermore," the writer whispered, soft as a lover's lament.

Beazle sighed in surrender. He didn't lose often, but when he did, it hurt. "He's going up."

The writer stepped into the blonde's elevator, the door closing with a quiet *whoosh.*

Beazle grabbed a fat cigar from his suit pocket. A Cohiba, a gift from Fidel himself at the Havana Film Festival. Beazle ran the wrapper paper under his nose and inhaled deeply. Not even burning sulfur smelled this good.

Beazle took a double guillotine cutter from his pants pocket and snipped off the cap of the Cohiba. He snapped his thumb and middle finger together, setting off a spark that engulfed the tip in flame. He drew smoke—his mother's milk—into his lungs, and held it there.

"There'll be others," he said, exhaling a cloud as black as coal dust.

There were always others, dying to sell their souls. Writers who dream of starlets and red carpets and their own insignificant names flickering across the screen. Vainglorious fools, every one, all destined to spend eternity in development hell.

—————————

PAUL LEVINE is the author of four novels featuring squabbling trial lawyers Steve Solomon and Victoria Lord. *Solomon vs. Lord* was nominated for the Macavity Award and the Thurber Prize for American Humor. *The Deep Blue Alibi* was nominated for an Edgar, and *Kill All the Lawyers* was a finalist for the International Thriller Writers Award. Paul also wrote seven Jake Lassiter novels. A screenwriter, Paul wrote twenty-one episodes of the CBS military series *JAG* and cocreated *First Monday*, a drama set in the Supreme Court. His latest book, set in the world of human trafficking, is *Illegal*. For more information, visit www.paul-levine.com.

The Deadliest Tale of All

Peter Lovesey

He wrote "A Troubled Sleep," stared at it for a time, sighed, and struck it out.

"The Unsafe Sleep" didn't last long either.

"In the Death Bed" was stronger, he decided. He left it to be considered later. A good title could make or break a story. He'd tried and rejected scores of them for this, the most ambitious of all his tales. "Night Horrors"? Probably not.

Then an inspiration: "It Comes By Night." *This,* he thought, *could be right.* He barely had time to write it down when there was a knock at the door.

He groaned.

The man from the *Tribune* was creating a bad impression. His manner verged on the offensive. "Have a care what you say to me. My readers are not to be deceived. I will insist upon the truth."

The inference was not lost on Edgar Allan Poe.

"Do you take me for a deceiver, then?" he said, scarcely containing his annoyance. He had consented to this interview on the assumption that it would prop up his shaky reputation.

"You will not deny that you are a teller of tall tales, a purveyor of the fantastic."

"That is my art, sir, not my character, and you had better make the distinction if you wish to detain me any longer. What did you say your name is?"

"Nolz. Rainer Nolz."

"Ha—it sounds Prussian."

"Is that objectionable to you?"

"It is if you are unable to temper your questions with courtesy."

"My family have lived in Virginia for two generations," Nolz said, as if that absolved him of Prussian tendencies. He seemed bent on establishing superiority. Overweight—fat, to put it bluntly—and dressed in a loud checked suit stained with food, he was probably twenty years Poe's senior—too old to be a hack, notebook in hand, interviewing a writer. A competent journalist his age should surely have occupied an editor's chair by now.

He threw in another barbed remark. "Since you raised the matter of names, yours is an odd one. Poe—what's the origin of that?"

"Irish. The Poes arrived in America about 1750."

"And the Allans?"

"The family who took me in when I was orphaned. Do you really need to know this?"

"It's not a question of what I need to know, but what my readers will expect to be informed about."

"My writing," Poe said, raising his generally quiet voice to fortissimo.

"On the contrary. They can always pick up one of your books. Anything from me about your writing would be superfluous. The readers—my readers—are interested in your life. That's my brief, Mr. Poe. I've come prepared. I have an adequate knowledge of your curriculum vitae—or as much of it as you have put in the public domain. You aren't honest about your age, subtracting years as if you were one of the fair sex."

"Is that important?"

"To posterity it will be. You were born in 1809, not 1811."

Poe smiled. "Now I understand. You've been talking to the unctuous Griswold."

"And you've been lying to him."

Rufus Griswold, self-appointed arbiter of national literary merit, had first come into Poe's life probing for personal information for an anthology he was compiling ambitiously titled *The Poets and Poetry of America*. At twenty-six, the man had been confident, plausible and sycophantic—a veritable toady. Poe had recognized as much, but failed to see the danger he presented. Writers with a genius for portraying malice do not always recognize it in real life. Griswold was a third-rate writer who fancied himself one of the literati, a parasite by now embedded in Poe's life and repeatedly damaging him. Ultimately the odious creature would take possession of the writing itself. At the time of their first meeting there had seemed no conceivable harm in embellishing the truth.

Nolz was a horse of a different color, making no pretension to charm. "But you'll oblige me by answering my questions honestly."

"Before I do," Poe said, liking him less by the minute, "I'm curious to know how much of my work you have read."

"Not much."

"The poems?"

"A few."

"The tales?"

"Fewer. I don't care for the fantastic and horrific. I prefer something of intellectual appeal."

"You think my work is not for the intellect?"

"Too sensational. At my age, Mr. Poe, one has a care for one's health."

"Are you unwell?"

"My doctor tells me I have a heart murmur. Too much excitement aggravates the condition. But I am here to talk about you, not myself. You are fond of claiming that you could have emulated Byron and swum the Hellespont because as a youth in Richmond you once won a wager by swimming a stretch of the James River."

Poe was pleased to confirm it. "Correct. At the mere age of fifteen I swam from Ludlam's Wharf to Warwick against one of the strongest tides ever known."

Nolz was shaking his head. "Unfortunately for you, I know Richmond. I have lived there. To have achieved such a feat you must have swum at least six miles."

"As I did," Poe answered on an angry rising note. "I assure you I did. In those conditions there is no question that my swim was the equal of Byron's."

"And I say it is impossible."

"Mr. Nolz, it happened, and others were there as witnesses. I was an athletic youth. Were I fifteen again and fit, I would not hesitate to duplicate the deed. Sadly, in recent months my health, like yours apparently, has suffered a decline. But I have achieved other things. Shall I tell you about 'The Raven'?"

"I would rather you didn't."

The sauce of this fellow! "Your readers will expect to be told how it came to be written."

"I know all that," Nolz said and smiled in a way that was not friendly. "I have a copy of your essay, 'The Philosophy of Composition,' which purports to explain the genesis of the poem."

"Purports?"

"The piece is self-congratulation, a paean to Mr. Poe. You omit to mention how much you borrowed from other writers."

"Name one."

"Miss Elizabeth Barrett."

"I am on the best of terms with Miss Barrett."

"You are on the best of terms with any number of ladies. And I am sure you are on the best of terms with a poem of Miss Barrett's entitled 'Lady Geraldine's Courtship' because in 'The Raven' you aped the rhythm and rhyme and offered not a word of your debt to her in the essay."

"She has not complained to me."

"As a critic you are quick to accuse others of imitation and lifting ideas, but you seem blind to the same tendency in yourself. You are also indebted to Mr. Charles Dickens. Allow me to remind you that you were planning to write a poem about a parrot until you read of the raven in *Barnaby Rudge*."

Poe was silent. The man was right, damn him.

"I suggest to you"—Nolz gave the knife a twist—"that a parrot saying 'Nevermore' would not have impressed the public. It might well have made you a laughingstock."

Poe said in his defense, "Whether or not the raven in the Dickens novel put the idea in my head is immaterial. I might as easily have seen one perched on a churchyard wall. The artist cannot choose the source of his inspiration."

"But he ought to acknowledge it when he claims to be expounding his modus operandi. I recall the scene in the novel where Barnaby is imprisoned with Grip the raven for company and the sun through the bars casts the bird's shadow upon the floor while its eyes gleam in the light of the fires set by the rioters outside. Somewhat reminiscent of your unforgettable final stanza, is it not? 'And his eyes have all the seeming of a demon's that is dreaming, And the lamp-light o'er him streaming throws his shadow on the floor.'"

"Would you tax me with plagiarism?"

"No, sir. Forgetfulness."

"How charitable! Is there anything else you hold against me?"

Nolz gave a nod, as if tempted to go on. Then he hesitated before saying, "Mr. Poe, you may not appreciate this, but I am your best hope."

"Best hope! God save us! Best hope of what?"

"Of a lasting reputation."

"Sir, my written work will ensure my reputation."

"Without wishing to be offensive, it has not achieved much for you thus far."

Poe sighed. "I grant you that. 'The Raven' is the most popular poem ever written, and I remain in penury."

Nolz spread his palms. "You were a fool, publishing in a newspaper without the protection of copyright. Any cheapjack publisher was free to reprint without redress."

"And has, a thousand times over." Poe put his hand to his mouth and yawned. "Put me out of my suspense. How will you improve my prospects?"

"Materially, not at all," Nolz said. "I am a journalist, not a businessman. I spoke just now of your reputation."

"It doesn't have need of you," Poe said on impulse. "It's second to none." Yet both knew the statement was untrue. He'd acceded all too eagerly to the request for an interview. He needed shoring up, if it wasn't too late already.

Nolz was looking at him with pity. The man had the power to unnerve, as if he knew things yet to be revealed. The world might be—ought to be—aware that the writer of "The Gold Bug" and "The Raven" was a genius, but this dislikable old hack seated across the table was behaving as if he were the recording angel.

"Who are you?" Poe cried out. "Why should I submit to your churlish questions?"

"I told you who I am," Nolz said. "And as to the questions, most of them have come from you."

"There you go, maligning me, twisting my words. Why should I trust you?"

"Because I have a care for the truth above everything. You have enemies masquerading as friends, Mr. Poe. They seek to destroy your reputation. They may succeed."

Much of what the man was saying was true.

"You keep speaking of this reputation of mine as if it matters. My work is all that matters, and it will endure. Poor Edgar Poe the man is a lost cause, a soul beyond hope of redemption."

"With a well-known flair for self-abasement. Coming from you, this is of no consequence. But when others damn you to kingdom come, as they will, you are going to have need of me."

"As my protector? You are not a young man, Rainer Nolz."

"Ray." He extended his fat hand across the table. "Address me as Ray. My fellow writers do."

Poe reached for the hand and felt revulsion at the flabby contact. "So, Ray . . ."

"Yes?"

"Are there any other failings of mine you wish to address?"

Nolz raised a shaggy eyebrow. "Are there any, Edgar, that you care to confess?"

"Plenty, I should think! When I drink, I drink to oblivion. One or two glasses are usually enough. I am a fool with women, writing love letters to one whilst pursuing another. I am hopeless with money. Are you writing this down?"

"It's too well known. Let's address some of the misinformation you have unleashed on the world."

"Must we?"

Nolz gave a penetrating look with his brown, unsparing eyes. "If I am to be of service, yes."

The examination that followed was uncomfortable, depressing, shaming, a ledger of Poe's falsehoods and exaggerations. Why did he endure it? Because Nolz, like the Ancient Mariner, was possessed of a mysterious power to detain. He dissected more of the myths blithely confided to Griswold and given substance in *The Poets and Poetry of America.* The myth that as a young man Poe had run away from home to fight for the liberty of the Greeks in their War of Independence against the Turks. The myth of a trip to St. Petersburg where he got into difficulties and was supposedly rescued by Henry Middleton, the American consul. All this in an attempt to gloss over two years in the ranks, of which Poe was not proud.

Nolz had said he knew the curriculum vitae, and so he did, in mortifying detail. He must have gone to infinite trouble to find out so much.

Finally he said, "Was that good for your soul?"

"Against all expectation, yes," Poe admitted. "I am tempted, almost, to ask you to absolve me of my sins."

Nolz laughed. "That would be exceeding my duties."

"I feel shriven, nonetheless, and I thank you for that."

"No need, Edgar. Instead of absolution I will offer a piece of advice. Beware of Rufus Griswold. He is not your friend."

"Ha! I don't need telling," Poe said. "After all his blandishments how many of my poems appeared in his book? Three. One Charles Fenno Hoffman had forty-five. I counted them. Forty-five. A man whose name means little to me or the public."

"I saw."

Poe was warming to his theme. "And who was offered and accepted my job after I was dismissed as editor at *Graham's*? Griswold."

"And the magazine suffered as a result," Nolz said, beginning to show some sympathy.

"He even shoulders me aside when I show affection for a lady. There is a certain poetess—"

"Fanny Osgood?"

"You know everything. The first I heard of it was that she had dedicated her collection of poems to him—'a souvenir of admiration for his genius.'"

"Why then, Edgar, do you continue to have any truck with a man who treats you with contempt?"

Poe rolled his eyes and eased his finger around his stock. All this was making him sweat. How could he explain without damning himself? "Griswold has influence. That wretched book of his must have gone through ten editions. Oh, I've tried cutting free of him more than once, but he'll remind me that I have need of him. Since you know so much, you must be aware that he put together another anthology, *The Prose Writers of America*."

"And invited you to contribute. To which you responded that he was an honorable friend you had lost through your own folly—*your own folly*."

Now Poe flushed with embarrassment. "Swallowing my pride. He included several of my tales."

"He continues to tell his own tales about you to all who will listen, shocking scurrilous stories."

"I know."

"Griswold will bring you nothing but discredit."

He nodded. He knew it, of course. He was destined for the sewers. But surely the work would keep its dignity, whatever was said of its creator?

"And you, Ray? What may I expect from you after this interrogation? Should I be nervous of what you will write in your newspaper?"

"The truth."

"Exposing the lies?"

"Oh, no. We disposed of them this evening. I needed to make certain. I am now confident that what I write has the force of verified fact. It will not be to your detriment."

"And when may I look forward to reading it?"

"Never."

Poe frowned, and played the word over in his brain. "I don't understand."

"You will never read it because you will be dead."

The statement was like a physical blow. His brain reeled. Deep inside himself, he'd feared this from the moment he admitted the stranger to his room. Nolz was not of this world, but an agent of destruction.

"You've turned pale," Nolz said. "I must apologize. It was wrong of me to speak of this."

"Tell me," Poe whispered, eyes wide. "Tell me all you know."

"Edgar, I know only what I have confirmed with you this evening."

"You spoke of my imminent death."

"No. I said you will never read what I write because you will be dead. I am a writer of obituaries."

A shocked silence ensued.

"You are my obituary writer?"

"It's my occupation. I was commissioned to prepare yours."

"By whom?"

"The editor of the *New York Daily Tribune*. You, as a journalist, will know that obituaries of eminent men are prepared in advance, sometimes years in advance. One cannot write an adequate account of a life on the morning a death is announced."

"My obituary! I am forty years old!"

"Ars longa, vita brevis."

"I don't want this," Poe said, panicking. "I wish I had never spoken to you. How can you compose my death notice when I am still of this earth? It's ghoulish. You've put the mark of death on me."

Nolz looked shamefaced. "I have committed an unprofessional act. I should never have told you."

"I'm still creative. God knows, I still have the talent."

The journalist cleared his throat. "With due respect, Edgar, you have not produced much of significance this year."

"I have not suffered a day to pass without writing."

"What manner of writing?"

"I revise my earlier work."

"Previously published work. All this tinkering with things that appeared in print ten years ago is the symptom of an exhausted talent."

"And poems. I wrote a new poem longer than 'The Raven.'"

Nolz lifted his eyebrows, allowing the words to resonate. "I doubt if anything you have written in the last six months is worthy of mention in the obituary."

"Cruel!"

"But true. I told you I must be honest." Nolz closed his notebook and pushed his chair back from the table. "I shall take my leave of you now. Take heart, Edgar. Your place in the pantheon is assured. In your short life you have written more masterpieces than Longfellow, Hawthorne, and Emerson between them."

Poe's next words were uttered in a forlorn cry of despair. "I am not finished."

"I think my hat is hanging in the passage."

"Damn you to kingdom come, I am not finished!"

Nolz crossed the room.

Poe got up and followed him, grabbing at his sleeve. "Wait. There is something you haven't seen, a work of monumental significance. I've been working on it for five years, the best thing I have ever done."

Nolz paused and turned halfway, his face creased in disbelief. "Unpublished?"

"You must read it," Poe said, nodding. "It's a work of genius."

"A poem?"

"A tale. It will stand with 'The Tell-Tale Heart' and 'The Pit and the Pendulum.'"

"One of your tales of horror? I told you how I feel about them."

"Not merely one of my tales of horror, Ray, but the ultimate tale. If you neglect to read it, you will undervalue my reputation, whatever you write in that obituary."

"What is the title?"

He had to think. "'It Comes By Night.'" He rushed to his desk in the corner of the room and started riffling through the sheets of paper spread across it, scattering anything unwanted to the floor. "Here!" He snatched up a pen and inscribed the title on the top sheet. "If I die tomorrow, this is my legacy. I beg you, Ray. If you have a shred of pity for a desperate man, give it your attention." He thrust the manuscript into Nolz's hands. "Take it with you. I swear it is the best I have ever done, or will do."

Shaking his head, Nolz pocketed the handwritten sheets, retrieved his hat, and left.

Two days later, the script of "It Comes by Night" was returned to Poe by special messenger. With it was a note:

Dear Sir,

I understand that you are the author and owner of these pages discovered in the rooms of Mr. Rainer Nolz, deceased. I regret to inform you that he was found dead in bed yesterday morning. The physician who attended was of the opinion that Mr. Nolz suffered some spasm of panic in the night that induced a fatal heart attack. He was known to have an irregular heart rhythm. In these sad circumstances it may be of some consolation to you that your story was the last thing he ever read, for it was found on his deathbed. I return it herewith.

> *Sincerely,*
> *J. C. Sneddon, Coroner*

Poe threw the script into the fire and wept.

Edgar Allan Poe himself died the next month in Washington College Hospital, Baltimore. The mystery surrounding his last days has baffled generations of biographers. He had been found in a drunken stupor in a gutter. Dr. John Moran, who attended him in hospital, reported that even when he regained consciousness the writer was confused and incoherent: "When I returned I found him in a violent delirium, resisting the efforts of two nurses to keep him in bed. This state continued until Saturday evening (he was admitted on Wednesday) when he commenced calling for one 'Reynolds' which he did through the night up to three on Sunday morning. At this time a very decided change began to affect him. Having become enfeebled from exertion he became quiet and seemed to rest for a short time, then gently moving his head he said, 'Lord help my poor Soul' and expired."

The identity of "Reynolds" has never been satisfactorily explained. Poe had no known friend of that name. In *The Tell-Tale Heart: The Life and Works of Edgar Allan Poe*, his biographer, the poet, critic, and mystery writer Julian Symons, wrote: ". . . this last cry, like so much else in his life, remains a riddle unsolved."

Just as the sudden death of Ray Nolz was never explained.

On the day of Poe's funeral, the *New York Daily Tribune* published an obituary announcing the death and stating "few will be grieved by it" because "he had no friends." Poe had been worthless as a critic, always biased, and "little better than a carping grammarian." This savage piece was balanced with praise of the stories and the poetry, but the impression of the man was devastating. He was likened to a character in a Bulwer-Lytton novel: "Irascible, envious, but not the worst, for these salient angles were all varnished over with a cold repellent cynicism while his passions vented themselves in sneers . . . He had, to a morbid excess, that desire to rise which is vulgarly called ambition, but no wish for the esteem or the love of his species."

The obituary had been prepared by Rufus Griswold.

And the damage didn't end there. The appalling Griswold approached Poe's mother-in-law, Maria Clemm, and by some undisclosed arrangement obtained a power of attorney to collect and edit the writings. The first two volumes were in print within three months of Poe's death, with a preface announcing that they were published as an act of charity to benefit Mrs. Clemm. She received no money, just six sets of the books. Griswold's *Memoir of the Author*, published in 1850, became for many years the accepted biography. It contained all of the old distortions and lies and added more.

Note from the writer: Rainer Nolz and "It Comes By Night" are inventions. Everything about Rufus Griswold has been checked for the truth.

Acclaimed author PETER LOVESEY has been writing for more than forty-five years, beginning with *The Kings of Distance*, a nonfiction sports book. He soon branched out into mystery stories when his first novel, *Wobble to Death*, won the contest that launched the Macmillan crime list in 1969. Since then he has published thirty novels, more than ninety short stories, had four collections of his short fiction published, and edited three mystery and crime anthologies. He has also won the Crime Writers' Association Silver and Gold and Diamond Daggers, the Barry Award, the Anthony Award, and the Macavity Award, and received the Lifetime Achievement award from Malice Domestic in 2008. His latest novel is *The Headhunters*.

Poe, Poe, Poe

John Lutz

'Twas a devilish rainy night, and the little man who burst through the tavern door seemed to bring the black and blustery weather inside with him.

Every head turned, if not toward the noise then toward the chilled, rain-flecked air that flowed through the place, over the old plank floor, beneath the worn, ruffled hem of the one dress on the one woman in the tavern, and around the corner where it swirled as a miniature whirlwind behind the bar.

"Shut the door, man!" shouted Eddie Reagan, bartender and owner of the Dark Destiny Tavern, as it proclaimed on the faded sign outside, hinged and creaking in the wind off the harbor.

The little gent did just that, stanching the flow of cold air, and removed his black derby. There was something about him that suggested he hadn't always been small but had wasted away from long and drastic ill health. He was quite pale, dressed well enough in a dark gray suit with a string tie and a reasonably clean white shirt with a starched collar. He had receding black hair with a lock combed across his forehead and a well-trimmed little black mustache. His eyes were deeply set beneath a bulbous brow and were dark and searching, as if seeking a way out of hell.

"A drink!" proclaimed the man, in a hoarse yet sonorous voice larger than himself. He squinted, peering around as if suddenly lost.

"The bar is this way, sir," said the barmaid, Mary Roper.

"If he can make it," said one of the male clientele, a sailor off the *Amontillado*, at her berth not far down the docks. He swaggered toward the little man as if to help him. Something in his bow-legged stride and the tight hunch and sway of his muscular body was vaguely and ominously simian.

The little man brushed him aside and made his way toward the bar, but at an unnecessary angle.

"He's drunk, all right," said the apelike sailor, staring after the man.

"Like the rest of you animals," said the barmaid. She gave the sailor a withering look. "Leave him alone, Apier."

The sailor, Apier, pressed both hands to his breast in a gesture of wronged innocence. "Would I not? I hear and heed you, Mary, dearest."

"You would rue the day that you did not," said she.

The intruder from the night reached the bar and leaned an elbow on it, choosing not to sit on the nearby stool. "Good whiskey," he said, "to drive the black night away."

"It'll seem to, anyways," said Reagan, the bartender, and poured two fingers of his best in a glass and placed it in front of the man.

Reagan was a large and mottled sack of a man, with bushy eyebrows and a ruddy, oft broken nose. He had jet black hair combed straight back and graying at the temples in a way that suggested wings.

The little man offered a hand, which the bartender shook.

"Your name, sir?" asked the man.

"Reagan," said the bartender. "Eddie Reagan."

The man tossed down his drink. "Another, please, Raven. One to ravish and one to mother, if you'll be so kind as to pour me another."

"Hah!" said Mary Roper. "A rhyme for us."

"It's Reagan, sir," corrected the bartender. "Not Raven." He leaned forward and looked carefully at the little man. "You remind me of someone. Have you been in here before?"

"He looks like that writer fella, Poe," said a grimy, bearded man named Dupin, seated six stools down the bar. There was a cynical turn to his lips, and a look in his eye that suggested he suspected everyone and everything. He was a Dark Destiny regular, half in the bag as usual. "Writes them po-ems, is what he does." He grinned with yellowed teeth at the little man. "You him?"

The interloper took a long swallow of liquor and then spoke with the exaggerated precision of the near-inebriated. "Am I Poe? Am I Poe? You can count it on your fingers; you can count it toe to toe. Am I Poe? Am I Poe? The answer's no, no, no." He squinted one eye and glanced around, as if just realizing where he was. He seemed slightly embarrassed. "That wasn't very good. I do apologize." He raised his glass and smiled, but more with sadness than humor. "Drink makes us all as others see us not, as do we ourselves who know our lot see others who see not."

"Drunk as a skunk," said Dupin.

"What'd that mean?" asked Mary Roper in obvious admiration.

Dupin, who presumed to know everything, ventured an opinion. "Lotsa drunks smell worse'n a skunk when they—"

"I was addressing our new arrival," Mary interrupted, still with her gaze fixed on the little man. "What you just said that sounded so wise. What's it mean?"

"Oh," said the man who'd said he wasn't Poe, "I would have a hard time explaining." Carrying his second drink with extreme care, he turned away from the bar and walked unsteadily to a table near the opposite wall, where he sat down so he had a wide view and was facing everyone. He drew from a coat pocket a pen and writing pad, and a small vial of ink, which he uncorked.

"It *did* rhyme," said Mary.

"As little else in life," said the man.

"I shall think and talk of you as Edgar Allan Poe," Mary said, "as I believe you're none other."

"Believe away," Poe said. "I neither confirm nor deny. I will be your mystery and you will be mine." He made a careless backhand gesture, knowing that by now everyone in the place thought him to be the bleak and famous poet. And yet they couldn't be sure, so enough of his anonymity was preserved. He would pretend to pretend along with them. He dipped pen into ink and scribbled some notes.

Another burst of foul, damp air swirled into the tavern as another customer threw open the door.

"Close the damned—" Reagan the bartender began, but the

new arrival deftly snatched the door and yanked it shut behind him. He strode boldly the rest of the way into the Dark Destiny and moved toward the bar. He was a tall man, broad through the chest and shoulders, and dressed as a laborer. His huge, callused hands suggested that was exactly his lot in life—physical toil. The bewilderment and agony in his dark eyes beneath arched black eyebrows suggested that mental toil went along with the physical.

He caught sight of Mary at the end of the bar and scowled. "So there you are, me dearest, where I thought I'd find you, perched like a harlot on a bar stool with a drink in your dainty fist."

"No need to insult anyone in my place," said Reagan, attempting to head off trouble.

"Ah, it's no insult to such as she," said the man.

Indeed, Mary seemed not at all insulted, nor even alarmed at the fearful appearance of the obviously agitated man. She was, in fact, looking at Poe. For his part, he was returning her stare and deciding that she was a handsome woman despite a certain coarseness to her wide features. Her eyes, the pure blueness of them, suggested far horizons and depths of uncharted sea.

The belligerent arrival followed the direction of her gaze. "And who might this be?" he asked, obviously directing his question to Mary, though glaring at Poe.

"That would be the famous poet, Mr. Edgar Allan Poe," Mary said. She pointed at the big man. "And this," she said, "is my husband, Mr. Montresor Pitt. Right now he's in a state of arousal and suspicion, but I think it fair to say there's no need to be afraid, as his moods tend to swing back and forth as does a . . ." Here she searched for words.

"Pendulum?" Poe offered.

"Why, just that!" she said.

"May I ask," said Poe, "why, if you are man and wife, do you not bear Mr. Pitt's last name?"

The belligerent man laughed. "Who's she calling herself to-night?"

"Roper," said Mary with considerable sauce.

There was another thunderous laugh from Pitt. "Sometimes she's Mary Roper, and sometimes it's Robard, and sometimes it's Roget. They're what you might call her professional names."

"I like that last," said Poe, and made a note.

"Then for you, tonight, I'm Mary Roget," Mary said.

This seemed to spur her husband to an even greater state of agitation.

"Raven," said Poe to the bartender, "pour Mr. Pitt a drink on my account."

"You don't have an account," Raven said. "And it's Reagan."

Poe drew a silver coin of considerable denomination from his pocket and placed it beside his glass.

"You have an account," said Reagan.

"Rum," said Pitt. "And I'll sit with Mr. Poe while I drink it."

So saying, he swaggered over to Poe's table, pulled out a wooden chair so its legs scraped the plank floor, and lowered his sizable bulk into it so he was facing Poe but could still see to his right, where his wife sat at the end of the bar. He didn't seem at all interested in what Poe had written, which suggested to Poe that he couldn't read.

Reagan poured, and it was Mary who carried the glass of rum over to the table.

As she started to walk away, Pitt reached out and clasped her delicate wrist in his huge hand. "So what do you think of my beautiful wife, Mr. Poe. Is she worth one of your poems?"

"Worth an entire story," Poe said, and raised his glass. Pitt studied him, and then tapped his own glass against Poe's, and the two men drank.

Mary yanked her arm from Pitt's grasp and strode regally back to stool and station.

The tavern door swung open again and, announced by a blast of wetness and chill, a man and woman entered. He was of medium height, about thirty, with sharp features and wavy blond hair. The woman was younger, with long, straight dark hair and sad brown eyes. She removed her rain-spotted cape to reveal a slim, attractive figure. When both man and woman noticed Pitt, they nodded. The man looked afraid.

Apparently they were also regulars at the Dark Destiny, because Reagan, upon seeing them, immediately drew two glasses of brew from the taps, which he placed midway on the bar.

"Those two newcomers," said Pitt in a loud voice, "would be Anna B'Lee and Chester Fortuna."

"I suspect that everyone here knows every other, and that I'm the lone stranger," said Poe, resting an elbow, as if casually, on his silver coin.

Pitt said, "I'd like not to think that my wife knows everyone."

It was then that a dark and dreary expression formed on Pitt's rugged features, and he seemed to enter into one of his mood swings that Mary had mentioned.

"It's a fact," Pitt said in a voice loud enough for all to hear, "that I came here tonight not to see my own wife, Mary, but to see someone she knows much more intimately than I've decided to accept. A man I deem no longer worthy of walking in this world. I vow that one of the two of us will not leave this place alive."

Raven (as he was now firmly fixed in Poe's imaginative mind) immediately hastened to the door. Poe assumed this was to summon a policeman. Instead, Raven bolted the door, and then turned and sought to calm Pitt.

"This isn't the place to settle your differences," said Raven. "The law has warned me there's to be no more such trouble on these premises, and I'm bound to see that there isn't any."

"See whatever it is you're bound to see," Pitt said, and threw back his head to drain his glass in a series of loud gulps that perhaps only Poe could hear. He made a sweeping motion with his arm. "One of these men leaves here only as a corpse." With a sudden lurch he stood up from the table, and from beneath his shirt he drew a long-bladed knife from a leather sheath tucked in his belt.

His merciless eyes swung from man to man in the suddenly silent tavern. Poe knew that of all the tavern's patrons it was only Mary who knew where that baleful and terrifying gaze would finally become fixed.

Raven had a stout club concealed behind the bar, which he used for just such rare occasions, but he was too far away to reach it. If he tried, Pitt would cut him down before he made it halfway across the tavern.

"Stop acting the fool, Pitt," said Mary. But she couldn't keep the quaver of fear from her voice.

"That's exactly what I've decided to do," Pitt said. "The fool will be the one who shared our bed with you, and he'll be a dead fool."

Dupin was obviously transfixed by terror.

Apier stood up from his chair and backed away.

Pitt merely smiled at both men, a smile of the devil.

It was then that Chester Fortuna bolted from his bar stool toward the rear of the tavern. His companion, Anna B'Lee, turned her head to stare after him. She seemed only mildly surprised. The almost deathlike calmness of her features much impressed Poe. Hers was a face he would not soon forget.

Mary tried to stop Fortuna but he shoved her away and ran past her. In one frantic motion he pulled open a thick wooden rear door and was through the exit, slamming the door behind him.

Pitt was at the door in a second, yanking at it, straining to open it. It seemed to be stuck.

Raven slowly approached, veering toward the bar until Pitt glared at him.

"Someone's on the other side, pulling back, keeping the door from opening," Pitt growled.

Standing very still, Raven said, "Fortuna thought he was escaping out a rear exit, but there is no back way out. He's entered a closet."

"Then he's trapped!" Pitt said.

"He must have something wrapped around the knob and fastened to a nearby iron bracket," Raven said. "You'll not be able to open the door."

"Trapped!" Pitt said again, with a malicious grin.

"And safe for now," Raven said. "Where he should remain until you've calmed down and reclaimed your sanity."

"Listen to him, Pitt!" Mary cried. "Please!"

Pitt aimed his evil, anticipatory smile at her, then looked down the bar to where Anna B'Lee still sat in repose on her stool.

"Shall I kill him?" Pitt asked Anna B'Lee.

"Do what you will," she said. "If he's been sleeping with another woman, he's earned his fate."

Pitt grunted and grinned at her.

"You there," he said to Apier. "Bring me a chair."

Approaching carefully in a crouching, simian manner, Apier slid a chair near so that Pitt might grip it. All the time, Apier stared at the knife. As his own hand released the chair, he danced well out of range of the blade.

Pitt gave the door another exploratory yank, and then shrugged. He wedged the wooden chair beneath the knob and kicked it tight with his big right boot.

Chester Fortuna was indeed now trapped in the dark closet.

Pitt faced Raven. "I've seen you knock the bungs from kegs of brew," he said, "so I know you have a hammer in the back room. Go get it, and hope you can find some nails."

Anna B'Lee said in a level voice, "Chester doesn't like close spaces. He'll surely go berserk in there."

"All the better," Pitt said. He pointed the knife as if it were a gun at Raven, who hurried into the back room.

The chair wedged beneath the doorknob inched forward. Pitt shoved it back in place. Realizing his predicament, Fortuna began pounding on the other side of the heavy oaken door. Pitt ignored the desperate drumbeat. He had the situation under control. There was no way out of the closet. And there was no way out the back of the building from the storeroom. Chester Fortuna was going nowhere. Raven would soon return with what Pitt had requested. Otherwise Pitt's knife would see some use.

No one in the tavern moved until Raven appeared with the hammer and a handful of nails. He laid them on the edge of a table near Pitt and quickly retreated to a safe distance.

Pitt gave each and every person a warning glare, then clamped the knife in his teeth, grabbed the hammer and nails, and set to work. He glanced to the side occasionally to be sure no one was about to attack him or might try to escape. The hammer now pounded the door along with Fortuna's fists, sounding louder, clearer notes of doom. Nail after nail went deep into the wood, fastening door to frame as if they were one.

By the time Pitt was finished, the pounding from inside the closet had lessened, grown fainter. Fortuna was getting weaker.

There was silence for a while. Everyone in the bar looked at everyone else.

Then a faint sound could be heard. A high, metallic clinking, over and over.

"Copper bowls," Raven said. "There are some copper bowls stored in there and he must be clanking them together to make noise because his fists are getting sore and bloody."

"He doesn't want us to forget him in there," Anna B'Lee said. "He couldn't survive the thought of that."

Mary moved closer to the closet door. Everyone winced, thinking Pitt would take the knife from where it was now tucked in his belt and go after her. But Pitt merely stood and watched her in grim amusement, knowing there was no way for her to budge the heavy door from its frame.

"Chester?" Mary called. "Chester, can you hear me?"

The faint metallic clinking seemed faster but weaker. It could barely be heard.

"You've got to stop this!" Mary said to Pitt. "Let the poor man out. He's claustrophobic. He's going mad in there!"

"As well he deserves to," Pitt said. He glared at his wife. "It's you who put him there, and there he stays."

Mary leaped at the door and gripped the knob. She began turning it, tugging it, accomplishing nothing. Finally, resigned that her struggles with the door were futile, she hurled herself at Pitt. He shoved her away hard, and she fell sprawling to the floor among overturned chairs.

She stayed down, staring up at her husband with a searing hatred.

"This has gone far enough," Raven said, but he didn't move.

"Try to stop it and you'll eat this knife," Pitt said.

The faint clinking of the metal bowls was barely audible now, along with another sound that might have been wailing.

"There's a bottle of wine in there at the back of the top shelf," said Raven, "if only the poor devil could find it in the dark."

"He could use it," Apier said. "Ease his pain and help him stay sane."

"He won't find it," Pitt said confidently. "He panicked and he's useless now. He's broken. It's a mercy not to let him out."

"Isn't breaking him enough for you?" Mary asked her husband, from where she sat on the floor.

"Not nearly enough."

"You're insane!" Mary cried.

Anna B'Lee got down off her bar stool and walked over to Mary, then helped her to her feet and stood with her arms around her while the muffled screams of Mary's lover became more feeble.

No one dared to move. They could only listen as another human being went mad. It wasn't difficult for them to imagine themselves in Fortuna's place in the dark closet. It was easy to understand that it was his vertical coffin. Occasionally the desperate screams were interrupted by the faint and futile clinking of the metal bowls.

"The bowls, bowls, bowls . . ." Poe muttered, hunched over pen and paper.

Then came the most chilling sound of all. The screams and clinking stopped, and Fortuna emitted peals of shrill and maniacal laughter. Whatever sanity he had left would soon cease to exist.

Pitt grinned. "See, he's laughing. Having a grand time in there, he is. Joking with us. Chester the jester."

No one commented. They could only be still and silent, paralyzed by the horrible cackling that wafted from the closet. Faint though it was, the sound was unbearable.

It was Apier who broke the horror of listening to it.

"You've got to stop this!" he shouted at Pitt. "You're driving us all mad!" Suddenly there was a long razor in Apier's right hand.

He swung it back and forth at the end of his dangling arm, and then launched himself at Pitt, who sidestepped and slashed with his knife in a swift horizontal arc.

The razor clattered to the floor. Empty-handed, Apier staggered backward and collapsed to a sitting position next to an overturned chair, his legs straight out in front of him. A long, sideways cut on his forehead spilled blood onto his shirt and pants.

Anna B'Lee took a step and reached to where a wadded rag lay on the bar. She bunched the rag tight and tossed it to the dazed Apier. It took him several seconds even to know the rag was on the floor beside him. Then he picked it up, folded it neatly, and held it to the cut in his forehead. It lessened the flow of blood, but not by much. Blood covered Apier's face like a mask of red death. He lay back, staring at the ceiling beams, holding the folded, filthy rag to his forehead.

There was complete silence now from the closet. In its way, it was even more terrible than Fortuna's muted insane laughter.

Grinning his own maniac's grin, Pitt made his way slowly to the tavern door.

"Get out!" Mary screamed. "Out! Out! Out!" Hers was a plaintive, shrieking plea beyond rage.

Pitt looked as if he might say something. Then he clamped his lips together, unbolted the door, and pushed outside amid an invading flurry of cold air and rain.

It was Anna who first approached the closet door, but once there she had no idea what to do. She reached out a hand and tugged at the knob, but the door was immovable. It might as well have been part of the solid brick wall.

Raven went back into the storeroom and shortly returned carrying a long pry bar. He picked up the hammer Pitt had left on the floor, and with it and the pry bar began removing nails from the oak door and frame.

Each of the patrons of Dark Destiny glanced at the others. No one was sure what they'd find inside the closet, what Fortuna might have become in the forge of his insanity, and they were afraid to look.

Raven cursed, then tossed aside the chair wedged beneath the knob and threw open the door.

Mary Roget screamed.

There was Fortuna, drawn back and curled like an infant in a corner of the closet. His face was frozen in a horrible mask of mad laughter, but he made only soft whimpering noises. His eyes were unblinking and without reason. He was seeing only inward to his private and eternal hell.

"I'll see if I can find Pitt," Anna B'Lee said in a sad voice. No one answered or looked at her as she went out the door into the night.

"She'll no doubt summon the police, or have someone do it for her," Raven said, and made his way behind the bar. He helped himself to a large drink.

There was nothing to be done for Fortuna but stay near him and perhaps provide some small comfort. This the patrons of Dark Destiny did, while one by one they went to the bar and tossed down generous drinks poured by Raven.

When it was Poe's turn, he tilted back his head and swallowed his whiskey in one gulp. The searing liquid plunged like purging fire to his stomach. He let out a long breath.

"Thank you, Raven."

"For once and for all, it's Reagan," said the bartender.

"May I quote you?" Poe asked. He extended his glass for a second drink.

"No more," Raven said, and took the glass and placed it and the bottle beneath the bar.

Shortly thereafter the police arrived. Dupin told them all that they needed to know, and then more. They led Fortuna away to where the poor man might be confined and treated, but held the patrons of Dark Destiny in the tavern for several hours, making sure everyone's story dovetailed with everyone else's.

Poe spent much of this time alone at his table, pondering weak and weary with paper and pen.

He paused when one of the policemen recited to the others a description of Montresor Pitt.

"There's a man matches such a description was wielding a knife five blocks from here," said a policeman with a massively bushy mustache. "Covered with blood, he was. When someone tried to take the knife from him, he cut his own throat and bled to death."

Mary's intake of breath was a shriek of pain. Pitt was, after all, her husband. After all his jealousies, her denials, his rages, her beatings, he was still a part of her soul and she would grieve his passing. In his way, he'd been as mad as poor Chester Fortuna, and as helpless.

Anna B'Lee was no longer there to comfort her. It was the beastlike Apier, with a lump of white bandage on his head, who sat by Mary and held her hand.

It was well into the night when everyone left Dark Destiny,

and Raven locked the door behind him. Though they went their separate ways, this dark and dreary night would maintain its hold on them always.

The rain had ceased, but the air was cool and lay on the skin in a way that made individual hairs tingle. The little man who'd pretended along with the tavern's patrons to be Poe paused by a boat rental dock. He stared at the paper on which he'd written the tale of the occurrences in Dark Destiny, decided his account was inadequate, and then crumpled it and tossed it into the water.

As he gazed after the crumpled white mass of paper, his eye caught something else.

The body of a woman floated faceup in the dark water. Her hair was fanned around her face and her clothes were blossomed out with air. Were it not for her paleness and wide-open eyes that saw nothing, it would have been easy to believe she was simply enjoying a swim, floating on her back.

Poe knew in an instant who the woman was—Anna B'Lee. And he knew that where she was floating, the current would soon carry her out to sea.

Home in his comfortable den, the man who'd written the tale of the man who'd written of the violence and death at Dark Destiny, and of finding the woman's floating body, crumpled the paper and tossed it into the fire blazing in the coal grate.

He stood slowly and stretched his aching back, paced restlessly a while before the fire, then poured himself another glass of wine. He sat down again at his desk and began to write.

All that we see or seem . . .

JOHN LUTZ's work includes political suspense, private-eye novels, urban suspense, humor, occult, crime caper, police procedural, espionage, historical, futuristic, amateur detective . . . virtually every mystery subgenre. He is the author of more than forty novels and more than two hundred short stories and articles. His novels and short fiction have been translated into virtually every language and adapted for almost every medium. His latest book is the suspense novel *Night Kills*.

The Tell-Tale Pacemaker

P. J. Parrish

"Nervous? Me nervous?"

I shifted, trying to get comfortable in the hard metal chair.

"Okay, okay," I said, lowering my voice. "I admit it, I get a little nervous from time to time. Who doesn't? But I know what's really going on here. You guys are *really* saying I'm nuts."

They all stared at me. Just sat there behind their table and stared at me. Alice Golub with her steely little eyes sunk in her pink pincushion of a face. Stan DeForest with his shar-pei puss and bad rug. And there in the middle, like some inscrutable shogun, fat fart Reggie Duncan. I couldn't believe my fate lay in the hands of this tribunal of twits.

I wasn't about to say anything more so I waited for them to speak. The charges had already been made. I had been accused of harassing my upstairs neighbor Morty Harmon. And I had been brought before the board to give my side of the story. That's the way it works in Florida condos. Somebody complains about somebody else and it goes to the board. I admit I had complained that my upstairs neighbor was making too much noise. That is how I came to this point—sitting on a folding chair in the social room of Esplanade-by-the-Sea Condominiums in Boca Raton, Florida.

But Zelda Shefferly had been the one who had turned me in. She was the ninety-year-old widow who had the unit next to Morty's, and the old bat made it her business to know everyone else's business at Esplanade. She claimed that I had "done something bad" to poor Morty.

The board members were huddling together and whispering. I picked a piece of lint off my sleeve and waited.

Let me take this time as my own. Can I tell you my side of this? Will you listen? I am sure that if you hear me out, you will sympathize with me, you will understand what I had to do. You won't blame me. Any of us can be driven to do the unthinkable given the right—or wrong—circumstances.

Those three people across the table? I know they won't listen. So let me tell *you* what happened and you be the judge.

It all started with my heart attack. See, I'm the youngest resident at Esplanade. I'm only fifty-six, just one year over the age minimum to even live in the condo. I bought the unit only because it was dirt cheap, in foreclosure after the previous owner keeled over during a bus trip to the Sawgrass Mills outlet mall.

I had been happy enough at Esplanade, keeping to myself, living my little life. That is, until the pains started and the EMTs carted me out with wires strapped to my chest. I was too young for a heart attack! The cardiologist told me I was fine. Sure enough, after an angioplasty and a three-day stay in the hospital,

I was back at Esplanade, playing my Mozart mazurkas, reading my translations of Proust, and exchanging barbs with my parrot, Jules.

But after a day or two, I noticed something odd. The heart attack had sharpened my senses. Suddenly, Sauternes were sweeter, Roqueforts more robust, colors more capricious. That wasn't bad at all. But above all, my sense of hearing was more acute. I heard everything in heaven and on earth. I heard many things in hell.

Am I nuts? Let me tell the rest of my story.

I don't really know when the idea first came to me. But once in my head, it haunted me day and night. I didn't have anything against the old guy upstairs per se. Morty Harmon and I mumbled a hello when we passed each other in the hall but because he was—like most of the Esplanade residents—a good twenty years older than me, I didn't mingle.

I would see him down at the pool every day. After my heart attack I went down each morning to swim laps and he was always there, playing gin with his wrinkled cronies. Morty had just gotten a new pacemaker implanted in his chest and he was proud of his new vitality. Popping Viagra like Tic Tacs, copping feels with the widows in water aerobics, trading his Arnold Palmer Performance Wear polo for a Tommy Hilfiger warmup suit. It was a ridiculous display. I have to say, I didn't give him much mind. Except . . .

Except for the antique ebony-and-gold cane he always kept with him. Morty had been in men's clothing up in Queens and thought of himself as Esplanade's fashion icon. Since retirement to Florida, his idea of sartorial splendor was hot pink Sansabelts. But that cane . . . it was exquisite. Not that I wanted it. I mean, I love antiques. My condo is filled with them. But for Morty Harmon's gold cane I had no desire. Passion there was none.

What bugged me about the cane was the sound it made. That constant *tap-tap-tapping* that announced Morty's every appearance.

I did my best to ignore the cane and its owner, ignore Morty's poolside peacock strutting. But in the end, I think it was his eyes that set me off. Yes, that was it. He had the eyes of a vulture, pale blue with a film over them.

And on that fateful Friday when we bumped into each other in the mail room, it was his vulture eyes that started it all.

Morty was there, depositing his mail into the outgoing slot. He had a habit that drove me crazy, a habit of feeding each letter, one at time, into the slot and watching it to make sure it went down. It took him forever, but I stood there, waiting, gritting my teeth. Finally, he was finished and turned to leave.

That is when those vulture eyes fell on me, and I saw myself. Saw myself getting old and foolish and useless just like him. Saw my heart turning to mush in my chest, and felt my breath growing faint. I saw myself in twenty years, like him, with a mechanical pump ticking in my chest, and my blood ran cold.

And so, little by little, I got this idea in my head to get rid of the old guy upstairs and thus rid myself of that cataractous eye forever.

You see, I could *hear* him. Not just the normal stuff that goes with the concrete floors and thin walls in a condo. Not just the *tap-tap-tapping* of his cane. No, I could hear every move Morty Harmon made.

I could hear the whine of his electric can opener when he made his Beefaroni lunches. I could hear the *snip-snap snip-snap* of his dog's nails on the ceramic tile over my head. I could hear the canned laughter of *Everybody Loves Raymond*. I could hear the slam of every drawer, the bang of every cabinet.

When I was in bed at night, contentedly reading the Moncrieff translation of *Swann's Way*, I could hear the rattle of every bit of trash he fed into the garbage chute. My bedroom, you see, is adjacent to the chute and whenever someone throws something down it, I can hear it. This didn't bother me normally. But Morty . . . he believed in saving the planet and, like his mail, he had the habit of feeding each and every bottle and can into the recycling chute one at a time. He'd feed a bottle in and watch it to make sure it went down. Then he'd feed in the next bottle, the next can. One by one, on and on, driving me nuts.

Okay, this is the part that gets weird. You think I am crazy. Just like the condo board thinks I am crazy. But could a crazy man do what I did? Could a crazy man have been able to pull this off?

I was never kinder to the old man than during the whole week before I killed him. I started by saying hello to him in the mail room. I reinforced it by feigning interest in his ugly pug dog, Winston, offering to feed the beast if Morty was ever away. Gradually, I gained Morty's trust. The fool even gave me a key, "just in case something happened" and Winston needed to be fed.

And then . . . then . . . one night, right after the ten o'clock news, after I was sure he was in bed, I went upstairs, unlocked his door, and opened it—oh, so gently.

I stuck my head in and shined the flashlight. Oh, you would have laughed to see me! I moved the light slowly, very very slowly, so he wouldn't wake up as I crept into his bedroom. Ha! Would a crazy person have been so smart?

I did this for four straight nights—every night at ten—but I always found him asleep. So I couldn't do it. Because it wasn't the old man and his noises that bugged me, it was his ugly, old-man cataractous eye. And I needed to see that eye when I killed him.

So I waited, biding my time for just that right moment. And every morning after, I'd see Morty down in the lobby when he was walking that ugly pug. I'd see him and call out, "Hey Morty, how's things?"

He never suspected a thing, never suspected that every night I looked in on him while he slept. Never suspected that I needed only the right moment for—

"Mr. Polk?"

I was drawn out of my memories and back to the condo social room. I looked at my accusers across the table.

"Do you have anything to say for yourself?"

I could only stare at Reggie Duncan and the others.

"Mr. Polk, I asked if you have anything to say for yourself?"

I shifted in the chair. "I have rights," I said. "I have the right to peace and quiet."

Fat Reggie pursed his lips. "This is a condominium, Mr. Polk, and we have to live in harmony here. We have to respect the rules, and each other's needs and lifestyles. We have to ask you to stop bothering Mr. Harmon."

I kept quiet, even as a kernel of a new idea was forming in my brain. Then it hit me in a flash! I needed to get away from this place. I needed to get away from this world of mah-jongg and casino nights, of petty tyrannies and peephole politics. The low price had lured me in, but it had been a mistake for me to buy here. I didn't belong among these stale pale people! I had life in me!

Alas, the Florida real estate market was in its biggest slump in decades and I knew if I put my unit up for sale now, I would take a bath. There was no escape—for now. I had to wait for the rebound.

I looked at my accusers, feigning contrition. I mumbled something about being a better member of our community. They let me go.

I had nothing more to say to them, of course. But you? I'll finish telling you what happened because I know you won't think I am crazy. I'll tell you because you understand what a hell my existence at Esplanade-by-the-Sea had become. I grew to hate the sight of the old men doing their tai chi on the lawn. Grew to hate the smell of the old women's Arpege. Grew to hate every shuffle of a foot, every click of a denture. For all of it reminded me only of my own creeping mortality. My screened-in porch, with its view of the eighteenth, seemed suddenly to me like a cage from which there was no escape.

As for Morty . . .

His *tap-tap-tapping* haunted me still. So I kept up my nightly visits. By the eighth night, I was going nuts. Here I was, creeping into this guy's bedroom every night and he didn't have a clue! Maybe he heard me, because sometimes he gave a little snort. You'd think I would have pulled back—but no! His bedroom was dark as pitch thanks to those heavy Sears blackout drapes, and his deaf dog never moved, snoring in its bed in the corner.

On this eighth fateful night, I was almost into the room when I tripped on the ebony cane and the old man sprang up in his bed, crying out, "Who's there?"

I froze. For the longest time I stood there in the shadows, waiting. Morty was just sitting up in bed, listening. Just as I had listened to him night after night, harkening to the sounds in the ceiling over my head.

Then, a groan. Not of pain or grief—oh no!—the low groan of mortal terror. I knew that sound. It was the same sound that swelled up in my own chest when, in the dark of night, when all the world slept, the terrors came to me. That awful feeling when my heart skipped a beat and I was sure I was dying.

So I knew what that old man was feeling and even as I felt sorry for him, I had to laugh because I knew that he had been lying there awake hearing me creep around his bedroom and now he was trying to convince himself it was nothing but his imagination.

Imagined sounds. The wind in the bathroom vent. The skitter of pigeons on the balcony rail. The hiss of the sprinklers out on the putting greens. But he could feel Death stalking him. He could feel my presence in the room. And as I stared down into that hideous blue vulture eye, I grew furious, and my ears started picking up a dull sound, like the *tap-tap-tap* of his cane on the floor.

But it wasn't his cane; it was his heart, and the sound of it just made me madder.

I'll tell you that the noise excited me to uncontrollable terror, growing ever louder so that I thought the old fart's heart would burst. And a new anxiety seized me—Zelda Shefferly, the widow who lived next door, would hear it! She heard everything! She knew everything!

Morty's hour had come. With a loud yell, I dragged him to the floor and pulled the mattress over him. His ugly deaf dog, Winston, came to life and ran yelping under the bed. I didn't bother to go after the cur.

Still, I could hear it—I could still hear that damn *tap-tap-tap* of Morty Harmon's heart. Then, finally, it stopped and the bedroom was quiet.

I shoved aside the mattress and examined the corpse. I put my head to his chest. No sound. He was stone dead. His eye would trouble me no more.

Well, let me tell you this. You might have thought I was crazy before this, but you won't when I tell you what I did next. I was so crafty in getting rid of Morty's body! First, I moved him to the bathtub. Then I cut him into pieces. I cut off his head and his arms and his legs. I cut the pieces into small pieces, and then even smaller pieces yet. It wasn't easy because the only tools I had were a Ginsu kitchen knife and a rusted hacksaw, and my heart was flapping in my chest like a dying baby bird from the effort.

But I finished the dreadful task. Then I stuffed the pieces into the extra-ply Hefty bags I found under the kitchen sink. I was careful when I dragged the bags out to the garbage chute in the hall. How convenient that Morty's condo was right next to the chute! How lucky that the old residents of Esplanade-by-the-Sea retired to their nasally sleep so early! How lucky for me that Zelda Shefferly did not emerge to see me in my grisly task!

There was nothing to clean up—no blood whatsoever because I had cut him apart in the tub—ha! ha! Just a good rinse and a swipe of 409. It was about four, still dark as midnight, when I slipped back into my bed, the sweet sound of silence hanging over my head.

It was two days later when I heard the knock at my door. I was sitting out on my balcony, watching the sun sink over the eighteenth green, finishing the Sunday *New York Times* crossword and sipping a fine Médoc (the resinol from the grapes is good for the heart). I was surprised to see Reggie Duncan, Alice Golub, and Stan DeForest at my door. But being ever the gentleman, I invited them in.

Reggie got to the point. He said Zelda Shefferly had complained about hearing noises coming from Morty Harmon's unit. Morty hadn't answered her knocks at his door and hadn't shown up for his gin game at the pool the next day.

I smiled—what did I have to fear?—and I told Reggie that Morty himself had told me he had gone to visit his son in Queens.

When Reggie insisted I accompany him to Morty's apartment, how could I refuse?

Using the super's key, Reggie unlocked Morty's door. I followed the trio in, confident there was nothing inside to condemn me. We went into the bathroom and then the bedroom and still I was calm, confident in my perfect triumph.

Finally, in obvious frustration, Reggie sat on the edge of Morty's unmade bed, clucking to Alice and Stan that it was odd that Morty had left so suddenly, especially since he was just saying down at the pool that he hated sleeping on his son's lumpy Castro Convertible. I stood there, nodding cheerily. Presently, they started talking about other condo business.

Then, after a while, I found myself getting pale and wishing they would be gone. My head ached and I heard a ringing in my ears. But still they sat there, not talking about Morty now but *tsk-tsking* about the cigarette butts on the pool deck, about how they were going to get everyone to cough up the five-hundred-dollar assessment to repave the parking lot.

The ringing became more distinct and I joined in the talk to drown it out. But the noise didn't let up—until, finally, I realized the noise wasn't in my ears. I felt my skin grow clammy—no doubt I was pale—but I talked more urgently and loudly. Still the noise grew and now it was low and dull and quick.

Tap-tap-tap-tap.

And it wasn't in my head now; it was coming from the wall— the very wall that adjoined the garbage chute!

I gasped for breath but they didn't seem to notice as their talk moved on to the issue of what could be done to make residents pick up their dog poop.

I jumped to my feet and started blathering about visitor parking spaces and bids for sprinkler repairs. But I couldn't drown out the noise. Why wouldn't they leave? I paced the bedroom, as if excited by the trivial concerns of these condo cretins. But still, the sound increased.

Oh God, what could I do? Inside my head, I swore, I raved. But the noise grew louder, louder, louder! And still the three twits prattled on. How could they not hear it? Almighty God, no, no!

They heard! They suspected! They knew! They were making a mockery of my horror!

But anything was better than this agony. Anything was more tolerable than looking at their derisive smiles! I felt that I had to scream or die! And now—again! Hark! That *tap-tap-tap*! Louder! Louder! Louder!

Finally, I grabbed a chair and flung it across the room.

The three of them—Reggie, Alice, and Stan—fell suddenly silent and stared at me. Then, as if they were one person, their eyes swung slowly to the spot where the chair had landed near the bed.

Tap-tap-tap . . .

Winston crawled out from under the bed. It had been his claws scratching on the floor that I heard. My heart seized up in my chest at the sight of him because between his slobbering chops there was a small object.

The deaf dog came forward, stopping in front of me. He released the object. One of Morty Harmon's bloated blue fingers fell to the floor.

"Villains!" I shrieked. "I admit it! I did it! I killed Morty! Go look down in the garbage chute! There! There! It is there you'll find the beating of his hideous heart!"

P. J. PARRISH, a.k.a. KRISTY MONTEE, is the author (with her sister Kelly Nichols) of two series of crime novels featuring biracial private eye Louis Kincaid and female homicide detective Joe Frye. Their books are *New York Times* bestsellers and have won awards from the Private Eye Writers of America and International Thriller Writers. Their short stories have appeared in *Ellery Queen's Mystery Magazine*, Mystery Writers of America's anthologies, and in Akashic Books' *Detroit Noir*. Like Poe, Kris has a love of wine and cats, an appreciation of all that is grotesque and depressing, and a distrust of critics (even though she once earned a living as one). Unfortunately, that is the limit of her kinship to Poe—unless one counts the fact that her second book was nominated for an Edgar.

Seeing the Moon

S. J. Rozan

I'd never even considered trying to take down Peter Boyd. Like everyone else in the art world, I'd heard rumors that his legit gallery trade was only half his business—not the lucrative half—and I personally knew he was a patronizing bigot. Every now and then in the course of a case, when I couldn't avoid calling him—and believe me, I tried—I got no help, just some gasbag lecture about whatever piece I was after as though he were the one with the degree in Asian Art. No question, the guy wasn't on my Christmas card list. But it wasn't personal until he messed with Molly Lo.

With leaf-filtered May sunlight dancing on my office wall, I was doing some creative Web surfing—due diligence on a new gallery a client was wondering about—when my iPhone tore through the calm, bellowing "The East Is Red." The first da-dah, and I was asking, "What's up, homegirl?" I don't keep Molly waiting.

"I have a problem."

"You need a shoulder?"

"I need professional help."

"I'm not touching that."

"Your profession, jerk."

"No kidding. The Thompson's calling Jack Lee? Or wait—you just want a background run on that new guy you're dating."

"For that I wouldn't call an art detective."

"You're right, he's no work of art. But for real? The museum needs me?"

"It just doesn't know it does—and I'd like to keep it that way."

"My lip is zipped. Should I come down?"

"Do you have time today?"

"Be there in ten minutes."

I wasn't showing off; my office is five blocks from Molly's. When your gig is strayed art, a Madison Avenue address gives your clients a warm and fuzzy feeling.

Molly and I met in grad school, U. of Chicago, East Asian Studies, two corn-belt Chinese kids bonding over *tangkhas* and Uta-maros. We passed through and out of an infatuation phase, and then, clutching our degrees, headed for New York as best friends. We both got the jobs we wanted most. Molly loved hers. Me, not so much. In Chicago I'd spent as much time auditing American Lit courses and shooting hoops as in the conservation lab. Molly says that should have tipped me off, and she's right: turned out the gallery assistant shtick bored me out of my skull. So I regrouped, went for a PI license, and now I have fun, making like Sherlock Holmes when someone's Tang horse gallops away. I'm still, you know, getting established, so my location-location-location office is a little spare, which accounts for dancing sunlight being the wall's best feature. But the emptiness just makes people think I practice Zen. And if I could sit still long enough I probably would.

Molly, though, beelined for the gallery ladder, climbing until she bagged her dream job six months ago: the Thompson, a small art museum based around an eclectic, to say the least, private collection. Gordon Thompson, a retired rich person, opens his double brownstone to the public four days a week, with rotating exhibits curated by none other than my rising art-world star, Molly Lo, for whom everything seemed to be coming up roses. Until, apparently, now.

Me, I'd only met Gordon Thompson twice, at openings Molly invited me to. But if he had a reason to think well of me, it would be kind of great. I locked up, grabbed a shot-in-the-dark from the Not-Starbucks on the corner, and sprinted to the rescue. I hoped.

Molly's assistant, Sherry—when you're as cool as Molly, you have people—led me through the front hall and up the grand staircase, past scholar's rocks and cinnabar boxes. Hasui's woodblock print *Kiba* hung at the landing and I stopped to admire it. No one, and I mean no one, makes you feel weather like Hasui Kawase. Sherry waited patiently, then led on, parking me in the Americana room. In case anyone was under the delusion Mr. Thompson was perfect, this room would shatter it. The one area that competes with imperial silks and Ukiyo-e for his attention, and his bucks, is a narrow slice of American history: artifacts of daily living, nineteenth century, eastern seaboard. Molly and I have a theory that's where he was in his last life. That could explain his enlightened-amateur approach to art, something you don't see much these days. And what else could explain this cheerful obsession with spitoons, riding crops, and doilies? Luckily Sherry didn't maroon me there long.

"I'm here to save the day," I announced, arriving in Molly's airy Qing-and-Ming office. "Could you cut down the dazzle, though?" I dropped into a scholar's chair.

"Too much sun?" She started to close the drapes.

"No, you. You look gorgeous. Trouble becomes you."

"Bullshit."

See why I like her? "No, really. Worry makes your cheeks flush or something. So what can I do for you?"

"I made a big mistake."

"Anyone dead? No? Then we can fix it. Tell me."

She sat, not behind her desk but in the other visitor's chair. I'm as Chinese as she is, but the chair looked better on her. "Two weeks ago," she started seriously, "I bought a bronze standing Buddha. Nepal, fifteenth century. It's in the center hall."

"Saw it. Didn't spend much time with it, though."

"Don't bother. It's a piece Mr. Thompson really wanted. There's a hole in the Himalayan collection right about there. We'd been making the auction rounds but nothing caught his eye. Then Peter Boyd called."

"Uh-oh."

She nodded. "He said he'd heard we were looking and he had something we might be interested in."

"I'm getting a bad feeling."

"You should. It's a fake."

"You must've vetted it before you bought it."

"Six ways from Sunday. Mr. Thompson's been in Asia for

awhile, Hong Kong, Shanghai, and Singapore, for the shows, but Boyd sent him photos and the piece grabbed him. He doesn't like doing business with Boyd—"

"Showing good taste."

"—but he really wanted this piece. You know how it is with collectors, something comes along and they just have to have it?"

I nodded; I did know. I count on that to pay my rent.

"He told me to have it looked at and to buy it if it checked out. It's the first time he's let me go ahead on my own. So I called in three different experts. It was the real deal. But the one in the case downstairs, not. Somewhere in there Boyd switched statues on us, Jack. I don't know how."

"How'd you find out?"

"I unpacked it. Cataloged it. Put it out. And then every time I walked by it I got the bad feeling you're getting now. I heard Hans Grolsch was in New York this week, so I asked him to come look at it."

"Happy Hans! I haven't seen him in ages."

"Well, he wasn't so happy with my Buddha. He confirmed it. Total fake."

"You called Boyd?"

"Of course. He said he'd put up with a lot from me already—'dicking around,' he called it—and he's not surprised to hear Hans Grolsch took a swipe at him."

"They have a history?"

"Boyd's very existence offends Hans. He thinks people who're only in it for the money and don't love the art shouldn't be allowed to get their grubby hands on it."

"Another man with good taste. Any possibility he's wrong about your statue?"

"No, and I told Boyd that. He said at this point, caveat emptor. And then, that bastard—!" She stopped, sputtering.

"Wow."

"Wow, what?"

"You're so mad your eyes are actually flashing."

"Jack!"

" 'That bastard . . . ?' "

"That *bastard* said Mr. Thompson was happy with the piece, wasn't he? So I should just leave it where it was, let everyone enjoy it, and no one would have to know the Thompson's new young director spent eighty thousand dollars on a fake."

I whistled. "That bastard."

"Mr. Thompson comes back in three days. What am I going to do?"

"For now, nothing." I unfolded myself from the chair. No great loss: Qing furniture's not all that comfy. "However, *I* am going to see Mr. Boyd."

You may be asking yourself why I bothered. What was he going to do—fall on his knees, confess to the fraud, beg forgiveness, and make restitution on the spot (with a little vig to cover Molly's mental anguish and my fee) now that Jack Lee was on the case?

But it didn't seem sporting not to give him a chance.

Peter Boyd Oriental—that's a bad sign already, right?—occupies a piss-elegant gallery on the same swank stretch of Madison Avenue as the Thompson and me. Boyd, wearing Armani, his short silver hair bristling and his tan glowing, issued a pained smile when he saw me come in. "Oh, my, Charlie Chan."

"If you have to throw around cheap stereotypes, Peter, could you at least go with Chow Yun-Fat? *Sex*-y. I'm here about that tin Buddha you palmed off on the Thompson."

"Oh? Molly Lo feels hard done by, so she's gone to Jack Lee, Boy Detective? That's some nice cultural solidarity there, Jack."

"You want to talk out here, or in private?"

"Given that there are no patrons in the gallery at the moment, that's a rather hollow threat. Still, come in back where we'll be comfortable."

He nodded to his gallery assistant, a faux-hawked kid in an Armani knockoff, and led me into his suite of offices in the back. This was the only gallery I knew with more back-room than front-room space. I mean, who needs a suite of offices? But part of Boyd's juju was to make his buyers feel like serious business was done here, where he showed them prints, netsuke, and graceful Han dancers that he disdained exhibiting in the front gallery for all eyes to see.

And another part was to sell prints, netsuke, and Han dancers of questionable provenance in deals better done where there were fewer eyes—at least that was the rumor.

He turned and fixed his beady stare on me. At five-eleven, I had four inches on him, but I'm such a beanpole our weight class was probably the same.

"The Thompson wants their money back," I said.

"Molly Lo wants the Thompson's money back. And she's not going to get it."

"You want the world to know you sold them a piece of junk?"

"They had it authenticated."

"And you switched it."

"Careful, Jack. You shouldn't make accusations you can't prove."

"You want me to shut up, switch it back. Bundle up the real one and I'll take it with me right now."

"Funny thing about that. I just sold a very, very similar piece to a collector in Singapore. Shipped it over two days ago."

I gave him my best level stare. "Then return the money."

"Come on. Eighty thousand dollars? That's pocket change for Gordon Thompson. As long as pretty Molly keeps her mouth shut, what's really been lost?"

"She can't do that, Peter. Unlike you, she has scruples."

"Oh, ouch."

"You'd better think hard about this."

"Or what? You'll go public? Jack, I suggest *you* think before you stick your foot in your mouth. If it comes out the piece is fake, I'll just say I had no idea."

"You're supposed to be an expert. You'll look like an idiot."

"Molly, Gordon Thompson, and I will all look like idiots, yes. So will the experts they took it to."

"Except Hans Grolsch."

"Good for Happy Hans." Boyd shrugged. "You know what, though? We'll all survive. We'll blush, look shamefaced, and go on."

"You think so? Then let's try it."

He held up a manicured finger. "Except, maybe, for Molly.

They did have it authenticated, so it's not my problem anymore. I won't take it back."

"Not just an idiot, a swindling, tightfisted idiot."

"Maybe. But Molly's problem will be worse. So young and untested, making a foolish mistake so early in her career?"

Bastard wasn't strong enough. "You counted on that, didn't you? That you could paint Molly into a corner."

"It's too bad, but you know as well as I that in situations like this someone has to be sacrificed. And the gods prefer pretty girls to stringy old men."

I met his eyes for a long steady moment. Then I broke off, sighed, and looked around the office. A Japanese scroll on the wall evoked trees and night in three flowing brushstrokes. The characters read, "Barn burned down: now I can see the moon." I let my gaze rest on it, then wander to a nearby case. Four long pipes of teak, gold, ivory, and silver; some slender jade needles; a tiny but elaborately carved whisk broom and pan. Opium paraphernalia, a cove off the Asian art sea. So much was destroyed in the late nineteenth-century anti-opium hysteria that what's left qualifies as rare. This was the only area where Boyd himself collected, working from gusto, not just greed. Whether he smoked the stuff I had no idea, but he was known to be addicted to the gear. Sensing a possibility, I turned from the objects of desire back to the man.

"Those things are beautiful," I said in a conciliatory way.

"Those 'things' are among your peoples' best contributions to civilization."

The compass? The civil service system? Gunpowder? Steamed

little juicy buns? But I wasn't here to debate. "Peter," I said, "is there any chance you have a heart?"

"No. Why?"

I rubbed my mouth, then sighed again. "Because your bogus Buddha is only part of Molly's problem. She'd kill me for telling you this, but she's in hot water already, or about to be. Last week she finished an inventory she probably should have started her first day there. But a big new job like that, you know . . . Anyway, now she's done, and it seems they're missing three Hasuis."

Boyd leaned back, eyebrows raised. "I'd say that's a problem. But maybe they disappeared before her time."

"Likely. But that's why you do inventories. Now she can't prove that."

"Gordon Thompson thinks she took them?"

"God, no. Molly? Anyhow, he's away, so he doesn't know yet. But at best he'll think she's been sloppy with his collection when he finds out. And then to discover she bought your piece of—"

"Which ones?"

"What?"

"Which Hasuis?"

I paused, then told him, *"Rainy Lake in Matsue District, Evening at Soemoncho,* and *Spring Night at Inokashira."*

"I didn't know Thompson owned those." Boyd himself is deep in Hasui. Not because he gives a damn about beautiful lines or subtle inks. But he knows an undervalued artist when he sees one. Some years back he bought up a few private collections, narrowing, if not quite cornering, the market. Thereby driving prices up. Hasui's prints are still not all that costly, in the mid-four or sometimes low five figures. But they're out of reach of, say, me, who can only admire them on gallery walls.

"Thompson's a big Hasui man," I told Boyd. "From before you locked them all up. He doesn't show many at a time—right now, only one—but he has twenty-seven."

Boyd smiled. "From what you say, now twenty-four."

"Peter—"

"No."

I gave him another long look. "You really are a bastard, aren't you?"

"So I hear."

I hadn't been back out on the street two minutes when my iPhone treated Madison Avenue to "The East Is Red."

"Did you get my Buddha?" I could hear Molly holding her breath.

"It already went to Singapore."

"Oh, no! Then my money?"

"I'm working on it. Listen, is Happy Hans still in town?"

"You didn't get anywhere at all with Boyd, did you?" she wailed.

"Well, the best he could do was repeat his suggestion that you leave the fake where it is and let Mr. Thompson enjoy it."

"I can't, and you know it. And now you want to double-check with Hans and see if he could have been wrong? He's not, I told you! Oh, Jack, you were my last hope. I am so sunk!"

"It's a little early for that level of panic."

"What should I do, wait until after lunch?"

"You should give me Hans's number. And then calm down. Go meditate or something."

She did the first, but not the second, and probably not the third. In her position, I wouldn't have either.

Now, you may be thinking Happy Hans is one of those ironic nicknames for some dour German who hasn't smiled since 1964. Not so. Hans Grolsch could be the picture in the dictionary next to *Jolly Dutchman*, if that were in the dictionary. White hair, chubby red cheeks, sparkling blue eyes, huge smile that you couldn't call quick in coming only because it almost never leaves. He's a dealer and appraiser from Delft, but what he really defines is a man who loves his work.

"Jack, my boy!" Hans raised a pilsner glass, already half-drained, when he spied me. We were meeting in the garden of a red-sauce Italian restaurant, food he claims he can't get in Holland. "You look well!" If I'd been at death's door he'd probably have said, "You look awful!" with equal enthusiasm.

"So do you, Hans." Sitting, I grinned, something no one can help doing around Hans. Except maybe Molly, yesterday.

"Ah, yes, the Buddha." Even Hans sighed after we'd ordered our spaghetti Bolognese, and Hans his second Sugar Hill, and I brought up Molly's problem. "They were rooked, you know. It's actually very good, bronze with an applied patina, I think a lost-wax casting from the original. Worth possibly twenty-five hundred dollars."

"Any chance you're wrong?"

He threw me a pitying look, tucked a napkin under his chin,

and reached for the bread. "It's a shame. Such a nice girl, Molly. But a man like Boyd—myself, I do not do business with him."

"Molly told me he gives you hives."

"Hives, he makes me itch? Yah, that's good, Jack! Yes, it's bad enough, the people who buy and sell art as a commodity, with no love. But to cheat also, this is abhorrent. Such men must be avoided. You cannot win against a man like that."

That pronouncement was downright gloomy, particularly considering the source. I contemplated it, then contemplated our antipasto.

"Let me buy you a drink after work," I suggested over the iPhone to Molly as I strolled to my office after lunch.

"Buy me a ticket out of town and a new identity."

"You don't need that."

"You made a miracle?"

"A couple of martinis and you'll think I did. Come on, it'll make you feel better."

"It'll only make me think I feel better. But if that's all I can get, I'm in."

Molly and I were up late, going from martinis to pad Thai to the late show at Drom, which involved more martinis. I shelled out for all of it. It was the least I could do.

I don't know when Molly got to work the next morning, but as I was stumbling along Madison toward my office sometime near noon, she called me.

"I just heard from Peter Boyd," she said.

"Do you have to bring him up when I feel like crap?"

"You shouldn't drink so much."

"You were three ahead by the end of the night!"

"I could always hold it better, why do you keep trying? Boyd wants me to go to his gallery."

"Oh." I rubbed my aching eyes. "Did he say why?"

"No. But I'm not going alone."

"Sigh. Okay, I'll meet you. Just give me time for coffee."

I grabbed a double venti, plus a bagel for belly ballast. By the time we rolled into Peter Boyd Oriental I didn't have any more of a headache than the one he usually gives me.

"Molly, my dear. And Jack." Boyd smiled like the shark he is. "Jack, you look awful." He said it with almost as much joy as Happy Hans would have, though for different reasons.

Molly, on the other hand, looked stunning in gallerina black, her hair flowing to her shoulders like ebony silk. She pursed her lips and allowed him to lead us to the office suite, where she sat primly and didn't speak. Boyd smiled again and didn't speak either.

Someone had to break this silence or we'd all suffocate. "Okay, Peter, we're here," I said.

"*You* weren't invited," Boyd pointed out. He turned to Molly. "I have something you'll want."

"My eighty thousand dollars?"

He chuckled as though he appreciated her funny joke. "No. These." From a folio he lifted three heavy sheets, each wrapped in acid-free paper. One by one he liberated them and laid them on the desk. Hasui, *Rainy Lake in Matsue District*, *Evening at Soemoncho*, and *Spring Night at Inokashira*. And good impressions, too.

Molly's jaw dropped, though she recovered fast. Shooting me a glare, she asked Boyd, "What makes you think I'm interested in these?"

"Your boyfriend here. Don't worry, I won't tell. Jack, try not to look so abashed. Truly, you did Molly a favor. If you slip these into the collection, Gordon Thompson will never know. Not too many editions of these three were made. The paper's all the same, the ink. What Gordon had was probably so close to these that he'll never be able to tell they've been replaced."

While Boyd was yakking on I examined the prints. They were the real thing, and breathtaking.

"Jack," said Molly icily, "I'm going to kill you."

"That would be all right with me," said Boyd. "But please pay for these first."

"How much?" I asked, to see if I could be useful.

"Fifteen thousand."

"For the three?"

"Each."

"Are you insane? Hasui's not going for anything near that!"

"Most Hasuis don't have the power to save a promising career."

"Thirty-five hundred each for these two, forty-five for *Inokashira*."

"Don't make me laugh. And this isn't a rug shop in the casbah. My offer's firm and it's not going to last."

"Where do you expect Molly to get that kind of money?"

"She can borrow it from you for all I care."

"Are you two through?" Molly's angry words sliced through

our dickering. "Jack? Shut up. Don't help, okay? And Peter, you can stick your offer in your vault." She settled back in her chair and gave a surprising little smile. "These are beautiful but I don't need them."

"Oh, how lucky," Boyd said mock kindly. "Gordon's have turned up?"

"No. But I have a line on something else, something he's so excited about he'll forgive me for the Hasuis, which aren't my fault anyway, and your scrap-heap Buddha, too."

"Is that a fact?"

Molly, crossing her awesome legs, arched a single eyebrow. I didn't know she could do that.

"All right, you want me to guess. Why not?" Boyd dripped condescension. Molly was being kind of obnoxious, though, I had to admit. Pretending to think hard, Boyd stared into space. "I know he's been looking for both cloisonné and carved jade lately."

"And you have some beauties to sell, I'm sure," I said.

"Jack," said Molly, "did I mention 'shut up'? I really don't need your help, or whatever this is. And Peter, forget it. Besides the fact that I'll never, ever do business with you again, this piece isn't even Asian. It's Americana."

"Oh." Boyd deflated. "Junk, you mean."

"To you, maybe. Not to Mr. Thompson. He's thrilled."

"Whatever it is, I suggest you buy these anyway. It can't hurt to have his Hasui collection intact when he gets back."

"If you were giving them away for free I wouldn't take them."

"Twelve each for these," said Boyd. "Thirteen for *Inokashira*."

"If I keep saying no, will you keep coming down until you get to free?" Molly looked delighted, as though this were a game.

"No."

"Then I might as well go." She stood. I noticed she hadn't said "we." "Hans Grolsch will be coming by with my new purchase. I don't want to miss him."

"Wait," Boyd said. "You're not going without revealing the secret of this wondrous artifact?"

"Oh, didn't I say?" Molly smiled and paused. I rolled my eyes. It was clear she'd had no intention of leaving the room without dropping her bombshell. "It's an opium pipe. Edgar Allan Poe's."

Peter Boyd blanched. Wow, I thought. Good for Molly.

Boyd, recovering, demanded, "What are you talking about?"

"And it's beautiful, too. Though Mr. Thompson would want it no matter what, for its historical importance. It's been in private hands since Poe pawned it in 1842. Never on the market before." Her eyes widened theatrically. "Oh, that's right! Peter, you collect opium paraphernalia, don't you? Would you like to see it?"

From her purse she took a sleek digital camera. She clicked on a stored photo and passed the camera to Boyd. She was smiling like the cat that ate the canary and when he saw the photo he turned apoplectic, like the cat that had been planning to. He stared at the screen and she stared at him and no one except me seemed to care whether I saw the photo, too. So I leaned over Boyd's shoulder.

Molly was right, the pipe was beautiful. A richly carved ivory bowl and mouthpiece, a silver stem inlaid with what looked like jade. "That's jade," Molly told Boyd. "On the stem."

Boyd looked up at her.

"Poe bought it one of the few times in his life when he was flush," Molly said. "Then pawned it when he went broke again. The pawnbroker was an admirer of Poe's writing. Gave him a good price and never sold it. It's been in his family since."

Boyd found his voice. "Where——"

"Happy Hans," Molly said. "That's why he's in New York. The family moved to England in 1896 when they started to come up in the world. Now they've come down again so they're selling off their art. Hans thought he'd do better with the Americana here than in Europe. He brought a few things, including this, specifically to offer to Mr. Thompson. He didn't know Mr. Thompson was away, but it doesn't matter. As you know, Peter, you stinker, Mr. Thompson will buy from photos, as long as he's sure the piece is genuine."

Boyd ignored the dig. "And this is?"

"Hans authenticated it. There's still the pawn ticket, for one thing. And a lab Hans consulted says that because of the chemical nature of opium residue there may be recoverable DNA. They haven't tested for that yet, though."

That undone test didn't seem to bother Boyd; he knew as well as anyone in the business that Hans Grolsch never signed off on a piece he wasn't sure about. Boyd turned slowly to look at the pipes and jade picks in his paraphernalia case. "That fat Dutchman. This is *my* area. Why didn't he offer it to me?"

"Because," I said, muscling in on Molly's victory, "Happy Hans is just one among thousands who won't do business with a worm like you."

Boyd must have been seriously rattled because he ignored my slur, too. "How much?" he asked Molly.

"What do you care?"

"How much!"

She blinked. "A hundred thousand."

"For a pipe?" Boyd snorted. "I've never paid more than fifty."

"Coleridge's went for a hundred and twenty-three last year," I reminded him. "And not to you, as I recall. You were beat out by Simon White in London."

"That fat Brit. Why is everyone in this business fat? Sit down. Both of you, sit down!"

Molly looked at me.

"Sit down!"

I shrugged. We sat down.

"I want this," Boyd said.

"Too bad," said Molly.

"No. Too bad for Gordon Thompson. What you need to do, Molly, is get in touch with Happy Hans and arrange for him to sell it to me, and only me."

"Why would I do that?"

"Because, little Molly, if you don't, I'll tell Gordon you were not only part of the scheme to defraud him of his Buddha, but that it was in fact your idea."

Total, total silence.

Finally Molly squeaked, *"What?* You can't. You wouldn't."

Boyd smiled thinly. "I think I'll even tell him you took the lion's share of the proceeds. If I sound aggrieved, you can be sure he'll believe me."

"Peter—" I started.

"Jack, let me echo Molly: shut up."

"No!" I jumped from my seat. "Listen, you can't do this."

"Watch me."

"Goddamn it—"

"Jack, if you want to be Sir Galahad and ride to Molly's rescue, why don't you stop yelling at me and convince her I'm serious and she should call Hans right away?" He was speaking to me, but looking directly at Molly.

"Peter," I said, "Hans won't sell you the pipe no matter what Molly says. Remember, he won't do business with you?"

Boyd's brow furrowed. "That's probably true. All right. Molly, you'll buy it and convey it to me. I'm not even going to insist that you dicker with Hans over the price."

Molly looked at him wildly. "I can't! Peter! Mr. Thompson wants it so much!"

"You can tell him he got beat out for it. It happens all the time. He'll get over it."

"But he'll be mad at Hans, and Hans will tell him he *did* sell it to me."

"That's your problem. Maybe you can offer Hans some other . . . consideration."

It was impossible to miss what that meant. Molly's cheeks flared.

I took a step toward him. *"Peter—!"*

"Oh, Jack, drop the histrionics. What are you going to do, karate-chop me? Go on, both of you, get out of here. Molly, bring me that pipe tomorrow, or—when did you say Gordon would be back? In three days? Or you have three days to find another job."

Molly rose in a wobbly way and stood for a moment. Then without warning she rounded on me, eyes practically shooting sparks. "This is your fault!"

"*Me?*"

"If you hadn't shot off your mouth about the Hasuis we wouldn't be here. He'd never know about the pipe!"

"I was trying to help."

"Thanks a lot!"

"Molly, my dear." Boyd stepped between us as though Molly were about to sock me, which she might have been. "Jack's not the one who brought up Poe's pipe in an effort to lord it over me, is he?"

That brought another silence. Molly was glaring like she'd make Boyd's head explode if she could.

"Tomorrow," said Boyd. "And by the way, I close at four."

"Wait," I said.

"For what?"

"First," I drew a breath, collecting myself, "you'll pay with a cashier's check."

"Jack! Don't you trust me?" Boyd broadly faked surprise.

"And second, you'll throw in the Hasuis."

Now the surprise was real. "I'll do what?"

"You can't leave Molly with nothing. She's got your junk Buddha and now she's lost Poe's pipe. Your *blackmail*," I snarled the word, "is supposed to save her job. If Mr. Thompson finds his Hasuis gone, too, that'll be the last straw. He'll can her, so why should she do this in the first place?"

Molly looked as if she were going to cry.

"Coleridge's pipe went for a hundred and twenty-three," I reminded Boyd. "Poe's at a hundred is a steal."

Boyd cocked his head and relented. "All right. Bring the pipe and you can have the Hasuis. They're not worth more than ten thousand together anyway. And of course I'd like to see Molly keep her job." He smiled. "Then we can do business again in the future."

The pipe did get conveyed to Boyd the next day, not by Molly, but by me. "I don't even want to be seen going in and out of there anymore," she said. So I waited as late in the day as I dared, just to make Boyd sweat, then brought the pipe and resisted the urge to shove it where it would do the most good. I made him give me the cashier's check, which I held up to the lamp to check the watermark, and the Hasuis, which I also examined, before I handed the pipe over. Seeing the love light in Boyd's eyes as he unwrapped it almost made me think he might be a human being. It was truly beautiful: the ivory bowl intricately carved, brought to a rich gold from heat and smoke; the jade inlays on the silver stem glinting provocatively.

"The paperwork?" he snapped at me, pulling his eyes from his new darling.

I handed over an envelope. Boyd slid out a cardboard square in a protective plastic sleeve—the pawn ticket, countersigned by the pawnbroker and the customer—and a Certificate of Authenticity from Hans Grolsch's gallery in Delft.

Boyd's forefinger gently rubbed the pipe's silver stem. Without looking at me, he said, "Jack, it's been a pleasure. Now get out."

• • •

When I got to Molly's office I found one of the Qing chairs cradling Hans Grolsch's beefy behind. I hesitated. Molly looked at me with anxious eyes. "Jack . . . ?"

Glancing at Hans, I handed Molly my portfolio. She opened it and, one by one, took the Hasuis out. Hans stood to look at them. "Well, these really are beautiful, aren't they?" he said.

Molly looked from the prints to me. I kept the stone face going another minute, then cracked. "So's this," I cackled, slapping Boyd's check down.

Molly drew a sharp breath. She put out a tentative hand, as though the check might bite her. Hans craned for a look. For a moment all eyes were fixed on that paper rectangle.

Then Hans laughed, a booming explosion of glee. Then Molly laughed, like chimes. Then I laughed. Then Hans whomped me on the back. I gasped for air as he said, "Jack, my boy! You did it!"

"*We* did it," I wheezed. "It would never have worked without you, Hans. But Molly's the real star. That eyebrow thing—did you practice in a mirror? And DNA in the opium residue! Where did that come from?"

Molly looked up from the ledger on her desk and smiled. "Just a little improvisation. Glad you liked it. Here, Hans." She handed him a check. "Are you sure it's enough? I hate to see you not make a profit."

"My dear, I'd have paid to be part of this! Twelve thousand is nearly what I could have expected for that pipe, so beautiful but without provenance. And the other eight will neatly cover the fee of Jack's delightful friend, who so skillfully created the pawn ticket."

"Abie does good work," I said.

"Yes. Though I must tell you, as pleased as he was with his results on the ticket, he became peevish when I insisted his forgery of my own signature be bad enough to be obvious, if need be. He made me promise to make *you* promise never to reveal the source of such sloppiness."

"The secret will go to my grave."

"I have one question, though," Molly said. "What if Poe's opium pipe does come on the market?"

I stared at her. "You just have to have something to worry about, don't you? First, if Peter ever gets his Jockeys in a knot over this, we deny knowing what the hell he's talking about. What pipe? We sold him a pipe? Never happened, he's tripping. What can he say? And Hans is completely insulated. Forged signature on no doubt stolen letterhead."

"People might even think it was Peter who forged it!" Hans grinned as the thought dawned on him.

I nodded. "But second, it won't. The pipe. Come to market."

"Why not?"

"God, I love that eyebrow thing! Because, as you'd know if you'd ever stepped outside Cochrane-Woods to take an American Lit course with me, there is no such pipe. Edgar Allan Poe never smoked opium."

"Come on. I thought he was a big druggie."

"Slander. Though he did take a little opium from time to time."

"That's what I—"

"But in the form of laudanum. Itty bitty liquid drops. He never smoked it. There is no pipe."

"Why, Jack Lee, you sneaky—"

"Hey, you two, lower the juice on the smiles, would you? You're blinding me."

We made plans to regroup at the Beatrice Inn in an hour, where Molly and I could get major mojitos, Hans could get draft Ommegang, and we could people-watch the coolest crowd in New York and not see anyone cooler than we were. We'd have gone right away, but Molly needed to put Boyd's money in the bank so the Thompson's account would be whole when Thompson got back. His Hasui collection would be improved, too; he'd never owned any of these prints, which is why I'd picked them to get this ball rolling. Molly was going to tell Thompson that I'd extorted them out of Peter Boyd in exchange for not exposing his switcheroo. That, plus Hans's lavish praise for her valor in calling him in to examine the Buddha even after she'd spent the money, and also the fine-tuned instincts that made her uncomfortable with the fake in the first place, would no doubt ensure her continued employment at the Thompson. Maybe even get her a raise. And next time I met him at an opening, Mr. Thompson might remember my name.

So we split to run our errands. I wanted to drop by my office, too; I had my own fee to deal with. Molly was adding only two Hasuis to Thompson's stash. Me, I was anxious to see how the full moon at the center of *Spring Night at Inokashira* looked in the sunlight dancing on my office wall.

S. J. ROZAN grew up in the Bronx and as a child visited the Poe Cottage many times, where she looked for but never found the Tell-Tale Heart. The author of ten novels and dozens of short stories, she's won most of crime-writing's major awards, including two Edgars, which make the cat-sitter so nervous he puts hats over their faces whenever S.J.'s out of town.

Challenger

Daniel Stashower

Annabel and I decided to mount an expedition to Mars. The idea came to me in fourth period social studies, and by the end of afternoon study hall I had drawn up plans for a homegrown version of the space shuttle, to be called *The Spirit of West Columbus*.

It would be difficult, I admitted, but not impossible. The crew cabin would be fashioned from the rusted-out Dodge Dart behind the mill. The oxygen supply would be continually replenished from empty Pringles cans stored in the trunk. The booster assembly would be a series of interlocking trash cans filled with a propulsive vinegar-and-baking-soda fuel of my own devising. I could see no flaw in the plan.

The *Challenger* disaster was still very fresh. The whole school had seen it happen on live television, during a science assembly. We'd been getting heavy doses of crisis management in the days following—letters to the McAuliffe family, poetic tributes to the brave men and women of NASA, that sort of thing. I was a huge space geek and I suppose it hit me as hard as anyone, but after a day or so the shock gave way to a kind of righteous indignation. That's when I decided to take matters into my own hands. When NASA grounded the shuttle program, it seemed that it was up to me and Annabel to put America back in space.

Annabel did her best to punch holes in the scheme. That was the pattern in those days. I had the big ideas; she had the common sense. I'd toss out some wild plan and she'd blow it apart, like shooting skeet. *Are you nuts? What makes you think we can build a rocket? The government spent billions of dollars on the shuttle! We only have $14.67 between us! How are we supposed to build a rocket?* That was the beauty of it, I explained. We were recycling. Also, we would sell tickets to the launch. In the end she went along with it. She usually did.

Annabel and her mother moved to the neighborhood when I was ten and she was nine. Her full name was Annabel Lee. The name meant nothing to me, but my mother, a substitute English teacher, went into raptures. "Oh!" she cried. "Annabel Lee! Like the poem!" She clasped her hands and tilted her head back, straining to recall the words:

> *It was many and many a year ago,*
> *In a kingdom by the sea,*
> *That a maiden there lived whom you may know*
> *By the name of Annabel Lee*

My mother did this every time she saw Annabel. Every single time. Annabel just rolled her eyes. It didn't make a whole lot of difference to me that she was named for a girl in a poem. In general, we managed to overlook the fact that she was a girl at all. She was a tomboy, complete with scabby knees and a Buckeyes cap, although from the first my mother had her pegged for a looker. "She'll break hearts, that one," my mother always said. "Just like the girl in the poem. *In her sepulchre there by the sea.*" I couldn't see it myself. Not then.

We spent most of our time in her backyard, where there was a tire swing and four or five decent climbing trees. In bad weather, we went down to the basement rumpus room, which somebody had done up with knotty pine and Def Leppard posters. We rarely went to my house. My house was boring, according to Annabel. My mother's idea of fun was carrot sticks and Yahtzee. If you'd been especially good—if, say, you finished your piano lesson early— you might get to watch *Family Feud*.

There were no rules at Annabel's house. A lot of the finer points of child rearing had fallen away with the arrival of Husband Number Three. His name was Todd and he was about ten years younger than Annabel's mom, so Mrs. Lee spent a lot of time trying to project a sense of youth and vitality. She wore leg warmers and listened to Culture Club on a Walkman. Somebody once told her that she and Annabel looked like sisters, and she clung to it for dear life. "Hey, Sis!" she would call out when we came through the door. "How was school, Sis?"

Todd mooched around the house in a pair of black jeans and a seemingly infinite collection of concert T-shirts—Pink Floyd, Jeff Beck, ELO. He drove an orange Pacer and spent a lot of time talking about "his journey of self-discovery," in which beer and pretzel rods seemed to figure heavily. I rarely saw him in the same room with Annabel's mom, and when I did, she treated him like some kind of newly arrived foreign exchange student. "Would you like some bark tea? Would you like to borrow my aroma therapy tape?" I was a kid who honestly believed that he was going to Mars, but even I knew this marriage was doomed.

Annabel and I worked on our mission plan for about five straight weeks. I filled a ream of graph paper with schematics and blowups of various phases of the design process. One particular drawing, which I labeled "Alpha Seven," seemed to me to be almost unimaginably sleek and powerful—a combination of an F-14 and Speed Racer's Mach 5. On the back of the page, I sketched out notes for the speech that I would deliver when we made our retro-burner landing on the White House lawn. I seem to recall that it made good use of the phrase "And lo! A child shall lead them!" Most of all I imagined the sensation of stepping out onto the surface of Mars for the first time—the thrill of weightlessness as we made our way toward a vast, uncharted horizon.

Launch was set for July Fourth. In my head, each step of the launch sequence took on weight and color. I could just about feel the surge of the primary ignition as we lifted off, and the concussive jolt as each booster phase flared up and dropped away behind us. What could go wrong? If anything, I told Annabel, the design was too ingeniously simple—I began to worry that someone else would get there first.

The only sticking point, I believed, was hitting on just the right formula for the booster fuel. We ran a series of preliminary tests using a balsa wood model from the rocket derby, and found that the familiar mixture of vinegar and baking soda would not provide the necessary lift. We expanded the formula to include any potentially combustible element we could lay our hands on. We started small with Rice Krispies, Pop Rocks, and some old perfume. Over time we strayed into more dangerous terrain— mashed-up firecrackers, ammonia, green "power pellets" from a rodent bait station. The idea was to get something that fizzed and spurted when mixed in an Erlenmeyer flask. The range of each splatter was carefully marked with a tiddlywink chip placed around the blast perimeter. The means by which these random spurts might translate into vertical thrust remained vague.

It struck me that Annabel wasn't quite getting into the spirit of the thing. She had been out of it for several days, pale and listless. I put it down to the lingering effects of the *Challenger* disaster—she had cried for a day and a half—or perhaps a steely, if tight-lipped, resolve to recapture America's lead in the space race.

It came to a head on the first day of spring. I was elaborating on a cunning idea to replace the shuttle's troublesome O-rings with a combination of duct tape and rubber cement. Annabel was lying facedown on a beanbag chair, and hadn't moved in about half an hour.

"Hey, lizard-head," I said. "Are you listening to me?"

She said something I couldn't hear.

"What?"

There was a vinyl creak as she lifted her head. "Do you think I'm pretty?" she said.

"Say again?"

"You heard me."

I looked down at my hands. I was holding the Alpha Seven drawing and a bottle of NuGrape. "Pretty?" I said.

She peeled herself off the beanbag chair and pushed the hair out of her eyes. "It's not a hard question, Doug. Do you think I'm pretty?"

I scratched a mosquito bite. I knew that we were drifting into uncharted waters. Was she pretty? I took a hard look.

"Yeah," I said. "I guess so. Whatever."

She wandered over to a cloudy mirror that was leaning against a pile of cinder blocks. She swiveled her shoulders a little and canted her hips. "Some people think so," she said.

"My mother says I'll grow into my looks," I said.

Annabel combed her hair with her fingers. "I need a boyfriend," she said. "Right away."

"A boyfriend?"

She turned away from the mirror. "God, you're dense today. A boyfriend. I need a boyfriend right away. Do you want to be my boyfriend?"

I set down my NuGrape. "Will it jeopardize the mission?"

Her eyes went flat. "No," she said. "No, Doug, it won't jeopardize the mission."

"What would I have to do?"

She gave an exaggerated sigh. "Nothing. You don't have to do anything."

"Then why do you need a boyfriend so bad?"

She looked away. "It's— There's this guy. He's bothering me. If I say I have a boyfriend, he'll leave me alone."

"How do you figure?"

"It's a guy thing. They call it 'marking your territory.' No guy would try to steal someone else's girl. Not if he's marked his territory. I'm surprised you don't know that."

I felt the back of my neck tighten. My spider sense. "Who is it? Am I going to have to get in another fight?"

Another fight. Sixteen months earlier I had been knocked backward over a balance beam. I'd stayed out of school for three days.

"You don't have to get into a fight. Believe me."

"Is it Rufe?" Rufe was one of those kids that they used to call special. He had a fuzz mustache and a bleached scar over one eye where a hammerhead M-80 had caught him.

"It's not anybody from school," Annabel said.

"Who, then?"

She shrugged. "It's not anybody you know. I just—I just need a boyfriend. You want to be my boyfriend or not?" She tapped her foot. "Don't let me down, here. I haven't got all day."

I glanced down at the Alpha Seven diagram. It was clear that we weren't going to get back to work until I gave her an answer. "Yeah," I said. "Okay. I'll be your boyfriend. Why not?"

She looked at me for a long time, nodding her head slowly as if making up her mind about something. "Show me your hand," she said.

I stuck out my hand and she turned it over, studying my palm.

"What are you doing?" I asked.

"Stop talking," she said. "For once."

With a sudden movement, she lifted her shirt and stuck my

hand underneath. The room turned. I felt something in my head drop away and burn. "This is what boyfriends do," Annabel said.

I don't know how long we stood there. Maybe five minutes, maybe an hour. I just remember that after a while the fluorescent lights overhead started to rattle as someone came walking through the kitchen above. Annabel jumped back just as the door at the top of the basement steps flew open. Todd's voice drifted down from the kitchen: "You kids down there?"

"Yeah," I said. Annabel flopped down on the beanbag chair and I picked up my NuGrape.

Todd came down the wooden steps, stumbling near the bottom. His hair looked as if he'd spilled shellac down one side. "Well, well," he said, "if it isn't Rat Boy."

Rat Boy. Because my father was an exterminator. Todd thought this was hilarious. "Rat Boy and the Princess," he continued. "In their magical laboratory. Doing magical things." He lurched toward the balsa-wood rocket on the launch pad.

"Leave that alone," I said. "It's secret."

He raised his palms in mock surrender. "Secret? Why didn't you say so?" He turned suddenly and snatched the soda bottle out of my hands. "What about this? Is this secret?" He held the bottle just out of my reach, daring me to try and stop him. "You got something to say, Rat Boy?"

I stared at the floor. "No," I said. My voice sounded strange to me.

"I didn't think so." He drained the bottle and gave a loud belch. "Now why don't you scurry along home, Rat Boy?"

• • •

Annabel avoided me for three days straight. At school she turned and walked the other way when she saw me coming. When I passed her notes, she crumpled them up and tossed them away unread. She signed up for field hockey so she'd have something to do after school—somewhere I couldn't follow. For a while I watched the practices from behind a chain-link fence. Whenever I caught her eye she'd look back with an expression of mild annoyance, as though I were selling band candy.

My mother wasn't used to having me around the house so much. She started inventing jobs for me, like sorting the loose nails on the workbench into mason jars, according to size. "It'll be fun," she insisted.

One afternoon while I was at my desk updating the Alpha Seven design, she appeared in the doorway, looking anxious. "Douglas, you haven't been getting into your father's work bench, have you?"

I leaned forward and brushed the remnants of a broken bait trap into a drawer. "No," I said. "Of course not."

"I was down in the workroom getting out the scrapbooks—I thought you might like to help me label them—and I noticed that some of the jars had been moved. Your father is very careful about those jars, Douglas. Very careful. They're his. For work."

I'd been experimenting with power pellets and other chemicals to form a new compound that I called Omega Twelve. It showed great promise.

My mother tapped her foot. "Because you know those chemicals are dangerous, don't you?"

"Of course. Duh. I know that." I looked up. "Really. I know that."

"All right," she said. "Just so we're clear." She turned slowly and walked away.

Three minutes later she was back with a plate of carrot sticks. "What's happened to the beautiful Annabel Lee?" she asked. "We haven't seen much of her lately."

"I don't know," I said.

She sat down on the edge of the bed. "Did you have a fight or something?"

"I don't know. Maybe."

My mother did her hand-clasping thing.

"I was a child and she was a child
In this kingdom by the sea;
But we loved with a love that was more than love—
I and my Annabel Lee—"

"Mom." I put down my protractor and swiveled in my chair. "Mom, could you stop that, please?"

"Stop what?"

"She's not a character in some sad poem. It's just her name. You keep—"

Something in my mother's eyes made me stop. She was looking at me as if she couldn't quite understand how I had come to be living in her house. She muttered something under her breath.

"What?" I said.

"Nothing. Forget it."

"No, what did you say?"

She blinked a couple of times. " 'All that we see or seem, is but a dream within a dream.' "

I just stared. Her eyes were wet. She kept picking at a thread on her sweater.

"Douglas," she said quietly, "we're all characters in a sad poem. That's the whole point. That's the whole goddamned point."

"What?" I said, but she had already left the room.

That night, I decided I couldn't stand it anymore. I went out back after dark and hopped over the fence into Annabel's yard, determined to have it out. Whatever it took, I would make it right. If there was some aspect of being a boyfriend that I needed to learn, I would learn it.

I brought a peace offering, and I had been practicing what I would say when I gave it to her. *It was right under our noses the whole time! The final ingredient for the booster fuel—it was right in this bottle! Grape soda! The carbonation was the missing piece! It forms an electrostatic energy field between the Pop Rocks and my Omega Twelve compound!* I imagined the joy on her face as I held up the NuGrape bottle and swirled the magic liquid, cloudy with chemicals and power pellets. *Oh, Doug! How could I have ever doubted you?* Then she would take my hand and lead me down to the rumpus room.

I had it all worked out. I would throw pennies at Annabel's window until she came down. I'd seen it in a movie, and it seemed to be the sort of crazy-fool romantic thing that girls liked. But as soon as I got over the fence I could see that something was wrong. The back door of the house was wide open and the garage door was up. Yellow light pooled under the basketball hoop. I could hear Mrs. Lee's voice through the open door, loud and strident, almost incoherent with rage. I distinctly remember the phrase *pencil-dick monster.*

I stepped closer. There were three cardboard boxes and a suitcase in the open trunk of Todd's Pacer. I fell back and pressed myself against the fence, suddenly afraid.

The screen door flapped and Todd appeared with an armful of clothes. He tossed them onto the backseat of the car and turned back toward the house, muttering. From inside the garage, a plastic Walkman sailed past his head and cracked against the concrete. He stooped to examine the damage, and spotted me in the shadows.

"Well," he said. "The boyfriend."

I didn't move.

He took a step toward me, squinting. "The boyfriend," he repeated. "Young Douglas. Rat Boy."

I found my voice. "I just came to see Annabel," I said.

"Is that a fact? You're out of luck, Rat Boy. The Princess is indisposed." He turned and stalked back through the garage. Mrs. Lee's shrieking continued without pause. I stayed pinned to the spot. After five minutes or so, Todd came back out and threw another load of clothes into the car. "Still here?" he called, slamming the trunk. "Can I give you some advice, young Douglas?"

I didn't answer. He came closer and put his hands on my shoulders, bringing his face close to mine. He smelled like a wet mattress. "Next time," he said, "you might want to mark your territory. You hear me?"

"I'm just here to talk to Annabel."

"So you said. You said that, young Douglas."

I closed my eyes. "I'm just—"

"Tough guy," he said. He snatched the soda bottle out of my hand and held it up out of reach. His lip curled and I could see a yellow stain on his teeth. "So? You got something to say, Rat Boy?"

Did I? I felt the back of my neck tighten. My brain was burning. I wondered what a proper boyfriend would say. I wondered if anything I said could possibly make any difference. I wondered if we were all just characters in some sad poem.

And then Todd put the bottle to his lips and drained it. "I didn't think so," he said, belching. "So why don't you scurry along home, Rat Boy?"

The empty bottle dangled from his fingers. I reached out and grabbed for it. For a minute or so we scrabbled over the bottle like two dogs with a stick. Then Todd let go, raising his palms to the night sky. "All right, kid," he said. "Happy now?"

I turned, suddenly weightless, and made my way toward a vast and uncharted horizon.

DANIEL STASHOWER is an Edgar Award–winning author whose most recent book is *The Beautiful Cigar Girl*, the true story of the murder of a sales clerk named Mary Rogers in New York in 1841, which became the basis of Edgar Allan Poe's famous detective story "The Mystery of Marie Roget."

Poe, Jo, and I

Don Winslow

I didn't read "The Fall of the House of Usher."

But that was typical of me back then. A junior in high school, I had flunked or hustled mercy D's out of most of my sophomore classes, but there I was in college-bound English taught by Miss Josephine Gernsheimer.

She was already old. This was her last year before retirement.

Anyway, it was, what, the first week of class. Early September in Rhode Island, the best time of year to be at the beach. The water was at its warmest, the tourists were gone, there was just enough surf to make it interesting, but there I was in class, listening to some old lady tell me to read something by Edgar Allan Poe. So I was already annoyed.

And Poe—hadn't he written some poem about a crow or a raven or something? Some black bird, anyway, with redundancy issues. "Quoth the raven," or some happy crap like that? *Quoth?* Freaking *quoth?!* What kind of pretentious bullshit was that?

Anyway, I wasn't much on talking animals. My sophomore year, I didn't read *Animal Farm*.

I wasn't going to read this story, either.

Soon as school was over, I drove down to the beach and caught the last of the waves, then I went home. After dinner I went up to my room, put on some Janis Joplin, and consumed the better part of a pint bottle of Teacher's Scotch as she banged out "Little Girl Blue."

I actually started to read the story. I got as far as the first sentence, something about a "dark, dull" day and then I put it down. If you live in Rhode Island with autumn approaching, you know more than you want to know about dark, dull days. The fog comes in around November and stays until about April, and it's darker and duller than the inside of an empty closet. Autumn was on its way, and so were my dark, dull moods, so I didn't need this pretentious Poe guy pushing the season.

So I hit the Scotch instead of the book.

Typical of me in those days.

Well, for a lot of days.

Next morning I got to class, hungover, and in a bad mood, and Miss Gernsheimer—she wasn't having the *Ms.* that was just hitting the culture then—passed out a pop quiz.

On "The Fall of the House of Usher."

I was screwed.

I didn't really care. My head ached, I was tired, and flunking English had become a worn habit. So I wrote on the top of the paper: "Dear Miss Gernsheimer. I could probably bluff my way through this quiz, but I don't want to waste my time or yours. Flunk me."

She did. The next day I got the quiz back with a big red F scrawled on the top along with an ominous note, the dreaded "See me after class." I lingered in my chair until the other kids left and then approached her desk.

Miss Gernsheimer had a face like a road map—there were lines all over it. She was deeply wrinkled and her skin was like old paper. Her steel-gray hair was done up in a stereotypical, severe bun. She was tall and gangly, her shoulders stooped from years of bending over books or student papers.

She looked up at me and smiled sardonically.

"Mr. Carpenter."

"Miss Gernsheimer."

"Why didn't you read the assignment?"

"I didn't feel like it."

Which was true for the most part. What I didn't say was that I hadn't wanted to disturb my drunken serenity with reading. What I especially didn't say was that I thought I knew what constituted worthwhile reading far better than Miss Gernsheimer, or certainly some anthology of literature.

I was reading Hemingway and Fitzgerald. Robert Ruark, James Michener. Jimmy Breslin columns. Shakespeare, with the exception of any play or sonnet I was assigned to read in school. Those, I wouldn't read.

"What do you have against Poe?" she asked me.

" 'Quoth the raven,' " I said.

"What about it?" she asked.

"It's stupid," I said. "First of all, ravens don't talk, except in Heckel and Jeckel cartoons, but those are cartoons. Second, if ravens talked, which they don't, they should just talk, not 'quoth.'"

"You find Poe pretentious."

"I guess so."

I didn't really care. My head was throbbing.

"Do you know anything about Poe?" she asked.

"'Quoth.'"

"That's it."

"It's enough," I said.

Yeah. In the arrogance of my youth I didn't know, couldn't know, that I would take much of the same path that Poe did; that, like him, I would lose myself in the bottle, throw away loved ones, walk dark, dull streets to nowhere.

"Well, you're honest, anyway," Miss Gernsheimer said. "You have an honest F.

"My failures are my own, Miss Gernsheimer," I said.

"You're also a pain in the neck," she said. "Don't come to class anymore."

I was sixteen and, of course, thought I had lost my ability to be surprised, but I was surprised. And delighted. "Don't come to class anymore"? A dream come true. A teacher had just looked me in the eye and told me to skip class. Saving us both the agony of my presence.

Smart lady, Miss Gernsheimer.

Then she said, "Instead, you and I are going to have lunch together every day. Be at my office at noon."

Then she looked back down at the papers on her desk.

I was dismissed.

I went to her office at noon. Chairperson of the English Department, she had her own office, a small narrow cavern at the end of the second-floor corridor. Her office was a mess, a complete dump—papers scattered haphazardly, open books on every available surface. She sat in an old overstuffed chair and motioned for me to sit down in the wooden chair beside her.

When I did, she handed me a copy of *The Atlantic Monthly*.

I had never seen *The Atlantic Monthly*. Coming from a little fishing village, I thought maybe it was some kind of professional fisherman's journal. There was probably a *Pacific Monthly* for guys on the West Coast.

"Read the article starting on page eighty-eight," she said. "Come back tomorrow prepared to discuss it. What do you have for lunch?"

"A tuna sandwich."

My mother was on a streak, alternating tuna fish and bologna sandwiches every day for the past two years. I usually threw them away.

"Really?" Ms. Gernsheimer asked, leaning over and peeking into my brown bag.

"Really."

"Hmmmm. I'll trade you."

She had Triscuits and chunks of Swiss cheese.

We had a deal.

I went home and read the article in *The Atlantic Monthly*. It had nothing to do with fishing. Then I read the rest of the magazine.

The next day we traded lunches again and she asked me questions about the article. Questions I couldn't answer, not because I hadn't read the story, but because the questions were just so hard. It became instantly, embarrassingly clear to me that she read on a level I hadn't seen yet. I would have to read deeper.

Read "critically," in Miss Gernsheimer's words. "Think critically."

That's the way it went. For the whole year. She gave me Triscuits and Swiss cheese in exchange for tuna fish and bologna, and she gave me *The Atlantic Monthly, Harper's,* the *New York Times Book Review,* and I struggled to respond half intelligently to her interrogations.

And we had conversations. She told me about growing up in New York City during the thirties and teaching in Appalachia as part of the WPA. Then she taught for years at a private girls' school on the Upper East Side before coming to Rhode Island twenty years ago. When I saved up some money and went to New York for three days over spring break, she was the only one who was really enthused.

She did retire at the end of the year. I went on to a senior Honors' class in English and proceeded to flunk most of my assignments—not reading the books that were assigned, drinking Scotch, listening to music, and reading just the things I wanted to read.

But I read them critically, and I asked myself questions, and most Wednesday afternoons I'd go to Miss Gernsheimer's house to eat Triscuits and Swiss cheese and talk about books.

I graduated high school only because I wrote a play that was a modest local hit. The administration was too embarrassed to flunk me and we negotiated a C in English. I went off to college in the Midwest.

Home for summers, I would visit Miss Gernsheimer, who told

me to call her Jo. She lived alone, had never married, had no children. She had a little miniature dachshund that used to fall asleep on her lap.

We'd sit in her backyard and talk, me inflicting my idiot opinions about writing on her, she patiently challenging my ideas. I don't know that Poe ever came up in those conversations. He wasn't my thing in those days—I was on Kerouac and Burroughs; spent a week canoeing down a river in Idaho, reading *Huckleberry Finn*. I had no idea back then that I would ever write detective stories, hadn't found my way to Hammett or Chandler yet, either MacDonald.

Or Poe.

After college, I was mostly overseas in Africa, or England or China, and I eventually lost touch with Jo. Hell, I lost touch with about everything, including myself. Those were my dark dull years, "when the clouds hung oppressively low in the heavens" and I lived in the bottom of the bottle. I ended up in New York and didn't know, couldn't know, that I trudged some of the same streets Poe had, in the same sad and drunken condition, had conversations with darker birds than ravens.

Years later, after I had put down the bottle and picked up the pen, my first book, a crime novel, was published. The bookstore in my little hometown, where I no longer lived, held a signing for me.

Jo Gernsheimer came.

I have a photo that my wife took.

Miss Gernsheimer, her face even more deeply lined, her shoulders stooped lower on her fragile frame, stands beside me. We're smiling at each other—my book standing on the table at our waists. Beside the book is the box of Triscuits that she brought. I love this photo because I remember it as one of the best moments of my life.

Of course, I knew Poe by that time. And Hammett, Chandler, the MacDonalds, and all the rest that had followed him. Realized that I had come from someplace, walked a trail that other people had blazed for me. I knew by then that he had died, alone and probably drunk, on a street in Baltimore. In the autumn.

When my first book was nominated for an Edgar, Jo wrote me a note. It said simply, "Quoth the Gernsheimer: Congratulations. Do you remember?"

Oh, I remembered. When I didn't win, I wrote her, "Well, he got me back."

We stayed in touch. I would visit her on the rare occasions that I was in town. When my son was born, I took him to meet her. He was too little to eat the Triscuits, but I did. He was far too young, of course, to have any comprehension of how important this woman had been in my life, but I hoped that he somehow absorbed it. And I wanted her to see him, to know that there would be continuity, to know that I prayed that he would be so lucky as to have a Jo Gernsheimer in his life.

By this time, she was in a nursing home, her health failing, her memory slipping from her as inexorably as a receding wave. She said good-bye in her own way, a letter with a poem:

Take this kiss upon the brow!
And, in parting from you now,

Thus much let me avow—
You are not wrong, who deem
That my days have been a dream.

It took me hours to dig out the source of the quote.

Poe.

Whatever Jo had lost, she had kept her sense of humor.

I was thousands of miles away when I heard that she'd died. Living in California, five novels under my belt, a family. Hope, anyway, that there would be no street in Baltimore for me.

The clipped-out obituary arrived in a letter from my mother.

I found some Triscuits and Swiss cheese, sat down, and read "The Fall of the House of Usher."

And cried.

During the whole of a dull, dark, and soundless day in the autumn of the *year, when the clouds hung oppressively low in the heavens . . .*

———————

DON WINSLOW was born in New York City but raised in South Kingstown, Rhode Island. At various times an actor, director, movie theater manager, safari guide, and private investigator, Don has done many things on his way to being a novelist. His first novel, *A Cool Breeze on the Underground*, was nominated for an Edgar, and a later book, *California Fire and Life*, received the Shamus Award. The film adaptation of *The Death and Life of*

Bobby Z, starring Paul Walker and Laurence Fishburne, came out in 2007. His upcoming novel, *The Winter of Frankie Machine*, has also been purchased for film, with Robert De Niro slated for the lead role. Don lives on an old ranch in the San Diego area with his wife, Jean, and son, Thomas.

Rue Morgue Noir
The possible—probable—struggles
Edgar Allan Poe might have faced while seeking
success as a talented new writer in the world of today

Angela Zeman

"Judith! Remember your promises? I can produce *un petite aide-mémoire* if required. I bought a digital recorder last week. With Lenore's tips," Ed added grudgingly. "You're not my first agent," he snarled into his cell phone.

He yanked his furry tail out of reach of a greasy-fingered customer, then bent close to the young face to chuckle appeasingly. He was able to look sincere by flashing on an image of the child breaking out in boils. Ed had a vivid imagination.

The eight-year-old birthday boy wailed, "Daaad, that monkey won't let me pull his tail!"

Ed moved further away, cell still at his ear. "Well, Judith?"

"You . . . *recorded* me?" Muffled noises came from the cell phone, then deep exhalation. "Eddie, sweetie, I understand your anxiety,

I really do. That's what we truly great agents do, we take burdens off our artists' shoulders. Are you, ah, recording me now?"

"Can't, I'm at work."

A sudden cacophony of whistles, drums, and squealing children drowned out her response. The many children and far too few adults sitting at the long rows of tables began howling, "Happy Birthday to yooooo."

"HANG ON," he yelled into his cell, and dropped it into his monkey tummy pouch. He raced for the kitchen, dodging a gauntlet of grasping fingers. School was out for the summer, and the tables were packed. The patrons of Chimps Ahoy! restaurant loved their waiters, but his monkey suit had to survive to the end of today's shift. And tomorrow's shift. And all the shifts until he sold his screenplay.

He bounded through the swinging doors and entered the relative quiet of the walk-in refrigerator. He retrieved his cell phone and shouted into it: "Any news? Gossip, rumors, *anything*?" No reply. She had hung up.

He walked slowly back to the kitchen door. Through the porthole he watched happy little customers gorge and scream and smear ketchup on each other.

That afternoon in his Bowery studio apartment, he hoisted his legs onto the twin bed that doubled as a sofa to allow Lenore floor space to step into her monkey suit. Her suit bore no species relationship to his monkey suit that he could see. She huffed as she hauled the rigid preshaped torso up the last few inches. "Zip me, sweetie?" He zipped, and she wriggled and plumped up body parts to fit.

Ed fluffed her long brown tail while she pulled up the fish-net stockings. "I never heard of a monkey wearing fishnets," he complained, mesmerized by her swaying rump inches from his nose.

"They hurt my skin. You never hear about that, either!" She popped the headpiece with the monkey ears atop her shimmering dark hair. "You called her today?"

Ed forgot her rump. "First thing."

"And nothing?"

Ed nodded.

Lenore shrieked in frustration. "It's *genius!* She promised she could sell it in two weeks! It's been *six!*" She pitched T-shirts and underwear into the air. "Where's my coat! I can't believe I let you talk me into being a monkey waitress. I *hate* being a monkey! I could make ten times more money at the Gold Bar. Especially in *this* outfit!"

"Well, true, but those men . . . Lennie, sweetheart, six weeks isn't—"

"In a monkey suit? Six weeks is forever! Call her again, Ed. Drive her crazy. You do *crazy* real well, I've seen it in your writing!"

He mumbled to himself, "Only in poems."

"Wall Streeters hang out at the Gold Bar, Ed. Bankers and brokers. Guys who're *already* successful!"

Shrugging off his good-bye kiss, she pulled on a trench coat and rushed out the door, slamming it behind her.

Ed took a deep breath, but just as he reached for his cell phone, it rang. He flipped it open. "Yes?"

"Whaddaya mean, *yes*? What way is that to answer the phone? Nevermind. Dan Dickens wants your screenplay."

Ed stood up straight, not a very long trip since he was a short man. "Dan Dickens of MELANCHOLY DEALS?"

"Any other producer named Dan Dickens?"

"You sound angry."

Judith heaved a great sigh. "I'm tired. The phone calls, the text messaging, the labor I've put in . . . I may add a few days' vacation to your tab, Eddie."

"How much?"

"A few days in Bermuda . . . not much."

"For the *film*. What kind of budget's he offering?"

"Darling, lovey, don't quit your day job. Hideous as it is. Too soon for money talk."

Ed heaved a sigh of his own. "So what now?"

"A phone meet."

He sprang to attention. "When!"

"For me, doll, not you. Call you back."

Ed passed the hours of the next day's shift in a morose mood, brightened only by an occasional sighting of Lenore across the room, although she ignored him. Finally, after watching yet another father of squalling brats pat Lenore's fishnetted bottom, he couldn't take it anymore. Trembling with fury, he raced to the kitchen to speed-dial Judith. Voice mail again. He retreated into the walk-in refrigerator to think.

Walter Hubbard, manager and owner of Chimps Ahoy!, whipped open the refrigerator door, then sprang back in surprise.

"Poe? Wha— HERE? You were hired t'be a monkey—for the KIDDIES! Not the cupcakes!" He waved a hand as large as a shovel around his head. "Get outta here!"

Ed strode out the door, skirting his boss's tall, hulking body. "Someday I'll bury you alive, Walt," he mumbled, knowing Walt wouldn't catch his words. Walt's hearing was impaired. Ed had never forgiven him for forcing the new costume on his female waitstaff.

Walter turned to watch Poe leave. "What? Did you call me Walt? Don't call me Walt!"

Ed waved to show that he got the message.

At eight p.m., Ed and Lenore slunk home together, smelling of hamburger grease and bananas. Just when Lenore turned her key in their lock, Ed's cell rang.

"Yes?"

"How many times I gotta tell you, that's no way to answer a phone! Nevermind. Dan Dickens is willing to pay ten grand for six months' option."

Lenore stared open-mouthed as Ed fumbled for a response. Finally he said, "Is that . . . it?"

" 'It.' That's what you call an option from the hottest producer in LA LA land? 'IT'? He's salivating for it, Edgar my boy. Salivating!"

Ten grand option, Ed mouthed to Lenore, who sank back onto her heels in disappointment.

No way! She mouthed back at him.

Ed braced himself, then spoke. "No deal. Move on."

"*What?* Tell Dickens no? That's crazy! Who's the agent here, young man!"

"I'm not selling it as an option, Judith. It's too good."

"It's *genius!*" yelled Lenore at the phone.

"But—but—" Judith snarled. "Oh all right." *Click.*

Inside the apartment, Lenore gazed at Ed speculatively, then announced she was meeting friends at the Gold Bar.

"No!" Ed commanded.

She left. Ed stared longingly after her, then shivered at the oppressive empty feel of the apartment. He pulled open his laptop, muttering to himself, "I'm a professional." He rotated his shoulders, then shook his hands in the air in a preparatory way. "I'm not crazy, I'm nervous, that's all. Nerves. I'm a professional. He typed experimentally, "D-r-e-a-d-f-u-l-l-y n-e-r-v-o-u-s."[1]

In the early hours of the new day, Lenore crept into the apartment. She pulled him away from his laptop and they fell into bed together.

Late morning, they climbed back into the monkey suits they had neglected to clean the night before, and arrived at Chimps Ahoy! smelling and feeling as if they'd already worked one shift that day.

At eleven thirty, as the tables began filling and parents began clamoring for waiters, Ed's cell phone rang. Flinging off the detaining hand of a mother, he darted for the kitchen, rushing past Walter, who growled with suspicion.

Inside the walk-in refrigerator, Ed demanded, *"What?!"*

Judith exhaled as if through clenched teeth. "That is *no way to answer*—never mind! Okay, so you're not so crazy. Steven Loessus

---

1 "The Tell-Tale Heart," by Edgar Allan Poe

wants your script for his company, Stet Productions. He'd also direct."

"*What?* That is fantastic! Oh, my God, ohmigod. Well. Not as good as Dickens, but—ohmigod!"

Judith, sounding much more pleased, said, "Yes. Thank God. So now we have to think about wardrobe."

Ed shook his head, sure he had misunderstood. "Um . . . ?"

"Steve's in town, again thank God, so you can meet him here instead of flying out to LA."

"I don't have money to fly—"

"Exactly. So breakfast at the Regis tomorrow, nine-ish. To you, that means exactly nine. I'll be there, too, don't worry. So what outfit will you wear to express your qualities as a writer, as opposed to a stinking deranged monkey?"

"Er . . ."

The refrigerator door whipped open, and Walter's big face appeared. His teeth were bared.

Ed shivered. "*Ha-ha!* Ha! Walter! Having a personal moment, if you could excu—"

"You like your job, Poe?"

"I'll brick up this grease pit with you in it," Ed mumbled. "Yes!" he declared loudly. "I adore my job." He grinned hard, thinking: *I adore eating.*

"You'll brick—what?" Judith exclaimed from his cell phone.

"What?" demanded Walt.

"Hang on!" Ed shouted at both his listeners. "Walter, ah, I'm fetching a carton of burger patties. Helping the, ah," he shuddered, "the chef. Orders are stacking up." He nudged a box with his elbow.

Walter drew back. Mists of chilled air wreathed his face. "Oh. Good. Hurry it up." He withdrew, leaving the door ajar.

Ed hissed into the phone, "Yes, wardrobe. Like what?"

"Best case, lovey, would be Armani. Dark neutral—this is New York, after all—casual and obviously this year—that would suggest you're used to earning high numbers. Therefore you're already successful but willing to consider working with Mr. Loessus."

Ed considered that. "What else?"

"As I suspected. Well, there's vintage. Cheap, but very 'in.' Expresses the quirky individuality of a creative too busy and successful to shop." She sounded tired.

"A *creative*?"

"Mmm."

"That sounds doable. All my clothes are old."

"Wear your oldest, lovey. Just looking ratty won't do."

"No ratty. Fine."

She hung up.

Ed ran to tell Lenore, and both worked the remaining hours of their shifts in a distracted haze. At home, he and Lenore shared their excitement in bed, and afterward ravaged his wardrobe.

At exactly nine the next morning, a marginally vintage-attired Ed stepped into the Regis breakfast room, which was much more yellow than he'd imagined. He blinked in the enhanced sunshine, and followed the maître d' to the correct table. Judith arrived five minutes later in a stone-colored suit that looked suspiciously like Armani to Ed's inexperienced eyes. Judith ordered coffee for herself, and they waited.

When Steven Loessus arrived an hour and twenty minutes later, he turned out to be a jovial man not much taller than Ed, with a fringe of white hair ringing his egg-shaped head. He wore a faded plaid shirt over khakis, both of which strained at the fastenings. Obviously, Ed thought with admiration, Loessus had nothing to prove to anyone.

Loessus had brought with him a polished young blonde of such flawless beauty—loyalty to Lenore stopped Ed's thoughts at that point. Dazzled, he rose to briefly touch her extended hand. "Marie Rogers! No one told me—I've seen every picture you—I can recite your dialogue—" he broke off, beginning to sweat. He gazed at Loessus with increased admiration and sat back down.

Loessus gave a coy smile. "I persuaded Ms. Rogers to join our little breakfast."

"Delighted!" Judith beamed at the childlike blonde in a way that made Ed think of a wolf licking her chops—not that Judith had chops. Surely not. "So, Ms. Rogers—you've read my client's screenplay?"

Ms. Rogers exclaimed breathily, "Simply . . . simply . . ." She groped for words. "Earthbreaking! No, Steve said *ground*breaking!"

Loessus glanced ruefully at Judith, whose gaze had drifted to the ceiling. Loessus murmured, "It's not bad. Nice little break-in role for the right . . . actor, do you agree, Mr. Poe?"

Ed, guessing Loessus's intention, blurted, "Sir, *Rue Morgue Noir* is written for a mature male protagonist."

"But!" Judith held up a hand as if to stop traffic. "Poe could reenvision the starring role for a woman. A young woman." She sat back. "For a fee, naturally. A lot of work, even for a writer of Poe's talents." She frowned at her manicure.

Loessus hesitated. Ms. Rogers laid one delicate hand over his.

Loessus didn't remove his hand, but glanced sourly at Ed. "What else have you done?"

Poe lifted mournful eyes to Ms. Rogers and quoted: " 'And his eyes have all the seeming of a demon that is dreaming—' "[2]

Judith waved her hand as if vigorously swatting a fly. "Never mind! Okay, he published some poetry—but he can handle this minor rewrite overnight. Right, Eddie?"

Ed's eyes widened in horror, but he nodded bravely. "Overnight."

Loessus sniffed.

Poe glared at Loessus. "A poet is no fool. If you think so, your opinion has been contradicted by the voice of the world."[3]

Judith glowered at Ed. "Eddie means, no problem. However, we've heard no offer. Capisce?"

Loessus sighed grandly. "With Ms. Rogers attached, Mr. Poe's career trajectory—"

Judith interrupted. "With the gorgeous Marie Rogers attached to *this* script, *you* would own a very commercial property."

Ms. Rogers cooed, "I adore dark thrillers."

Judith smiled. "You and the rest of the globe. Meaning this film will translate overseas, Steve lovey. 'Dark' is a money machine these days, and Ed does 'dark' as if he invented it. And

---

2 "The Raven," by Edgar Allan Poe
3 A discussion of this idea can be found in "The Purloined Letter," by Edgar Allan Poe.

his characters—ingenious, if a bit insane. Five big money scenes, FIVE. Immaculate dialogue, emotionally satisfying plot, and the ending? A shocker."

"But *organic*," added Ed.

Judith blinked as if she'd forgotten he was there, then smiled at Loessus. "Indisputably. *Organic*."

Loessus sat brooding for a minute, then looked up as if someone had spoken. "Oh, my! We haven't ordered breakfast! Let's see the menu." The waiter, who'd been standing four feet away while they talked, leaped forward and handed around large cardboard sheets.

Judith, Loessus, and Ms. Rogers all leaned back in their chairs, looking relaxed and complacent, mulling their menu choices. Ed stared at them in bewilderment. Suddenly Judith's pointed shoe connected painfully with his ankle. He forced himself to also sit back in his chair. He stared blindly at the menu.

Eggs Benedict, raisin bagels, flaky croissants, he told Lenore later, in bed. She exhaled far more euphorically than she had moments earlier.

He grimly added, "And two days to turn my male protagonist into a young female. For free."

Lenore snapped upright. "Free!"

"Judith says since it's my first script, and on spec, I'm lucky to do it at all, even for nothing. But," he kissed her hard, "who's your genius, eh?"

Sullenly she replied, "You are."

He snapped open his laptop and stood stretching his back, waiting for the machine to boot up. "Sooo . . . a tiny bit longer at Chimps Ahoy! Tell Walt I'm sick, will you? Forty-eight-hour flu."

Huffing angrily, Lenore struggled into her monkey suit. On her way out, she slammed the apartment door so hard it bounced back open. Ed glanced absently at the broken latch, then began typing.

Two days later, Ed's cell phone rang. He pulled it out from underneath his pillow and stared at it with sunken, bleary eyes. It rang again.

"Mmmph?"

"Edgar. That is no way to answer . . ." Judith inhaled noisily. "Never mind. Dan Dickens is having second thoughts."

He yawned. "Too late. Walked the new script to Loessus"—he yawned again—"an hour ago. Listen, Judith. Fired if I don't work . . . today . . . famished . . ."

"Never too late when you're dealing with Loessus! He's a last-second signer, notorious for it! If Dickens wants to deal—nothing holding us back!"

Judith heard a faint snore.

"Edgar! Snap out of it! *Dan Dickens!* Whatsamatta, you been up all night?"

Ed blinked. "As a matter of fact—"

"He's salivating for it!"

Silence. "Didn't he salivate when he wanted that option?"

Judith shrieked, "Okay, he panted! Sit up! Are you sitting up?"

Edgar pulled himself upright, suddenly noticing he was alone. "I guess."

Her voice became low and urgent. "Dickens heard Marie Rogers was attached. He's been obsessed with her since that short she did for Sundance. He's sal—he's hot to sign her to something, anything, and *she's* hot for *your script*. Hah!" Silence. "Edgar?"

"How much?"

"Ah, he's awake! Nevermind, Eddie! Two horny guys? I win! I mean, *we* win!"

Click.

Edgar stared at his empty bed and then at his Radio Shack alarm clock. When had Lenore left? He grabbed his chimp suit and hurried to get ready for work.

At Chimps Ahoy! Ed was so relieved to find Lenore he grabbed her and shouted, "Dan Dickens and Steve Loessus both want Marie Rogers and she wants my script and . . . and . . ." He sat down suddenly. "When was my last meal?"

Lenore shrieked, "Eddie, my *genius!*" and wrapped her arms around him in a fierce clutch.

Walt trundled over. "Here, cut that out! Get back to work!" He gripped Lenore's tail with a beefy hand.

Ed jumped to his feet and pushed Lenore aside. "Watch where you're putting that hand, Walt!"

"Don't call me Walt!" But he let go of her tail.

Lenore thrust her small face close to Walter's large one. "We quit."

"*Quit? What?*"

Lenore began jumping up and down, squealing, *"Quit! Quit!"*

Ed's hollow stomach suddenly growled, causing him to wince. "Wait. That's right, Walter. Quit groping the girl chimps or you'll find yourself in a sexual harassment suit!"

Walter turned his good ear closer to Ed. "What? What's that?"

Lenore gasped. "We don't quit?"

Ed glanced desperately at her. "So far, Walter's the only one paying us!"

That night, Ed's cell phone rang. Ed didn't raise his head off the pillow, but Lenore smacked the phone against his ear. "Answer it!"

"What," he answered feebly.

"Someday I'll teach you phone manners," came the snarling reply. "Dan Dickens is considering low four figures against high five if the final script gets made."

Ed struggled to wake up. "Low four . . . four five . . . if what?"

Lenore, listening in, jerked on his arm. "Make her spell it out!"

"Spell it out, Judith."

"Opening salvo, lovey, that's all. It's a lust war, didn't you listen? Dickens and Loessus are in a death match over *la femme* Marie." She snorted. "Always *cherchez la femme*, great for capital gains. Now focus. Dickens is faxing me notes at this very moment. My messenger will be at your place in half an hour. Pay him, will you? If we work this right . . . maybe we could even finagle some points."

She chortled. Ed heard music and glasses tinkling in the background. Judith was at a party.

"Really? Points?" Ed asked.

Lenore shouted into the phone, "What are points?"

Ed mouthed, *"Shares of gross profits,"* at Lenore, then continued with Judith. "Why rewrite for Dickens? If he wants Ms. Rogers to star, I wrote that already for Loessus."

Judith murmured something syrupy to someone at the party then resumed briskly, "He has a different idea—just look over his notes. You must expect rewrites. That's the business, lovey. Everybody gets rewritten."

Ed sighed. "Does the 'business' ever pay their writers?"

"That's the great part! Dickens and Loessus both are doing the redeye from LA. We'll do breakfast at the Regis again, this time with *everybody* there. Give Dickens his new rewrite, I know he'll love it. And since Loessus already loves *his* rewrite, the battle will be on! *Somebody* will sign a check right at the table! *There's* your money, babe!"

Ed paused, eyeing Lenore. "We'd like to burn our monkey suits, Judith."

"Tomorrow morning, I promise!"

"She promised before," whined Lenore in Ed's other ear.

"Nevermind, lovey! Get started on Dickens's rewrite the moment the notes arrive. Meeting's set, tomorrow at the Regis. And, ah, wear different clothes from the ones you wore last time. It won't do for Loessus to think that's all you own."

"Nine?"

"Naturally. Don't forget to tip the messenger!"

Click.

At a quarter to nine the next day, Ed, unable to finance a subway ride and armed with his original script plus the two new versions, was trudging his way up Park Avenue when his cell phone rang.

"Lucky I caught you! Thought you'd be in the subway."

"Lenore wouldn't loan me her Metro card. She gets cranky when she's impatient."

Judith sounded as if she was running. On a treadmill, guessed Ed, hearing a rhythmic thump. Sweating off those cocktails, he thought resentfully. He patted at his damp forehead with his wrist. "What now?"

"Oh, dear, so tetchy. Well, you'll love my news. Loessus canceled. He decided to rush *his* script to Fantasy Prod, Stet's parent corporation. He thinks it may be too big for Stet to handle."

"*His* script. It's not his yet!"

"Well, the version you wrote for him. As opposed to the version you wrote for Dickens."

Ed sighed. "Are you telling me there's no breakfast meeting?"

"Why yes, lovey!" She sounded astonished. "We can't have a bidding war with only one side showing up! Dickens will just have to wait."

He turned around and started walking back downtown.

Judith continued, "We may not need Dickens anyway. *Fantasy Productions*, Eddie! A bigger production company means a bigger budget, and that means hotter actors," she burbled in her enthusiasm. "A bigger *movie*! A bigger percent for *us*!"

"Nobody's given me a nickel yet."

"Still, it never hurts to have a backup producer. Messenger over Dickens's rewrite, I'll get it to him for you. You know, if you bought a fax machine things would be so much simpler," she complained.

"Send me some money, I'll see what's on sale," he snarled.

"Never mind."

Click.

Two days later, Ed found himself confronting a formidable trio of men across the Regis's best table. Two he recognized from photos in the trade papers: the tall, tan, burly Dan Dickens of Melancholy Deals; and a shorter man, homely with his Manhattan pallor and yet drenched in charisma—the superstar of Ed's dream movies, the man on whom he'd secretly modeled the hero that Ms. Rogers desired to replace, Robert D'Wolfe. Mr. D'Wolfe smiled at Ed in a mischievous, un-wolfish manner. Mr. Dickens's carnivorous grin, however, caused Ed to shift his chair closer to his agent.

A smallish third man who Ed had heard of but never before seen sat between Judith and Robert. Alden Derrik, the director. Or, to Ed's dazzled mind, THE DIRECTOR. The man who'd directed the two films for which Ed's hero, Robert D'Wolfe, had won both Golden Globes and Oscars. Ed somehow managed to shake Mr. Derrik's hand, straining to look undaunted. In truth, he was very daunted.

Mr. Derrik was slim, rakishly handsome, with overly long dark hair. The silver wings sweeping back from each temple made his Malibu tan look even darker than Dan Dickens's. Three movie icons, each oozing confidence from their fifty-something but still invisible pores.

Ed's right hand crept toward the pimple on his twenty-year-old forehead, but he caught himself and instead hugged his revised scripts to his sunken chest.

He'd ordered water for his dry mouth. Everyone else had ordered omelets, Canadian bacon, croissants, crème fraîche, homemade jam, and coffee. The pitcher of mimosas, proclaimed Judith, would counter the bacon's ill effect on arteries with loads of vitamin C.

Robert leaned toward Ed. "*Rue Morgue Noir* is great, son, just great."

"Egh?" croaked Ed. He took a gulp of water.

"Yeah, and I love the new sidekick."

"That's what Mr. Dickens asked for." Ed tried to laugh. "Heh heh." He stopped trying.

"And I like how you *did* it!" Robert's smile became hearty. "I heard you were considering turning the protagonist into a female?"

Ed nodded glumly. He hesitated, then rushed to say, "Mr. D'Wolfe . . . in truth, I wrote the protagonist with *you* as my model. You are my hero, my most . . . I admire every role—" He choked, overwhelmed.

Judith smacked the table next to Robert's plate. She declared, "Edgar's talent is BIG!" *Smack!* "His script is BIG!" *Smack!* Satisfied that she'd made her point, she added, "Steve Loessus agrees. In fact, he agrees so much, he's taken it to Fantasy Productions. Too big for Stet."

The three men rumbled polite compliments. Ed brightened.

"I won't be acting in this, you understand," added Robert casually.

"You wouldn't?" Ed drooped.

"No, no. I'm here to *participate*," said Robert. "We're in partnership. DDD."

Dan Dickens bared all his teeth again, bringing to Ed's fevered mind the image of a maddened gorilla. "We've waited a long time for a script like this. A good fit for DDD. And . . . it's got legs. Derrik really wants legs!"

Derrik straightened his half-unbuttoned white dress shirt. *"Sequels!"*

Robert lightly punched Derrik's shoulder and laughed. "Alden's always dreamed of out-doing *Star Wars!*" He leaned toward Ed. "See, if I participate, Alden attaches."

Ed said blankly, *"Star Wars?"* Then, "Oh! My God, are you serious? Alden Derrik would direct?"

Judith declared, "Sequels! Fab! So what's stopping you?"

Alden shrugged. "I haven't seen what I'd consider a final draft."

Ed said nervously, "Final—"

Robert said, "Derrik's got the power to green-light. I just throw in my two cents." He added, "Dickens would produce."

Ed gaped at the men, who, shoulder to shoulder, loomed like Hollywood's Mount Rushmore—minus one. He squeaked, "All three of you?" and dove into his bag for paper and a pencil.

Judith barked, "Ready Ed? Okay. What bothers you fellas about the script?" Judith chose a chocolate croissant and sat back.

Ed spent the next thirty minutes scribbling while the others ate and squabbled over ideas. After getting down the last comments, he looked up, blinking, and realized the men had left. Only Judith remained, and she was reapplying lipstick. The waiter was removing plates. Ed shoved his papers into his bag and rose to leave, but Judith stopped him with one hand and handed him the bill with her other. "Well, *this* meeting was worth recording. Someday historians will want to know what was said here today." She paused. "You, ah, ever *erase* your recordings?"

"No. I download them to my computer. Like podcasts."

"Oh. Well, Derrik wants to see your rewrite tomorrow."

Ed dropped his bag onto the littered table, making the crystal teeter and ping. "Tomorrow! Don't most screenwriters get weeks or months to do rewrites?"

Judith nodded. "Usually."

She slid her status bag onto her arm, then paused. "Edgar. Do you want D'Wolfe, Derrik, and Dickens? Or a pat on the head at Sundance and an indie budget?" She scanned the tables to see who else was power-breakfasting, then swaggered from the room on her stilettos, radiating accomplishment.

Ed handed his only credit card to the waiter, then signed the charge slip, crossing off the automatically added tip. The waiter glared. Ed sighed. "Sorry. Just be grateful you're not a monkey."

An hour later, Lenore gasped in all the right places when Ed relayed the story of his morning, making him feel more optimistic and even macho about surviving his ordeal. Fueled by the adrenaline Lenore always brought out in him, Ed spent another hour making Lenore gasp some more.

Afterward, while Ed panted in recovery, Lenore suddenly said, "I want to be in your movie."

Ed sat up. "You're no actress."

Lenore sat up, too. "Oh, Eddie, nobody's *born* an actress. They *become* one. With experience. Practice."

"Nobody practices in my big break. But—but I'll buy us an apartment with a full bathroom!"

Lenore gazed at him coolly.

"And an elevator!" Ed, watching her stare back at him, felt like he was coming down with a fever.

She began wriggling to untangle herself from the sheet.

"And, and—a designer gown to wear to my Premiere! Okay?"

She smiled. "Sure. You're my genius, aren't you?" She dressed, then tossed her monkey costume and other things into a shopping bag. "Get to work, Eddie."

"Where are you going?" he asked.

But she was gone.

Ed pulled himself off the mattress and rebooted his laptop. He gripped his head with both hands while he studied his notes. "I'm a professional!"

Around five that afternoon, Ed's cell phone rang. He pushed it against his ear with a hunched shoulder, his mind still on his computer screen. "What."

"Walter here. Remember me? Your boss? Just checking on whether you're fired or not."

"What do you mean?" Ed straightened.

"You working the late shift tonight? Or never again?"

"Oh." Ed thought of the screaming children, the smell of rancid grease . . . "Walt—er, um, I'm still awfully weak from that flu—"

Walter snarled, "Take all the time you need to recover. You're fired."

Lenore's voice shrilled in the background, "Shove your job! Ed's making a movie! He's going to be BIG, and he's taking me with him!"

Walter growled, his voice faint to Ed. "The movie mogul taking you with him right this minute?"

Ed mashed the cell phone receiver against his ear. He heard Lenore shriek, "Ed! If I stay away from the Gold Bar, support you until your first paycheck, would you put me in your movie?"

"N-n-n-no."

Walter's voice boomed in triumph. "He said no!"

"NO?"

"Back to work, Chimpette," snapped Walt, and the connection broke.

Ed stared at his cell phone, feeling sick to his stomach. His empty stomach.

At four a.m., Ed printed out the revised script and rushed it to a twenty-four-hour Kinko's. Not waiting to confirm that Judith had received the fax, he returned home and slammed into bed. A Lenore-less bed, he noticed only after his cell phone rang and woke him four hours later. Bleary and disoriented, his anxiety rose as he considered where she could be.

"Lenore?"

"Not in *your* blood-soaked daydreams."

"Judith."

"Derrik LOVES it."

Ed rubbed his aching head. "Cripes, doesn't the man sleep? Well, thank God."

"He wonders how it'll work with the female as the murderer."

Ed sprang to his feet. "WHAT? That changes the whole character dynamic of the story!"

"He'll pay three hundred—."

Ed sputtered.

"—thousand."

After a pause, she added, "Extra."

Ed cleared his throat and sat. "When would I get this, ah, extra money?"

"Dickens pays. He's the money man of the group."

"Yeah, so . . ." Ed prompted.

"When Derrik gets the script he wants."

Ed considered this. Slowly he lay back on his pillow. "Okay. After one good night's"—he eyed the bright sun outside his one small window—"*day's* sleep. I'll start on it tonight. Don't messenger it back to me, I've got it on computer."

"He's got notes."

Ed groaned.

"Don't start until you see his notes. And tiny catch, he wants to see it tomorrow after lunch–ish. He's at the Regis Hotel."

"Surprise," muttered Ed. "What about his buddies, D'Wolfe and Dickens?"

"They'll do whatever he says."

"And Loessus?"

"I'm working that out."

Ed envisioned a deep dark pit yawning at his feet. He shut his eyes. "Send the notes." He flipped his phone shut and curled around his pillow in a fetal position.

• • •

The next afternoon, in Alden Derrik's hotel suite, Ed crouched in a half-comatose state on a feather-cushioned sofa and watched Alden read. Alden paced and occasionally broke into a loud, buzzing ramble of dialogue. He seemed to be acting out the various parts at high speed.

Suddenly, Alden sat down and gripped Ed's arm. "What an ending. What a *story*! You write— I felt every word. Intense. So intense. What if you made the female's son the murderer?"

Ed's voice was faint. "When . . ."

"Oh, I'm—let me think—flying to Rio Friday noon. Anytime before then."

"This is Wednesday."

Alden grabbed Ed's hand and shook it. "This script." He searched for words to describe it.

"Mad?" suggested Ed, tugging to get his hand back.

"Yes!" Alden pumped his hand harder.

"Deranged?" Ed yanked, this time successfully.

"That's it!" cried Alden.

In the hours between Thursday night and Friday morning, Judith's voice squawked in Ed's cell phone receiver, "Stop! Don't write another word. Loessus made a better offer, dependent on one eensy-weensy change! You'll love it!"

Ed would've let his head fall back on the pillow, but it was already there. He'd taken to writing in bed. He felt especially free to do so, since he hadn't seen or heard from Lenore in a few days.

"Judith. Bludith, exudith, Judith."

"Are you all right, Edgar?"

"What could Loessus possibly want that I haven't already written?" he grumped. "Derrik's nutso convoluted script is almost done. You know, Marie Rogers isn't old enough to have a son old enough to commit this murder. Derrik forgot that."

"Meeting! Absolutely everybody there, lovey. The dueling directors, et al!"

"Judith." Tears welled. He breathed, in and out, in and out, until he regained control. "If this script sells, and it gets made, and it does okay . . ."

"Yes, poor lovey," she crooned. "They'll let you sleep between rewrites. Breakfast, at the Regis."

"Nine," muttered Ed.

"You guessed. Alden's plane leaves at noon, if you remember. And lovey? Wear whatever you want, nevermind what I said before."

Edgar hung up.

Wearing jeans, a sleep-wrinkled Gap tee, and unlaced dirty cross-trainers, Edgar padded into the Regis dining room, waving off the maître d'. When he got to the table, though, he stopped. His mouth opened but no words emerged.

Lenore sat ensconced between Alden Derrik and Dan Dickens in a skimpy blue sundress. She beamed up at him. Her dark hair glimmered in the buttery light of the room like a river of silk.

"I called Judith, Eddie. She mentioned the meeting, so I . . ." She wriggled her shoulders. "I just thought I'd come, too."

Dan Dickens loomed over her as if she were the last mimosa

on the table. Derrik, whose arm casually oozed across Lenore's chair back, said, "Happy addition to our party."

Belatedly, Ed remembered reading about Derrik's marital and extramarital antics in the *Star*. He tried to signal Lenore, but she was looking elsewhere.

"Except this isn't a party," said Marie Rogers in a withering tone, which sounded wrong coming from her soft young lips.

Judith said briskly, "No indeed. Business." She smiled at Loessus, who sulked on Ms. Rogers's left. "Shall we order?" Loessus brightened. Judith jerked her head in command at Edgar, who hurriedly seated himself on her right.

After all plates were loaded, even Ed's, who'd caught on to the rhythm of breakfast meetings with film execs, Loessus casually dropped a bomb. "Ginger Grant phoned my office yesterday."

Derrik's, Dickens's, and Marie's forks paused in mid-air. Judith inquired brightly, "Oh? For what reason, Steve, dear?"

Ed froze. Her question sounded rehearsed. He'd always been sensitive to atmosphere, and he definitely felt this one cooling down.

"Said she'd heard about Poe's script." Loessus shoveled a pile of bacon into his mouth and began slowly chewing. Obviously he felt no further comment was needed.

D'Wolfe swung around to stare at Derrik. "I've always wanted to work with Grant."

At this news, Ed's fork slowed, although it didn't stop.

"Ah?" Absently Derrik began stroking Lenore's bare arm.

Ed cleared his throat as if in the last stages of tuberculosis, but Lenore's gaze stayed adoringly on Derrik's face. Derrik said, "Marvelous as Queen Bets last year."

"My God yes. Oscar, Best Actress," murmured Dickens. "Went to cable. Brilliant miniseries."

Loessus glanced at the stricken Ms. Rogers and swallowed his bacon. "Grant's interest would depend on the part."

D'Wolfe waved a careless hand. "Poe could enlarge that. Think of the *draw!*"

Ed's eyes squeezed shut. *Enlarge.*

Loessus nodded. "You and Grant as costars? *Mmm!*"

Ms. Rogers looked around the table for a champion, and finding none, blurted, "Steve? Alden? I mean . . . She's too *old!* I earned this part! Promises were made! *Favors* were exchanged!" She glared at Loessus, then Derrik.

Derrik smiled vaguely. "Oh, sweetie, you know."

She slammed her napkin onto her plate and rose.

D'Wolfe watched her stalk from the room. "She'd make a great dead body, Alden."

Derrik turned to stare at Ms. Rogers's retreating back. "Oh. I didn't think of that."

"Hey! I'm still here!" said Lenore. Nobody looked at her. She pushed herself up and left the table.

Ed half-rose from his chair. "I could write in *Ms. Rogers* as the murderer. As—as Mr. D'Wolfe's daughter? Really, anyone could kill, given the right circumstances."

Robert D'Wolfe cast Ed a wounded glance. Dickens picked up

the check, to Ed's relief. Judith pulled Ed aside, murmuring into his ear, "Don't lose *this* recording!" She shooed him away before he could mention that he didn't have the recorder anymore.

Ed couldn't find Lenore, although he darted through the hotel lobby and into the street, looking.

He walked home.

The next Monday, midmorning, while Edgar lounged in bed with his laptop, trying to digest the ketchup soup he'd had for breakfast, Judith called.

"It's here." She sounded breathless with excitement.

Ed echoed blankly, "It's here."

"Yeees, lovey! Our deal!"

Ed sat up. "Signed?"

"Almost. We've got Grant interested if you can enlarge her part to costar with D'Wolfe—"

Ed flopped backward onto the bed. "God, I knew it. Okay. I'm honored. Humbled. Awed. What's the deadline, tonight?"

Judith said, "And then about Derrik. Well . . ."

"What? He's still directing, right?"

"His wife doesn't like the location."

"Location? *Location?*" Ed trembled with fury where he lay. "The movie *is* the location! Why do you think the roles can be switched around like three-card monte, it's because *location* is the genesis and the exodus of the whole damned STORY! It's called *Rue Morgue Noir*, NOT *Petaluma Parkway Noir*! Or *Main Street USA Noir!*"

"Mmm. Well, nevermind. Maybe another writer could do it."

After a long silence, Ed began to massage his forehead. "Understood."

"You see, Derrik once shot another movie there—"

"Nineteen ninety-eight. *Time of Death.*"

"Yes! And a supporting female lead, not to name names, but there was litigation, an aborted abortion. And, well, to leap to the denouement, the woman bought herself and her new son a house, Derrik picking up the tab. She still lives there." She hesitated. "Ed, lovey. Mrs. Derrik is an athletic type. Tall, too."

He studied his tiny feet. "She's bigger than her husband, and he's scared witless."

"You *do* understand! Oh, and she mentioned San Francisco, Chicago, and Austin. The one in Texas."

"When does he find time to direct?"

"And a few other places. I'll messenger over the list."

Ed rolled off the bed and began to pace. "Let's rehash, and I use the word *hash* precisely. New location—thus a completely new storyline. Enlarge the new, older female's part to costar with Robert. Keep the male protagonist role at equal star level despite new partner. Ditch the young female version totally, but practice makes perfect, right? Wait, I'm confused. Is there still a son, and is he still the murderer? Is Robert the boy's father? Or is Derrik?"

"Oh, lovey, you're the writer, isn't the story your job? And you'll have tons of time to sleep and eat! No more cause for complaint. Healthy and happy."

He stopped. "Define happy."

"Derrik is busy with another project now, so mid-July is your new deadline."

"July! A month? Judith, I have no job! Lenore's vanished, along with her tips and Metro card. She even took the digital recorder. I ate my last ketchup packet this morning! Where's that extra check? Any check?" He thundered, *"Show me the money!"*

Judith hung up.

Ed mused resentfully on the example set by Cuba Gooding Jr.

"Oh, so fashionable now!" cooed Loessus, eyeing Ed's gaunt figure, the ponytail stub at his neck, and the beard shading sunken cheekbones.

"This is New York, after all!" snapped Ed as he took his chair. He gestured for the waiter, who came hurrying. After ordering, Ed seized a roll from the basket and frowned at Loessus. "Are *you* supposed to be here?"

Loessus sat back in his chair, smiling amiably. "I breakfast at the Regis whenever I'm in town."

D'Wolfe came up to the table, trailed by Dickens, Derrik, and a perspiring Judith, who was trotting to catch up. After all were sitting and had caught their breaths, in sauntered Lenore.

Ed jumped to his feet and cried with joy, " 'Oh my radiant Lenore, my rare and radiant maiden!' "[4] He sat again. "Where've you been in the last month!"

She slid cozily between Dickens and Derrik and sat. "Getting a screen test." She snuggled close to a beaming Derrik and added, "I'm going to be a star. Alden promised."

---

4 "The Raven," by Edgar Allan Poe

Ed sneered, "You fell for that cliché?"

She held up a rectangular metal box and waggled it. "Got all his promises right here. Like I should've recorded *yours!*"

Judith said coolly, "You've definitely been spending time with Alden. It shows."

Lenore giggled. "Thanks!"

"I meant your chest," drawled Judith. "His favorite size."

Lenore's smile vanished. She sat back and began picking at the strawberries on her plate.

"Everyone having fun?" came a gravelly, female purr. Heads snapped in the direction of the door.

Derrik leaped to his feet. "Linda! Dear wife!" Ed suspected *wife* had been pronounced with special volume, because Lenore suddenly switched to a chair on the other side of Dickens.

A woman, six feet tall in kitten heels and a clinging summer dress, strode across the room with a feline hip swivel that brought attention to her tiny waist and long perfect legs. Ed noticed that her bust was the same shape as Lenore's, except . . . more. A sheet of glossy caramel-colored hair almost hid one eye.

She touched the chair vacated by Lenore. "Anyone sitting here? I'll join you then." Her husband gave her a dutiful peck on the lips. "Am I crashing a party?" She gazed, eyebrows high, at Lenore, Judith, and Ed.

Her husband cleared his throat. "Hopefully, we're putting together the world's next great film, dear."

"I hate that we can't smoke," she said distractedly. "You mean the one whatsisname is attached to?"

Silence.

Alden Derrik buttoned a button on the front of his dress shirt. "Who do you mean, dearest?"

Linda was studying the menu. "Oh, you know. That hunky guy who wins all the awards. Murphy. Warren Murphy?"

Again, silence.

Judith sucked air through puckered lips. "Mrs. Derrik, how do you do. I'm Judith Ravenna, representing Edgar Poe. What did you hear about Murphy? If you don't mind my asking." Her tone was light and ingratiating.

Linda gazed at her. Then at Ed. "Is this Mr. Poe?"

Judith said, "Yes, it is. He is."

Ed gestured and said firmly, "And that's my girlfriend, Lenore."

"I'm not his girlfriend!"

Linda considered Lenore. "You like them young. Perky breasts," she added politely to Lenore. She looked back at Judith. "If his name is Poe, it was your client's script I heard about. Murphy is attached for the male lead." She shrugged. "They say it's a groundbreaking role. *Rue Morgue Noir*?"

Loessus stood. "I must make a phone call. Excuse me." He rushed from the room.

Robert D'Wolfe eyed Dickens. "Well, he could be my sidekick. I guess."

Ed said, "I wrote out the sidekick. There is no sidekick now. Now there's a *mature* female costar."

Dickens studied something in the far distance. "Sidekick . . ."

Derrik said, his eyes darting nervously from his wife to D'Wolfe, "You're forgetting the son. And he's the killer."

Ed said, "Nobody confirmed that so I didn't write it."

D'Wolfe brightened. "Yes. Murphy could be the son. Well," he added archly, "with heavy makeup." He frowned. "But I'd rather be the killer."

Loessus returned, looking thoughtful, and sat.

Ed said anxiously to D'Wolfe, "I could do that. You were supposed to be the killer in the first place!"

D'Wolfe sighed. "Jeeze, but if Murphy's the son *and* the killer, why would I . . ." He lifted his shoulders unhappily. "Why would I bother with it, then? What's in it for me?"

Derrik smacked the table. "If you're out, so'm I."

Ed sighed.

Judith paled and searched for words.

Loessus drawled, "Don't you three have a formal contract with each other? Partnership thing, one for all? What d'you call yourselves, DDD?"

D'Wolfe nodded absently. "We're official. No worries there."

Derrik's wife made a kissy shape with her mouth and wrapped her long fingers around her husband's neck in a grip Edgar felt uncomfortable watching. Derrik looked terrified. "I'm the one suggested the woman be older, Linda dearest. No young women in this one."

"Hang on," Lenore said, her voice harsh. "I was promised a part in this thing!"

Judith eyed her in distaste. "By whom?"

Lenore merely held up the digital recorder. "And it's still on."

Derrik nibbled at his croissant, cowering under Linda's basilisk gaze.

Loessus said, "Four major stars." He stroked his puffy jowls. "Consider *The Dirty Dozen.*"

"*The Magnificent Seven,*" said Dickens, catching on. "*From Here to Eternity. Ocean's . . .* et cetera."

Loessus waved a hand in the air. "Exactly. A bevy of stars, unforgettable, unforgettable. Of course, you'll need more financing. Fantasy Prods *would've* been willing to take part," he finished wistfully. "But, of course, you're all signed with each other."

Judith said excitedly, "So what? Producers coproduce all the time for tent poles! You could bring in Fantasy, couldn't you Dickens?"

Dickens considered Loessus. "You consider Poe's script a tent pole?"

Judith said, "I do!"

Loessus glanced in irritation at Judith. "Very possibly, Dan, very possibly. However. Alden would have to invite Ms. Marie Rogers back—with a large public apology—"

Lenore let out a shriek. "Me! I can be the dead body!"

Linda smirked at Lenore. "You do tempt me, dahling." She thrust her mimosa flute high in the air. The waiter lifted it from her fingers. "No orange juice," she ordered.

Loessus sighed. "If, as I say, *if* Marie played the dead body, well! What a picture."

D'Wolfe asked plaintively, "Which role would Murphy play?"

Dickens hmmphed. "Nobody signed Murphy, I'm telling you!"

Loessus smiled. "I did."

Dickens swiveled around to look at him. "When, by God?"

"On the phone just a minute ago. After hearing Mrs. Derrik's news. I knew his signing was a rumor, but I loved the idea. However, when I spoke with Ms. Rogers——"

Dickens snarled, "I might've expected something like this from you!"

"What's wrong now?" asked Poe, bewildered.

Linda Derrik laughed. "Oh, Stevie's so deliciously twisted. He's stealing the movie!" She glanced sideways at Dickens. "He's famous for it. Be careful, Mr. Poe, that he doesn't rewrite your screenplay under his own name. He does that to writers and then they're so surprised when they see the film credits. Did you register your script with the WGA?"

Ed nodded.

"Won't help. Can't copyright ideas, as Steve knows far too well, don't you, dahling?"

Loessus added, "Luckily, I signed nothing despite our *charming* breakfasts. Because . . ." He smiled faintly at Linda. "Marie Rogers is filing suit against DDD."

D'Wolfe's mouth dropped open. Dickens rose from his seat, angry. "Why would Rogers sue us?"

"Breach of professional promises." Loessus cleared his throat and carefully looked nowhere near Derrik. "With proof. Because our conversations were recorded, weren't they Mr. Poe?"

Poe reddened. "Until Lenore took the recorder."

Linda Derrik cooed, "Recorder! So Mr. Poe, you're twisted, too. What is it with these writers' minds?"

Loessus said, "And, after Poe's girlfriend took it, *she* no doubt recorded everything too? Oh, oh, oh."

Derrik managed to croak out, "She—people—can't tape people . . . without permission. Not legal. Is it?"

Silence.

Loessus gave a polite cough. "Ms. Rogers wants reimbursement for loss of income, if the film in which she'd been promised a role becomes a hit. I suggested she also sue for damage to her professional reputation. She might be considered difficult to work with after this, lose jobs."

Derrik chewed on his lower lip. "I can't apologize."

His wife folded her arms. "Of course not, don't be naïve. You apologize to her, you'd have to apologize to me, and I won't be made out a fool in public."

Dickens's face twisted. "I can't believe I almost stooped to work with a crass commercial prodco like yours, Loessus!"

Loessus smiled. "Don't blame yourself. The money's so tempting. Ms. Grant might consider taking a groundbreaking, costarring role with Murphy, if one were to be offered." He forked a grape into his mouth and chewed. "Ms. Rogers could make an interesting sidekick for Grant. Or more of a buddy role." He mused. "In one movie or another."

Judith leaned toward Dickens and spoke in low rapid hisses. Although Poe couldn't hear much, he caught enough to know she was flogging other writers she represented to DDD's "money man."

Poe hunched a shoulder against this betrayal and studied the others.

Linda Derrik was languorously enjoying both her champagne and Lenore's anxious glances at her husband. Derrik sniffed, rigid in the embrace of his wife. D'Wolfe examined his image in a wall mirror across from their table. Despite Judith's assault on his ear, Dickens glared at Loessus, his face ruddy and swollen.

Loessus gazed with detached interest at his omelet, now nearly demolished. Ed wondered if he was reimagining the script so he could steal it.

Imminent detonation of the project hovered over the table like a mushroom cloud. The *Enola Gay* could've done no worse. Poe saw clearly that he would be the only fatality. Nothing and no one else would die. Everyone else would go on to put together new deals, seize and milk other star-quality scripts. Scripts with legs. More sequels than *Star Wars*. Murders in all kinds of Rues.

Their waiter had drafted a busboy's help, and they were now darting between bodies to reach cups and plates.

Poe rose. "I'm proud you thought so much of my talent that we had these discussions. I've learned a lot." He began shaking hands around the table, skipping Lenore. "I never thought I'd get the chance to meet you all. Steve, Dan, Alden, Linda." He paused, imagining all those vulnerable versions of his script nesting in their fax machines. "Especially you, Robert. Been some good moments."

Loessus asked, "Do you have anything else in development, dear boy?"

"Oh, yes. Another murder mystery, this time based on a real case, very dark—"

Loessus patted Ed on the back, smiling kindly. "Dark's your forte, Poe, not surprised!"

"—and a sort of dream poem, possibly drug influenced, I haven't decided yet, of a man grieving for the love of his life. She dies. A nightmare I guess."

Judith beamed. "Keep 'em coming, Ed, keep 'em coming!"

A pause bloomed and became awkward.

As Poe threaded through the tables to leave the room, he heard Derrik say he would head up to his room now. Jet lag.

"That Ed's a real professional," he heard Loessus comment. Without looking, he heard more chairs being pushed back. The group was breaking up.

He loitered outside near the entrance for twenty minutes, but Lenore did not emerge.

Ed walked home.

"What," said Ed the next morning, his voice flat. "You woke me." He'd pulled the ringing phone from under his pillow, but he hadn't been asleep.

Lenore would never again call, and he worked such long hours he had no other friends. It had to be Judith.

"WHY can't you just say hello? *Eddie!* Oh, Eddie you'll never in a million years . . ." Judith's voice was shrill. "So tragic! The shock! I can hardly . . . Well, I know you don't have television, and rarely see a newspaper, so I called . . . Derrik. It's Derrik."

"Alden?"

"Linda. She, ohmigod. She missed her flight to LA, or . . . or changed her mind after a phone call, something like that, I paid no attention. What do I care? Anyway, Alden must've felt safe . . . he and Lenore . . . well, Linda shoved the crown—you know the pointy crown of those crystal Miss Liberty statues the Regis puts between their upstairs elevators?—right into his chest. Well, the crown's largish. His neck got a few of the points."

Unlike me, Edgar couldn't help thinking.

"Carotid artery. It's made in that famous crystal that's so expensive. I never understood why. Is their crystal better than other crystal? It's just glass, for heaven's sake . . ."

"What statues?" murmured Ed. "When could I afford to stay at the Regis?" Although he had visited Derrik's room, Judith would never remember.

"Oh. OH." Judith's voice brightened. "Right. Of course not. You can't even afford a TV. So—Alden's out of the loop. And Linda's in jail. No bail."

"How's Lenore?" asked Ed, yawning.

"Fine. She wasn't there at the time."

"She wasn't? Then why did Linda kill him—"

"Underwear was found. Embroidered. Lenore's. Obviously Linda saw it . . ."

"Oops. I gave her monogrammed underwear for Valentine's Day. My bad."

"So Steve Loessus says—"

"He called?"

"Right before I called you. You really caught his eye, Edgar! And with no one left to object to your script location, which saves your story line . . . he wants to meet."

"Not at the—"

Judith's voice was firm. "Nevermore! The Mondrian. I hear they have organic waffles."

ANGELA ZEMAN, primarily a short story writer whose work often appears in anthologies, is the author of *The Witch and the Borscht Pearl*, a novel developed from stories published in *Alfred Hitchcock's Mystery Magazine*. These and her suspense stories have been praised often in *Publishers Weekly* and other venues. One story published in Jeffery Deaver's *A Hot And Sultry Night for Crime* was selected by Otto Penzler and Nelson DeMille to be included in *The Best American Mystery Stories 2004* (Houghton Mifflin). She also contributes nonfiction articles to various publications, including the award-winning *The Fine Art of Murder*.

Copyrights